'Here she be then,' ⟨...⟩ you wanted. Tek her ⟨...⟩ back room. An' no a⟨...⟩ bought her—' He ch⟨...⟩

'How much?' The ⟨...⟩ voice.

'Half a crown, wife. How's tha' f'r ee?'

'Too much by half. You fool. Come on, you—' to me, 'let's have a look at you.'

Exhausted, but realising the need for compliance, I struggled up the narrow stairs. She put out a large coarse-palmed hand, and peered at me under the flickering light. I shook back my hair, lifted my chin, and faced her. She gave a grunt. 'Ha. Some gentry's whore, is that it, girl? Well, there edn' no gentry here. Only work. *Work*, I said. Hear me?'

I didn't answer; I couldn't think. The dark landing seemed to close in on me suddenly, and I could hardly breathe. For a few moments I lost consciousness, and was recovered only by the sting of spirit in my throat. After that I was pulled to my feet again, and taken to a musty small room hardly larger than a full-sized cupboard with an old mattress on the floor and a chair of some sort in one corner . . .

MARY WILLIAMS

# Dark Flame

SPHERE BOOKS LIMITED

A SPHERE BOOK

First published in Great Britain by
William Kimber and Co. Ltd 1988
Published by Sphere Books Ltd 1990

Copyright © Mary Williams 1988

Reproduced, printed and bound in Great Britain by
Cox & Wyman Ltd, Reading

ISBN 0 7474 0397 X

Sphere Books Ltd
A Division of
Macdonald & Co (Publishers) Ltd
Orbit House, 1 New Fetter Lane,
London EC4A 1AR
A member of Maxwell Macmillan Pergamon Publishing Corporation

In Memory of
beloved Ronald

# Contents

# I

## Katrina
## 1813

*1*

I was sold at a fair like any trumpery piece of finery or second-hand goods – *me*! Katrina – daughter of a brave Spanish sea-captain and a noble mother I'd hardly known, for she'd died when I was but a baby.

Three years had passed since the wreck off Cornwall, when I'd been found, a sixteen-year-old girl, the only survivor – lying half gone myself among the rubble of the lost merchant vessel. From there, on that wild and desolate shore, I'd been taken by Squire Pencorrin and had served him well and faithfully as servant, and wife in all but name – the latter to be legalised as soon as his first one, poor ailing creature, died. Three months ago she'd passed away, and I was already with my second child. The eldest, a boy, Rupert, had been a toddler then, and after the mistress's death a minister had been sent for by the Squire and things had been said that I'd taken to be marriage vows. Only later was I to learn the truth. He'd wed *me*, and was already pledged to a fine and wealthy woman in London. On that fatal day though, when we set off for Penjust Autumn Fair – 'A trip out', Penncorrin said – I took everything in good faith, but instead of merrymaking found myself tethered among sheep and cattle, and put up on a barrel to be auctioned for all to see.

The wind blew my black hair wild, and my green eyes blazed from the sun that was harsh and strong on my face, bitter-sweet from the salt and sea winds. I pulled the silk cape tight round me – the cape Pencorrin had given me in a moment of passion. But greedy fingers grabbed and tore so bosom and thighs showed clear and firm, but slender still through my thin dress. There were lewd remarks, laughter and shouting as the crowd milled round, nodding and grinning – smirking male faces greedy with desire. Most were drunk by then; Richard Pencorrin perhaps the worst of them.

The bargaining went on. 'A penny? – Two? Or mebbe a shillun? – What about that?'

'Two? Three?'

'A good bit o' flesh theer!' and fingers and thumbs pinched where they had no right. Forgetting my manners, I spat on their reddened, befuddled faces, and a roar of laughter went up. I lifted my head proudly, in an effort to quell the rising sickness in me. And it was then the deal was settled.

I was sold for half-a-crown to Thomas Trengrouse and carried off to the small farm and kiddleywink he owned on the wild north cliffs.

*

The journey, though not more than six miles, took two hours' rough ride in Trengrouse's cart which was laden with stuff he'd picked up, including a young sow pig for breeding with, clucking fowls, and sacks of this and that, including myself, although before we'd gone far he stopped his old nag, and lifted me from the cart to sit beside him.

'Jus s'long as you behave,' he said thickly, 'an' try no tricks. You're mine now, see? Bought fair an' square with good money. So doan' you go fergettin' et.'

I had no chance. If my hands hadn't been bound behind my back I'd have made an effort to escape. But there was no opportunity, and anyway I was so shocked and sickened by events that the only thought in my mind was of hatred and revenge. Hatred for Richard Pencorrin and what he'd done for me. So I sat there huddled into my cape, while Trengrouse muttered and sang, stopping at times to take a long swig of whisky. On several occasions we followed a wrong track, and there was swearing as he turned the cart into a different direction.

The night air was cold, and the watery moon filmed by rising cloud. On either side the moor stretched bleak and dark, with a wild sea breaking on the distant coast. The smell of liquor was thick and strong. Like a nightmare it was, peopled only by creatures of the elements – the great stones and menhirs reborn

as legends from the past, and the wind whining through briar
and gorse.

At last we reached it – 'The Travelling Man', a low squat
building with a barn and shed or two about it, presumably the
'farm'.

Trengrouse drew the cart to a halt, lumbered out with
difficulty, and before stabling the nag or getting his livestock
and screaming pig to the sheds, heaved me to my feet and
somehow bundled me through the door of the kiddleywink.
An oil lamp still burned from the interior, revealing a smoky
tap room on the left, where one or two drink-sodden figures
lay unconscious on the floor. A woman appeared holding a
candle at the top of a narrow stairway. She was broad and dark
as a giant toad peering from its hole.

'Here she be then,' Trengrouse shouted. 'The help you
wanted. Tek her an' bed her f'r the night th' back room. An' no
arguin' mind. Fair an' square I bought her—' He chuckled. 'A
good bargain.'

'How much?' The voice was gruff and low. An ugly voice.

'Half a crown, wife. How's tha' f'r ee?'

'Too much by half. You fool. Come on, you—' to me, 'let's
have a look at you.'

Exhausted, but realising the need for compliance, I
struggled up the narrow stairs. She put out a large coarse-
palmed hand, and peered at me under the flickering light. I
shook back my hair, lifted my chin, and faced her. She gave a
grunt. 'Ha. Some gentry's whore, is that it, girl? Well, there
edn' no gentry here. Only work. *Work*, I said. Hear me?'

I didn't answer; I couldn't think. The dark landing seemed
to close in on me suddenly, and I could hardly breathe. For a
few moments I lost consciousness, and was recovered only by
the sting of spirit in my throat. After that I was pulled to my
feet again, and taken to a musty small room hardly larger than
a full-sized cupboard with an old mattress on the floor and a
chair of some sort in one corner.

There I was left, with the sound of a bolt being pushed from
the other side of the door. I collapsed on the rough bedding
and before I knew it was in a heavy sleep. It was only when I
woke that I remembered my son, little Rupert. And then I
cried.

*

Mistress Trengrouse – she insisted on my calling her 'mistress' despite her more-than-ample size and slatternly appearance – had cold and calculating little beads of eyes peering from her fleshy countenance. I soon learned that I was not only expected to shoulder the cleaning and what washing and scrubbing there was, but to be busy frequently in the taproom at nights, serving the customers, who were a motley crowd of seamen, adventurers, pedlars and sly-eyed looking vagabonds with plots to hatch and information of an evil kind to give in exchange for a tot of whisky or rum.

Occasionally one of the gentry might arrive, swaddled discreetly in a black cloak and high riding boots. Coins were jingled then and exchanged to the accompaniment of winks and nods among low-born avaricious accomplices. There would be a bawdy woman or two on most nights, out to tempt lusting male desires with glimpses of a bare bosom or a stout white thigh, for a drink or coin in the pocket. There would be throaty laughter, vulgar comments, and sometimes a fight. It was nauseating, and I hated it. But still I stayed, because I'd been purchased officially by Trengrouse, and until I could see a safe way of breaking free, was determined to make the best of it. I had a bed to lie on in the miserable cubbyhole, food of a kind, and a haughty way of dealing with any man trying to take liberties, that kept them off.

This angered the repulsive 'Mistress' Trengrouse. 'You wan' brought here jus' for what little you do with two hands,' she told me. 'Why can't you act reasonable an' do a bit o' pleasurin'? A lusty man needs moren' a quaff o' liquor to pay right. Those wi' gold in their pockets visits here, girl, an' tes up t'you to see it comes our way.'

'Yours, you mean,' I said sharply, 'and I don't sell myself.'

'Ha! No wonder that theer man o' yours put ee up for auction, then,' she said sharply. 'A fool y'are. An' I doan' tek easily to such.'

'Leave the girl be,' her husband interrupted sharply at that point. 'She does well enough. If you had more'n half her guts an' will in that lumberin' great body of yours we could have a nicely run inn an' a payin' small-holdin' by now. But you're lazy, Annie – an' that's the truth of it. Lazy an' a shrew into the bargain. A sodden gin-drinkin' shrew.'

He turned and walked from the room heavily, and just for a moment I felt a stab of pity for him. Since that first night when he'd brought me from the fair so sodden with drink he'd hardly known what he was doing, I'd been given a completely different impression of the man. Tidied up behind the bar, and in his bottlegreen coat with a clean cravat, his gingerish sideburns clipped close on either side of his broad fresh-complexioned face, he could have been quite a respectable 'mine host' of a better tavern than The Travelling Man, as he served behind the bar. And with no thanks to his wife either. I'd seen him washing his aprons himself in the back scullery more than once, while she drowsed with her gin by the kitchen fire – if you could call that small stuffy place a kitchen. And although gruff, sometimes surly, he'd appeared to keep his own drinking habits well under control, and had not said a wrong word to me.

For the small-holding Trengrouse had only the help of a simple-minded lad from a nearby farm. I didn't mind helping outside, in fact I preferred it to the thick odour of the tap room where the lewd gossip provided a constant undertone against the murmur of dark and dangerous talk.

Occasionally a Revenue official – one of the King's men – ill-disguised as a traveller appeared, to glean what information he could of deals in smuggling and other illegal practices. But it was seldom he had much success. Strangers were viewed suspiciously, and more frequently than not conversation subsided when any were about the premsies. Whether Trengrouse ever got himself involved I didn't know. In a small way maybe he might have been open to bribery, but if so he was clever enough to keep clear of suspicion of the law, even making himself agreeable to any visiting member of the authorities. Debauchery he accepted, though strangely, from the very beginning of my time there, he did his best to steer me clear of it. Perhaps he regretted his rash action at the auction, realised that in bidding for me he'd mistaken me, in the state he was, for the usual type of low-born pathetic creature usually displayed on such wretched occasions.

On the other hand, my fate could have been worse. I could

have landed up with some tyrannical master whose aim was to treat a woman like a slave, beating or raping her as the mood took him, and paying her nothing into the bargain. Oh, yes, I'd soon learned the nature of certain individuals frequenting The Travelling Man, and Trengrouse was certainly not one of them, thank God. In fact, there were times when he was almost polite. One night he said as we were clearing up the tap room after a particularly bawdy evening, 'A proud wumman you are, edn' you, Kat? What made you tek up with Pencorrin in the first place?'

'He rescued me. He seemed lonely. His wife was no use to him – a dying ailing creature. When she went he said he'd wed me, and he *did*. But it seems he didn't really want me.'

'I wonder.'

'What do you mean?'

'Wed you. They say Zaul way the banns be up for his marriage to a certain Lady Angelica Leach. Known her for a long time – used to visit in London. Funny you didn' guess somethin' o' the sort was goin' on.'

'Why should I? He married me legally in front of a minister. I had the lines.'

Trengrouse laughed. 'A bit o' paper mayhap, an' a rogue bribed to dress as a cleric. But lustin' noblemen like him doan' go marryin' such as you, girl, with not a penny in her pocket. That fine estate of his needs a deal of gold spent on it, an' no wonder. That with his gamblin' ways. Oh, I know for sure what's goin' on there – made it my business to do a bit of pryin' into his affairs. There edn' no record of any marriage, Kat. You was had there, an' no mistakin' it. So when you was sold to me, he hadn' no right to put thee up – not in any way.'

'You mean—' I paused a moment in astonishment, before continuing, '—you mean it wasn't a proper bargain?'

'Yes,' he agreed somewhat grudgingly. 'That's just what I *do* mean, girl. As far as th' law's concerned I reckon you be as free as they sparrows peckin' 'bout in the yard. More fool me for sayin' it, an' that's the truth. You've bin useful 'bout this place, an' in a way I've come to d'pend on 'ee – brought a bit o' brightness to life, 'stead of always that old harridan on me tail, on an' *on*, always natterin' an' naggin'.'

I couldn't speak for quite a minute, then as the full import of his words sank in, I said slowly. 'So young Rupert then, my little son, he's a bastard—'

'Oh, think nuthen o' that. There's many a—'

'There's only one *Rupert*,' I interrupted. 'And he's mine. *Mine*.' I could feel the colour burning my cheeks. I faced Trengrouse very straight in the eyes, and with my chin set defiantly, said, 'I've got to claim him, get him back!'

'Now, now, Kat, doan' thee be goin' off on a wild goose chase. If he's truly Pencorrin's son—'

'If – *if*—' I almost screamed, 'of *course* he is. What do you think I am? What insolence to imply I could have lain with anyone else – *me*? Katrina, daughter of Captain Marriac. Oh, yes, maybe I *was* mistress while the wife lived, maybe I shouldn't have been. But I was alone in a strange land and needing the things any young woman does. I thought he'd come to care. I had to have food, a shelter, and a home. But obviously he was a good actor, Pencorrin was. At first I was content just to work in the kitchen and help the old woman of a housekeeper with the cooking. There was only one other servant, a man kept mostly busy in the stables. Then, when I saw how things were – no marriage any more at all – just a slowly dying woman in a sick room – why, then it seemed sensible for him to turn to me and I gave him all I'd got to give, affection, service and trust. Yes, I *trusted* him. But if what you say is true—'

'It's true all right,' Trengrouse affirmed and I believed him, 'but how you'll ever get hold o' that boy if he wants to keep him is a problem, girl. And anyway, how would he fit in here? Thought o' that? With Annie f'rever cursin' an' grudgin' a friendly word from me, an' on your tail wi' wicked words an' ways. There'd be no future for a young un. B'lieve me, he's best where he is. Maybe Pencorrin wants to be sure of a son, an' in your Rupert he's got one, edn' he? Well then! my advice is – let well alone, Kat, unless you do want to trek the road an' live as tramps.'

'I *could* do that, couldn't I?' I said. 'Take to the roads, I mean. Join the gypsies if I wanted to.'

Trengrouse gave a long searching look, then agreed grudgingly. 'Maybe you could, if you fancied it. But getting the little lad! – you wouldn' have a chance o' that, girl. Pencorrin'd see to it, an' if you tried, likely as not he'd have y' before the Bench, an' then what d'you think it'd be? – Transportation, or wuss. They have the ways an' means, these high-up families.' His voice faded. He turned away. 'Well, think on't. You think *well*, Kat. With you around here reckon I could make more of a tidy respectable place than tes. It'd tek time, but—'

'And how would you get it, tied as you are to *her*?' I couldn't help saying contemptuously.

There was a pause in which the shadows settled on his face with brooding dark intensity. It was as though his eyes were turned upon the future, searching for – or seeing there – a pattern I couldn't know. Then he said in emotionless tones, 'Maybe the day'll come sooner than you d'think.'

And there was a sense of deadly purpose in his manner that brought a brief shiver to my spine.

## 2

It was strange how the relationship between Thomas Trengrouse and myself developed. I suppose our mutual dislike of the overbearing and repulsive Annie had something to do with it – that, and the awareness that Thomas really *did* have it in him to act like a civilized human being once he could assert himself above her bullying influence. His periodic attacks of drinking became fewer and as I helped him get the kiddleywink cleaner and in better order there were even periods when we had a rare moment or two to talk together of our past lives. Not that there was much I could divulge to him of mine, though he *did* make a point one day of how strange it seemed I should speak English so well when my father had been Spanish.

'He was a clever man,' I explained, 'and for so long as I sailed with him, since I was a child of four, we spoke three languages, French, Spanish and English. He had a notion once of writing a book about our travels. Part of it was already done, when the ship sank. Oh, I loved my father dearly. He was a real scholar as well as a brave tough character, but I think the sea always meant the most to him.'

'An' your ma?'

I shook my head. 'I don't know. He never spoke of her, except that she was grand and beautiful. He showed me a miniature once – she had a proud face and dark eyes under shining piled-up black hair. But I've a feeling they weren't happy. "Forget her, Katrina," he said. "Remembering can be a torment. Best to live in the present and take each day as it comes – wind, rain or sun – chasing the waves and wind, Carissima. That's life!" And he was right.'

The trouble was that I was no longer free to do that – even if I wished. I had to think and plan, because of the coming child, Pencorrin's legacy of which Thomas Trengrouse was so far unaware. I carried the child easily, and well to the back, which had enabled me so far to keep my secret to myself, making use of my full working skirt and coarse hessian apron for hiding the developing curves. But I fancied one day that Annie had her suspicions. Her narrowed gaze recently had held a shrewd, speculative glace whenever I passed; the sly watchful look of her had intensified, and I knew the time had come when I must tell Thomas. I did so at the earliest opportunity.

'So it's about time I was away,' I ended by saying, 'That is, if you'll allow me to pay back the halfcrown you gave for me at the fair. Quite honourable money it is – earned honestly in the tap-room for giving a smile and polite speech, nothing more. No one's been allowed any liberties where I'm concerned, Mister Trengrouse.'

'Say Tom an' be done wi' it,' the man told me curtly, adding heavily, 'Well, I'll be damned. You with a kid in your belly. Could've told me before, couldn' ee?'

'I could, but I wanted to bide here for a bit. It suited me – under the circumstances.'

'In spite of *her*? – Annie?'

'She doesn't frighten me.'

'She will though – she *will*, if I do let her. Your life'll be hell on earth, girl. An' the little un—' He sighed, gritting his teeth and pulling his whiskers, a habit he had when he was rattled.

'I just doan' know, an' that's fer sure,' he added. 'A pretty kettle o' fish we've been landed in, an' no mistake.'

'Not at all,' I drew myself up, and my voice was strong and firm when I said, 'You must let me leave, Thomas – today or tomorrow. I shall be all right. And I wouldn't stay here, not for the world, to bring a young life into such a den of wickedness and ill-temper. There'll be work I can do travelling round. Healthy jobs like broom-making and helping in dairies, or maybe as I said going with the Romanies from door to door, once I get northwards. Don't you fret about me. There's no cause.'

'But I reckon there is, Kat. I got thee here, an' rough-an'-ready as the place still is, no one'd tek it as the same dirty den that old witch o' mine had it. An' it's goin' to stay as it isn, d'ye hear? I won't have ee leavin' me now just at a time when the fresh air's got in, an' I doan' need the rum no more to kip the madness away. *Her!*' His jaw had an aggressive thrust. 'Let her kip out of our way, yours an' mine, girl, an' go to hell f'r all I care. I'll show her, Kat, I'll show her who's master here. You wait, you just wait, I say, and see.'

And that's what I did.

\*

On an afternoon when Annie sat slumped in the small parlour, bleary-eyed, and sodden with gin, I put on a cape – a thick wollen one Trengrouse had brought me from Penjust Market – and went for a walk to get a breath of sweet air into my lungs. Where Thomas was I didn't know, and if Annie aroused herself sufficiently to miss me I didn't care. Something independent and strong in me drove me recklessly without thought from the drab confines of that beer-smelling interior towards the open moor where the cold wind shivered between the great boulders and bent clumps of heather and gorse, whining and singing with the tiny stream down the slope. Halfway up the hill there stood the gaunt dark shape of what at some time might have been a dwelling house. A large farm, perhaps? Or had it once been part of an estate comprising the derelict mine works a mile to the east which I'd learned had once produced a fair yield of copper, but had been deserted and left derelict following some major mishap.

Curiosity impelled me upwards. And as I climbed, the late rays of a dying sun sent elongated shadows snaking from the granite walls where gaps of windows were briefly lit to flame. At no time could the building have been decorative structurally. There was no suggestion of period about it, no turrets or terraces – only one ugly squat tower poking above an otherwise square frontage, and a small barn-like erection projecting separately on the left from a mass of twisting elder and tangled undergrowth.

I pushed through a partly open and broken gate, and took a flagged path mostly covered by weeds, to the door which was slightly ajar. The building was two-storied with three windows on each side of the ground floor, and three above. One or two had the glass broken, but the place was in no way a ruin – just derelict, neglected, and dark from damp and the buffeting of elements. I stood for minutes staring up at the thin slimy streams of water trickling down the granite bricks. Such a waste, I thought for a house to be left so – unwanted and unloved – something that must originally have seen life and held purpose abandoned to the decay of a slow death.

The door was ajar. I pushed it and heard it groan as I went in. Mould and crumbling wood and plaster filmed the interior. Cobwebs, weeds, insects and the unmistakable smell of rot pervaded the atmosphere. Yet curtains, though worn and torn in parts still draped the windows, and as far as I could judge the foundations were still sound; a few stones had fallen to the floors, there were obvious signs of rats, and when I pushed through the entrance to what had probably once been a parlour, a grey shape lumbered from the shadows, and with a bleat brushed by. Only a sheep, but my heart lurched.

Once accustomed to the poor light, I saw the furnishings might have been quite handsome in the past, though cobwebs now draped thick veils over the decaying upholstery, and yellowed muslin at a side window hung in shreds. Only the marble mantelshelf and surround appeared intact. The hands of the grandfather clock stood at twelve o'clock. How long had they remained static with their ancient time-keeper stilled? And whose childish arms had once held a doll in a blue dress, minus an arm and leg, that lay on the floor near a once richly embroidered footstool? The poignancy of such unanswerable questions roused strong emotions in me, dispelling a first sense of gloom into awakening excitement. Even now it was not too late. With hard work and care the house could be brought to life again. Where one child had played in the past, others could follow. Floors could be washed and walls cleaned. The rotting windowsills could be repaired with new wood, and repainted – new covers made for furniture, and glass fitted where it had been broken.

But whom did it belong to, I wondered? Thomas would surely know. Living so near in the fold of the moors below he must have knowledge of the family who'd resided there. I'd ask him as soon as I returned to The Travelling Man. Meanwhile I made a brief survey of the two floors. On the top there were six bedrooms and a washroom with a closet that at some time had probably been used as a linen room. Although the wooden stairs had been holed in parts, the landings and walls were in a surprisingly good condition. Even a tapestry hung almost intact in a recess, and my only shock there was when a raven or crow, with a flurry of sooty dust, flapped squawking down a chimney of the largest bedroom.

The kitchens were at the back downstairs, and there was a dairy leading off, with marble shelves, and hooks projecting from the ceiling. A milk can lay tumbled in one corner. The cold floor seeped with damp; moss and lichen pushed between the flags. But nothing was beyond repair, and a sudden truth occurred to me, how wonderful it would be if this forgotten dwelling – that was how I thought of it – 'forgotten' – could be restored so my child could be born there. My heart quickened, and my cheeks burned rosy red through the cold. If it were possible – if I could conceive some wild plan that would induce Thomas Trengrouse to take the matter up and see me settled there, I might even succeed in claiming Rupert from Pencorrin.

*Pencorrin!*

How I hated him.

The indignity and shame he'd caused me renewed its angry tide in my veins. I would do anything – *anything* to thwart and humiliate him in return. Whatever Thomas said, I determined somehow to deprive Pencorrin of my son. I was not Captain Marriac's daughter for nothing; and I knew, in that moment of stark truth, that there was nothing short of murder I wouldn't commit in order to gain my own ends.

The sun had left a blaze of orange lighting the western rim of hills when I swung down towards the inn. To my surprise Thomas was busy with some barrels at the door, but it was obvious he was watching for me; he kept turning his head towards the moors, and his face wore a creased angry look when he saw me.

'At last,' he said. 'I was gettin' worried – wonderin' whether you'd taken off. Where you bin, girl? Annie's in a fair rage. We've got a crowded bar already, an' she doan' like havin' to take over "out of hours", as she puts it.'

Rather to my own surprise I was not at all put out by the thought of Annie's annoyance. I felt strong, and strangely confident.

'It won't hurt her having to lift a hand for a change,' I said. 'I've done a good deal of thinking during the last hour, and there are things I've got to know, Thomas.'

'Hm! Then it'll have to be later.'

'All right. But there's one thing you can answer now. Who owns that old house up on the moor there?' I turned and waved a hand to the darkening slope.

'Rookswood, d'you mean?'

'I don't know what it's called. But it's a good house – well built. I went in and saw for myself. It seemed funny, seeing it so empty and desolate. I thought—'

'You needn' go havin' thoughts 'bout that place. Doomed it is. Got a bad name. Nothin' good'll thrive there. So forget it, Kat, an' go an' appease Annie if you can an' I'll be theer in a few minutes.'

But I wouldn't be put off. 'Whom does it belong to? That's all I asked.'

'Very well then. It's on *my* land. Once 'twas thrivin', a kind o' small manor farm you c'd say, wi' cattle an' crops, an' 'twas *my* folk, the Trengrouses, as owned an' ran it. But things happened; things best forgot. So you just do that – forget it an' get on with what's to do here.'

Matters were left then, temporarily. But the next day I managed to get Trengrouse for a few minutes on his own, and learned what I could about the building. Thomas was by no means forthcoming, but admitted during his great uncle's day a particularly nasty murder had occurred there, which had given rise to strange tales of curses and hauntings.

'Don't b'lieve them myself,' he told me, 'but it doan' alter the fact that nothin' to do with the Trengrouse family's prospered since. Gradual decline you could say. An' anyway with Wheal Clara fallin', there wasn' nuthen left t'run the place.'

'Wheal Clara – what's that? That old mine, do you mean, further along the coast?'

'That's right.'

'What happened?'

'A landslide or sumthen of the sort. Levels gave through a tumble o' rock an' was taken into the sea. There wasn' money enough to get it goin' again, an' since then 'tis bin left.'

My mind was whirling.

'Do you mean there's tin still there to be worked?'

'Not tin, girl – copper maybe, or maybe not. Who c'n tell? Anyways, no one's interested. So let's forget it, shall us?'

'No,' I replied very, very definitely. 'For the present we'll have to put any thought of it aside, I suppose. But the house – that's quite different.'

'Now then! What's got into you? What d'ye mean by such a notion?'

Very briefly, but with wild enthusiasm mounting in me, I put my plan into words, ending with, 'I know you'll have difficulty with your wife. But you're a man, Thomas. And that house is your heritage, don't you see? With hard work and putting it into repair it could be made productive. At the start everything would have to be on a small scale – but *gradually* it could become a *paying* concern. And the position's between Zaul and St Cory. There could be accommodation for passing visitors. With a few good milk-yielding cows, there could be butter for villagers and other produce – I know how to churn – I did that at Pencorrin's – and the kiddleywink could be run in conjunction in some way, *reputably*. You could become a respectable and well-recognised landlord and land owner, Thomas. Think of it – the Trengrouse name redeemed.'

I broke off breathlessly, feeling my cheeks flame and my pulses racing. 'And my baby could be born there, Thomas – if you give me permission. From this day on I'd work and slave for you – and for us, myself and my child – with all the energy I've got; oh, Thomas, *do* think of it.'

There was a long pause before he said, 'I will— Yes, all right, I will, Kat. By all that's holy, and old Nick hisself, I'll give my mind to it. Where did you get it, girl, that knack you have o' givin' flame an' fire to everything? Eh?'

I smiled, thinking back to my father who was never deterred from a course once he was set on it, and further back, far, far further, to my unknown mother whose proud rich blood also ran in my veins. Why had my father been so reticent about her origins, or never even divulged the name she was born with? All I knew of her was her great beauty which had been proved by her portrait, and by the expression in the Captain's eyes and in his voice on the rare occasions when he'd spoken of her?

Perhaps one day I would know. Fate had already taught me that life, indeed, could be unpredictable. When would the next surprise occur, I wondered, and what would it be?

I didn't have to ponder long. That same week something occurred that was to change the course of events in a manner I certainly had not expected.

*

The weather had turned mild and heavy for the time of year. Fog crept in a thickening blanket to the moors from the sea. Tempers had become surly on that certain evening, and a brawl had ensued, resulting from the arrival of an exciseman who'd taken a seaman in custody following information given concerning a smuggling spisode planned for the same evening. As soon as the official party was out of sight and hearing, the informant – a sly-eyed looking fellow with a nose as sharp and pointed as that of a fox or ferret – was attacked, and beaten up by the sailors' comrades who'd lost a good deal in contraband – through his loose tongue.

Slippery Sam, as he was called, was known to be open to bribery by the law if it suited him, and there was little doubt in the minds of those present that he was the guilty one on this occasion. So mercy was slow to come. Thomas, with the aid of a burly farmer, was eventually able to stop the shindig. Sam was hoisted on to the back of his nag standing outside, safely roped astride to the animal's neck, and sent off, half conscious with a shout and whack on the horse's rump, to find his own 'bloody way home'.

After that the kiddleywink soon emptied, - but Annie, fortified by more gin than usual, started a tirade of such violence and hatred against her husband that I was sickened and made a hurried exit to my small room. I pushed the bolt firmly, and flung myself down on the narrow lumpy mattress. Even with my hands to my ears the noise was shattering, a crescendo of thick, coarse shouting, dying at moments to a mere rumble then starting up again more violently than ever.

How long the fury of the quarrel lasted I didn't know. There was no clock in the small room I'd occupied since moving from the available cubby-hole, and time was lost in the cacophony of screaming, shouting – of thumps and the crash of breaking crockery. I couldn't sleep; I didn't even try, but just lay there rigidly with my eyes closed trying to think of other things. It was no use. Any form of relaxing was impossible. Not until a sudden silence followed by what sounded like a harsh cough, could I summon sufficient initiative and go for a drink of water from the cracked ewer.

After that, in an attempt to dispel a suffocating sense of claustrophobia, I crossed to the narrow slit of window and peered out. A faint glimmer of watery moonlight struggled behind the mist. Nothing was clear; but against the greyness of the moor a dark shape moved stealthily dragging something heavy and sack-like through the thick furze. The outline was furred and uncertain. At first glimpse it could have been some large animal with its prey after a kill. But as the mist lifted momentarily, I knew otherwise. The form was human. The other? – Nausea rose to my throat. I turned away suddenly, before the cold proof could properly register. I didn't *know*. I didn't want to. I was not involved; if later, questions should be asked, I would deny any knowledge or even suspicion of the evening's events.

So the night passed, and dawn came – a winter's dawn of fine rain and sullen skies.

Thomas was at the breakfast table when I went down. He looked paler than usual, a little grim, but his manner was controlled, despite the bags of exhaustion under his eyes. Of Annie there was no sign.

I didn't enquire about her. I didn't have to.

'She's gone,' he said suddenly in heavy tones. 'Annie's gone, an' she'll not be back. Heard it all, did you?'

'The noise? Yes. No one could help hearing.'

He sighed. 'Mebbe I should explain. Seems to me you've the right to know.'

'*No.*' Even in my own ears my voice sounded fierce. 'I want nothing of it. What's done is done, and Annie was no friend of mine. Let the past rest. Thomas. Today has to be got through, and tomorrow, and the next day, and the next. Let's make the most we can of what's left to us. I know naught, and have no blame for you in any case. Just leave me in ignorance, please.'

He stared at me, half opened his mouth to speak, then thought better of it, and slowly nodded his head. After a long pause he said, 'Mebbe you're right. I'll get us a drink then; sumthen hot an' cheerin'.'

And from that point I forced myself to plan for the future realistically, and with a strength of purpose I hadn't known I possessed, effectively smothering any lingering shred of conscience that could have thwarted my plans for using Thomas as a means to my own ends.

*3*

During the weeks following the violent night of Annie's disappearance I was careful, as much as possible, to give all the support Thomas needed to help him to a practical frame of mind and able to maintain an easy manner before regular clients of The Travelling Man. Her absence was commented on, of course, sly winks were occasionally passed, nudges, and teasing remarks concerning the missing woman. But mostly his explanation that she'd taken off for a time, to visit a niece in Plymouth, was accepted without suspicion, and I never referred to it. Anyway, the kiddleywink minus her unsavoury presence was considerably pleasanter than having her bulky weight and carping tongue forever causing trouble, and I managed to be bright and pleasant in the tap room, at the same time affording no liberties, or cheap innuendoes concerning my character.

Thomas began to eye me speculatively, warily at first, as though doubtful of my intentions. Sometimes, when he was off his guard, I fancied a look of fear cross his face; his eyes would travel momentarily to the moor; then at a quick word from me, he'd come to himself again and attend to the matter in hand. I got through twice the work I had done before, and there would be times he remonstrated, implying that in my condition I should see I had more rest.

'Rest?' I said one afternoon. 'Why? – I'm strong and healthy, and the child's going to be the same. Hard work hurts no one. And you and I have got a deal of it ahead.'

He peered at me questioningly, before saying, 'What're you referring to, Kat?'

'You know very well. The house. I told you, didn't I, that I'd like the baby born there, in a proper bed in a clean room. I meant it, Tom. And there are things to get. Fresh blankets, and a proper cradle. Are you any good at carpentry?'

He shook his head slowly. 'Now what's all this mean, girl? You're not on again 'bout movin' there, are you? How do you think it'll be paid for? Eh?'

I smiled. 'I don't know. We can't use what you haven't got. And it would take something including a trip to Truro. We could use the waggon for the journey, though. But – *have* you any money? Anything more than what comes weekly from this place?'

He considered for a moment, then decided to confide in me. 'A bit. Quite a *good* bit, you could say. Gold. Hidden under the floor boards. Annie never knew. Greedy as she was, an' smart in her way, she never cottoned on to my little hoard.' He gave a gruff chuckle, then continued in sober tones, 'It was my only escape – knowing when things got unbearable I'd enough stored away to get started again in some other sort o' way. I *had* to do it, Kat.'

There was a kind of pleading in his voice that softened me, indeed, in an odd friendly way I was becoming very fond of Thomas Trengrouse. There was something about him, beneath his bluff expression crying out for affection. I could never be in love with him, of course – he had no glamour, sophistication, handsome looks, or even youth. But he was a man who'd been hurt, and who was still vulnerable. He needed me, as I needed him, but in a different way; and although I'd hardened myself against sentiment following the shame and suffering caused by Richard Pencorrin, something soft and hungry at the deep core of my being couldn't help but respond to his male loneliness.

'I know,' I agreed. 'I understand. But – it's not going to do much good – that gold of yours, lying among the dust and cobwebs, is it? And what I plan isn't only for myself, but for *you*. Thomas Trengrouse. I can see it, so clearly – a half-way hostelry – *that's* it, the name! – Meaning "halfway between Zaul and Crink". Near enough to be seen and visited by travellers along the high lane above those on business in Crink, and the visitors that are starting to come to Cornwall. Oh, run properly we could get a tidy trade, and I'd *work*, Thomas. Like I've told you before, there's nothing I wouldn't do for us – you, me and the children, the one in my womb – and others maybe, one day. Rupert too. Yes. Whatever happens I mean to get that son of mine from the rake who sired him.'

My manner obviously impressed him. I could feel my chin rising proudly, and my heart beating firm and strong beneath my swelling breasts. As I jerked my head thick dark coils of hair broke from their combs brushing my neck sensuously. Light seemed to flood my veins with spreading warm energy, as though sunlight fired it.

'My God, Katrina,' I heard Thomas saying almost with awe, 'you're a handsome woman.' A finger touched my firm forearm where the skin was bare beneath the short sleeve. 'Where did you get those green eyes from, eh? – I've a great yearnin' for thee, girl, know that?'

Yes, I knew. And from then on, though not without great effort, I realised also that things were going my way. And so the business of getting the house habitable began. Much of the time, of course, was taken up by helping Thomas with the bar, in return for which he spent an hour or two each day searching for wood suitable for making simple furniture, and set to work on it whenever he had the chance in a nearby shed. None of his gold was wasted or used carelessly, and every opportunity was taken for making money from sidelines.

For instance, the boy employed at the kiddleywink was sent with the cart to collect sand and weed for which payment of 3d a load was paid to William Theack, a large farmer of the district. The mixture was used as valuable manure, and the lad was grateful to take a halfpenny for himself from each delivery. So there was no complaint of being tired or over-worked. Meanwhile, when I was not cooking or cleaning, or helping in the tap room, I was scrubbing, and doing things about the big house, such as putting fresh clean curtains up at the windows, made from odd lengths of material supplied cheap by Billy Noakes, the pedlar, who called regularly at The Travelling Man.

Whispers began at the inn, of course. But in time Tren-grouse's statement that Annie had died of fever in Plymouth was accepted. Dark things still went on there – plots were still laid of an evil nature, I knew that, but I kept my eyes and ears shut to such, and slowly a façade of comparative respectability reigned there when I was around.

Thomas was mystified. 'It's as though you'd got the magic in you,' he said more than once. 'To hear that bawdy lot sayin' "yes, ma'am," "no ma'am," – even a touch o' the cap on occasion. An' you as you are – so near y'r time. How d'you do it, girl? Heavy with child yet able to slave an' serve *an'* keep control just as though you was Cap'n an' the rest your crew.'

I smiled. 'Someone has to be Captain, Thomas. But I'm not that – not really. *You* are. I'm just a kind of mate to see things go right for you.'

He shook his head. 'You're more'n that. Much more, Kat. Little I knowed when I bid that halfcrown for thee I was gettin' such a rare jewel of a woman. Never would I've believed it possible a slip of a girl would've had the power to transform my whole life, or anyone else f'r that matter – cos that's what you've done, Kat – an' gettin' me to move up there as well. There's time when I still can't realise the truth of it.'

'You'd better,' I told him. 'A week or two now, and the child's due. And by then – I promise you – we'll be biding safe and snug as possible in your old family home. Not that it will be finished by any manner. But the time will come. Oh, Thomas—' a deep tide of gratitude and affection overcame me. 'I do thank you for going along with me. Truly.'

'There's nothin' t'thank me for,' he said gruffly. 'If I've done thee a bit of good, then that's a kind o' leveller, I reckon—'

'*Leveller*, Tom? Now what do you mean by that?'

'Never you mind, girl. But doan' you go thinkin' I haven' sinned at all in my time. I *have* – like men do, an' mebbe darker than most.'

He was staring broodingly past me into things I did not see – but set me remembering the grey moor on a dark night when I'd refused to acknowledge the bent shape with its burden trudging round the corner of the hill into the fog.

I resolutely pushed that picture to the far recess of my mind. 'Now don't be morbid, Thomas Trengrouse. None of us is perfect, and I'll not have this new beginning ruined by – past things. Think of me and the child – and the future, Tom. It's what you owe yourself, and me—' I forced a smile, '—for not adding another sixpence when you bid for me.'

The shadow slowly lifted from his face. He took both my hands, letting his own slowly travel from there up my arm to my warm shoulders. 'Wed me, Kat,' he said, with the heat of him suddenly close, his lips and rough brush of his sideburns close on my skin. 'Be my wife an' take a name for thyself an' the little 'un comin'—'

I pushed him away gently. 'I can't do that, Thomas, and you know it well. How do you think you'd get away with it? Folks have accepted the story about your wife's death in Plymouth now. But *marriage*! You couldn't risk it, as you must know very well.'

'But I want you so bad – I never thought to need a woman as I need you.'

'After the baby's come,' I said, 'we'll talk of it. But I – I – don't love you, Tom, not in the way you mean. I might lie with you and find a certain peace; but—'

'I'm no handsome young gallant to fire a girl's imagination,' he interrupted wrily. 'That's all right by me, Kat, I understand, just so long as you do care a bit and are willin' to share what you can with me.' He paused before adding, 'Not frettin, still for that high-an'-mighty lustin' braggart Pencorrin, are ye?'

'*Him*?' I said scornfully. 'I hate and despise him. And one

day – I swear I'll make him suffer for what he did.' The fury
and a wild despair in my voice had a subduing effect on
Thomas's ardour. His arm fell away from me. He sighed
heavily. 'Ah, Kat, seems to me you feel more still than what you
do admit. Theer's a shadder in y'r heart yet, an' a flame not
properly put out—'

'Because of Rupert,' I interrupted angrily. 'While my son's
there, with his – his father – I'll never be rid of it, the shadow,
as you put it, or the flame. I *want my son*.'

'There, there, steady on now. A time'll come mebbe, when
he's older, and he'll be lookin' for you himself. Besides—' he
came close again, and took my chin in his hands, 'You've got
the other one to think of now – it'll be with us soon, safe in y'r
arms, an' I'll do my best for the two of you, I swear it, Kat.'

My figure slumped. I felt suddenly weary. His arm came
round me, and I was content to rest against him briefly, with
my face pressing against his shoulder. I was lucky, I told
myself, to have found such a haven, a man content to care for a
woman wild-at-heart, like myself, who could offer so little in
return. Yes. Things could have been much worse. But they
could have been better too – sweeter, more fulfilling, and rich,
heady still with the passion kindled in me by Richard Pencorrin. Much as I hated him, I couldn't forget how he'd held
and caressed me and taken me on a dark tide of desire.

When I allowed myself to look back, the memory was
torment, filled with a wild surge of waste and squandered
sweetness followed by black emptiness. So I forced memory
away becoming firm and hard again, determined to make the
best of what was left. Thomas allowed me more than I'd
expected for making two rooms up at Rookswood – it had
been called that, he told me, in the old days – presentable, and
by the time the child was born in late April 1814, I was already
installed and ready for the birth.

Most of the furniture in the bedroom was sturdy and
primitive – either made by Trengrouse's own hand, or by a
friend of his, a carpenter in Zaul. I'd stitched the hangings,
linen, and bedclothes myself, and the cradle was a wooden
rocker covered by a woollen quilt. Little frivolities supplied by
the old pedlar had been added to give a feeling of womanly
charm. A simple room, it was, by no means elegant, but

somehow warm and welcoming, safe from gales and storm, like any young animal's or bird's nest. Thomas of a necessity spent his days and evenings at the kiddleywink, returning only when he'd managed to shut its doors on any late 'callers'. When he got to Rookswood it was to bed down there in the kitchen, not liking to leave me in 'that ramblin' ole relic' on my own.

To me it was no 'rambling relic', but home. The sound of the wind moaning round its granite walls held no fears for me, nor wild things' cries from outside. The shadows of the copse on the east side bred no terrors, of lurking thieves or vagabonds waiting to invade; I felt secure; secure with a future before me to build for my child, as recompense for the past and salvage for my wounded pride. For Thomas, too, I would reclaim a heritage. One day every corner and room in the abandoned house would be cleared from dust and decay and brought to life again, and not so far ahead either. Coach wheels would stop at the high lane above, and later a drive down would be made. It would be hard work, but together we could manage it, Thomas and I, and then I would feel competent and ready somehow to fling my contempt and achievement in Pencorrin's face.

Oh yes, however wild my dreams were, they could be practical given the ability and will to achieve them. Even the mine! − I could see it thriving in a far-off, perhaps, but foreseeable future, with the pumping rod moving rhythmically against the sky, and bal maidens of an evening winding their ways along the moor, singing, to their grey cottage homes.

I did not as yet mention the mine to Thomas, as it would have seemed a wild and irrational thought of mine to have such an idea. But it was in my mind that spring evening when my pains began. Thomas wasn't back, and there was no one in the house but myself and a young fox I'd taken in, that I'd found wounded weeks earlier with a gunshot wound, and nursed back to health.

'Rusty', I called her. She was a vixen, with a sharp nose and bright eyes that seemed to hold even a warm glint of affection in them. One day, however, I knew, before long she'd be away again, to start her own life, with a mate. But that evening she followed me up to the room I'd prepared, and there was a

strange comfort in having her around. Though she could do
nothing, she was there, head on paws, watching me –
something living and real to talk to when the pangs were at
their worst.

The birth was not difficult. An hour before Thomas arrived
the babe was lying at my breast in the bed, an independent
minute human being free to suckle and kick tiny limbs, with
the umbilical cord sundered, and hungry small mouth drawing the milk from my full nipples. There was little tidying up to
do for Trengrouse. He stared in amazement, a kind of wonder
on his face.

'It's come,' he said. 'A real babe. An' you alone, girl – all
alone.'

'There was Rusty,' I said, indicating the fox just loping away
and suddenly, though tired, a welling up of joy and laughter
broke from me. 'Don't look so scared, man. It's not so rare
after all, having a child; although—' I paused to glance down
at the soft thatch of dark hair in the crook of my arm, '*she* is.'

'She?'

'Yes – it's a girl, Thomas. Look at her; just look – that small
face, and tiny nose. I think she's going to be beautiful – a real
rose of a girl. And that's what we'll call her, don't you think? Or
maybe Rosanna. I like the sound of that.'

Thomas pushed a finger into one clutching tiny hand.
'Rosanna,' he murmured thoughtfully. 'A bit of a mouthful.
Still – if you want it, Kat, let it be so. Yes, Rosanna.'

There was a pause, while a gentle wind stirred the curtains,
bringing a drift of spring – of heather, bracken, young gorse,
ferns and growing things from the moor into the room. I lay
back, briefly closing my eyes. From somewhere nearby a
cuckoo called; then, through slowly deepening peace, I heard
Thomas say, 'An' to think of all this happenin' to me.'

I smiled sleepily, and opened my eyes. 'And for just half a
crown,' I couldn't help reminding him with a quirk of
humour. 'But I've a feeling it's only the beginning. Yes, I'm
sure of it. There'll be more to come, dear Tom. You just wait.'

And then before I knew it, I was drifting into sleep, and
when I woke it was early dawn.

It seemed symbolic somehow that the date of Rosanna's birth should correspond with demonstrations throughout Cornwall and elsewhere celebrating the entrance of the Allied army into Paris and dethronement of Napoleon Bonaparte. In the evening the skies around Penzance and Marazion were alight with bonfires and their illumination, and on Thursday the bells of St Michael's Mount Castle were set ringing again after a lapse of many years. An effigy of Bonaparte was burned in Mousehole, and miners and workpeople of various districts were treated to free beer, roasted ox and other savoury victuals.

'Like as if a king'd been born,' Thomas remarked, at the window, staring across the valleys and moors to where rosy flames and fireworks lit the rugged coast to flame.

'Or a queen,' I retorted proudly, gazing on the small downy head by my side. 'And here she is. She's going to be a beauty, Thomas, my baby — and a proud one. I know it.'

Trengrouse came to my bedside, and patted my hand, saying wistfully, 'Mebbe there'll be another — to keep her company soon.'

I glanced up, saying absently, 'Maybe.'

But it was not until two years had passed, in 1816, when all gossip had died down and I had been married to Thomas a year, that I bore our son, Drake, who was as unlike Rosanna as two children could be. From the very first Rosanna had been stubborn, wild-tempered, loving and impulsive, whereas Drake was amiable, blue-eyed and with a thatch of hair so gold it was almost silver. He had a sudden swift smile, warm and winning as sunlight, and a quiet manner of getting his own way that was more effectual in those early days than Rosanna's stormy approach.

Th·mas, who I realised had a special place in his heart for

his son, was careful nevertheless, to show him no partiality. To the contrary, because of the blood tie he was inclined to be more strict with the boy, spoiling Rosanna quiet unnecessarily.

'She's wilful, and must be disciplined sometimes,' I pointed out. 'You're doing her no service giving in to all her quick tempered moods.'

'Like you, she is,' Thomas said, 'that's why. I s'pose I'm tryin' to make up for the ill I did when I bid for you like common merchandise.'

'Only good will come from that day,' I told him, 'and Rosanna isn't like me. She's like—' I nearly said 'Pencorrin', but held the word back; it wouldn't have been true. She had, even in babyhood, a challenging way about her that resembled her father, but her eyes were different, neither bright green as mine were nor caressing brown like Pencorrin's, but deep darkest violet.

'Yes?' A note of jealousy tinged Trengrouse's voice. 'Like who?'

'Herself,' I retorted firmly.

'Ay, well! Mebbe that's as it should be.'

'Of course it is, and you should see you don't let your thoughts wander any more to the past,' I retorted. 'Not when the present looks so good.'

Indeed it did. Apart from failure of my one attempt to claim Rupert from his father – Pencorrin had been away in London when I called, and the house shut – there was no obstacle to my contentment.

By the time Drake was a toddler of two, we'd managed somehow to get the house simply furnished and sufficiently comfortable to take two or more travellers – folk either prevented by storm, or tired and jaded from journeying to Crink or elsewhere – for a night's rest and a meal the following morning. Thomas had enclosed some of the moorland for the few cattle we had, and in fields for the production of wheat, turnips and potatoes. He'd had an argument at the start with the leases of the tithes by a certain deanery, but the outcome had been in Trengrouse's favour. Originally a portion of the land had belonged to his own family – the rest counted as barren heath, coming under a statute of Edward III's day which provided such heath was exempt from tithes until seven years had proved fruitful. So no tithes had to be paid. With the aid of a girl – daughter of a mining family Penjust way – and an extra youth to help with the land, Rookswood showed promise of developing as I'd intended into a thriving small estate. Thomas rented out the kiddleywink but made sure he kept his eye on it. We were a happy enough couple, although I could never find it possible to respond with passion to his need of me, my fondness for him was genuine, and I never denied my body.

One thing disturbed me that for the sake of any peace of mind I had to force to the back of my brain. But occasionally, when the weather was sullen, or twilight crept to the darkening hills, I remembered; remembered an afternoon before Rosanna's birth when I'd taken a walk in a certain direction slightly below Wheal Clara and Rookswood. The land immediately round there was said by Thomas to be dangerous and full of sucking bog.

'Never wander that way,' he'd told me more than once. 'If you took a wrong step the moor'd swallow thee up, an' no one'd hear ee cry. Remember, Kat—' and he'd looked so stern and yet fearful, I'd laughed and said lightly:

'As if I'd chance risking my life in such a manner – especially *now* with things going so well for us.'

I hadn't definitely promised, though he'd taken my words as such, and on the day mentioned there had been a longing in me to be free of bonds and restrictions of any kind. By then I was used to the moor. True, there were treacherous places that could be nasty, but forewarned could be forearmed, as the saying went, and with care I knew there was no danger.

So feeling confident and slightly rebellious – a rebellion intensified in me by the weight of the child I carried, so soon to be born – I'd made my way along a narrow sheep track that appeared thread-like between clumps of heather and twisted wind-blown gorse, at moments clearly defined, the next lost in a tangled briar, then suddenly shimmering again in the fading light by stone and furze.

The ground was mostly springy underfoot, but at intervals became slightly soggy with damp, from underground streams. A thin grey mist was creeping over the landscape, through which deep purple shadows from boulders and standing stones emerged slowly, heralding evening. I'd known I should turn back, but something deeply instinctive drew me on, and suddenly with a shock I felt a tangle of weeds and briars give beneath me. I'd sprung lightly, in spite of my weight, to the far side of the treacherous patch, and when I turned my head, glancing down, saw, with a lurch of my heart, a yawning hole of blackness only half covered by the undergrowth. Another step or second and I should have been claimed not by bog, but by the gaping deep chasm of an abandoned mineshaft.

I'd waited for seconds until my pulse and nerves had steadied, and was about to move cautiously up the slope and make for Rookswood, when a shiver of wind rose, momentarily disturbing the mist, to send a quiver of light clarifying the yawning abyss so dangerously near my feet. Was it my fancy, or was there really a bundle of something that had once been human reflected through the blackened water and mud at the bottom of the long shaft? I wanted to rush away before I knew; but my eyes were riveted against my will — concentrated on the half-visible suggestion of grasping claw-like fingers resembling those of a dead hand, and deeper still holed eyes and open mouth thick with seeping green slime. I shuddered, and clutched the cape tightly to my neck, trying thus to dispel the horror. But still I could not force my legs to move.

The mist had thickened again, and it seemed to me that a mournful admonishment like the croaking of a giant frog issued in an eerie monotone from the desolate depths. Then the thin wind intensified, creaking and moaning through the heather, bending the undergrowth so the morbid tomb was once more covered and taken into darkness.

Horrified and shaking, trying to believe I'd suffered an illusion but knowing I hadn't, I'd made my way back to Rookswood.

Mercifully Thomas had been late in returning from the kiddleywink that night, and when he did, I pretended sleep. During the days that followed I fortified myself with the possibility that what I'd seen might not have been, after all, Annie. A dead sheep, perhaps? Could a sheep have appeared so? I realised the suggestion was mere wishful thinking, but

I'd clung to it, until Rosanna was born. In any case, common sense told me, if the grotesque corpse or 'thing' had been Trengrouse's wife, she had probably died from her own rage in the quarrel at The Travelling Man on that distant night. It was somehow unthinkable that Thomas, however near to murder he'd been driven, could have intentionally killed her.

A year later through curiosity and morbid desire for certainty or a desire to have my mind forever at peace, I visited the spot again. The shaft by then had been filled with earth, and concealed its mystery, except for an indenture of the soil where the gap had been. Thomas had been busy during the long evenings when he'd spent hours about the fields. If anything ever were discovered in the future it would only be a bundle of old bones which by then could have been those of anyone or anything, either animal or human.

So I turned my will entirely from gloomy conjecture, although an indefinable shadow lingered between myself and Thomas, forbidding any complete confidence – except the rebuilding of the future between us.

Because of that one dark incident which returned intermittently at rare intervals to haunt me, I worked all the harder to restore a measure of Rookswood's lost posterity, and by the time Drake had passed his first birthday the house itself was unrecognisable as the derelict broken-down place where his sister had been born. What cattle and crops we had were thriving, and 'Half Way Hostelry', as Rookswood had become known to travellers, was a respectable, comfortable visiting place run by myself with the help of the girl and a man, though nominally remaining the property of 'mine host', Thomas Trengrouse. I saw to it that in the daytime my blue cotton gown was always covered by a clean white apron for dairy work, ready to be quickly discarded should any unexpected travellers appear. In the evenings I changed into my best black silk, cut decently wide on the shoulders, but sufficiently modest to be dignified, giving no false idea that any man might dare take a liberty with me.

I was friendly, of course, to all clients, but remote. It was brought back to my ears that the general opinion concerning Mistress Trengrouse was that of a proud, strange, woman, but a good hostess nevertheless.

When I confronted myself through the mirror I could well believe it. Although only in my early twenties, through determination and hard work my face had thinned, emphasising high cheek bones beneath the elongated emerald eyes. My lips had a serious firm set above my rather too pointed chin, and I wore my thick glossy hair drawn severely back from a wide forehead held by combs on top, leaving only a few curls to brush my cheeks.

Was I beautiful? Not exactly. But I knew men admired and secretly lusted for my body which had filled out at the bosom, leaving my waist still slim above the swelling curve of thighs.

Thomas, I think – no, I'm sure – had become a little in awe of me.

'I shall never quite understand you, Kat,' he said one day. 'You c'n be so safe an' gentle when any poor creature or animal needs help, yet underneath there's somethin' hard an' cold as steel. What made you that way, woman?' He never called me 'girl' now. 'It's as if you was bound for great things – things far beyond my reach that I'll never know.'

I allowed myself to smile.

'You've come a long way, Thomas, and so have I, I grant you. But without you I couldn't have done it.'

'Ah, but you could. Rookswood edn' *my* creatin', it's yours. If you hadn't set your mind so fiercely on makin' it the mansion 'tis now it'd still be a moulderin' old place half tumblin' to ruin. An' the land – the crops, the cattle, the fine dairy, an' the butter you do churn with thy two hands – what *drives* thee, Kat?'

If I'd been honest I could have replied, 'Hatred mostly – hatred of a man who sullied and shamed me. A bit of love as well, though, for you – Thomas Trengrouse – who offered me the chance to raise myself up again, and who helped replace the son I'd lost, by giving me Drake.'

Yes. I must never forget Drake. But I said none of these things. Instead I replied, 'Determination that good land shouldn't be wasted; and one day, somehow, we'll have that old mine going once more. You just wait, Thomas, this is only the beginning.'

And so it was. But not for Trengrouse.

In the autumn of 1819 he died of a seizure, leaving me a widow, mistress of Rookswood, with two young children to bring up in a future that was to hold more dramatic problems than I could have remotely guessed.

5

I was wearing red the morning that Justin King first appeared at Rookswood's front door on a spring day in 1820. My cheeks must have been flaming as bright as my gown, for I'd just had a scene with Rosanna following a wilful escapade when she'd wandered off with a tinker's boy, knowing I'd forbidden it. She'd been absent for two hours, leaving me in a state of anxiety that had exploded into anger when she'd returned looking bedraggled as any adventurous small boy with her apron torn, one shoe missing, and her skirts hitched up over her bare brown knees. There was a smudge of earth on one cheek, and a green woollen cap with a feather in it on her dark curls.

'I'm Puck,' she'd announced with her violet eyes turned unswervingly up to mine, 'like the Puck you told me about in – in Mr Shakespeare.'

I'd scolded and shaken her, and sent her to bed, because of my fear and worry for her, and because just for an instant it was as though Pencorrin was mocking and defying me from the past. Then I'd thrown the tinker's cap on to a pile of rubbish to be burned, and to ease my strained nerves picked up the shears to prune a few more bushes that were straggling round the porch.

It was then that I saw him swinging up the path towards me – a tall broad figure wearing a black cutaway coat, white stock and shirt and high black boots over fawn breeches. He had no hat, and the morning sunlight lit his dark hair to richest, deepest copper. His face, too, was brown – as though he'd been in the hot sun for a long time. He smiled when he drew near, and held out his hand.

'Mrs Trengrouse, can it be, ma'am?' His voice held a trace of an accent which I took to be American. But it was not that which startled me. It was his eyes. They were the keenest, most brilliant blue I'd ever seen and in that very first moment it was as though a shock ran through me like that of lightning. For this very reason I assumed a coldness I did not feel.

'Yes. I'm Mrs Trengrouse. Can I help you? Are you in need of accommodation, or what – Mr – Mr—?'

'Justin King,' he answered easily, with his gaze fixed unblinkingly on me. 'And, yes, I hope very much you can. It's about the mine – that derelict place on the moor there to the west. I've heard it's on your land.'

'Wheal Clara? Yes. It happens to be part of my property, Mr King.'

'Then maybe—' he smiled, revealing the flash of very white strong teeth, '—maybe we have something mutual to discuss, ma'am.'

'I can hardly see in what way it could concern you,' I answered, suddenly resenting his interest.

'So may I have the chance to explain?'

I hesitated, sensing a quality that could be overbearing about him, yet I was curious, unwilling to be manipulated, but magnetised at the same time by a certain male charm that roused my senses, and a manner I was quite unprepared for and certainly did not appreciate. The little smile hovering about his lips faded, leaving his strongly carved face sterner, and considerably older looking. Indeed in those few moments between us I judged him to be in the region of thirty or thirty-five.

'Well, Mrs Trengrouse, madam?' Was it my imagination, or did a hint of mockery tinge his voice.

'All right,' I said coolly, lifting my chin an inch higher, 'you'd better come in.'

'I take it my horse will be safe at the side of the house there? I tethered him to a tree.'

'I hardly think any horse thief is likely to be lurking around my premises,' I told him acerbically. 'In any case, I'm sure what you have to say concerning Wheal Clara will take only a few minutes. And as I happen to be extremely busy—'

'Ah, yes,' he said, following me into the hall, 'roses.'

He was amused. I was instantly unreasonably annoyed. I

opened the smaller parlour door and with a rustle of red silk raised an arm showing him in.

He gave a short bow. 'After you, Mrs Trengrouse.'

I shrugged, and entered the room, annoyed with myself for feeling so exasperated. He followed.

'Do sit down,' I said, indicating an armchair. The room was simply furnished with oak table, chest, and chairs made by Thomas. There was an oak settle along one wall facing the fireplace, and curtains and cushions were maroon velvet. Justin King – I wondered where on earth the name came from – did not at first comply. He walked to the window, stood for a few moments with his hands behind his back, legs a little apart, surveying the scene outside which gave a wide view of the brown moorland now spattered with young green and golden gorse. The mine was a dark spectral shape overlooking the sea in the distance.

I waited for him to turn. He did so suddenly, and said, 'I've a deal to propose, ma'am. But please do seat yourself. I was forgetting my manners.'

'Not at all, Mr King,' I said icily, 'and perhaps you'll do the same. The sooner we get down to your – proposal, deal – whatever it is, the quicker we can dismiss the project, so we may as well be comfortable while doing it.'

'Oh, I don't think you'll get rid of me quite so easily and quickly as you think, ma'am,' the calm cocksure voice continued as he settled himself on the bench, head thrust forward, eyeing me closely, 'in fact, I'm pretty sure when you've heard me right you'll there's a good deal in it for you.'

There was a pause.

'Well?' I said sharply. 'Continue. Tell me.'

'I want either the mining rights of that place – Wheal Clara, don't they call it? – Or to buy the whole area thereabouts, lock stock and barrel, as they say—'

'But—'

'Listen to me.' He lifted a hand peremptorily, 'I know all about land, and mining country particularly – had a "nose" for it since I was a boy, and took off ten years ago to the Americas; California to be precise, where I tried my luck – and found it – at streaming, not for tin or copper, but *gold*, Mrs Trengrouse – *gold*. My instincts proved right. Subsequently I made – quite a fortune, you could say.' He grinned, and the years momentarily fled leaving him once again youthful-looking, and filled with the enthusiasm of the adventurer, the prospector. 'Now I'm back, back to my own land. Yes, I'm Cornish born and bred, and there's a great urge in me to try my skill here.'

'But *why* if you're so rich? And what possible chance do you think there is of making Wheal Clara productive again? I used to wonder about it in the past. But it's *dead*, Mr King. It would take quite a fortune to reconstruct and even get the engine and new shafts workable. And the ore isn't there – the lodes are practically dry anyway. I've made enquiries, so did Thomas, my – my late husband. All the local folk know. What you're suggesting is quite impossible. Ridiculous.'

Her chin came out doggedly. The startling blue eyes were hard – compelling on my face.

'No. As I've just said, I've a nose for land. I *understand* it. If you give me – sell the rights, I'll prove you wrong. And I'm willing to pay well.'

'Then you must be very sure,' I said tartly, 'in your own mind, that is. But what makes you assume I'd be willing to sell any inch of the Trengrouse estate? I've worked hard to help my husband salvage it in the last few years. And if there *were* more benefits to be had, then I think I'd have claim to them.'

'To a portion, yes,' he agreed surprisingly. 'Whatever terms we could come to over the actual mine, I would have a document made out, legally, assuring you of half the profits. In the meantime, I'd have involved considerable capital in building, in sinking new shafts – exploring fresh levels, and in consultation with a top-rate engineering firm concerning possible yields. To my way of thinking an important adit could be made directly into the sea—' He broke off, and shrugged. 'But why bore you with such details. The point is – are you interested?'

I faced him squarely, excitement mounting in me, knowing that my colour had deepened and that my green eyes must be blazing. After all, wasn't this what I had always wanted since my marriage, to have the old mine working again? And if what this reckless adventurer, Justin King, proved to be right – then I could be rich; richer than imagined in all my wildest dreams.

Nevertheless, I did not intend to give in too easily.

Challenge, I sensed, was at the very root of Justin King's character, and would make him not only more acquisitive where the mine was concerned, but to have a share in my personal interests.

And myself? Beyond a throbbing inner excitement, I felt nothing but triumph and enjoyment that something was happening at last – something beyond the ambition and a determination to rise above past shame. Behind the hard veneer I'd cultivated, the girl stirred again; after all, I was still comparatively young – but twenty-six, and however crystal clear my mind might be – the joyous ridiculous yearnings of my body broke into sudden confused flowering. I knew nothing of this man – this stranger daring to storm my privacy. Neither did I trust him. But his precocious confidence, his swagger and cool assumptions I'd go along with his plans fired my imagination and set my blood racing. There was a certain danger already in the contract, that made us at once both adversaries and partners in an unpredictable future.

'Well, Mrs Trengrouse?' I heard him say after a pause.

'I shall have to think about it,' I managed to answer in steady tones.

He smiled again. 'Good.' For a second his lips tightened. Though my expression never changed under the answering appraisal of his gaze, I could feel the warm colour once more staining my face. 'Don't take too long, though,' he told me. 'I have other alternatives in mind, but my preference is for Wheal Clara. However—'

'I will let you know tomorrow,' I told him more coldly, 'if you can wait that long.'

He inclined his head, 'Of course. I'm staying at The Marriner in Zaul, and can ride over any hour you wish.'

I pulled myself together, named a time, and after a few more businesslike questions and answers, he departed, leaving me in such a whirl of confused emotion that without knowing the reason, I lifted my skirts above my ankles, ran up the stairs to my bedroom, and stared in astonishment at my reflection through the mirror.

What I saw at first almost affronted me – determined expression with narrowed green eyes above grim set mouth, but with damp curling tendrils of hair broken free of their combs about my temples, as though mocking any show of severity.

Suddenly, irrationally, I dropped the façade, and laughed. Happiness broke from me, unashamed and free. He could be difficult, I knew. He wasn't even handsome in the strictest sense – craggy-looking rather, but those eyes – the message in them. 'Ah Justin King,' I thought. 'We're not so unlike after all. We each know what we want.'

How strange that it should prove to be the same thing.

And in more ways than one.

# II
## Justin

### 1

I wanted the mine, and wanted the woman.

Both.

The mine because after ten years in the gold fields I had a 'nose' – an instinct you could say – for the earth and what it held, also because an inborn passion for Cornwall and my home had pulled me back with the means to restore and reimburse the estate my elder brother had so recklessly squandered. I had never cared for my handsome kinsman who'd been a bully and a snob of the first water – a braggart and womaniser with the charm unfortunately to win my father's complete confidence and enslave my poor mother into an adoration that lasted until her death.

I had always come second in parental esteem and affections – if indeed I'd ever truly had anything of either. So when, after obtaining an engineering and science degree at Oxford I'd decided to take off to the gold fields of either Africa or America, I'm sure relief had been felt in the family bosom. With a reasonable cheque in my pocket and a friendly pat of bonhomie on the shoulder from my sire, I'd walked bag in hand through the door of Heatherfield, stepped into the waiting brougham and been driven to Falmouth where I'd found a boat almost immediately bound for the Americas. Any regrets I'd had about leaving the place I'd secretly loved with such passion through my twenty years of life, were stifled by a hard fanatical determination to return one day, and redeem what remained of it. For I knew, even then, that when my father died, my sibling would soon make ducks and drakes of his ill-deserved inheritance. And without gold in my pocket I'd have no means of saving it. So I must have gold. And gold lay waiting under the dry hot sun for any man with determination, guts, and the constitution of an ox, to dig and work, fail and start again, enduring privations and fever, disappointment and all the other obstacles sent to deter him before good luck struck.

Well – I'd been such a man. And the goal had given me the drive. News had reached me from time to time through various and devious channels that my insights concerning Heatherfield had been correct. My brother's debauchery since our father's demise was allowing an estate that had once been the pride of our forefathers to fall into debt and ruin.

Hatred of all he represented mingled with memories of his cruelty and bullying when I was a child – of his suave behaviour and the elegant front presented to my parents, had given zest and almost inhuman energy to my resolve. So I'd worked and sweated and suffered and overcome. And in the end it was there.

I was rich.

Rich enough to buy up the whole of Cornwall if I wished. But I didn't wish. And Cornwall wasn't for sale. It belonged to the inheritors: sons bred from the ordinary folk who'd streamed for copper and tin, the early Celts from whom I, too, was descended, the farmers and miners, toilers of the earth.

It seemed natural, therefore, that I should covet Wheal Clara which stood stark and abandoned on the fringe of the north cliffs only twenty miles as the crow flew, from Heatherfield. Experience and calculating insight told me that with new shafts and a fresh adit at a lower level running to the sea, and a powerful pumping engine the site could be made not only lucrative but extremely profitable. The expense would be considerable, but my pocket could well spare it. from the records it was made quite clear that the problem initially had been water. Water had caused the main collapse of levels. Searching through accounts of the final disaster which had led to complete closure I'd had no firm evidence that the copper had run out; on the contrary – and my intuition worked here – I'd sensed there could still be a wealth of it, and very likely tin, beneath.

Tin.

Yes – there could very likely be tin below the copper. The mine had formerly been worked down to 200 fathoms. It was possible to go considerably deeper. Anything was possible providing the woman could be persuaded to sell or at least co-operate.

The woman!

As I walked away from her glorified farmhouse that spring morning, both my body and imagination were alight. Strong and sturdy she'd appeared as she'd stood at the door with the sunlight striking sideways on the bold outlines of her face, and edging her black hair with flame. Yet the lines of her figure were desirable and curved in all the right places. There'd been a peculiar dignity about her – a withheld quality that nonplussed me. I'd wanted to run a hand down from the golden-brown forearm, feel her stir in response, and bring a softening to the expresison in her long cat's eyes. She was a widow, I knew, with something in her history that stopped men gossiping when her name was mentioned.

Why?

What was there so different about her from any other of the women I'd known and desired? I'd met many far more beautiful and certainly more forthcoming and eager to charm. This one appeared not to care a rap. And it wasn't natural. During my years abroad I'd had experience enough to calculate pretty accurately within the first five minutes of meeting a girl, to which type she belonged – the warmly accessible, cool and superciliously flirtatious, hard to get, or frankly promiscuous. Katrina Trengrouse fitted into none of these. She appeared outwardly haughty, yet at the same time with a flame in her startling eyes, a sexual defiance of movement and timbre of voice that belied the chill façade. And from her proud stance I knew she'd be difficult to win. But I warmed to the task. As I said, I wanted her. And I'd never been the man to resist a challenge or lose, once I set my mind to it.

I'd heard she'd not long been widowed, and that her life before marriage still remained a bit of a mystery in those parts. No matter. That she was intrinsically virtuous I had no doubts. Perhaps that very quality in her caused the hard lines of bitterness about her mouth and narrowed censure of her gaze.

Never mind, I thought, there'd be additional gratification in bringing sweetness to the hungry lips – for she was hungry, I knew that, too. The desire between us was mutual, and in the end she'd succumb.

Meanwhile there was the mine.

I spent the rest of the day until early evening, taking a further survey, with the help of the books and information I had gathered of the land round Wheal Clara, assessing expenditure and labour required for reopening, the mileage of past levels and making a rough estimate for the number of new shafts and large Watt pumping engines necessary, once confirmation had been obtained from the proper quarters.

Rebuilding would include not only more powerful pumps and boiler houses, but an enlarged count house, a miners' store and smith's shop. The number of workers – miners and their families necessary for such an ambitious project, would require cottages and I envisaged, to the east, a new village emerging for this specific purpose. Oh, there was no end to the dream and none of it was impossible, because I had the means.

*Gold.*

Gold to produce copper, tin and new life for poor folks needing work, and for the Widow Trengrouse – the woman I'd seen and in the first instant recognised was the only one I'd ever wished to make my wife.

*

The following day she was waiting for me when I arrived in the afternoon at Rookswood promptly at the hour suggested. One glance at the slightly tilted lips suggested she intended to be at least co-operative – a suggestion endorsed by the frilled white dress and softly bunched dark curls which gave a seductive enchantingly feminine quality to the slender waist below the full breasts and throat. But the penetrating green eyes were enigmatic, and I knew that before any assent was given to my offer, there might be quite a tough bargaining session, if only for her vanity's and pride's sake.

When the usual first polite formalities had been exchanged, I came to the point abruptly, saying, 'Well, Mrs Trengrouse, what is it to be? Yes or no?' The double-edged question appeared not to disconcert her in the least, although I fancied a tinge of rose coloured her complexion.

'Regarding the mine, do you mean?'

'Exactly. You know, roughly, my proposition. It's a good one, and if you've a business head—' I eyed her speculatively, '—which I'm sure you have, there isn't really any great problem where *you're* concerned. You risk nothing, I a great deal. However—' I had a sheet of plans and details ready, which I laid forthwith on the parlour table – 'if you wish me to go through each point one by one I'm quite willing to do so. They are subject to amendment, of course, and would have to be legally drawn up. But first of all it's essential you make your feelings clear. There's no point in either of us wasting time if you're determined to be set against the idea.'

A hint of quick temper lit her eyes and voice as she replied sharply, 'I would not be discussing the matter at all with you if I wasn't prepared to consider the proposition, Mr King. And should I agree—' She paused then, and I knew that she would ultimately, '—naturally my own solicitor would have to be present at any settlement.'

I bowed my head slightly.

'Naturally.'

She might already have a solicitor, she might not, I thought, with a quirk of amusement. Meanwhile she was now playing a very titillating little game of 'hard-to-get and hard-to-win', by exercising any feminine trick she could think of to enslave me, although possibly she was less aware of it than I gave her credit for. The first stiffness of pose and speech had softened slightly, and as we talked of quite mundane and unnecessary points, her every movement indicated an instinctive sensual quality betraying the woman behind the bargainer. The golden sheen of skin, and subtle slow turn of head – the rounded rhythmic motion of arm and shoulder as she emphasised some quite unimportant fact were more indicative of her inevitable surrender, than any formal statement of words could have been. She was like some beautiful hungry wild-cat driven by instinct to exploit herself before a mate.

And consequently innocent, as all intrinsically untamed creatures were. Therefore I wanted her all the more' not only for b·siness but for myself. Had the pristine naiveté been lacking, her allure for me would have been considerably less. As it was I put up with her childlike pretence and bartering with as good a will as I could muster.

Eventually my patience wearied. I got up from the chair abruptly, folded the paper and replaced it in my case, then I said, 'I think you've had plenty of time. We're getting nowhere. Maybe I should look elsewhere for a mine.'

'No.' The one word came out with a snap. 'I've had time to think – as you've just said. Very well, I'm not averse to giving you the "rights" as you call them of Wheal Clara, but first, wouldn't it be a good plan to look over the site together?'

I almost laughed aloud.

'I agree with you, of course. When?'

'What about now? You can ride over – it's only a matter of two miles, and I'll follow presently. I've something to do first—' She broke off vaguely and I wondered what was in her mind.

'You could ride with me onNero.'

'I'd rather not, if you don't mind. I feel like a walk – on my own, Mr King, and it shouldn't take me more than half-an-hour.'

So I agreed, and five minutes later was cantering across the moors towards Wheal Clara.

Once there, I had time to reflect more objectively on the project ahead to weigh the pros and cons less personally, away from the disturbing presence of Katrina Trengrouse, but I didn't make the effort, because my mind was already made up. The only problem, as I then saw it, was to make the mutual assessment sufficiently agreeable and tantilising to her for there to be no argument about the sharing basis. I had no intention at all of allowing her a complete half of the profits. One or two other 'adventurers' would be involved, which would make a safe business of the company, ensuring that should the wilful young madam attempt to push her nose into business matters that didn't concern her, the majority vote, including mine, would overrule any wild idea she might have.

I also meant to *buy* – not loan – the land around. She might not like it, but in the end I reckoned she'd respect me for my inborn acquisitive streak. Beneath that proud air of hers she was a very feminine woman who'd appreciate that in business a man was meant to wear the breeches, just as in the home a woman held power through the lure of feminine skirts. And it was in those long voluminous affairs that I'd thought to see her coming along the moor that day to meet me at Wheal Clara. Indeed, I was to receive a shock when a jaunty bold figure appeared round a bend of the hill attired in breeches, tall boots, with a cape flying behind her from her shoulders, and her hair pushed up under some fantastic pointed cap, looking for all the world like a character from one of Shakespeare's plays.

'Good heavens!' I said, when she stood before me, lips twitching humorously, eyes bright with a sparkle of mischief, 'I didn't recognise you.' And indeed at first glance I hadn't. But only for a second. The stance, and swing of shoulders had been unmistakable, and, close to, no one could have taken her for a boy.

'Why? Because of these?' She glanced down at the breeches. 'In case you didn't know, I've spent quite a time getting Rookswood into some sort of order, inside the house and out. It would be folly, don't you think to get my gowns torn to shreds by thorns and briars? Moors are not gentle places, Mr King, neither am I the gentle type of a well-bred woman. Also I have had to study expense. Do you understand?'

I was beginning to.

'I wouldn't want you to get a wrong idea of me,' she continued, 'or to think you could fool me in business or otherwise. Once it would have been all too easy. But I learned my lesson the hard way.' Her smile had vanished. She was once more the slightly defiant creature of our first meeting.

'I never intended to fool you,' I said abruptly. 'But it's imperative you should realise and appreciate that in the long run *I* am the only one standing to lose, should the copper yield prove disappointing. You will be considerably the richer either way it goes, once you've put your signature to the agreement.'

'*If* I do.'

'Of course. *If.* Pardon me.' I could hardly refrain from laughing outright. She sensed it, for she said immediately, 'Don't play with me, Mr King.'

'As if I would.'

'Oh, I think you might, if you thought you could get away with it.'

'You're a very bitter young woman,' I told her, 'which is a pity. It doesn't suit you.'

She bit her lip, shrugged, turned her lovely head away, displaying a few dark curls nestling at her neck beneath the stupid cap, and said, 'Well, shall we get on with it?'

'With what, Mrs Trengrouse?'

'The site. You wanted to look over it.'

'If I remember, that was *your* suggestion. I'd hardly have put any proposition to you if I hadn't already studied the area many times already.'

'Then why did we bother? As I've already told you, I'm an extremely busy woman, and—'

'Which makes it all the more complimentary to me that you should have bothered dressing up and tramping the wilds to meet me here alone at such a very desolate spot,' I answered.

She flushed.

'We're wasting time, Mr King.'

'Yes, Mrs Trengrouse.'

The next moment I'd put an arm round her waist, drawn her close, tilted her chin up towards mine, and my lips were on hers, gently at first, as warmly seductive as possible, then deepening firmly until her luscious mouth was sweet and eager under mine – hungry for fulfilment.

\*

I must make myself clear.

It was for no reason of man-made morality that I did not seduce Katrina Trengrouse during our auspicious moorland meeting on that spring afternoon of 1820.

It was more a matter of good sense and taste – of savouring the vintage before relishing the full intoxication on the marriage night. A passionate mistress can be extremely satisfying as I'd discovered, conveniently, during my years abroad. But the full enjoyment of possessing a wife demands a completely different approach, and I was determined that for both of us it should hold all the sensual and physical delights of an exciting emotional journey of discovery.

That I might be sticking my neck out in assuming she would

marry me did not occur to me, simply because I knew by that first kiss she was already committed.

I did not even have to say, 'Darling, will you be my wife?' Simply, 'When is it be then?' At the same time letting a hand travel downwards from her shoulder over one ripe breast wondering meanwhile at my capacity to keep control.

She released herself and said with the trace of a tremor in her voice, 'You are proposing to me, I take it?'

'Exactly.'

'You don't waste words, I must say.'

'Not unnecessarily.'

She laughed then, 'You certainly have a nerve.'

'Part of my nature, Katrina. If I hadn't I wouldn't now be where I am – rich enough and wise enough to assess my chances in a fortuitous deal and take a risk.'

'So that's what I am? A fortuitous deal?'

I gave in then, and pulled her to my arms again. 'God, no. Listen. Don't taunt me too far or I might just mount my horse and ride away. I want you, Katrina – need, desire you in a way I never thought to feel about any woman. Love? What's that? A *word*, no more, just a sentimental tit-bit used as a trap to lure respectable couples to the altar. But we're different to that, you and I, not particularly respectable perhaps, merely flesh-and-blood; *real*. Now – answer me. *When?*'

'Just whenever you like, Justin King,' she said softly, demurely, but with a wicked glint in her eyes.

'I suggest next week. No need to delay things. A short breathing space to get the formalities settled and introduce you to my family – at Heatherfield, and then—'

I could feel her stiffen, grow rigid against my chest.

'What's the matter?' I asked. 'Shy? Surely not.'

With her face averted she replied almost coldly, 'I'd rather not, if you don't mind.'

'*What?*'

'Go to Heatherfield.'

'But *why*? It's not a bad place, and as it happens to be the Pencorrin family home I'd assumed you'd not be averse to living there.'

'Did you say *Pencorrin*?' she asked, still in the curiously icy tones

'I did, and why not? Are you afraid of disapproval? If so, I can put your mind at rest in a few words. They'll eat out of your hand, metaphorically speaking, because I wish it. Have you forgotten what I told you of my background and my brother's dastardly neglect of the estate? And of my aim to get it on its feet again? Well? – That's just what I'm doing—' I broke off, confused, almost shocked, by the tightened, contemptuous set of her face, her blazing eyes. 'Pencorrin,' she said. 'You mentioned Pencorrin. But you said your name was King.'

'So it is. Justin King Pencorrin. I used the 'King' abroad, because it sounded simpler, and had a better ring to it. I've kept it on for working purposes. Damn it, Katrina, what's it matter? An abbreviation? A *name*? I don't understand.'

She walked away a few yards, stood with her back to me, looking down, and playing with a branch of flowering thorn. Then she turned and said, 'You're quite right; I'm being stupid. A relation of mine a long time ago had some sort of misunderstanding with your kinsman. That's all.' Her voice had become natural once more, controlled and quite steady. 'All the same, I *would* prefer us to be married first – before meeting a bunch of relatives—'

'Hardly a bunch, just my brother, his wife, Angelica, and his son Rupert by a former marriage. I never knew her, she was French, and he divorced her when the boy was young – little more than a baby.'

She snapped off a twig of white blossom sharply, held it to her nose, made a play of sniffing it, then reiterated, 'They would be sure to want a fuss – something showy in Church, a public ceremony. And I don't want that, Justin. I haven't been widowed long. Surely it's not much to ask – a quiet ceremony, then, afterwards, the meeting at Heatherfield Grange.'

Was it my fancy, or did a hint of triumph emphasise the last two words.

I shrugged. The issue wasn't really so important and it was perhaps understandable she wished the event to be kept on as low a key as possible considering the short time that had elapsed since Thomas Trengrouse's death. Women, the most feminine of them, were unpredictable creatures harbouring strange phobias and fancies at times of emotional crisis. And there would be a certain stimulus after all – a kick – in the fait accompli, by presenting Katrina unexpectedly as Mrs Justin Pencorrin to my rake of a brother and his petulant high-born wife.

So it was settled.

Katrina and I were married five days later by special licence. That same evening I took her by chaise to Heatherfield Grange, leaving the two children, Rosanna and Drake, temporarily at Rookswood in the care of the kindly housekeeper and what domestic help was employed there.

## 2

Possibly an intelligent and beautiful woman is bound to be in some way or another unpredictable. Certainly this proved to be the case on my new wife's first introduction to the family. After professing to me such a shy dislike of there being any fuss or outward show of celebration, she insisted on appearing – to my inner amusement and approval – in an outfit of deepest luxurious-looking jade silk, bought two days previously, with a ridiculously smart but intriguing concoction of flowers and plumes on her head that gave her the air of a duchess rather than a young unsophisticated widow brought suddenly to the status of a country landowner's wife.

That Richard looked intrigued as I led her into the drawing room is an understatement. His mouth gaped in astonishment, his eyes – which had become slightly protruberant through years of indulgent living – stared as though hypnotised. As usual these days, he smelled of whisky. He was no longer the outstandingly handsome bully I remembered, but an overweight edition of a libertine who still could not resist the sight of a beautiful woman. Angelica, his wife, pale, pretty and bored-looking, with a certain contemptuous droop to her petulant mouth, extended her hand indifferently, although she gave an abrupt start of surprise when I said, with

a motion of my hand '—my wife, Katrina. Katrina, love, meet
my sister-in-law, Angelica, and my brother, Richard.'

Richard got to his feet, poured a glass of whisky, and
quaffed it down automatically, as though habitual, which of
course it was. He was wearing a velvet maroon-coloured
jacket that emphasised the sudden rise of colour to his
face. Then he remarked. 'Really! *Wife*. You're joking, of
course.'

'Certainly not,' I answered coldly. 'Katrina and I were
married this morning, in Penzance, so I hope it will be possible
to have the guest rooms made ready as soon as possible for our
retirement. I should have let you know earlier, but we were
both anxious there should be no fuss or show. Katrina has no
liking for pomp.'

'So I observe.' Richard's voice was heavy with sarcasm. For a
second or two he eyed me with something of the old
challenging bravado; then abruptly he shrugged, turned
away, and said to Angelica, 'You'd better inform Mrs Heron.'

Angelica sighed, but before leaving the room said coldly,
'This is all very difficult – at the last moment. You *should* have
let us know.'

'So we should.' Katrina spoke with the sweetness of a tiger
about to spring. 'But please don't weary yourself too much on
my account. I'm really quite used to facing emergencies; as
long as the sheets are dry and there's water in the ewer, I'm
sure neither Justin nor I will complain.'

With a rustle of pale blue skirts, Anglica went to the door
and slammed it sharply as she left.

Katrina and Richard stood facing each other, and there was
something in the pause between them that I just couldn't make
out – and something I damned well meant to interrupt before
it developed into downright hate. That my brother's nose was
put out of joint I could understand. He'd probably hardly
contemplated me marrying anyone. That I'd done so at last,
and without his knowledge, and taken such a vibrant alluring
creature as wife into the bargain would be sufficient reason to
breed antagonism. Katrina might well bear sons, and although
nominally his precious boy, Rupert, would be heir, he would
be dependent entirely financially on the goodwill of any heirs I
might produce. Yes, I could well indeed understand his

chagrin, but the narrowed gleam of Katrina's eyes, the set of Richard's fleshy bold chin and distinct tremor of his hand suggested there was more to it than that.

Later, when we were alone in a hastily prepared suite facing westwards, over the moors, I questioned Katrina about her past references concerning former family trouble with the Pencorrins. She was preparing herself for a late evening meal, and apart from a lingering kiss, during which I'd allowed one hand to travel exploratively the lines of her body, I'd refrained so far from explicit marital overtures. In spite of my goldmining days – or perhaps because of them – and a natural erotic appreciation of physical allure, I was at heart something of a sensual romantic. To have crudely made a sudden show of asserting 'male rights' would have dulled the ultimate pleasures of consummation. I had also been mildly irritated by the over-charged atmosphere of antagonism between my brother and my wife, which had suggested a deep inner conflict of which I had no knowledge or understanding.

She was at the dressing table loosening her dark hair about her shoulders when I said, 'What exactly *was* the trouble between our family and yours, Katrina?'

'Oh!' she gave a short laugh that had a high ring about it. 'Does it matter? – Nothing. Nothing at all really. Something about land, as I've said – I don't know, I forget.'

I took her face firmly between my hands and turned her head round so her eyes were forced to stare straight into mine.

'It seems odd,' I commented, 'that you never mentioned it before.'

'There hasn't been much time, has there?' she parried. 'And until a few days ago I didn't even know you were a Pencorrin, Mr King.'

'Ha!' I took her point. 'You've got me there.'

'Yes. And if we both have to go into unimportant family incidents of past history I'm afraid there's going to be a good deal of time-waste, don't you think?'

'But—'

'*Really*, Justin! If I was abrupt with your brother it was because I didn't particularly like him. As for the family trouble – that little incident hardly deserves mentioning. Anyway, I was a child then – I don't even remember.'

'You could hardly do so, I suppose, since you spent your life on the sea with your father?'

'*Most* of the time,' she pointed out. 'I told you, my mother died. And sometimes I stayed with my – my aunt and uncle – they had a farm not *very* far from Penjust, but it was only quite small, comparatively speaking. It was demolished years ago. And I thought—'

'Yes?'

'I thought we'd both agreed not to discuss the past. Whenever I referred to Thomas you seemed to object. Now it's some stupid little argument from my childhood.' She jumped up suddenly, jerked herself round challengingly, and said, 'What's the *matter* with you? Do you want a book of memoirs, or something? Because if you do, I'm afraid you'll have to wait for some years. I'm no stuffy writer of books.'

Her outburst of temper was irresistible; she looked so young and fiery with such a wild colour, and light in her eyes, I forgot my prudent resolve, and drew her to me, pulses hammering, with hunger, lust and adoration all clamouring in one surging tide of desire.

To say we were both perfectly adjusted in every way is an understatement. I'd always, until that first full experience with my wild and beautiful Katrina rather shied at the word 'love', which had suggested to me sentimentality, and a shy reverence between man's attitude to woman which all too often proved a mockery in the bedroom, and under certain other circumstances nothing more than crude hypocrisy. Sex – either titillating or as a simple necessity to normal life – had been the one vital impulse behind the façade of fancy phrases and protestations of enduring passion. But my feelings for Katrina went far, far deeper than mere sex. Before that first act of mutual possession I had never believed in any bond superseding the physical. But our union soared with the flesh to a wild sphere also of fiery spiritual fusion that revealed me as a new man – a human being reborn.

I knew that it was the same with her – just as I had to accept that the knowledge – the first pristine glimpse of this new state of awareness must inevitably relax shortly into a more mundane acceptance of the entirely normal satisfying man-and-woman relationship.

Such was life.

In that brief period of time, however, I had learned that life itself did indeed include the much maligned word 'love', and that through Katrina I had found it.

During the days following I was intrigued by my wife's aptitude for gradually taking control as chatelaine of Heatherfield. Although Angelica by rights was mistress, she was far too languid and concerned with her own extravagant indulgences to be bothered by Katrina's obvious capacity and desire to assert herself in household affairs, and only occasionally did a hint of venom tinge her well-bred voice when she bothered herself to show priority concerning any orders of Katrina's given to a servant in her presence.

Eventually even incidents of this kind practically ceased. She was a vain, bored woman, who appeared not to care a rap that the very substantial dowry brought on her marriage to Richard had already been absorbed by the high life-style she'd demanded during their first years together. I'd managed to curtail certain expenditures pretty ruthlessly when I'd discovered just how badly the estate had suffered. Debts had been paid, which Richard had accepted with a wry, sarcastic show of gratitude holding no sincerity whatever. 'Thanks, old boy,' he'd said, after the first hurdle had been crossed. 'Must give you no end of a kick, eh? Being able to step in and retrieve the family fortune and honour. What?' He'd been slightly drunk at the time. His manner had been insulting, his eyes hard and cold.

'Just see you don't run up any bills in *my* name,' I'd answered, 'and try and din a little sense into that wife of yours, or—'

'You'll send me packing lock, stock and barrel, as they say. Is that it? No, brother dear. Simply because you can't. I was born, and remain, heir to Heatherfield, and nothing you damn well do on behalf of its poverty-stricken acres can alter that legal fact. If you're fool enough to spend your precious nuggets on me and mine, good luck to you. Only don't nag my wife. She's of the élite, remember – which is more than can be said of yours, if what I hear is correct.'

I'd lifted my fist, and almost brought it hard against his jaw, but restrained, because just at that moment Katrina had entered the room, and stood staring, with two bright spots of colour on her high cheekbones.

'What—?'

Richard had given an unsteady mock bow.

'I was informing your spouse, my overbearing sibling, that you both would do well to remember on occasion that my wife has prior rights in this household,' he remarked, 'and in future that you will not be allowed to go your devious way in checking what vintage liquor is taken to her room. I hope you understand, Katrina dear. It would be regrettable if I had to play a very important card I hold, to ensure your co-operation—'

'And what the devil do you mean by that?' I demanded with some heat, taking a step forward.

Katrina pulled me back. 'No. Don't, Justin. Take no notice. He's just—'

'Drunk,' again the silly bow. 'True. Too true, but only slightly.' He drew himself up, and walked over carefully to the door. 'Think it over, sister-in-law,' he said before leaving. 'I should hate to discomfort you.'

'Now what did he mean by that?' I asked Katrina when the door had slammed.

She was very pale, and her emerald eyes were very cold and clear, almost blazing, when she said, 'He's just a mountebank, Justin. It's obvious he's going to do his best to drive a wedge between us. Take no notice, if you do you'll merely be playing into his hands. Nothing would please him better than to succeed in discomforting you, and—' she smiled faintly, intriguingly, 'and it wouldn't be very flattering to me, would it, knowing you didn't entirely trust me?'

For a moment she looked so very temptingly seductive I could hardly resist taking her to the bedroom there and then. Instead I said with assumed remarkable coolness, 'I didn't realise a matter of trust was involved.' I could feel my lips tightening as I continued, 'but as you've raised the subject, my love – no. It would certainly not be either flattering or for your own good. I really believe if I discovered you'd been playing with me in any devious way I would either beat or kill you. The first probably. And then throw you to—'

'The lions, as the Roman emperors did,' she interrupted. 'Oh, Justin, what a way to talk.' She laughed.

'Never take a statement of mine as just talk, Katrina.'

She sighed. 'Darling, what's the matter with you? Look at me.' She reached up, and with both hands round my neck forced my face down towards hers. 'Kiss me, Justin. I love you so much.'

Kissing her was no problem; in fact it was an effective way of ending such a totally unrewarding conversation. Her lips under mine were luscious and sweet, her body soft and yielding. Already desirous and hard for her, I yet managed to firmly disengage myself.

'Not just at the moment, love,' I said, with an effort. 'Later – at a more convenient moment, when I say so.'

I knew she was annoyed, but the fact didn't trouble me. I was no callow youth, and had learned long since that in one way most women were alike – even Katrina. They respected and desired a man all the more for asserting the male prerogative of being the dominant partner.

After that incident I noticed with inner amusement a certain reflective assessing glance in my wife's eyes at rare intervals, indicating my point had registered, and that she was sufficiently wise to leave the initiative in sexual matters to me, although sensually she had the subtle power always to rouse me.

And so time passed; a busy hard-pressed period in which I spent hours each day dealing with estate matters – of visiting and re-housing tenants whom Richard had allowed to live in hovels under poverty-stricken conditions, subsisting entirely on what they managed to grow for themselves from a poor patch of earth, and in finding jobs on the site at Wheal Clara for any men once employed there who were still capable physically of wielding a pick or a spade.

One new shaft was already partly sunk at the mine, and two more had been scheduled, on the advice from engineers up-country. Ground had been sifted and examined and found to contain copper. At a deeper level than formerly worked, I'd been assured there was certainly tin.

The major undertaking still was drainage, but this problem was not insurmountable, and it was exhilarating to me to note the dulled resignation in men's eyes lighten to expectancy and hope, as the project proceeded.

I had expected – or rather hoped for – some slight show of

interest or gratitude from my brother. Occasionally he accompanied me to meetings at the new count house, but mostly he continued with his indulgent life of lassitude and cynical acceptance of a status quo which he had no intention of discarding.

'It's all right for you,' he said one day, 'you're still young – comparatively. I did my share in the past, and have no intention of slaving for the rest of my life at a white elephant – and that's what Heatherfield is, Justin. You just wait. You'll find out. Then maybe you'll appreciate my little weakness for a game of cards and the bottle.'

'And your wife? And son?'

'Ah! Rupert. The legal heir.'

I didn't like the way he looked at me.

'He will go to Oxford, I take it,' my brother continued, 'following Eton, or Harrow? I presume you wouldn't wish the inheritor of Heatherfield to lack the usual educational benefits due to his station in life?'

'At my expense, of course.'

'Hopefully, brother dear, seeing I'm unlikely at this stage to go knock-knock-knocking at the earth for little lumps of gold in America or far-off Africa.'

I gave up.

'You're impossible.'

He gave his short satirical laugh.

'I happen to be the quite predictable result of years coping with a mean old devil, who happened to be our papa leading a penurious existence because of some bible-thumping illusion that to enjoy life was sin, while you conveniently disappeared to make your little pile.

'Have you ever seen things that way? Naturally not. But don't blame *me* for squandering a few pennies when I got the chance, and don't lay it at *my* door that tenants and the estate suffered. If you'd had the guts you pretended to have when you were a kid, you'd have stayed where you'd belonged instead of running away. Oh you fancy yourself as the brave tough colourful saviour of the family name, but in reality you're the same sneaking shirker I did my best to beat into shape in the old days. So no preaching if you please. I never liked you, and it's the same now. But we'll never be rid of each other simply because I mean to enjoy what I can of your ill-gotten gains.'

He waved a hand tipsily, 'And don't deny it. I'm not a fool. You're no saint, brother – just a wily hypocrite who's had the damned good luck to pull off a risky deal or two bringing a tidy fortune into the bargain.'

The glimmer of his teeth shone in the travesty of the grin I'd so loathed when he was a boy. For a second, though, he looked almost handsome again, and I remembered occasions in the far-off past when that same smile had heralded some sadistic trick to torment me.

I walked away abruptly, saying, 'Now you've made your little speech, I advise you to pull yourself together – for Anglica's sake. Also it's almost lunchtime.'

'Angelica,' I heard him say before I reached the door. 'Ah, yes. Poor pretty little Angelica. No looks any more, no brains. So sad she can't even give me a son. Still, there's always Rupert. Thank God for Rupert. What say you, brother dear?'

I said nothing, but slammed the door, with the temper rising in me, because it seemed he was using his son as a challenge to discomfort me, and I resented it. Contrary to what might have been expected I quite liked the boy; he was a good-looking youngster with a certain boldness about him that appealed to me. He showed as well, even in those early years, a love of nature and appreciation of the domain which, once free of his father, boded well for the future. Yes – I didn't resent that my nephew would eventually have certain nominal rights in the estate denied to any children of Katrina's and mine, and I wished she could find it in her heart to show more friendliness to him. Her attitude held a certain aloofness where the boy was concerned that was mildly disconcerting. It was almost as though she was afraid to have contact. And quite clearly he noticed it.

'Can't you be a little more forthcoming with the boy?' I asked her one day, in mild irritation. 'You may not care for Richard – that's *your* affair, and I can't say I blame you. But damn it all, Katrina, that Rupert has such a bastard of a father isn't *his* fault. Usually you're good with children – perhaps rather overstrung with Rosanna who gets slapped far too often, but at least there's something between you – a *bond*. But with Rupert—'

'Rosanna's my daughter,' Katrina interrupted sharply.

'Don't try and tell me how to bring up my own child, Justin. As for Rupert—' her voice faltered, I noticed she swallowed before continuing, '—he's not my concern.'

'But he's your *nephew* – by marriage. And in one house all the children in it should be treated equally.'

'I *try* to be fair,' she persisted.

'You may try, but you're not. Rupert has no mother, and needs affection. Angelica as step-mama is a travesty, and through your over-possessiveness of Rosanna the child's becoming too often wilful and defiant. As for Drake, spoiled little brat, he's quite likely to develop into a real mother's boy. A prig.'

'Drake will never be a prig. He's the same as his father – stubborn, but even-tempered and gentle. Just like Thomas.'

She spoke with such prim assuredness and admiration of that other man's son I had a swift jealous instinct to give my lovely wife a taste of the medicine she'd delivered so sharply to Rosanna that very morning, and put her over my knee.

But I didn't. It would have been sensless and unfair.

Instead I said coldly but meaningfully, 'Listen to me, my love. The last thing I intend to have in our home – yes, *ours* – yours, mine, the children's, Richard's, and Angelica's – the whole lot – is quarrelling or ill-feeling. I won't have it, you understand? There may be difficulties at times, almost bound to be. You've dealt with them pretty effectively so far. But lately it seems to me you've become a bit too—' I broke off, struggling for the right word.

'Yes?'

'Too overbearing,' I told her.

'*Overbearing?*' she laughed. '*Me!* well *really*—!'

'Yes, *really*, my love. And—' I took her chin in one hand, '—it's got to stop. *You* rule here, you know that. *They* know it now – the family, and the servants. Well, try using tact and diplomacy with your power, and don't ever raise a hand to Rosanna again. You understand?'

'But—'

'Say yes, darling, and have done with it, or there'll be trouble.'

She sighed, softened and murmured with grudging mock-meek ess, 'Oh, very well, tyrant.' And I knew by her faint smile and the over sidelong glance of her eyes that she hadn't really minded giving in, and that to keep our passion bright and glowing a little show of male dominance on my part might be necessary at times.

Following that short incident between us Katrina *did* appear to unbend somewhat towards Rupert, and Rosanna was left more freely to enjoy herself in her own way. She was a beautiful young creature with a good deal in her of Katrina, but with a quality of sensitive allure holding none of my wife's bold assurance. There was a pride and shyness about her allied to an adventurous streak that frequently drove her to wandering off by herself over the moors to haunts that she knew were strictly forbidden. Somehow I contrived on more than one occasion to intercede between her mother and herself when the young truant returned after an hour or so, with a torn hem to her skirt and her dark curls tangled with tiny twigs and briars.

'Where have you been?' Katrina demanded once, with the old fiery gleam in her green eyes. 'Just look at you—' She took the little girl's shoulder and pointed to the soiled blue dress. Rosanna's small chin came out, her huge violet eyes stared up at her mother with a hint of rising defiance.

'Now, Rosanna,' I interposed. 'It's all right. You'll not be punished. Just tell the truth.'

'Dancing,' Rosanna replied. 'Just dancing.'

'*Dancing? Alone?*'

Rosanna nodded. 'At first. In that green place – by the stone. Then *they* came.'

'Who?' Katrina's voice was as sharp.

There was a pause before the child answered, in soft wondering tones, almost a whisper, 'Just *them*. They wore coloured clothes, and said funny things in words I didn't know. There was an old woman smoking a pipe, and a – a boy in a coloured cap like Puck—'

Katrina sighed, shaking her head.

'What *do* you *mean*? Why do you say such wicked things? They're not true, are they? You're making it all up.'

'Oh, no, *no* I haven't. I'm *not*. They were *real* – truly, mama, they were. And one of them played a fiddle, so I danced again and they clapped, and it was lovely. Then—'

'Yes?'

'Then I stopped and told them I must come home. They didn't *want* me to, but I remembered what you said, so I did.'

Thinking back I realise more may have been said, but the gist of it was there – in what I remember now. I guessed the truth pretty quickly, that Rosanna had been entertaining a company of gypsies – there was a fair on at Trywenna – but I didn't mention the fact to Katrina, who luckily accepted Rosanna's explanation with unexpected docility.

Time passed. During the next few years, Richard pulled himself together sufficiently to put on a façade of respectability to tenants and the outside world, making a show of interest in the estate by riding round – when he was sufficiently sober – on Major, one of the best horses in the stables, attending the local hunts, looking every inch the ageing gentleman squire, while I made it my business seeing all was well at the Wheal Clara mine and with workers of the agricultural community.

Many farmers of the district, indeed throughout the country, were suffering disasters due to the low price of agricultural produce and excessive taxes which, added to payment of rent, rates, tithes and enormously increased poor rate, made living hard. In 1822 a petition was organised on behalf of farmers, to which 482 signatures were given, including holdings of thousands of acres, to some in the region of only four. A point was also made in the press of the unequal state of the representation of the people in the Commons' House of Parliament.

Seeing personally how things were, I was able to alleviate a good deal of anxiety in the vicinity of Heatherfield by dipping into my own pocket. And in doing so did not lose. Satisfied men – like miners, with minds free of worry and good food in their bellies, produced more and therefore the estate not only survived financially, but flourished comparatively.

During those years I did not perhaps spend as much time in Katrina's company as she wished – journeying to and fro to Wheal Clara alone took up certain hours each week, but our life together was rich and vivid, our passion still as bright a flame. Naturally, we had occasional temperament battles, but the coming-together again was all the sweeter for a little petulance on her part and quick-tempered dominance on my own. In 1821 she had borne me two children – twins – Dominic and Juliana.

In 1822 there was an outbreak of typhus fever at Penzance and in the surrounding district, which Angelica, after a day's shopping in the town, contracted, and from which she died. Katrina, through nerves and anxiety for the rest of the family, especially myself and the children, was on tenterhooks and decided to take the youngsters off to Rookswood for a period to escape infection.

I didn't try to dissuade her. A new adit had been opened at Wheal Clara, which I decided to keep my eye on, and in close contact with the manager, Joe Gorran, and my being comparatively on the spot for part of the time would certainly help matters. Only Rupert who was eleven, objected.

'I don't want to go. I'll stay with papa,' he said stubbornly.

Richard flung me a hostile but triumphant look. 'You see? I can't be all that bad, can I?'

Katrina opened her mouth to object, then shrugged and said coldly, 'Very well. You're his father; it's up to you.'

And so it was. My wife and family went off to Rookswood, which we'd retained as a holiday home, Rosanna rather resentfully, leaving Richard and Rupert behind with most of the staff.

When we were all reunited again it was springtime.

\*

No one could have helped noticing with the passing of years how fond of each other Rupert and Rosanna were becoming. In many ways they were alike – both dark, good-looking, and occasionally imperious. Both had a tendency to be headstrong, although Rupert could be lack-a-daisical when it suited him, whereas Rosanna showed always a passionate determination to go her own way. She still insisted on lonely periods when she would wander off, dreaming, I guessed of romance ahead, when some young gallant would appear to win her heart and wed her. Not that social events were very frequent at Heatherfield those days. Katrina had developed an unexpected sense of snobbery where her children were concerned, and made it quite clear that mere farmers' sons, however prosperous, were not in the right category to have aspirations as future sons-in-law.

So parties at the house were rare. A few of the minor gentry in an accessible area occasionally accepted invitations, and there was one son of an honourable – weedy, pleasant-looking, but ineffectual young man of Rupert's age attending the same public school near Truro – whom my wife cultivated very obviously. His name was Charles Cornfield. His grandfather in his time had made a fortune from iron and through wealth and cunning good works had won a baronetcy. I was amused at the way Katrina's quick mind worked, although irritated by this newly-discovered quirk in her character which I'd never before suspected. But she was firmly determined for Rosanna, when the day came, to make a 'good marriage', and Charles, quite clearly, though possessing nothing outstanding about him, was already on her list of 'possibles'. By the time of Rosanna's fourteenth birthday, Charles already appeared at Heatherfield for the occasional weekend, presumably as a friend of Rupert's, deviously contrived by Katrina.

'God! Uncle Justin,' the boy confided to me one day, '*why* does Aunt Kat have to make such a fuss of Cornfield? He's a bit of an ass really – we haven't a bloody thing in common, honestly.'

'*Rupert*,' I said sharply, 'watch your tongue. 'It's for your aunt and Rosanna to choose who they want invited to the house. Now if Charles is considered nice company for your cousin—'

'For *her*?' Rupert interrupted with a high colour flooding his handsome face. '*Nice*? Rosanna doesn't care a fig for him, I can tell you that. In fact, she bloo – sorry – I didn't mean that – she despises him, Uncle Justin. The truth is—'

'Yes?'

'He spoils our time together. I used to jolly well like the rambles we had at weekends before *he* had to muscle in. Now it's all – "Rupert, dear – what about you and Charles going with Rosanna together for a bit of a walk before lunch", or – "I'm sure Charles would like Rosanna to show him those old paintings in the library" – you know, that sort of thing. Oh! it's so stupid! Why is she so damned eager to have this threesome. Maybe twosome's more correct, though. Yes, that's it – she's trying to nab an "honourable" for a son-in-law.'

'Don't be silly,' I told him shortly. 'Your cousin's still only a child. It will be years before any idea of marriage is *thought* about.' I knew I was lying, but went on, 'And another thing, young man, you must learn to control your speech, or I'll have something to say to your father—'

'*Father*? Don't make me laugh. And don't tell me Rosanna's a child any more. She isn't. She's not my cousin either, is she? Just a step-cousin. That's right, isn't it, Uncle Justin? Her real name's Trengrouse, like Drake's.' He paused before adding in rather strange reflective tones that had a curiously adult ring about them: 'Rosanna Trengrouse. Rosanna Pencorrin. Which do you think sounds the best, Uncle Justin? Pencorrin, I think.'

It was then that I first began to sense the truth – Rupert and Rosanna had an emotional relationship already transcending that of the brotherly-sisterly order, or of normal cousinship.

I wasn't unduly perturbed; if anything serious developed between them in the future there'd be nothing to gamble or worry about. I was fond of both youngsters, to keep them as a couple in the family would be an agreeable state of affair rather than otherwise.

Katrina, I'm sure, had no suspicions concerning a sentimental tie between the two; her mind was far too occupied in encouraging the friendship with Charles. Rupert's presence during those early years made the 'threesome', as my nephew had referred to the situation, respectable and natural. He was the link – the means by which, hopefully, she would eventually gain her ends. And as the months went by it became clear that the quiet but pleasant Charles Cornfield was becoming infatuated with Katrina's wayward and lovely daughter.

Shortly before Rosanna's seventeenth birthday the first indication of impending crisis arose.

I arrived at Heatherfield one evening after a day in conference with shareholders at the mine to find Katrina and Rosanna in a heated argument. The very feeling in the atmosphere was tense as I entered the long hall from the back. Except for the rise and fall of shrill voices from the large parlour all was curiously quiet, and when my footsteps were heard approaching, I noticed a maidservant hurriedly move from the shadows by the door of the room. She had a dustpan in her hand and scurried by me with a pretence of being busy, but I knew she had been listening.

I gave her a brief, surprised look, then walked in.

Katrina was wearing a dress I'd not seen before, of some thick gold-coloured silk material that showed her proud well-corseted figure off to perfection. She was somewhat stouter than when we'd married, but the extra pounds in no way detracted from her grace which was almost statuesque. Above a still slender waist her ripe bosom rose, defiantly feminine, undisguised by the frail lacy shawl draped over her white shoulders. Her cheeks were pale, tinged only by two spots of angry colour on her cheekbones, her glossy hair as yet free of grey, was held by combs studded with brilliants that flashed as brightly as the green of her eyes. Rosanna, shorter by three inches than her mother, stood a slender nymph-like creature in something flimsy and green – or it may have been blue, I can't remember – her dark curls tied back by ribbons, yet in no way appearing a child. Her hands were clenched by her sides, her delicate small chin raised stubbornly. One cheek had a crimson glow to it, as though it had been slapped. I glanced at Katrina warningly. Both heads turned towards me. The tirade of words died suddenly as I entered, the last being – 'No, I won't, I *won't*,' from Rosanna.

'What's this?' I demanded. 'What the devil's going on? I've noticed far too much arguing between you two these last few days. And I won't have it, do you hear?'

Katrina remained firmly belligerent for a moment or two while Rosanna cried impetuously, the words rushing out, 'It's *her*, papa. She just *won't* leave me alone about Charles – and now this birthday party I've got to have! I *won't* give the supper dance to that boring creature. I don't even like him – I've said so, time after time. And I don't want the party either. Why can't I be left alone? I hate it – all this fuss, this "do this, do that – you must learn to be a lady". I'm *not* a lady. I don't want to be—' She broke off with a glitter of tears in her eyes. I turned to my wife enquiringly.

'You *see*!' she said, her voice cold with suppressed anger above the quick rise and fall of her breasts. 'She's quite

impossible. And it's your indulgence that has helped. She
should have been—'

'Beaten. Yes, I know what you'd like,' Rosanna blazed
before Katrina could finish. 'You're jealous – that's what it is –
you must be. Jealous because of Rupert—'

Katrina stared in genuine astonishment. '*Rupert?* Whatever
do you mean? Whatever has Rupert to do with it? And how
*dare* you talk to me like that?'

She took a step forward, but I pulled her back.

'Stop it,' I said. 'You should be ashamed, both of you!
Rosanna, leave us a moment. Go upstairs and quieten down.
When you've got your temper under control we'll all three
have a talk about this little business of Charles. But rationally
and calmly. You understand? And don't ever talk to your
mother in such a way again. That's an order. Now go along. Be
a good girl.' My voice softened. '*Please.*'

After a moment, picking up her skirts, she ran with the
lightness of a dancer to the door, and went out.

When the latch had clicked I turned to my wife and said
heavily, 'You're getting impossible these days, Katrina. What's
happened to change you so?'

'Happened? Nothing. Except that I can't—'

'Manage your own daughter. Obviously. And why? Can it be
true, what she said?'

'*What?* – what are you implying?'

'That you're jealous.'

'Why should I be? How *ridiculous*.' Her voice held contempt.
'*Jealous!*'

'That she's young, and you're not any more,' I told her
honestly. 'That she has all her life ahead – whereas you have
only me – with a bit of luck.' The words may have seemed
brutal, but had to be said.

She flushed. 'You're insufferable. As if I could be jealous of
my own daughter – and as if I wanted anything, anyone but
*you.*'

I knew she thought she was speaking the truth.

'But you *do*, Kat,' I insisted. 'For one thing, having your own
existence isn't sufficient anymore. You're determined on
running Rosanna's too. And it can't be done. It's unfair to her
to try. This Charles Cornfield, for instance! Why have you got

to push him on to her? He's really rather a colourless kind of fellow. Makes out to be a friend of Rupert's, I know. But Rupert gets more than a bit bored with his company. He just happens to be too polite to say so.'

'That's another thing. What did she mean in that remark about him? – About Rupert, and me being jealous?'

'Oh, heavens, Katrina, don't ask me to even *try* to explain the reason for an emotional girl's hasty remark. She and Rupert get on well together, that's all. And maybe she fancies you resent it.'

'Why should I?' Katrina's lips had become a thin line, I'd seen that look on her face countless times before whenever my nephew's name's cropped up in conversation. It was one of the enigmas of her character I'd never properly fathomed. She seemed always to make a point of keeping aloof from him as much as possible, yet at times when no one else probably noticed, I'd caught her eyes riveted upon him with an intensity that was bewildering.

It could be merely an over-protective intention on her daughter's behalf, of course. Rupert was quickly developing into an extremely handsome young man added to a charm that was emphasised by that certain amused tolerance which in Richard, my brother, had become so obnoxious. I wondered about that first wife – Rupert's mother, who'd been divorced when the boy was too young to remember her. What had she been like? I'd heard nothing of it from Richard except that her family was of no consequence, he'd met her at some social function or other, and that the marriage couldn't have worked.

'What a nosy one you are,' he'd said on one of the rare occasions I'd thrown out a question. 'We were only together a year or two anyway. You're as bad as any fussy old spinster wanting to know the colour of her eyes and hair, and if she came of a decent family attending church on Sundays, or a fancy bit I picked up at a fair? Eh?' He'd grinned in his usual unpleasant way, and continued, 'Well, brood on it, man, if it's so important to you. Ask the servants – oh, no. You can't, of course, I got rid of 'em all before I went to London for a period. But don't bother me. To tell you the truth I can't recall a bloody thing about her except that she had an eye for the men, was a bit of a fool, and made herself a nuisance – to *me*, old boy. So—'

'Yes? So?'

'Well – she took off didn't she? To other climes. So forget her if you don't mind. She was a whore. No more than that.'

I'd shrugged the matter off, but at intervals through the years curiosity had still pricked me. The unknown woman after all, had been my sister-in-law, and Rupert's mother, yet I didn't even know where they'd been married.

Rupert, too, had pondered over the question. 'It's a funny thing, isn't it,' he'd said reflectively one day when we were out walking together, 'that there's no portrait, not even a picture of my mother anywhere in the house? And I don't believe my father has one either. He never talks about her – he won't allow me to. And when I asked her name he said "What's that to you? It's all in the past. Dead things are best forgotten." After that I didn't mention her again. What was the point? I tried to think he was funny about the thing – you know, being *so* secretive – because in spite of everything he loved her too much to bear hearing her name spoken. But I'm not sure.' The young, strongly carved, face looked thoughtfully, almost broodingly ahead.

'About what, Rupert?' I said.

'About the love,' he answered. 'Maybe it was just hate he felt. He looked so – old, somehow, aggressive with his chin stuck out, and eyes narrowed. Well, I guess that sort of business *can* make a man bitter. If she *did* let him down – I mean if he divorced her because of some other man, and it *could* be that, I suppose – well, in a way, you can understand.'

But Rupert didn't. That much was quite clear to me. However, we dropped the subject; there was something far too resilient and outgoing about my nephew to dwell on any piece of family history having little bearing on the present. Probably I could have sounded out one or other of the early farm tenants for information concerning the quick marriage and its speedy ending – once, indeed, I'd brought the subject up deviously to old Will Drew, a smallholder. He'd wrinkled his forehead and replied ambiguously, 'I saw 'er once or twice. Just a girl, she were – tha's all I do remember. Didn' go out much. B'longed to a seafarin' family, I do b'lieve, an' took off

with a sailor – tha's what was put 'bout in these parts. But folks
is careful with their tongues 'bout Squire's affairs. See? Doan'
pay to gossip. *No*, surr.'

And that's as far as I got.

*3*

In spite of Rosanna's petulance and assumed boredom concerning the proposed birthday party arrangements went
ahead, as I knew they would, Katrina having set her heart so
determinedly on the event. In any case I realised that Rosanna
was not so uninterested as she appeared to be, and when the
subject of Charles was dropped she even began to show an
awakening interest in her new gown and the hair style
proposed by Katrina which was to be up-to-date, presenting
her at last as a young woman about to enter society, rather than
the wayward unsophisticated girl she was and would remain, I
suspected – under the new image.

There was a good deal of whispering and conspiratorial talk
between herself and Rupert at this time, which Katrina – for
which I was thankful – was far too busy to notice, although
others in the household did, including Drake.

He ran into the hall from the garden one evening looking
very flushed and breathless, almost knocking me over in the
hall. He was a nice-looking boy, rather quiet and shy, but with
depths of feeling in him which I'd grown to appreciate during
the years, and in appearance still as fair as my own son
Dominic was dark. A real cuckoo in the nest, Richard had
described him once in his callous withering way.

'Good for him,' I'd replied. 'The Pencorrins are all the
better for a breath of fresh air in the house. New blood's
necessary for healthy stock.'

'My God! you talk like a cattle-breeder. Of course, I suppose
that's the way in those far-off gold climes. Anyway—' Richard
had added as a parting shot, 'young Drake's really nothing to

do with you or the Pencorrins, is he? Just an off-shoot of a
rustic sire and that merry widow you married.'

He'd meant to be insulting, and for a moment my blood had
boiled. Any memory that Katrina had once lain in wedlock
with another man still rankled secretly, although I'd made it
my business to ignore the fact for most of the time, and had
determinedly treated Drake in every way as my own son,
favouring him on occasion above the twins, just because he
wasn't. So we'd managed to form a steady good relationship,
he and I, and when he bumped into me that autumn evening
so evidently disturbed I was more than a fraction surprised.

'Hey now,' I said, grasping his shoulder, 'what's all this
about? Why the hurry?'

Drake stared up at me with the flush deepening on his fair,
faintly freckled face.

'Nothing,' he said. 'Nothing really. It's just – it's very hot,
isn't it?' And he wiped his forehead where the sweat trickled in
a generous stream.

'Not particularly,' I answered, 'but you are. Come on now,
young man, out with it. You look *scared*.'

He would have pulled away, but I kept a firm hold of him,
and in the end he muttered, 'It was only – only that I saw
Rosanna, and – and she didn't see me, because – well, I don't
think she'd have wanted to.'

'*Why* do you think that?'

'Well!' He paused before answering grudgingly. 'If I say –
has mama got to know? She's so *stuffy* about some things.'

'That depends on what it is, and whether *I* think she should.
Now, Drake, don't be stubborn. You're hiding something, and
that's not like you. I don't believe for one moment Rosanna
was doing anything she shouldn't – especially in our own
garden. If she was I'll handle it myself – yes, I'll do that. Now
then, out with it.'

In the end he told me. Quite unintentionally, while waiting
quietly behind a bush watching for a night-bird to leave its nest
– he was a keen naturalist – two figures had run almost
soundlessly across the lawn to the shadows of a cedar and
stood close against the massive trunk, linked suddenly in each
other's arms and kissing passionately.

'I got away as quickly as I could,' he said, 'without them

seeing,' he ended. 'And that's – well, you know now. And I've let her down, haven't I! – Rosanna – in telling on her.'

'No,' I answered firmly. 'I forced it out of you, and there's nothing wrong in two young people tasting a touch of romance. The most natural thing in the world.'

'And you won't – you'll keep it from mama?'

'Of course. It's not my affair – or yours, and certainly not your mother's.'

'But she's so set on getting Rosie and Charles together. You know – because he's an honourable and all that! *I* think it would be quite – nauseating.' For a moment a spark of Katrina's fiery spirit lit his blue eyes. 'Don't you?'

Against his straight clear gaze I couldn't lie.

'Not at all what I'd choose,' I agreed. 'But I don't think there's any fear of Rosanna being pushed into the arms of anyone she doesn't want. So let's forget the little scene in the garden. Rupert goes up to Oxford in a month or two, and that will give him time to get things into proportion, Rosanna too. Whether anything serious develops between them or not doesn't really matter. As for Charles—' I grinned, 'you can get him out of your hair once and for all then where your sister's concerned. I'll wager by the time her birthday party happens he'll have got the message.'

But as things turned out, he hadn't.

The occasion arrived – a perfect spring evening. The gardens, hall and conservatory were lit by fairy lanterns, and Heatherfield's largest reception room cleared for dancing, with an extravagant buffet supper in the dining room, and the large drawingroom, next to the powder closet, subtly and discreetly arranged under shaded candlelight for romantic couples wishing to 'sit out'.

Katrina had certainly managed to create an 'atmosphere', and although the guests were largely represented by families of the upper class yeoman farming and hunting fraternity, my wife had contrived to gather a small smattering of true gentry – mostly minor, but extending to one or two possessing handles to their name.

The latter, naturally, included Charles Cornfield.

To say that Rosanna behaved badly would be an understatement. From the very start of the dancing her behaviour was outrageous. Intrinsically I couldn't have cared a rap, but Katrina recently had developed a quite ridiculous sense of what was done, socially, and what wasn't. I'd hoped it was only a phase, and would pass. But I must admit that on this occasion she had cause to be put out, and I knew there'd be a scene afterwards in which I'd be expected to be on her side.

My wayward step-daughter, defying any pretence or modicum of good manners refused pointedly to allow Charles a single dance, or even a smile. She sharply jerked her little card away – yes, Katrina had insisted on every conventional detail being observed – turning her pert chin in the opposite direction and gazing warmly into the eyes of another admirer – a tenant farmer's son, to whom she allowed the privilege of scribbling his name down more than once. Then she lifted her fan, wafted it before her face several times and wandered off, the arrogant little hussy – a dream in pink satin – to where Rupert waited by the conservatory door, lifted her face and was kissed, not modestly on one cheek, but in full view of everyone, very possessively on the lips. The next moment at a signal of a hand from Rupert to the hired orchestral trio, they were whirling away across the floor together watched by outraged matrons, astonished papas, and other young couples, who after a moment or two joined in – making joyous pageantry to the romantic melody.

I glanced at Katrina; her face was deathly pale, white round the lips, her eyes so vividly cold a green with anger, I feared for Rosanna afterwards. She stood still and silent as a statue for minutes, and when I touched her shoulder, turned to me fleetingly, saying, 'She shall pay for this,' before making her way to an abject Charles who was trying to hide his discomfiture and disappointment behind a small crowd of watchers. She caught him before he left, and I watched her making placating gestures, and apologies, doubtless for her daughter's behaviour. I couldn't hear what was said, but the poor young man, very red-faced, obviously was in no state to be placated, and I didn't blame him. He managed to disengage himself, with I'm sure, the politest of excuses, and without a word, or nod in my direction, left the room and was seen no more that evening.

The rest of the party, for my wife anyway, was no more than

a farce – a charade of colourful enjoyment,and on her part a show of assumed dignity which would have deceived anyone who had not known her very well.

I was sorry for her in a way. And yet I'd sensed for quite a time that something of the sort was bound to happen if she persisted in trying so ruthlessly to govern Rosanna's emotions and her future. In a way I felt a certain relief. The streak of ambitious snobbery in Katrina's character, of which I'd been unaware until the last year, had not only irritated me, but lessened the joyous bond of understanding between us that before had been unquestionable and completely natural. Somehow, I'd known it would have to be broken, or we could easily drift apart as the years passed, and if that had happened – well, there was no point in conjecturing. Through Rosanna's defiant gesture of rebellion, Katrina's ridiculously proud spirit had received a jolt which just for once put her in her place.

Pride, maybe, was not the term to be used. Wilful conquest was more apt, and I wondered about the underlying cause for the growing passion for power that had developed so ruthlessly during the past year or two of our marriage. I still loved her, but the former complete trust between us had become faintly tinged with jealousy on my part. Before, I had been content to accept her sensuous allure as just an unimportant perfectly natural characteristic.

Now, at odd moments, I wondered.

The climax to my developing doubt came abruptly on the day following the party, when Katrina insisted on summoning Rosanna to the large parlour for a confrontation concerning her wild behaviour the night before. I'd managed to keep the two apart for the few hours until the morning; the celebrations had not ended until two-thirty, and by then my step-daughter had locked herself in her room. All night, or what was left of it, Katrina had been restless and not slept, getting up from time to time, and pacing up and down the bedroom.

'I'll never forgive her,' she'd said, '*never*. We shall be the talking point of all Cornwall—'

'Oh, don't be stupid?' I'd retorted. 'What on earth's the matter with you? What the devil does it matter if society *does* gasp and gossip a bit? Rosanna's just behaved like a high-spirited girl, that's all – flouted the conventions because she's sick of her mother's continual insistence on domination—'

'She's behaved without any manners or consideration at all,' Katrina had interrupted sharply. 'She's not too old to be spanked thoroughly, and that's what she deserves—'

'Neither are you,' I interposed, 'and don't forget it. Remember this – I'm having no violence. And to make sure I shall insist on being present at the argument between you.'

'*Why?*'

'Because I think you're neurotic and unbalanced over your petty passion lately for cultivating the right people, which is becoming a damned bore.'

'*Me?* A *bore?*' Just for a moment her lip had trembled – she'd looked younger, more like the Katrina I'd married.

'Yes,' I replied shortly. 'Now get back into bed before I have to carry you.'

She obeyed meekly, like a lamb then. But in the morning, despite lack of sleep, her fighting spirit had returned. Though little was said between us before we entered the parlour – indeed she was curiously silent – by the set of her chin and rigid stance I knew she was preparing for the attack. No one else was about. We were, after all, a few minutes early for the stupid domestic drama, and it was hardly likely Rosanna would be waiting before time. I went to the cabinet, took out a decanter, with glasses, and offered a drink to my wife.

'No, thank you,' she replied in cool precise tones. 'What I have to say needs no stimulus.' She could have been, in that moment, a tragedy queen out of Shakespeare, or, better still, some lofty-minded young madam from an erotic stage melodrama.

I quaffed my whisky quickly, and a moment later, following a sharp tap, the door opened and Rosanna, bright-eyed, cheeks flushed, rushed in, not alone, but with Rupert, her hand firmly held by his.

Katrina, astonished, let her pose drop for a second as she said, 'I think Rupert would be advised to keep out of this. Rupert, would you mind leaving?'

'Yes, I would,' he answered, facing her with eyes as bold and bright as her own, but with a darker fire. 'What concerns Rosie from now, concerns me. I'm sorry, step-aunt,' there was a challenge in the rich young voice, 'but you may as well know now – both of you – we love each other—'

'Yes,' Rosanna interrupted, 'and we're going to get married – whether you like it or not. I hope you won't make a fuss or anything – it would be nice if – if we could all be happy. Oh, mama—' her lovely face became temporarily pleading, 'won't you please—' the words faded, lips tightened again, against the fury of her mother's gaze. It was ironic, that at the same moment, Richard should appear, blundering into the room under a guise of surprise.

'I beg your pardon,' he said in slightly blurred tones, 'do I intrude?'

Katrina wheeled round to face him. 'Not at all. You've come most opportunely for taking your son away. There is a private matter I have to discuss with my daughter—'

'It's not private at all.' Rosanna's interruption rang defiantly on the air. 'It's for everyone to know – *every*one.' She paused only briefly to get her breath, before continuing, 'We're getting married – Rupert and me, before he goes to Oxford—' the words came out with a rush, 'and I shall go up there to be with him. We shall—'

'You certainly won't,' Katrina cried, and there was something hysterical, something in her voice and manner I couldn't fathom, which seemed reasonless, out of all proportion. 'You can't. It won't be allowed, do you hear? You and Rupert can never be married – never, *never* – not in this world—'

I put a restraining hand on her arm. 'Katrina—'

She pulled herself away fiercely, and rushed forward towards Rosanna. Rupert, like a young lion defending its mate pushed himself in front, saying between his teeth, 'And why not? You just tell me why not—'

Then Richard spoke.

'Tell him, sister-in-law,' he said, with a thick insulting amusement in his voice, 'just explain that according to—' he swallowed tipsily, '—according to the laws of the land – and of – of God presumably – a man may not marry his sister.' Katrina blanched; even through my bewilderment, not yet shock, I noticed her extraordinary pallor.

'Stop it,' she whispered in a low voice. 'Stop it.'

Richard's eyebrows shot up in mock surprise. 'But *why*? Such an unexpected turn of events demands a truthful answer – surely?' He turned to me, with both hands held out, palms upwards, and said with a pretence of self-effacing mock supplication, 'Prepare thyself for a shock, bro-brother dear—' He reached for a further drink – although by then God knows how much he'd already had, drank it – pulled himself together with an effort, and said loudly and clearly, 'My son and your charming daughter are bred of the same stock. Before you took her to bed I had already lain with her times without number. Yes indeed. Both are fruit of my loins. I would have spared you the shock of knowing for the sake of Heatherfield. Now, regretfully, unless I take me another wife to breed from – you will step into my shoes as heir when I shuffle off this mortal coil. Poor Angelica was a disappointment alas! However—' He poured another glass of brandy, which I knocked out of his hand, sending it smashing to the floor.

'You *lie*!' I shouted, and plunged my fist hard against his jaw. He staggered and fell back against the table, one hand to his bleeding face. Then I turned to Katrina. She was staring straight before her, eyes wide and terrified in her white face, mouth slightly opened in shock. But even in that ghastly moment she was beautiful.

'Tell me,' I said, 'tell me, do you hear?' My voice was rising, I could feel it thudding in my ears, with the blood pounding at my temples heavily, turning the whole world temporarily dark and frightful. I put my hands on her shoulders and shook her. 'Well? *Well*? Speak, can't you? Either deny it, or—'

I broke off as she said faintly, 'Don't Justin – don't – it was so long ago – it—' She hardly knew what she was saying, I realised that. But I knew in that same agonising revelation of the past, that Richard hadn't lied. Only Katrina – the wife I had worshipped and believed in for all the years of our marriage – the one I'd thought beyond reproach. She'd not only lusted and conceived with my own brother, but connived and succeeded in deceiving me.

Katrina, my beloved, a cheat, and a whore!

What happened afterwards was a nightmare. I remember vaguely seeing Rosanna rush from the room in tears, followed by Rupert who paused at the door for a second to shout in a voice of knife-edged hatred, 'I'll *never* forgive you for this — *never*.'

There was a slam and he'd gone. After that I just stood for a time with my head bent in my hands, then without another word marched out, went straight to the stables, saddled Major and rode out across the moors, galloping wildly, not knowing or caring where, but ending up in a fall near Wheal Clara, where I lay conscious only of a darkness and fiery stars piercing my head in sparks of searing pain.

I must have lain there in the heather for the rest of the night before I was found by workers to the early shift at the mine the next day.

I remembered nothing. But weeks later at Heatherfield, memory returned, and I knew I could never again look on Katrina with desire.

Our life together was over.

# III

## Rosanna

### 1

When I was a tiny girl I wanted two things more than anything else in the world – for mama to love me, and to dance. I suppose in one way my mother *did*. Love me, I mean, but in a possessive over-passionate and strict manner that I didn't want. I longed for her to be gentle and soft, and willing to listen when I tried to explain the complicated emotions of my developing youth, of how the wild urge flooded me sometimes to wander off by myself so I could be free to dance in secret moorland places where foxgloves and bluebells grew among the tall green ferns.

I wanted to tell her of a shining pool hidden in rocks where a stream trickled and an otter swam; there were baby badgers too, over the rim of the hill, and old Pete Nancegollan, a shepherd, showed me a fairy ring of short pale turf near his hut where he said the 'small folk' had danced one summer night. I'm not sure whether or not I believed in the 'little people', but I'd have liked to ask mama about them. I daren't, though, because she'd have been cross and stopped me talking to old Pete.

That was the trouble; she was so often severe with me, although she could be sweet and loving with Drake. I used to wonder why, and decided it was because Drake was good and amiable and never seemed to be bothered by the wilful strange moods that were part of my character. So for a time *I* tried hard to be good, desperately, hoping mama would notice and pull me close to her, just as she did my brother. It was no use. After a repressed period of restraint and doing none of the things I really wanted to, I'd go all wild suddenly, and run away so I could dance and dance to my heart's content – dance with the ferns and the leaves and the wind, with the heather and thyme smelling sweet about me, and the tremble of lovely unknown music singing in my ears 'the music o' Nature,' old Pete called it.

But mama never understood, and sometimes I was spanked. For that there were times when I almost hated her. Discipline she called it, and to keep me from falling down dangerous mine shafts. Well, perhaps the latter was true. And, of course, I knew I could never *really* hate her, but as I grew older the rift between us seemed to widen — perhaps 'void' is a better word. I had a governess, Miss Grey, the daughter of a clergyman; she lived with us at Rookswood, then when mama married my stepfather and became Mrs Pencorrin, she went with us to Heatherfield. She was calm and kind, rather colourless, and I'd soon found, a little frightened of mama, so I did my best to obey her and not get her into trouble. When he was old enough Drake had lessons from her too.

Life became easier with my new papa. I called him 'papa', while I was small, although I knew he wasn't. My name, of course, was 'Trengrouse'. Once a servant girl had told me *he* hadn't been my papa either. I'd asked mama about it, and she'd said, 'Nonsense,' and promptly dismissed the girl. After that I stopped prying and wondering about the 'father business', and was content to regard Justin Pencorrin as an 'uncle' figure — a firm, strong character who did his best to keep mama in order, and gave me extra love to make up for what I didn't get from her.

I was seven-years-old when the twins, Juliana and Dominic, were born. Juliana was fairish and plump, not pretty exactly — although as she got older she improved, and became good-looking in a vague way, blue-eyed like her father. Dominic was different — fierce-looking, even as a baby, very dark and thin. He screamed a lot, but mama, strangely, didn't seem to mind. She called him her 'little princeling' — which I thought was stupid — and hugged him to her, patting his back, and giving him her finger to suck or maybe, when he was old enough, a bon-bon from her reticule.

Jealousy would gnaw me temporarily, but it never lasted. After all, I was growing up. There were other people in the world to love, apart from mama. Rupert, for instance, my step-cousin. It was easy to love Rupert; he was so handsome and brave and confident somehow. And clever. Clever in a way I wasn't, and never would be. Although when he was at home from school he had many adventures that could have landed him in the most awful trouble, he always managed not to be found out.

'That's the spice of it – partly,' he told me once, 'getting away with things.'

I didn't know exactly what those things were, but one night when I couldn't sleep I looked out of my window and saw him climbing up the wall by the side of the house where there was a gnarled old cherry tree, before disappearing into his own room. The moon slipped from the clouds for a moment and he looked like a giant bee or spider, with a black cap pulled over his ears. In the morning I heard my stepfather telling mama there'd been a smuggling operation that night – brandy and lace taken ashore from a French vessel in small boats to Blackman's Cove where most of it had been secreted or driven away on donkeys before the Preventative got there. Justin said local men had been involved, but none had been caught.

'Thank goodness,' mama said, and she was actually smiling, with a gleam in her eye I'd not seen for a long time.

Papa laughed. 'I'm surprised at you, Kat. Such a stickler as you are for discipline and good behaviour.'

'No, you're not, Justin Pencorrin. You know very well that at heart I'm a—'

'Wayward creature. Yes,' Papa moved towards her and touched her cheek. They seemed oblivious of my presence. I stood very still, feeling embarrassed, yet curiously excited too, because mama looked so strange and young and beautiful suddenly – with a softness in her eyes I'd never seen before, but always longed to. Then, just as quickly they remembered me and broke apart.

'Rosanna!' my mother exclaimed, brushing a curl from a flushed cheek. 'What are you staring at? And so quiet. As quiet as a mouse. I believe you were listening—' She paused, not knowing whether to scold or smile.

'Yes, mama,' I said boldly. 'About the smuggling. It's exciting, isn't it?'

'It's very wrong,' I was told abruptly. 'And if any of the men are caught they'll be severely punished – imprisoned, perhaps even flogged, or sent to Van Diemen's Land.'

I shivered, remembering Rupert, and thinking how dreadful it would be if he was tied to a post and whipped or sent to some horrible prison place where I'd never see him again.

I knew I'd have to warn him, and at the first opportunity did so.

He gave me a lazy charming grin, put his arm round my shoulder, and said, 'So you know. You *saw* me, Brighteyes!' – that was his name for me often – 'Brighteyes'.

I nodded.

'Well! So what? A fellow has to know what's going on around him. And that's just what I did. Found out. Mixed with the crowd as you might say. Think of it as my duty, if you like.'

'But it was wrong, wasn't it, Rupert?'

He considered me thoughtfully for a few moments before replying, 'As wrong as your little adventures, dancing before the gypsies. Only I take care not to be found out, and that's what *you* must do. So we'll call it quits, shall we, become partners in crime, and never, *never* tell on each other?'

I nodded vigorously, with a wild warm glow stealing through me. 'Oh, *yes*, Rupert. *Yes*.'

And from that moment the relationship between us assumed a more subtle deepening significance.

\*

When I was sixteen both Rupert and I were desperately in love. Being a reckless character, I wanted the whole family to know it instantly, so we would be married as soon as possible. It was so hard to keep the truth to ourselves, when just being together meant the whole world changed – the wind seemed to sing with joy, and each day, as the pale light of dawn rimmed the moors with gold, I'd run to my window wanting to cry, 'Rupert loves me – loves me – loves me—', then I'd put on a wrap quickly and steal out into the gardens where the dew was still silvery thick on the grass, without anyone knowing, and wait in some hidden place until he joined me, and lifted me up into his arms. My head would rest against his shoulder, and I'd wriggle with delight, pressing close against him, my hair tumbled over his arm. His lips would be warm and sweet on mine, draining such love and desire from me nothing registered any more but longing and wanting to be his completely.

'Why can't they know now?' I asked him one day. 'Why, Rupert? I'm sixteen. Lots of girls are sixteen when they're married.'

'A *few* more months,' he said. 'until you're seventeen and I've got Oxford ahead. Then we'll be independent – sort of. Of course, I shall depend on papa for my allowance. I mean we won't have any money for luxuries or anything. We'll have to live in rooms. But maybe the old man will cough up.'

'Cough up? What a funny expression. But, anyway, if he doesn't, Justin, my stepfather, will. He's fond of you. There won't be any trouble. There *can't* be. There's no reason. So let's tell them. *Please.*'

'What about your mother?'

'Mama?' The thought sobered me temporarily. 'Well – I expect she'd be stuffy at first. She always is, when I want anything very much. But she'd come round. She'd *have* to, if papa Justin took our side. Which I'm sure he will; and he's boss, you know – in any *serious* argument mama always has to give in, in the end.'

'Hm! you may be right. All the same, something tells this cunning brain of mine it'd be better to hold our horses just for a bit longer.'

I sighed. 'Oh, *Rupert!* you do use such funny phrases. What has holding horses got to do with *love*?' I laughed, pulled myself from his grasp, and lifted my arms in the air. There was a mist that morning, and everything was kind of mysterious and magical, and, so filled with happiness, I couldn't argue with him any more.

'All right,' I agreed, 'if that's what you really want. And now I'm going to dance. Dance to our future.'

I kicked off my slippers, and with the damp sweet turf tickling my toes I twizzled and turned, and leaped and pranced until I caught a toe on a thorn, and gave a little squeak as I flung myself to the ground to examine it.

Rupert was kneeling down beside me in a second.

'There! You see,' he said with mock severity, taking my foot in his hand, 'And you expect me to take such a foolish one for a wife.'

'Well!' I looked up at him. 'Fools are sometimes much more fun than clever folk like you—'

I got no further. He was kissing me in a different way from ever before, with just the tip of his tongue touching mine. My heart was beating wildly. I could feel his thudding too – thump, thump against my breasts.

Oh, how I longed for him; but suddenly he jumped up, and said breathlessly, 'You're a wicked sprite. A temptress – that's what. And now you'd better be off quick, dress and make yourself look decent – if you can.'

I sighed, shook my curls, then shrugged and reached for my slippers. 'Decency's such a bore,' I said.

Rupert was straightening his tie and smoothing his hair as he remarked jokingly, but still in a breathless way, 'Wait till we're wed and you can be as provokingly indecent as you choose—'

'Like making love naked on that leopardskin rug in the library – or two fishes in Winsey Pool. No – not fishes – mermaids – only you'd be a *man* – a mer*man*, with green hair and fins to tickle my tail—' I laughed at the vision because it was easier to laugh than be serious just then, with such a yearning riotous confusion of emotions in me.

'God! What an imagination you have,' Rupert remarked, staring at me. 'Hurry up now. They're already rattling things in the kitchen, and you don't want to be found like this, for heaven's sake—'

'I don't care at all,' I retorted. In truth, I'd rather have liked it, and then perhaps Rupert would have let the secret out. But to please him I quietened down, and a minute later was making my way to the house, while Rupert, being properly attired, went the opposite way in the direction of the moors, presumably – if seen – on one of his frequent early morning walks.

So it was like that.

For weeks, months, things continued in such a way, with secret meetings that made mama's insistence on having boring Charles to the house on every opportunity just bearable, but only just.

Before, when we'd been younger, I hadn't resented him –
he'd been interesting in his rather old-fashioned way –
knowledgeable about things I cared about, like wildlife and
nature, and legends and history of the district; but when that
adoring gleam came into his eyes – half-planted there, I'm
sure, and encouraged by mama, I began positively to find him
a nuisance. Once, when we were out walking, he stopped
suddenly, touched my hand, drew me forward saying something in a stuttering kind of way that was so silly I just gave him
a push sending him on his back into the long grass. Then I ran
and ran and ran, and when he caught up with me, he said,
'Why did you do that?'

'Just fun,' I answered, feeling a bit sorry for him. 'A game,
that's all – like friends have. And that's what you are, Charles, a
*friend*. Don't forget.'

He took me all wrongly, of course.

'Oh, no,' he said. 'I won't. *Indeed* I won't – and it's a privilege
being your friend, Rosanna. Believe me, I *mean* it. More than
that – an honour.'

Oh! he could be so stuffy.

However, I somehow managed to put up with Charles and
mama's domineering 'intentions', until the day of my birthday
when I was seventeen.

And it was then, that evening, the crisis happened. The
crisis that was to bring such tragedy and alter the whole course
of my life – and all so unpredictable, because Rupert and I had
planned for things to be so different.

I suppose, looking back, that I *did* behave rather badly. I
ought to have acted more kindly to Charles at my birthday
party, and saved both his and mama's dignity for that one
evening. But then what use would it have been in the end? The
terrible truth would have had to come out eventually, I
suppose. Or would it? Would mama have kept silent for fear of
papa Justin's reaction? If I could have been sure of that I
wouldn't have cared *what* relationship Rupert and I were to
each other. I loved him so desperately, and anyway we needn't
have had children. It isn't just having a family that's so
important when two people are in love, is it? It's *they* –
themselves – knowing that no one else in the world could
count in the same way, ever.

Oh! when I rushed out into the garden that evening
following the fearful row I didn't care one iota about rules and
regulations, what the law allowed and what God thought. Who
was God anyway? Perhaps it was blasphemy thinking like that
but it didn't matter. Nothing mattered to me but that the
grown-ups and their horrible rules and quarrelling had
spoiled the loveliest thing I'd ever known or would again in my
whole life. Mama had won after all; she had separated Rupert
and me.

Even in those first dreadful moments of revelation I sensed
– or rather *knew* intuitively – that however much I protested
and fought for our love, Rupert would give in. He'd *have* to.
Knowing I was his sister would be bound to affect him. He'd
still care for me – but very gradually the caring would change
into something different – something protective and gentler.
A nobler emotion altogether. I knew him so well, you see –
knew that beneath his dash and daring and fire, there was that
*protective* streak. And perhaps – a sense of rightness. And I
didn't want *protecting*, or morality, or to be his affectionate
sister, I wanted *him*; wanted him so dreadfully my nails bit into
the tree trunk where I was standing, until blood trickled over
my wrists, and I hated them all – especially my mother, for
deceiving me and letting out the secret when it was too late.

How long I stood there alone I don't know. It could have
been minutes or hours. It was Uncle Richard, my father, of all
people who found me. He slipped his arm round me and said,
'Come along now, Rosie. Cheer up. 'Tisn't the end of the
world, you know. I'm sorry, girl—'

'Sorry – *sorry*?' I struck out at him wildly, battling against his
chest, hitting his face where my stepfather earlier had struck
him. 'How can you be sorry? You caused it all. And I hate you,
yes, I do.'

I was gasping and breathless. Something in my face must
have scared him. He backed a little, and at that same moment
Rupert crossed the grass and came towards me. He looked
very white. His face was set and grim, with a kind of despairing
helplessness on it that told me I'd been right in my deductions.

It was the end.

'Leave us,' he said to his father. 'It's better so.'

Richard turned and walked heavily to the house, shoulders

bent, almost as though in contrition. For the first time I saw him abject, with all the mockery and bravado dispelled, leaving merely the shell of the reprobate braggart he'd appeared for so many years.

Alone, Rupert and I stood staring, desolate, before I rushed into his arms. He held me, and I could feel him trembling. Tears fell from my eyes then, salty against his coat; his lips rested on my hair for a moment, while I managed to control great gulping sobs.

At last I said helplessly, 'It *can't* be true, can it? It's not, is it? It's some trick of mama's?'

'I'm afraid it's no trick,' Rupert muttered. 'She's confirmed it – Katrina. And there are other things, things I didn't notice at the time—'

'What things?'

'Oh, remarks from here and there. I'll make sure, of course.'

Hope stirred in me. 'You mean there's a doubt?'

He shrugged.

'Not much – my darling love, you mustn't hope. We've got to—'

'What? *What?*'

'Accept the truth. I shall make enquiries. Go into facts concerning your birth and our – Katrina's marriage to Trengrouse – and things like that, when a woman was sold at a fair—'

'What do you *mean?*'

He shook his head. 'Rumours get about, Rosanna, that are kept secret until a crisis arises, and lately—'

'Yes?'

'Lately an old servant returned to the district who was employed here in the past, during my father's *supposed* first marriage. He'd been dismissed with the rest of the staff before Richard took off for a period to town. Well – he can be pretty talkative in his cups, and—' Rupert broke off suddenly and put a hand to his head. 'Oh, God, darling. What a mess, what a bloody infernal mess. Why the *devil* should this happen to us?'

'It hasn't yet, though has it?' I cried, clutching at a straw, *any* straw, that could stave off the nightmare. 'If this man – if he knows anything that could help and could prove it—'

Rupert shook his head slowly.

'If he can prove anything I very much fear it will be no help to us.'

'Then you mean you're just going to accept what they – what Katrina and Richard say – and – and—' I broke off, unable to finish.

There was a long silence; a silence of hopelessness between us. Presently I heard Rupert continuing in dulled matter-of-fact-tones. 'I'm due to leave for Oxford in a few weeks. Under the circumstances, I think the only sensible thing is to go earlier. I intend to do so at the weekend.'

'*Leave?* But, Rupert—'

'I *have* to, Rosanna. There's nothing else for it. Feeling as we do, what's the point of prolonging the agony? Don't you *see*, love? The situation's impossible. I just couldn't take it, having to face you every day, knowing I've no right to touch you, and you—'

'But you *have* a right, you have,' I interrupted wildly. 'We *love* each other, don't we? *Don't* we?'

'Love can change,' he said, gently but firmly pushing me away when I would have rushed passionately into his arms, drawing his head down, so my lips could be sweetly desirous under him as they had so often been. 'We can both come to terms – eventually,' he continued. 'We *must*, we have to.'

'*No*. I never will.'

'It will happen,' he told me. 'In time. And one day you'll find someone else—'

'I won't, though. That's where you're wrong. *You* may. But not me.'

We continued protesting and arguing, until all the words possible had been said. Then, very slowly I turned and went back to the house.

The whole day was a terrible one.

The next morning Justin was found unconscious by the mine following a fall from his horse. When he recovered consciousness he did not know where he was, or recognise any of us. I had meant to run away that day, but under the circumstances felt I couldn't. He had always been kind and loving to me, and I determined to stay by him till he was better, and somehow learn to endure Katrina's presence.

Rupert left for Oxford on Friday, as he'd planned.

Life went on.

But for me there was no joy in it any more, nor would there be, I knew, until – if ever – the day came when I might feel the urge to dance again and somehow express my emotions – deep hurt, anguish, and passion in movement, rhythm, a bitter-sweet fulfilment. Then, maybe, I would manage – not to forget – but no longer care.

During the next few weeks Justin recovered sufficiently, physically, to get about the house tackling routine jobs – even conversing mechanically with Richard about affairs of the estate. But his memory was severely impaired. When he was told I was his brother's daughter he merely looked puzzled, as though dim signs of recognition stirred somewhere at the back of his brain, and said, 'My niece. Of course. Sorry I'm so dull.'

Naturally Katrina tried her utmost to make contact, passion-ately insisting that he must recognise her as his wife. I happened to be there on the first occasion, and was embar-rassed by his polite rejection. 'Surely you're joking, madam. I don't recall going to the altar. There's no need – no damn need at all for this emotional how-de-do? I've had a slight mishap, that's all. Such things happen in the goldfields. An accident, leaving me temporarily confused. But it'll pass. Still, I'm flattered by your attentions – only don't press me too hard. I've the devil of a headache.'

I was temporarily embarrassed, and tried to pull mama away. But she *would* go on – pleading, arguing, forcing herself upon him, even although the doctor had warned her not to. And in the end he turned completely against her, saying to me, 'Keep that woman out of my sight. She may mean well, but I don't trust her. Don't trust her an inch.'

Oh, it was pathetic, distressing, and frightening all at the same time, because mama eventually put all the blame on me.

'It's your fault,' she cried one day after a particularly unpleasant scene, screaming. 'It's all because of *you* this has happened. If you hadn't made such a disgusting show of yourself with Rupert none of it would have occurred; because of your selfishness you've destroyed my life, and driven Justin mad. Don't you understand, you wicked girl? I'll never forgive you – *never.*'

Her cheeks were flaming, her green eyes blazing with rage

and unhappiness. When I trembled, with the tears clutching at my throat, she moved forward as though to hit me, but didn't. With one hand clenched she went on, 'I've given you all the love I could. Cared and worried over you, tried to make sure you'd have security for the rest of your life and never have to endure what *I* did – thanks to your wretched father – and all I get from you is *this*: Justin, the one man I've ever truly loved – hating me.'

I put out a hand. 'Mama, please—'

She struck it away fiercely.

'Leave me. *Go*. I can't bear to look at you.'

I did just that.

As I ran from the room she was still standing by the table, but drooping, with her face in her hands, dark hair tumbled from its combs, sobs at last tearing at her whole body. I ran upstairs blindly, almost knocking into Drake on the landing.

'Hey,' he said, 'what's the matter?' as I rushed by.

I didn't answer.

I said nothing to anyone anymore in that house.

Until the evening I stayed in my room, ignoring knocks from the servants and thumps and questions from Richard.

When the rest of the household was at dinner and the servants occupied in the kitchens, I crept down the back stairs wearing a bonnet and dark cloak over my blue everyday dress, and left Heatherfield by a side door with only a small case and my reticule containing all the money I had. The dying sunlight threw long shadows across the drive and lawns, giving ample coverage for my flight. No one saw me leave, and I doubted that anyone would care very much. Papa Justin was still too bemused to miss me, and mama would feel only relief at my disappearance. Richard, my real father would quickly ease any pangs of conscience – if he had any – through the whisky bottle. The twins might question and wonder. But the only one who might grieve a little – just *might* – was Drake; and maybe when I reached some destination, wherever it was, I'd contrive to get a message to him.

So I walked on, away from love and hatred, grief and loss, into an unknown future, while evening crept to the moors, encompassing the world with a kind of half-dream bearing little relationship to reality. I saw and met no one, except a few sheep dotted here and there about the granite stones.

When at last tiredness registered I noticed a red glow curdled with grey smoke below me, some distance down the valley.

I limped towards it instinctively. One foot was already sore and blistered in its thin boot.

So it was that I came to a gypsy encampment and fortuitously met the Petra family.

2

I had walked a very long way; I was tired to the point of complete exhaustion, although I'd never fainted in my life. The brown faces and figures moving between the waggons and pitched tents had the strange half-real appearance of a backcloth to a play, and yet I knew they were real, human beings with emotions and feelings who could give food and sanctuary. What a word to come to mind so suddenly, yet that was what I felt: sanctuary from the hatred of my mother and Rupert's desertion from common sense, from the quarrelling and anguish and betrayal at Heatherfield. Yes, everything had been betrayal, and I knew I'd never be free of it until I was far away where Katrina's taunting voice couldn't follow, and I'd no longer have to watch daily the pain and torture of realisation register and deepen in Justin's eyes.

So I simply said, as I blundered forward and clutched at a tree branch for support, 'Please can I join you. I'm tired and hungry. I've gold – I can pay.'

No one appeared impressed by the mention of gold. They just stared silently for what seemed an age with dark, narrow penetrating eyes, while the rosy flare of logs burning lit their boldly carved features to transient mobility for a few seconds, then faded, wraith-like in the scene into misted curdling grey.

I waited, and a crone came forward. She was bent with age,

wrapped in a black shawl, with a long claypipe held in one gnarled hand. Tiny gold rings glinted from her ears where locks of grey hair straggled over her shoulders. She could have been a witch from *Macbeth* although her gaze was steady and unblinking, filled with the ancient primitive wisdom of her race. How such details should register through my extreme weariness I don't know. But I was aware of an instinctive stirring acceptance that put me at ease suddenly, causing my strained muscles to ease and tremble.

'Come thee hedre, gorgio one,' she said, beckoning, 'and keep talk of gold to thyself. There's food'n shelter for any rawni lady needing help of the Petras though by morning mebbe it's a Romany chal thee'll be—'

I had no idea what she meant, but I followed her willingly to her tent, while a group of her kin stood whispering together in a tongue I didn't understand.

After a liberal portion of stew and rabbit cooked with herbs, I slept well that night amply covered by rugs and sacking in a small tent from which moonlight gradually replaced the dying glow of the rosy sky.

In the morning I was woken early, and told by the old woman that I must either have my hair cut short as a boy's, and my face stained brown, or else take the road on my own again.

''Tis the p'lice,' she said. 'They sneakin' critters be lookin' a'ready for a fine runaway gorgio lady. But a Romany chal?' she smiled, showing a row of broken yellowed teeth, 'No one'll suspect a fine younger feller such as thee'd be once old Esther's done with thee.'

Esther turned out to be the old one's grand-daughter. She was tremendously stout, with her black hair falling over her shoulders in two pigtails. Her face was high boned, with not a wrinkle to be seen on the nut-brown rosy flesh, yet I learned as she snipped my curls off ruthlessly that she had borne fifteen children, who had enlarged the Petra family by producing in all so far twenty great-grandchildren. She had lost only three sons; one in a wrestling match, one in a brawl with a horse dealer and the other at sea. He had married a worthless gorgio slut, I'd been told, and therefore been banished from the tribe – 'bitchedy pawdel' – which had resulted in his sailing away.

Her voice was deep and gruff, but with a kind of dark music

in it, and as she snipped away until only a fringe of small curls covered my head like any boy's, I listened in a kind of dream, hardly believing it was myself sitting there in that small tent while others of the tribe – from young to old, moved about outside, cooking, building fires, and preparing to leave the next day for a place near Truro, where a fair was on. Her speech was partly incomprehensible to me, interspersed as it was by strange words and phrases, in her native Romany language.

'Thy name shall be Chiknoo,' she said at one point, 'and thee'l help while thee's with us – stirring the pot and sortin' herbs. We take thee because Bebee – the ancient one – says we must.'

'Bebee?'

'My grandmother who took thee in last night. Her own father was a great Romany Kral – one of the greatest the world has seen. His tribe has travelled many countries. Here we be but a handful of the family – twenty at most, from young to old. But it's enough for one camp. Although thee'l pass for a young chal it seems a strange notion to me that Bebee shud've so taken to thee. A gorgio woman!' The snipping stopped all of a sudden. 'From what are thee flyin' from?'

'From hatred, and unfairness, and – love,' I answered, simply.

'Love? Pah!' she snapped her fingers. 'Love be a soft word, daughter. Race and pride be stronger, good faith and health, and lungs and eyes to savour the riches of the earth. *Love?*' she laughed contemptuously. ''Tis weakness to speak so.'

'I don't think so.'

She was silent then, and presently after my chin had been stained, I was attired like a youth, in breeches and jerkin, and presented to the ancient woman as 'Chiknoo'.

The old creature was sitting outside her own tent which was a little apart from the rest, behind a clump of thick furze and twisting elder.

'Come here, rawni,' she commanded, 'and listen to what I say. A story maybe, but a true one.'

I seated myself on a tumbled tree trunk beside her that served as a bench. She took a puff at her pipe, then eased herself into a position where her black beads of eyes could stare quietly into mine through the thin coils of grey smoke.

I waited.

From yards away the clatter of tins and murmur of voices mingled with the piping of a blackbird, and the stream's ripple over the stones.

'In thy face it's all writ,' she said at last. 'Recognition. The blood. You be the child of terrible passion, dordi, passion which bred thy mother at the big house, and her mother afore her—'

'What do you mean? How do you know? What has my mother to do with you?'

The old creature shook her head and answered, 'How? Because the true Romany has ways of knowin', an' I've kept check, daughter. Katrina. Mariac? Was that her name?'

'Yes. But—'

'She's of our kin, dordi. Her grandmother was my own sister, Leonora, whose child Anyana married a gorgio sea captain Mariac, and was made bitchedy-pawdel by the tribe. *Outcast.* She was a dancer, girl, a true dancer of the Flamenco and her own wild nature, and already betrothed to Tawnos, her blood cousin. So it was a crime she committed, and for that she suffered. When the captain was at sea she was taken in lust by another and thy mother was conceived.' There was a pause. 'Because of it, daughter, Anyana died.'

At first I tried to dismiss the story as mere fabrication. I couldn't accept it; just couldn't, it seemed too fantastic to be believed. Yet all the time a strange excitement was stirring – a deep inner comprehension that somehow made a logical pattern and understanding of my mother's conflicting moods and attitudes to myself.

'But the captain?' I persisted. 'Captain Mariac. He was father to Katrina when she was small, only a baby, cared for her and when she was old enough took her with him wherever he sailed.'

'Ha! A kindly gorgio fool,' the old woman said harshly. 'A man with pity in him that was greater than his pride.'

'Did he *know* about her – about my mother's true father?'

'He knew, dordi. Before she died she confessed, and wrote, too, to my father, the great Kral, for forgiveness from the tribe. But there was none. So she took poison, and that was the end.'

The end.

I shivered. The words were spoken with such fatality, held such hard unrelenting doom in them.

I stood up, with the wind shuddering through my shorn short locks, and was about to move away, when I remembered something.

'Who was my *real* grandfather?' I asked. 'If you know so much, perhaps you know his name also.'

'Yes, I know it.'

'Tell me.'

'Louis de Marchère.'

'De Marchère? Isn't that French?'

The old woman took the pipe from her mouth and spat contemptuously.

'A rich gorgio rogue with a fancy title and English wife – what matters it to thee? 'Tis all gone now, with the Revolution. No Vicomte any more. No airs an' graces to shame honourable well-born Romany folk such as we. Forget them all, dordi. An' her also who betrayed the tribe.'

'No,' I said. 'I can't forget. If you're speaking the truth—'

'And why would I lie to thee? Besides I have that which speaks clearer than words.'

'What?'

She stared at me for a moment, then went into the tent and returned with something hidden, screwed up in her hand. I watched spellbound as she uncurled her brown fingers. A gold locket lay there on a thin chain, with something that looked like a crest engraved upon it. She handed it to me and said, 'Open it.'

I did so.

Two exquisite small portraits confronted me, painted in a fashion of many decades ago – the woman with luxurious curls threaded by ribbons, a half-smile on her lovely lips, eyes dark and shining, and finely carved features unmistakably resembling Katrina's. The other – he, too, bore a certain resemblance to mama. The haughty expression on the proud face was similar. But the eyes were different. The eyes, seeming to stare into mine, though painted on such a small scale, were deep, dark violet.

*My* eyes.

And it was *my* countenance, only stronger, looking up at me.

I stared for moments, until the old woman said, 'Turn it over. Read.'

I closed the locket, and did as she said.

Inscribed on the back were names, 'Anyana and Louis'. There was a date too, but it had become indistinct through scratches and the passing of time. I let the tips of my fingers hover over the surface for a second or two, then handed it back, saying, 'So those – *they* were my – my grandparents.'

'Thy kin. Thy cursed kin, daughter.'

'Cursed?' I echoed. 'But they must have – have cared – to have those portraits done. And—'

'Tch! she waved a hand contemptuously. 'He was rich – thy grandsire, with many ways o' temptin' an' beddin' a foolish girl. And once he had her – but it didn't end there, did it, dordi? And now thee's come to prove it.'

'How did you get the locket?' I asked.

'Sent to me. Those of our race have many friends in many countries,' she answered in thin cracked tones. 'And when Anyana died 'twas there, in that small room, a place no decent Romany'd choose, with a few of her things, a shawl, an' slippers, for she could always dance, daughter. Ah! there was no fine gorgio lady in any place of the world who could dance as Anyana did. 'Twas in the blood, see? Like the wind in th' trees an' moonlight slippin' between shadders. She was all music an' fire an' laughter with the tears brimmin' bright as the streams in spring rain. For Anyana's kind, love can only bring tragedy. An' that's why I say, daughter, forget love. Take this back, dordi!' she handed me the locket. ''Tis thy true heritage. An' when a gorgio's sly words tempt thee to weakness, remember thy kind.'

I took it hesitantly.

'But you could – it's *valuable*,' I ventured to point out. 'You could sell it.'

'For gold? An' why would I be needin' gold, lady, when I've shawls for my shoulders and broth for my belly?' She took a puff of her pipe again, and continued, ''Tis all around me – what I want – a roof of sky, and good grass for my bed. An' when winter comes, there's a tent or waggon for our vardo. What else in all the world does an old body need?'

There seemed no answer to her question. All the same it was there – in my heart and mind. I accepted the gift as a kind of pledge, because I knew from that moment to do in life.

I would be a dancer.

And no man, ever, would break my heart again as Rupert had done.

*

Although I had not intended to, I stayed with the gypsies for many weeks, helping with all manner of odd jobs when we took to the roads, travelling by-ways and lanes mostly to vicinities of fairs or markets where pegs, baskets, brooms and other commodities could be sold for a reasonable price. I would have liked to dance, as Izonne did on the fringe of a moorland fairground near Bodmin; she was a grand-daughter of Esther – a wild-looking beautiful girl with black hair falling below her waist, who could twirl and leap in her crimson skirt and coloured petticoats, looking like some fiery exotic bird, with her beads and earrings jangling. She earned many coins, some of them silver, and mostly from men. She was strictly moral and pledged to Romano, her cousin, who was an adept at knife-throwing. Oh, how I longed to dance too.

'*No*,' Christos said, when my wish was made known. 'The rozzers are still searching, and though as a lad thou looks well enough, at best thy blood is diddikais, and the rozzers have sharp eyes. Travel with us if thou wish it, but well in shadows of the vardo or tents.'

Christos had more power over his tribe than even Bebee the old woman. As a true Romany Kral he was complete ruler, although out of reverence for her age and ancient heritage, he made a show of asking her opinion on important matters, knowing she would comply with his. He was a lean dark-skinned man, not tall, but with fine muscles and a skill at many crafts with his hands. He spoke very little, and when he did it was mostly in Romany.

So I remained to all intents and purposes a kind of jack-of-all trades, helping put up the tents in any new place we visited, collecting wood for fires and cooking, polishing the bright brass in the large waggon or vardo, learning the look and smell of herbs, searching, sorting them and stirring the immense pot that was kept simmering till all mouths were fed.

It was a strange life. Always when I woke up at early dawn it was with a start of surprise to find myself in the open among such a band of strange-looking people instead of in my pretty bedroom at Heatherfield.

The weather grew chill. Soon Christmas would be upon us. My hair now had grown into tiny curls all over my head. I knew I could not much longer pass as Chiknoo, a boy; realised also that the nomadic period had only been a brief interlude, just a prologue to that other life I was aiming for, as a dancer for sophisticated audiences on a wide stage.

Strangely, I felt no stirring of compassion or worry on account of the family I'd left at Heatherfield, except perhaps for papa Justin and Drake. Justin anyway had shown no sign of softening to anyone during his brief periods of consciousness, only of dislike of Katrina. When he recovered – *if* – he wouldn't miss me, but would probably be thankful to be rid of my presence, since I, initially, was the cause of his accident and marital disaster. Drake would worry, perhaps, but when I got to London, which had been my intention from the start of my flight, I'd write him a note, giving no address, saying all was well with me.

So the time came when I abandoned my youth's attire, and once more put on my own clothes covered by the dark cape and the bonnet which I wore low to the brow shadowing my face.

Christos refused to accept any of the gold I had with me – rather at Bebee's wish I guessed – and before parting added a blessing in Romany.

We were then on the outskirts of Exeter. After bidding farewell, and with some regret, for a romantic period had ended, and those strange mysterious people had been good to me – I found a respectable inn where I stayed the night, before taking the postchaise next morning for London.

When I counted the money in my reticule I found I had more than sufficient for my fare, and to establish myself in the city while deciding how to start on my new career.

Career?

For an instant a tug of apprehension swept through me. I knew no one, had no knowledge at all of the ways of the theatre, or any contact likely to be of assistance. All the possessions I had were in my bag and reticule: a minimum of necessary clothing, a handful of gold, and a precious locket which, as old Bebee had said, was my heritage. Apart from that I had to rely only on one thing – my capacity and passion to dance.

This in itself was sufficient temporarily to drive any niggling fears away. And so it was that two days before Yuletide, I arrived in London, young and determined, a slightly dark-skinned girl – for the stain had not yet completely worn off – with a totally unknown future before her, in a world of strangers.

Alone.

## 3

There was a dense fog when the coach reached the fringe of the city. The driver refused to go further, drawing the vehicle to a halt outside an inn, The Golden Cow, where, with other passengers, I was forced to spend the night. I had to share a small room with a stout yellow-haired woman who told me she was on a visit to her daughter who kept a coffee house near Camden Town. 'Very respectable place,' she announced, when she'd sufficient breath, after loosening her stays, wiping the perspiration from her ample stout cheeks and taking a liberal draught of spirit from a flask. 'No funny goings on like there are in some. She's got on, our Carrie has. Always had a good head on her, our Carrie did. Took up with a fine gentleman who set her up so she's settled for good if she likes.'

'Oh. Married him, you mean?' I remarked and realised I'd said the wrong thing immediately, from the deepening crimson of her broad countenance.

'What's that to you?' she asked sharply. 'I don't go asking

questions 'bout Carrie's life. The faithful sort she is, no flighty little besom trippin' from one man's bed to another's. Oh, Carrie knows which side her bread's buttered, I can tell you.' And she ripped her chemise open revealing an expanse of mottled pink bosom that made me turn away in embarrassment.

'No need to be shy, dear,' the woman continued again in familiar more conciliatory tones. 'Two gels together isn't no disgrace.' When I didn't reply she continued with awakening curiosity, 'Young, ain't you, to be travelling alone? What's your business, love, if I may ask?'

'I'm – I'm going to visit friends,' I lied, hoping she'd believe me and ask no more questions.

But she didn't.

'Now, now,' she said, almost reprovingly. 'Don't try to fool Auntie, dear. To my way of thinking no friends'd allow one of your kind to travel alone on such a journey without so much as a welcome at the end of it. What part o' London do they live in, dear?'

I thought wildly and answered, 'Oh – the west end – somewhere—'

'*Somewhere?*' The heavy eyebrows, several degrees darker than her hair, rose in astonishment. 'But haven't you their proper address, then?'

'It's at the bottom of my bag. I can't bother about that now.'

The full lips drew themselves into a small button.

'Then I think you should, dear. Because it seems to me—' she paused significantly before continuing, '—it seems to me you're not telling the truth. Now that's it, isn't it? You're on the run, and not knowing where to. Now that's a fact, isn't it?'

By then she was unfastening her skirt and petticoats, showing a pair of crimson flannelette drawers that had no pretensions to elegance or style. Everything about my enforced companion was crude and extremely vulgar. If I hadn't been so weary I'd have left the stuffy bedroom there and then and spent the night hours in the taproom. But the sounds from below were male and raucous, the odour of ale and spirits, sweat and smoke so strong, I feared worse things might happen there, and steeled myself to endure the lesser evil.

I did my best to divert the unwelcome probing, but the woman, who called herself Mrs Maria Perkins, wouldn't desist.

'What are you afraid of, dear?' she said, seating herself on the bed that sagged and creaked under her enormous weight. 'Auntie won't harm you. And that's what I could easily be – your auntie, love. Think of me that way. You just tell me what's bothering you, and maybe I can help.'

'I'm quite all right,' I answered, mechanically, though I didn't feel it. The journey and uncertainty, the knowledge of what I'd done in leaving Heatherfield began to register, and if it had been possible, if I'd been alone, I'd have flung myself on the none-too-clean bed, and wept; wept for life's irony, the loss, and desperate longing for Rupert. As it was, I bit my lips, and decided on admitting to a half truth. 'There's no need to bother about me, Mrs Perkins,' I continued. 'I have friends connected with the theatre. But I'm not quite sure—'

'*Ah!*' a great gruff exclamation of understanding broke from her. 'A young lady wanting to be an *actress*. Now that makes sense, dear. Yes – certainly sense, in *your* case, because you have looks of a kind, in spite of your hair. Very short, isn't it, dear?'

'Yes. You see—'

'And your face, love?'

'What about my face?'

'Oh – well now!' Suddenly, quite unexpectedly, she reached for my shoulder and pulled the neck of my dress open. 'Yes, I *thought* so. Very white – your skin. Yet those cheeks of yours! Well now, at first I almost believed you to be Italian. But that's not so. There's been a bit of acting *already*, hasn't there, dear?'

After that, somehow, part of my secret leaked out, and eventually I found myself admitting I'd run away from home because of unpleasant happenings, and was determined to be a dancer. By then she was half-reclining completely, and to me disgustingly naked, on the bed. I kept my eyes averted as much as possible from the heavy sagging breasts and immense thighs.

Once she laughed, and said, 'Never seen a body before as the Good Lord made it, dear? Come now. Don't be so queasy. Soon we'll be snuggled warm and cosy as two bugs in a rug together. I won't touch you, dear, if you don't want it. Keep strictly to my part o' the snuggery.' She laughed, a throaty chuckle of coarse good humour, continuing, 'though my part'll take two-thirds of this old creaker, and that's a fact.'

I turned my back on her, slipped off my dress, and presently, after a cold wash from the ewer, slipped into the bed beside her still wearing my loosened corsets and underwear.

Her mound of a figure heaved round to face me. 'Cold, dear?' she enquired solicitously, ''Fraid these mucky sheets are damp, or of me? Surely not that.'

'I don't think I'm going to sleep well,' I said honestly. 'I may get up and walk about a bit.'

'Now that'd be daft, if I may say so. You just lie quiet for a bit, and listen to me. I've got an idea. Seeing as how you've no plans at all – except for the dancing lark, what about coming with me to Carrie's?'

'*Carrie's?*'

'Yes. Why not? As I said, Carrie runs a fine place and has connections. Oh, many grand folk are clients of hers and perhaps – just *perhaps*, mind you – she could put you in touch with someone knowledgeable about the theatre.' She paused significantly, watching me shrewdly from her small eyes – ''Cos you don't really know, do you?'

'You mean, an actor or actress?'

'Oh, more important than *them* my dear. It's the influential ones as count, managers, men of wealth and taste who know a bit of talent when they see it, and I've a feeling you have some of that, dear. Soon as I saw you I thought, "There's a young woman who could get anywhere given the right treatment and management." Yes, that's what you need, a bit of smartening up, a friendly word in the right quarter, a bit of a push as they say to give confidence, and style, and there you are! You've got *class*, dear. And class always tells in the end – *if* you grab the right chance when it comes. And it may be I'm that chance, dear. Think about it.'

Well, with strange wild thoughts whirling through my brain I did my best to view the prospect of meeting Carrie objectively, with commonsense. But it was difficult to get things into any kind of proportion so tired I was, and that dusty interior so stuffy and lacking fresh air. The gruff voice of my companion faded eventually into heavy breathing and snores, enabling me to slide out of bed unseen and cross to the small window. Behind a drab blind, curtains of thick yellowed lace were looped by shabby velvet ribbon. I pushed one aside and peeped out. Nothing was visible but pin-points of light with the muffled silhouettes of chimney pots and tall windows beyond. The air, momentarily, didn't appear quite so dense, revealing a yard and further ahead the vague suggestion of a street with two shapes lurching along obviously drunk, to be swallowed up the next moment by a returning veil of fog. There was the sound of shouting, accompanied by raucous laughter followed by an oath and rattle of cart wheels and horses' hooves from the distance. I moved away and returned to the bed where Mrs Perkins' mound of a body still heaved and grunted. At first I decided to lie on the floor, then reluctantly perched myself on the very edge of the mattress, where eventually, towards dawn, I fell into the disturbed sleep of exhaustion coloured by restless dreams and imaginings in which Katrina was screaming at Rupert and Justin, and a large figure looking like a huge doll with yellow hair was laughing and waving a bottle in the air shouting, 'Carrie – Carrie – Carrie' while I hammered at the door of a strange room crying to be let out. There was no sense in the dream, and when I woke my head was aching and my heart beating violently. Mrs Perkins was already standing by the cracked mirror, buttoning up her chemise above the red drawers. Hearing me move she turned round. 'Ah! so you're awake at last. Slept well, dear?'

'No,' I answered.

'You should've taken a tot of my tiddly,' she said cheerfully. 'That'd have put you out proper.'

'You never offered any,' I said crossly.

'Didn' I? Oh, really now, that was remiss of me. Never mind, dear, when we get to Carrie's she'll see you get all you want.'

'I didn't say I was going to Carrie's,' I retorted in as lofty a voice as I could manage.

'Oh, but I think you will, dear, 'cos you've nowhere else to go, have you? And if you want to meet up with any theatre folk it'd be daft to turn the chance down. That's what I say.'

As I dressed as hastily as I could, because I didn't like her prying at my limbs and underwear in so initimate a fashion, I realised there could be a degree of sense in what she said.

After all, if Carrie's establishment proved a disappointment or in any way offensive, I could easily leave and look for suitable lodgings somewhere.

Somewhere. *Somewhere!* what a lonely word that was. For the first time since my flight from Heatherfield I realised the full implications of what I'd done. With the gypsies I'd at least had colour, company, excitement and something to do. But London, in the light of day, suddenly appeared a frightening wilderness empty of friends and true human contact. Desolate and grey, and hostile to a seventeen-year-old girl's ambition to be a dancer. In a weak moment I longed poignantly to be back in the world I knew of moorland and sea – for a glimpse again of familiar faces – even Katrina's – which could be so bitter and cold one second, the next softened by a glimpse of affection from Justin's eyes. And Rupert! Oh, how I longed for Rupert.

But Rupert had gone, and Justin no longer felt affection for anyone. No one cared really. No one. Not even Drake, because he was too practical and sensible to waste time being miserable over anyone, especially a wild, unpredictable half-sister like me. So I must dance. Yes, I must – I *must*. If I couldn't have love I would show the world I didn't care! No one, nothing mattered to me but the chance to express the pain I'd suffered, the passion I'd felt and all the lovely past joys of youth's awakening to beauty and desire. I would be a poet through movement and my body's music, holding vast audiences spellbound before breaking into wild applause. And my name would be 'Anyana', in memory of my grandmother who had died so tragically. Yes! somehow I'd achieve it, and if Carrie could help, why not?

So, with the decision made, I set off in the cumbrous vehicle that morning with Mrs Perkins for her daughter's establishment near Camden Town.

Carrie, to my astonishment, was not at all like the rather coarse yellow-haired creature of my dream, but an elegant young woman, a trifle hard-looking perhaps, tastefully – almost demurely – attired, although her eyes of a clear very pale blue held an unblinking sophisticated stare of cool appraisal. Her coffee-house which was situated in a comparatively quiet byway cutting off from the main thoroughfare, was set back from the road at a slightly lower height than most

of the houses which were grey and flat fronted, looming
behind patches of pavement or dusty gardens.

A façade of innocuous respectability hovered over the area,
curiously without obvious character, although the very
drabness was discomfortingly intimidating, the square lace-
shrouded windows suggestive of purposefully withheld intimate activity. Beyond Carrie's place I'd noticed the buildings
dwindle in size becoming interspersed with occasional small
stores and shops. From the distance the faint tinkling sounds
of a barrel organ penetrated the air; a man carrying papers
and wearing working-class clothes trudged in heavy boots over
the cobbles. A cab rattled along to the clip-clop of horses'
hooves. Everything seemed depressingly impersonal. Never
here, I thought, would be the chance of meeting the individual
of influence referred to by Mrs Perkins, who might assist me
on the first step to fame as a dancer. Even the few trees
bordering the street appeared wan and lifeless lifting their
leafless tired branches to the damp grey sky.

Yet, when I stepped through the door of Carrie's house,
everything changed. From appearing outside as just a rather
meagre commercial dwelling, the interior became subtly
exciting. Perfume and scent, mingled with the odour of
coffee, permeated the atmosphere. The decor, mostly contrived in gilt and blue, with rosy lights penetrating lace
curtains at alcoves and doors, suggested affluence and mystery
that to my naive mind already held the promise of
theatredom.

Mrs Perkins, assuming an air of pompous authority,
ushered me past the entrance of quite a large lounge, where
fashionably dressed men and women drank and chattered at
small glass-topped tables. Not only coffee was served there, I
noticed, but also wine, and I would have liked longer to stare,
but my guide propelled me forward.

'Later,' she said. 'Later, dear, we can join the company,
when you're better equipped like,' she gave me a quick, not
entirely, pleasant glance. 'Neither of us is fitted for such style
as we are. Your clothes is drab, dear. But don't you worry. Just
follow me an' trust Carrie. Carrie'll see you dressed properly.'

And that, to my great surprise, and not entirely to my liking,
is what happened.

Bewildered and hardly able to believe I wasn't dreaming, I followed – or rather was pushed by – Mrs Perkins into a smaller room down the hall. Unlike the lounge, there was nothing ostentatious or at all elegant about it. It was probably similar to countless parlours of that area and period – comfortable in a conventional way, with chairs and sofa upholstered in red plush, lace draped windows with an aspidistra in an ornate pot standing on its own small pedestal. There were numerous ornaments about, and a gilt clock on the marble-topped mantelshelf above the fireplace. A few papers lay on the crimson velvet cloth covering the mahogany round table in the centre of the room. A fire burned cheerfully in the grate.

'There now!' Mrs Perkins said, relaxing with a wheezy sigh and creaking of corsets on to the sofa, and indicating a chair for me. 'That's better. Carrie, my dear, this young lady and I've had quite a time of it – quite a time – what with the fog and travelling so far the first day in that old boneshaker. But you can depend on it – it's been worth it – and if you listen to me, you'll agree; that's for certain. Because there's business in it for all of us—' she gave a knowing wink in my direction. 'Isn't that so, dear?'

'Well,' I hesitated. 'I'm not sure, Mrs – Mrs Perkins. It depends. I – you see, I—' I broke off at a loss, not knowing what was in her mind. Did she fancy me as a lodger for her daughter, some sort of paying guest, or as a help, a waitress to assist in serving customers for my board, with the possibility I might eventually make contact with someone of influence beneficial both to the coffee house and myself?

'She wants to be a dancer,' Mrs Perkins suddenly stated, without further preamble. 'I thought you might be able to give a helping hand, so to speak, knowing that your – clientele—' she got the word out with difficulty – 'is of such quality, and seeing as you know so many fine gentlemen.'

'Oh!' Carrie's cold eyes viewed me critically. 'Has she any experience?'

I jumped up from my chair hurriedly and said, 'No. Not professionally. And I don't want *any* gentleman's help who isn't interested in – in talent. Just that. If you thought—' I felt myself crimsoning, 'if you thought anything else I'm afraid you're quite wrong, and I really think I should be leaving—'

'But *where*, dear?' Mrs Perkins queried, apparently all innocent solicitude. 'Where? Nowhere to go, you said – those very words, nowhere, except to some friends, "*somewhere*". But you haven't got any have you? Not in London. I'm sure there's no need to get huffed, dear. All I'm trying to do is to get a contact for you through *Carrie*.'

'But I don't see why,' I protested. 'And business. You mentioned "business for all of us". What business could there possibly be in it for you?'

'Ah, now. That's a good question. A very good question indeed. You've got a bit of a head on you after all, under those tight little curls of yours. Listen to me then. It's this way. If you've got talent – which I don't doubt for a moment dear – still it's *if*, after all, and Carrie takes the risk – well—' She paused to get breath. '*If*, as I say, you're a success, dear, after a bit of training, Carrie'd get a small, a very small commission. Now that's sensible, isn't it? You gradually getting more famous on the stage every day, and your manager paying Carrie a weeny-teeny sum for putting you in touch in the first place. Do you understand?'

Dimly I was beginning to. The way her mind was running *could* make sense, and her daughter certainly didn't appear to have much interest in any mutual plan her mother might have. Indeed, to the contrary. Before I could reply Carrie remarked casually, 'I'd hardly like to sound *any* of my clients on the possibility of launching an unknown girl on the stage. It isn't etiquette in the first place, and as you've already said, ma – mama,' she corrected herself quickly, 'your young friend's without experience. If she'd had training it would be a different matter altogether.'

'Ah! but then suppose – just *suppose* Gusta'd take her? For a bit of that? The training lark? And suppose, just *suppose*, she made it. What about that, eh?'

Again the cool appraising look on me from Carrie's cold eyes.

'*Augusta*?'

'Why not?'

For some moments Carrie appeared doubtful, then after

apparently considering the proposition she agreed with no sign of enthusiasm. 'I suppose we could *try*. But she'd have to look more presentable than she does. That cloak and bonnet! *Really!*'

'You take her upstairs, love, and find something else. Beneath that old-fashioned blanketty thing she's got quite a figger on her, *that* I can tell you – for all her modesty and primness when we was abed together last night,' she laughed coarsely.

I flinched and was on the point of refusing, when Carrie, sensing my displeasure, smiled apologetically. 'Don't be bullied,' she said, 'Ma – mama – can be over-blunt sometimes, it's her way. But if you really *want* what help I can give, you should look just a little smarter before I take you along to Augusta's. She's a friend of mine who runs a training school. So shall we go to my bedroom? I've quite a wardrobe. And I suspect you're very slight. I'm sure there'll be something to suit you, and turn you into a very glamorous young lady.'

Titillated by a feeling of curiosity marred only by a shadow of apprehension I followed Carrie into the hall and up a flight of steep stairs, bordered by a rail of gilt painted bannisters – to give an impression of luxury, I suppose, to visitors from below.

Carrie's bedroom reflected a different Carrie from the business-like good looking character who'd received us. The air was pungent with heady perfume, the walls papered in stripes of pale pink and grey. Against walnut furniture satin cushions and glass figurines glinted from rose coloured lamps. A lace gown looking like a bridal dress lay over the silk quilt on the canopied brass four-poster bed.

Carrie picked it up and placed it in a box filled with tissue paper.

'Now,' she said reflectively. 'How are we going to fix you up? Take off that terrible bonnet and cape thing, for heaven's sake.'

I noticed that her voice, turned slightly irritable, was a little coarser; she no longer attempted the ultra air of refinement so obvious before.

I did as she told me, revealing my ordinary everyday frock. 'My God,' she gasped, 'what a frumpish thing. Where have you lived all your life, girl?'

Lifting my head, and with anger rising in me, I answered, 'Cornwall. And if you remember, I've been travelling. And I really don't think—'

'Huh!' she interrupted. 'Don't get fussed. I meant no harm. But you're quite a beauty in your way – know that? The point is, though, you obviously haven't the *first* idea about *dress*.'

'I haven't needed any, until now,' I answered more quietly.

'That's what I mean. If I'm taking you to my friend's, we must see you reasonably presentable, as my mother pointed out. Now just step out of that monstrosity, and I'll take a look at my wardrobe.'

I unbuttoned my bodice half-reluctantly, and unfastened my skirts at the waist. When Carrie was back with two gowns over her arm, one of a peach-coloured chiffony thing, the other in pale sea-green silk, I was seated on the bed, looking ludicrous, no doubt, in just a cotton chemise, stockings, long drawers, and with my boots still on. Carrie put a hand to her mouth to stifle a guffaw of laughter.

'Oh, my God! Sweet Jesus! What a blooming funny sight.' Then she sobered and said in her assumed lady-like way, 'You must forgive me. My apologies. I don't often let off stream. But what on earth's the *matter* with you?'

'What do you mean?'

'Are you *shy* or something? Of *me*? Now, girl – what did you say your name was, by the way? – strip off. I've got proper things here.' She went to a drawer in a chest, pulled it open and returned with flimsy-looking underwear which she flung on the bed. 'What's your name. You've got one, surely?'

'Anyana,' I answered on the spur of the moment, recalling in a sudden flash of memory the one given me by the old gypsy woman, of my tragic long-dead ancestress.

'Hm? I don't believe it for one moment. But Anyana! – it sounds good. It will do.'

So from that moment I was no longer known as Rosanna, and somehow the change in name seemed to give me fresh identity and courage, and an hour later, as I went downstairs attired in the sea-green silk gown under a violet velvet cloak, with an intriguing little hat of flowers and feathers pushed forward slightly to one side over my forehead, I was already forgetting my secret fears and experiencing a new and bewildering excitement.

As we entered the small parlour a waitress hurried up the hall carrying a tray to the lounge. She gave no start of surprise when she saw me, but then she *wouldn't*, I told myself, she'd merely accept such elegance as natural, and what she was used to, from frequenters of Carrie's place.

Mrs Perkins was all approval when she saw me, nodding with satisfaction, and almost purring, like some great greedy cat.

'Good,' she remarked, 'good. I knowed from the start you could have style, given a bit of assistance. Those ospreys tickling your curls'll tickle *their* fancy all right—'

'Whose? What do you mean?'

'Now, now, dear. No need to take such a hoity tone. Remember girl – what d'you call yourself?'

'Anyana,' Carrie replied promptly.

'Oh. An' whose idea was *that*? Yours or Carrie's? Well, it don't matter. It's got style – mystery. Sounds foreign-like. But as I was saying, remember, I'm your *friend*, dear.'

She tapped my shoulder in an almost predatory way. I drew myself away quickly saying, 'Are we going into the lounge *now*, for that coffee?'

'Oh, I don't think there's any need after all,' Carrie answered in matter-of-fact equable tones. 'You've proved yourself already – in looking the part, I mean. The sooner we reach Augusta's, the better, I think.'

'That's true,' Mrs Perkins agreed. 'The quicker things're settled less likely there'll be any arguing. After all, you never know.'

What she was referring to by that last remark, I'd no idea. But ten minutes later, in the company of Carrie, I was being driven by cab to meet the influential Augusta at her training school for young ladies apparently needing tuition in etiquette, sophisticated manners and for making a fashionable impression in any particular careers of their fancy.

Mostly, I learned later, the tuition in particular was for enticing and pleasuring men of wealth and a fancy for beautiful women. Maybe in a subtle way I already sensed, but would not acknowledge it. However, I didn't, at that point, delve too much into probabilities, but was concerned primarily in being a success and when it came, in using it to my own advantage.

One fact was already clear and determined in my mind. I would be no man's slave – *ever*. My life would be my own. My one aim that I should prove myself as a dancer. Love I had already known and would never feel again. Sex was immaterial. The flame in me for rhythm and self-expression burned clear and strong; a pure fire of flesh and spirit, single-minded in dedication, for which I would follow any demanding and tireless road to reach its zenith.

*4*

Augusta's Theatrical Academy for Young Ladies was situated off a main thoroughfare in a district not unlike Carrie's Coffee House, except that most of the houses were terraced and balconied which gave a vague air of past elegance to the area. Here was no sign of a shop or commercial activity. As I dismounted from the cab, a top-hatted gentleman walked smartly across the small square opposite where a few plane trees reached naked networked branches to the lowering sky. A hansom cab rattled by, its shape slightly blurred by the mist which still hovered over wet pavements and cobbles, taking the whole vista into deepening uniformity.

I noticed, before Carrie gave a tug at the bell-pull, the discreet lettering over the door, which could easily have passed unnoticed except for those interested and in search of tuition. The front of the house was wide and tall with windows indicating the interior would be three-storied. It was also detached, unlike most of the other buildings, with paths – almost narrow drives – leading on either side to the back.

A maidservant, modestly but attractively dressed, opened the door to us, and I was surprised at the dim lighting of the wide hall, which unlike the coffee house, gave no suggestion of glamour or fashionable company. To the contrary, everything appeared extremely ordinary and discreet – the kind of interior one would expect of a doctor's or solicitor's dwelling. Anything less like a dancing establishment could not be imagined. But then, I told myself reasoningly, I didn't *exactly* know what training Carrie's friend, Augusta, was prepared to give – all Carrie had suggested concerned deportment, and learning to dress and behave in the manner demanded by high society – *men* in particular. The slight uneasy feeling returned to me, emphasised by the brooding quietness of the scene! For a second or two I felt trapped.

Then the girl who'd tapped and poked her head into a room opposite a wide flight of stairs, returned and said, 'Madam will see you now, Miss Carrie.'

We followed her, and a minute later found myself facing the much discussed 'Augusta', or 'Madam', as I learned later she was known to her business acquaintances and clients.

She was tall, rather severe-looking, late-middle-aged or perhaps more, with a pale complexion, fine features, a thin mouth, and extremely shrewd eyes darting between narrow long lids like some predatory bird's; hawk's eyes. She was dressed all in black, with jet earrings hanging below upswept coiled black hair pinned with a jewelled comb. Her gown was styled to no set period, but when she moved there was a rustle of heavy silk, a fleeting flash of diamante, and glitter of a diamond brooch near her throat. Everything about her indeed was distinctive, but curiously ambiguous. I realised in those first few moments of contact that she would be an impossible woman to know intimately. Her air of breeding was belied only by the grasping claw-like motion of her restless thin white hands, which, though cared for, were heavily ringed, suggesting the acquisitive quality of a hungry peasant out for all she could get.

I didn't like her, and sensed that the feeling was mutual, although if she could she would use me unscrupulously for her own ends.

Carrie was brief and to the point concerning the reason for our unexpected visit, and while she was explaining my ambitions for a dancing career, including pointedly that I had no friends in London, nowhere to stay, and that she was sure I would be an adaptable girl if Madam considered me suitable as a residential trainee, I was aware of the hard bird's eyes darting here, there, and everywhere over my person, considering my potential.

At length she agreed it was possible – just *possible*, a trial period might be beneficial to both of us, *providing* I agreed to all conditions and rules she might impose.

'For instance,' she said in husky, rather rough-edged tones, though her pronunciation was perfect, 'diet is important for retaining or producing a good figure, and sleep, plenty of sleep. My girls – my *pupils* – must be abed at eight o'clock *every* night, unless she has permission from me for any well-chaperoned celebration with an escort likely to advance her future. Morning sessions of deportment, movement and manner are strictly enforced. Elisse, my head instructress, will put up with no slacking. She was herself a ballerina until, tragically, she broke a foot that put an end to her stage life. Nevertheless, during her appearance at various theatres she became acquainted with many discerning patrons of the nobility, some of whom, if you are lucky, you may meet in the future—' On and on Madam's voice droned until my head and ears rang through trying to absorb exactly what I must and must not do. As a number of her 'girls', for instance, were truants from home like myself, no true identity must be divulged, not even to herself. We all studied under assumed names. Mine, for instance, 'Anyana', must not be given.

'Oh, but that *isn't* my name, not my real one,' I interjected. 'It's—'

'Hush,' she put up a finger warningly. 'I don't wish to know. There could be nothing more distasteful to me than being accused of abduction, which just *might* happen if I was aware of any legitimate connection with your parentage. To me you will be, then, if accepted, Anyana, a girl without means, ties, or duties, willing – no, *anxious* – to be launched on a profitable dancing career.'

Her statement silenced me. By then I knew her plans for me were devious and certainly to her own advantage, but curiously, being aware of this didn't deter or in any way intimidate me. I would obey whatever rules she imposed, up to a point. If a time came when they seemed excessive I'd find a way of escape, and by then I surely would have sufficient knowledge to take the first stepping stone to success.

So it was that I became a pupil of Augusta's Dancing Academy for Young Ladies, and on my first evening there met a number of the companions who were to share my daily life.

*

First of all I was conducted to my room, which was certainly the most luxurious I'd ever slept in, being furnished in rose pink and grey with all the requisites of a bedroom combined with a 'retiring room', as Madam described it, including a chaise longue and ornate rosewood writing table as well as a large velvet upholstered easy chair, canopied wide bed, wardrobe and dressing table with a muslin-draped mirror and glass shelves containing numerous bottles of lotions and cosmetics. When the wardrobe was opened, Augusta waved a thin hand to where numerous garments of a flimsy nature – wraps and dresses – were hung. A fire was burning in the grate.

I gasped.

'But so many!' I exclaimed. 'And – why? Whose are they?'

'For you. Who else?'

'But you didn't even know I was coming.'

'Not anyone called Anyana, certainly. But *some*one, yes. I knew that; this establishment is much sought after, and always I make sure my girls are suitably equipped to master the art of—' She paused before adding, '—graceful allure, shall we say?'

'But *please*—' I insisted. 'All I wish to learn is to dance—'

'I understood you knew that already, up to a point.'

'Yes, yes. In my own way. But when Carrie, Mrs Perkins' daughter, suggested bringing me here it was – well, I thought it was to have *stage* instruction, and introductions to managers looking for talent.'

'That is so. But managers, as I'm sure she must also have pointed out, would not take a second glance at such a little brown bird as you appear. No wonder your manner is somewhat distraught. My dear girl—' Her voice lost its cool authority and became irritable, almost harsh, 'have sense. Your complexion at the moment is quite ridiculous, in spite of those flowers and feathers meant to disguise it – at the instigation of our mutual friend, no doubt?' Sarcasm broke from her with a slight lift of her upper lip in the suggestion of a sneer.

'Carrie gave me – loaned me these clothes, yes.'

'I thought so. She has incredibly bad taste. Presently, when you've washed, I'll send Janetta up to you. She's one of my most successful pupils, and extremely knowledgeable about style in clothes and make-up. She will do something about your skin, and advise on what you wear for introduction to your companions at dinner. Meanwhile, do rid yourself of those ridiculous frills, and put on something more elegant. This perhaps.'

She took an exotic-looking embroidered wrap from the cupboard and placed it on the bed. 'There. Undress and see how you look in it—'

'But I – it must be very expensive,' I remarked hesitantly. 'And I haven't much money. You see I – oh, I don't think I *ought* to – really. I shall need different underwear, too. You see—'

Madam's mood changed. She patted my shoulder almost affectionately.

'You're bewildered and tired, child, that's all. You must forgive me. I suppose everything *has* come as something of a shock to you. But you mustn't worry. And any talk about expense is *nonsense*! Sheer nonsense. You pay for nothing. The only payment I demand is gratification in your ultimate success. Everything in this room is for your use. Your very own. As for underwear, it's all there, but in actual fact you will need very little—'

'What *do* you mean?'

'This establishment is kept warm, my dear. No flannel petticoats or drawers, just flimsy bits and pieces, the merest minimum of pull-ons to ensure comfort for routine practice in the studio which is on the top floor. It covers the whole of this establishment. Later Janetta will escort you upstairs and explain the daily routine.'

Conversation between us continued for another five minutes or so, then with a swish of black silk Madam left me sitting alone on the bed, still wearing the ridiculous little hat which I pulled off a minute later and threw to the floor.

I stared bemused at the satin wrap lying beside me, suddenly completely exhausted, with my head whirling; and was still there when Janetta arrived. She was small, dainty, with a very white skin, long dark eyes, and a dazzling smile, foreign-looking and attired in a loose black robe, belted and ankle length, dotted with tiny stars. Jewelled combs held her very black shining hair, and when she spoke it was with an entrancing accent from which I deduced correctly she must be French.

'I am so veree pleased to meet you, *chérie*,' she said, smiling in a warm intriguing fashion. 'And you must not too much notice if Madam Augusta appears a trifle – shall we say – important on occasions. Times when she chooses to watch – what you call, I suppose – rehearsals. Yes?' When I gave no reply she laughed softly, and continued, 'The important thing is for us to be friends. And with Elissa, too. Elissa is very knowledgeable, so when she directs you must follow carefully.'

'Do you mean when she directs the dancing?' I enquired.

Janetta shrugged. 'Oh, yes. *Mais oui*. But there are other things too, things you must already have been told by Madam: behaviour, etiquette, and how to please our patrons. *Now?*' she paused, with one finger to her dainty mouth, surveying me from every angle, and then said, 'Slip off those unmentionables, and put on the wrap, then we'll have that veree lovely hair pinned as it should be, and we'll take a quick look together at the studio before the real work begins of getting your own countree skin fair as a lily. Eh?' Again there was a tinkle of laughter. I did what she said, and as my last undergarment was removed heard her say approvingly, 'You have a nice figure. Good. Slim, but not *too* slim where there should be the curves. I shall look forward to dressing you, *chérie*.'

There were a few more complimentary remarks, which I accepted in embarrassed silence; then we went along a wide corridor, thickly carpeted, passing many doors, each with a name on it, and up a flight of stairs to an immense room with a glass roof and a platform at one end, obviously used as a stage. There was also a practice rail along one wall. The floor was varnished and shining, the decor pale blue, and except for curtains at Gothic-styled windows, and several chairs at the opposite end facing the stage, no furniture at all.

'There, you see—' Janetta said, indicating the platform.

'When rhythm and movement, dancing, if you like to call eet, is over, one by one each pupil demonstrates alone before Elissa, and Madam sometimes – to see how everee one of us progresses. *Now!* – do not look so *serious*, little one. You will be accustomed to it in no time, and a favourite with our most influential gentlemen, I am sure.'

But would I? I wondered. Everything was so strange and unlike what I'd imagined a dancing academy would be. I hadn't anticipated the emphasis there'd be on rules, looks, clothes, and above all, in pleasing patrons and male clients. Still, during the process of being bathed, scrubbed, powdered and scented, with a special cream applied to my face, neck, hands and in fact, over my whole body, to make it soft and so disguising any remaining signs of the gypsy boy 'Chiknoo' – I was too flurried and occupied to fret over the 'whys' and 'wherefores' of my future at Madam Augusta's, but obeyed Janetta's instruction automatically, and when night came, was presented to the company of pupils – a new character altogether, even to myself.

I was wearing a loose negligée of exotic purple satin – chosen by Janetta because, she said, it emphasised the shade of my violet eyes. With ten other girls – likewise simply but elegantly clad, I ate a simple but well-served meal in the communal dining room, headed by Elissa. Diet, I'd already learned, though nourishing, was limited to foods conducive to retaining a good figure. It was the wish of Madam we should all feel at ease and relaxed for any social events that might arise during the evening; therefore negligées or wraps were the rule before the chance arose of being called upon to display our attributes to our brightest and most pleasing.

When the meal was over I was once again directed to Madam's parlour and informed that naturally I needn't fear having to appear in public for some time.

'Your introduction to any influential patron will not be until I consider your performances in every way to be beyond reproach or any chance of failing to impress,' she stated in precise practical tones. 'In the meantime, watch closely, learn from those more knowledgeable than you, and be careful never to disobey instructions.'

It was like being reprimanded in advance by a headmistress

of some strict finishing school, although, as I already guessed, and was to discover later, any respectable headmistress of a young lady's establishment would have been horrified at the aims and particular type of tuition provided at Madam Augusta's.

## 5

During my first weeks at Madam Augusta's I learned many things; I learned that the girls there – *presumably* pupils – were known only by their first names – Estella, Cora, Juliet, Marianne, Linnet, Sheena, Laura, Lilianne, Marguerite and Paula. And, of course, Janetta and Elissa. I was informed, also, that *never*, under any circumstances, must domestic affairs be discussed outside the precincts of the establishment, or with any friend allowed to escort a particular young lady to the theatre or supper. Day time, except for luncheon and two hours' relaxation in individual bedrooms, was specifically for *work* – the work including not merely dancing and deportment lessons in the studio, but for special studying concerning care of the complexion, massage, and learning all the arts of allure; especially the latter. No one was allowed outside, except in the company of Elissa for personal shopping; the high walled-in garden at the back of the house was large with a lawn, a spreading cedar tree and a gazebo at one end, where, if we wished, we could stroll, and relax during recreation hours. No letters, except when censored, were allowed. This rule was strictly enforced by Madam herself, and any maidservant bribed secretly to take one to the post and discovered, was dismissed immediately, under some false accusation of theft. So chances of contacting the outside world were meagre. In any case, female servants employed at the Academy were generally ex-pupils who had not quite 'made the grade', as Elissa described their position, so there was little likelihood of disobedience to Augusta's wishes.

If my ambition and curiosity hadn't been so acute I'd have resented such a claustrophobic existence. As it was, being on the alert for any information likely to advance my future, kept me occupied. It soon became apparent to me that a good deal of quiet activity went on in the house following eight o'clock bed-time. There was the soft thud of male footsteps on the landing – I knew they were male, because of their widely spaced tread – and because once, defying the danger of being seen, I opened my door the merest chink, and observed the broad back of a gentleman's tailed-coat disappearing into Marguerite's bedroom. He had a top hat in one hand, and carried gloves and a cane.

Oh, very respectable in daytime, no doubt, probably a man of repute and property with a lady wife and family living in one of the more select squares of London, but when evening came demanding something more titillating than respectability, such as Marguerite or Cora, or any other of my willing companions. Yes, I'd learned a lot in a short time, from whispers, nudges, subtle comments and muffled laughter behind closed doors. Were they all the same? I wondered frequently, or was there anyone of our company like myself wishing only for a career? The façade of academic dancing tuition, of course, was retained, but I couldn't help realising it was merely an act to most of the trainees. On the occasions when Madam visited rehearsal times, I sensed the underlying boredom of the event, noticed the blank expressions on colleagues' faces as she referred to the mystique of Maria Taglioni as La Sylphide, and Fanny Elssler's sexual and physical allure. They weren't really interested in pirouettes, entrechats, or mastering true technical ability. Choreography to most of them meant no more than a means of attracting – or ensnaring – male attention when the opportunity arose. I strongly suspected that, except perhaps for Juliet and Linnet, Augusta's protégées had no serious dedication to the dance whatever, only to the subtle means of attaining eventually some wealthy protector willing to set up a mistress in a secure little establishment of her own as payment for her sexual favours.

You could say, I suppose, that I lost most of my illusions during my time at Madam's. But that wouldn't directly be true.

Although, communally I shared and was part of the day-to-day life there, I remained strictly 'my self', and never forgot for one moment that another world and people existed outside, with different values and aspirations that I meant one day to contact and conquer eventually as Anyana. Finding love at seventeen, had, in a sense, shaped my future. I knew there could be no second best for me. Rupert, through a bitter twist of Fate, was lost to me, but the fire, the sweetness, longing and despair of passion, still burned as a bright flame that somehow had to find its own firmament.

The dance.

*My* dance of life.

And so time passed, while Madam watched me, I knew, with more than the general interest she showed in her other girls. The secret assignations concerning the rest of the company continued. I became used to the furtive night-footsteps echoing down the well-carpeted landings -- the faint creak of doors opening and closing, and occasions when Cora, Laura, Liliane, or any particular favoured girl of the moment was allowed openly to be escorted to the theatre, or some late supper date with an affluent-looking male 'relative' purporting to be a sophisticated elderly 'uncle', under the approved glance of Madam Augusta as they left. Such occasions were rare, and never referred to afterwards, although Madam remarked to me casually one day, when she had been commending me on my progress, that *Cora*'s 'uncle' was an extremely influential and wealthy man, who would most probably see she was presented at court when he considered that she had all the necessary charm and manners to do him credit.

By then I had no illusions about the 'uncle' business or the actual relationship between Cora and her escort. Whether Madam guessed this of me or not, I did not know, but she went on to remark in more intimate, slightly insinuating tones, 'It will not be long now, my dear, before I may be able to arrange a very important introduction for *you*.' She paused, while I waited, apparently calmly, but inwardly with a growing sense of excited anticipation, for the conclusion of her statement. Her glance, though veiled and inscrutable, was concentrated unblinkingly upon me for a prolonged pause, and when I remained silent, she added with a faint trace of irritation, 'Well, aren't you interested?'

'Of course, Madam,' I replied politely. 'I didn't wish to appear – pushing, that's all.'

'Ah, I see. Modesty.' She gave a flicker of a thin smile. 'But I don't believe it for one moment. You are just clever, Anyana. But try not to appear *too* innocent when the great moment comes. Subtle, yes, and well-behaved. But it would be a pity to let the great man think you a fool, would it not?'

'It would depend, Madam.'

'*Indeed?*' she appeared nonplussed, even taken aback. 'On what, may I ask?'

'On the man, Madam,' I replied. 'Whether the advantage would be mutual to us both.'

Her usually yellowish-pale countenance betrayed a flush of anger.

'Do not be impertinent with *me*, dear,' she said tartly. '*I* am the judge of whom you will meet, and whom *you*, in your turn, will do your best to oblige. A great deal depends on your success there – and if you fail or become unco-operative then I'm afraid you'll quickly realise your stupidity and find yourself in the street.'

'I don't think I shall fail,' I said quietly.

'I sincerely hope not. Now – after this rather unpleasant turn in our conversation, let me divulge my news.' She pulled herself together, and smiled again acidly. 'All being well, you will meet this influential, wealthy, and most charming gentleman in, shall we say, about a week's time. He is not only high up in the social scale, but a great patron of the theatre who was a famous producer himself in the past. His name, indeed, is international. To you he will be known as Mr Black. Mr Theodore Black, or 'sir'. His real identity will not be divulged until considerably later when he's had time to assess your potential and grow to know you. Do you understand?'

I wasn't sure, but my mind worked quickly, and I answered, 'Mr Black seems a very *ordinary* name for anyone so famous, Madam.'

'Ah, child!' she tapped the table irritably with her long thin fingers. 'You're very *inquisitive*, Anyana, and are not being at all helpful. Do you wish for this introduction or not?'

'Oh, yes, of course, I'm sorry,' I apologised. 'I didn't mean to be awkward. But it's just—'

'I know. I know. You were taken by surprise. All these months you've accepted training and life here as a pleasant occupation which would continue indefinitely. But the time has come for you to face the test. To prove having you here has been worth all the time and trouble spent in seeing you were equipped for your true career. Well, Mr Black will be able to judge.'

'Thank you,' I said automatically. 'I shall be – pleased – grateful, I'm sure, to meet him.'

But I was not sure at all.

And during the following few days I thought out my plan.

# 6

The evening arrived when I was to meet Mr Theodore Black. I didn't doubt Madam's assertion that he was a man of influence – the gleam in her eyes told me it was true – and that he had a certain knowledge of the theatre which would tempt me into playing my cards well – Janetta's comment – therefore ensuring considerable benefits for both myself and Augusta.

This I was quite prepared to do, in my own way, and dressed for the occasion in the manner directed by Elissa, at Madam's command, in a flowing gauzy-looking gown of rainbow shades that had the flimsy quality of a butterfly's wings under the carefully contrived subtle lighting of my apartment. My glossy hair was carefully pinned, with a few stray curls brushing my shoulders. From Janetta's careful handling and massaging with soothing lotions my skin glowed smoothly, faintly tinged with pink, almost pearl-like. Oh yes! I looked my very best – almost, or perhaps *quite* beautiful. And seeing my reflected image in the mirror I had a momentary desperate longing for Rupert – to feel his hands on my satin-soft shoulders, and the pressure of his body closer, closer against mine, his lips warm against my cheek murmuring,' My Rosanna, my own lovely rose—'

But I wasn't his any more, and I wasn't Rosanna. I was 'Anyana', a girl trained for the art of seducing a strange man at Madam's command, and for my own particular purpose. This time, though, matters would not quite follow the usual pattern of such erotic occasions at the Academy. This time it would be different. So I thrust all thought of Rupert aside, and through the mirror I saw my violet eyes darken, my small chin set decisively under the secret smile of my lips.

Madam entered at that very moment for inspection.

'Turn,' she said as the door closed. 'Let me see. *Vite!*' This '*vite*' was a word she had learned from Janetta, I supposed, and used when she wished to be particularly impressive.

I moved, lifting my head slowly at a graceful seductive angle to face her.

She stared at me for some moments critically, with appraisal. Then, after a thoughtful nod, she said, 'Walk across the room, smile, then turn again with one arm lifted towards me as though in welcome—'

She waited, while I did my graceful best.

Both of her thin hands went out in a gesture of negation.

'That is not right. The pose? Yes. You possess all the arts of movement. But your attire, Anyana. All wrong.'

I stared at her in astonishment.

'Why? What's wrong? Don't you like the dress?'

'The dress? Oh, there's nothing to dislike in that. But what you have underneath! That lace petticoat and chemise. *No*. Take them off immediately. And anything else you are wearing.'

'How *can* I? Why *should* I?' I gasped. 'I would look awful! Cheap – ridiculous. This dress is so thin it would show *everything*!' A hand went to one breast defensively.

'That's just it, my dear. You have a beautiful body, and your business is to show it. You are not a little girl going to a birthday party, you know.' Her lips pursed critically. When I didn't speak she asked tartly, 'Did you hear what I said?'

'Yes, Madam.'

'Then kindly do as I say.'

Reluctantly, realising that my career, and indeed my whole

future, might depend on those next few moments, I obeyed, and when I hadn't a shred on, flung the garments towards the bed, and pulled the flimsy see-through affair over my head, with my back to Madam.

'Ah, that's better,' I heard her remark in more soothing tones. 'Now, Anyana, turn round, if you please. There's no need to sulk.'

Once more I did as she said, and strangely, with the soft warm-scented air brushing my skin through the ethereal material, annoyance in me gave way to a slowly welling-up excitement – a feeling of freedom – an impetus to rise on my toes and dance with erotic emotion, floating, reaching with arms like wings raised to the window and open sky beyond.

Almost simultaneously, Madam lifted the lid of the ornate French china music-box standing on a small rosewood table near my bed, and a joyous tinkle of sound gave impulse to my desire. I stood high on my bare toes, and a second later was twirling round, with the feather-light gown billowing cloud-like round my breasts and long curved thighs.

When the tune suddenly ceased, I stopped, and saw Madam's hand close the lid abruptly. She was smiling. 'That was good,' she said approvingly. 'And you enjoyed it, too. You see, my dear, you are not at all the little goody-two-shoes you pretend to be. You have the potential of Taglioni's Sylphide, or Fanny Elssler's La Esmeralda – pagan but bewitchingly alluring. Spiritual or of the earth? What does it matter so long as you have the great man at your feet. And remember, dear—' her voice became harder, more practical, 'for such a favour you must see you give something in return – be generous and see he is satisfied in every way.'

'I shall do my best to please him,' I answered ambiguously, with a façade of demure acquiescence.

At last she was content.

I was left alone to prepare for Elissa's approval before the arrival of my hoped-for patron.

\*

Mr Theodore Black was of average height, late middle-aged, I judged, with a tendency to portliness. He had a rubicund complexion, long reddish sideburns almost – but not *quite* –

joining his somewhat fleshy chin. His eyes were small of a bright blue, peering inquisitively from under busy eyebrows. He wore a double-breasted dark tailed-coat, above an embroidered waistcoat and a frilled high cream collar reaching to the lobes of his ears. His striped twill trousers were elegantly cut, narrowing at the ankles to cover the top of his pointed black shoes. Over his stomach hung a gold fob, and in one hand he held a slender ivory-topped cane, in the other a tall shining top hat.

Such details of course registered in my mind only later. My first impression was merely that of a demanding vital individual used to power and obtaining what he wanted without argument, and for a brief pause my senses tensed. I had a swift desire to run away – to rush down the corridor and stairs, straight through into the street before anyone could stop me. But I couldn't move; I stood transfixed to the spot between the dressing-table and bed as though my limbs were glued to the floor. Something must have shown in my face, for his voice was surprisingly soft, a cultured – even kindly voice, when he said. 'My dear. How charming you look.' He held out a hand. 'Come now. Don't be nervous. I was assured you were a most sociable and – ambitious young lady. Isn't that so? Well, then we should both be gratified for the chance of being acquainted. Or have I made a mistake?' The smile on his lips faded.

I pulled myself together abruptly, and with an effort answered apologetically, 'Of course. Forgive me, Mr – Mr Black. Please—' indicating the large velvet padded chair, 'do sit down. It's just that I'm not used to—' I glanced down at the shimmering flimsy gown lit to flickering gold from the candle-light – 'to Madam Augusta's choice of attire for receiving a celebrated guest,' I ended bluntly.

'Ah! an innocent. How really refreshing. And how fortunate – for me.'

Courage returned to be suddenly.

'Why for you, sir?' I asked, lifting my head an inch higher.

His bushy eyebrows rose with rather comical-looking arches of surprise.

'Because the pleasures of teaching you the ways of the world – of a man and a woman about to experience a most rewarding relationship, will be all the more titillating,' he remarked. 'I am sure you have much to give. And I, in return—' he shrugged and spread both hands out significantly – 'will see you benefit in every way possible from the power I have to help you. Do you understand, Anyana? I believe that's your name?'

'Yes,' I answered, 'of course. But I don't think *you* do – quite. Oh, I don't mean to be impertinent. Please don't be angry—'

He came towards me and touched my shoulder gently, letting his surprisingly long slender fingers travel a few inches downwards over the gauzy material and linger for a few moments on my flesh.

'Angry? Why should I be angry? You wish to be a dancer, and I wish for *you*, my dear. Both wishes I'm sure can come true, and be made exceedingly pleasurable.'

I broke free of him quickly and ran lightly across the carpet on my bare feet to where the music-box stood, waiting to be played. I lifted the lid, and the silvery tones tinkled out, in a haunting French tune that held something in it of sadness, joy, and a coquettish invitation to dance. Then I twirled round and faced him.

'There?' I said, lifting my arms. 'Listen, and look, sir. Oh, please watch – just for a little time, a few minutes. No one has seen me dance this way before – *no* one. It is my own – and you will be the only one, the very first to see it. You see, sir – Mr Black – I'm not like the others, Madam Augusta's pupils. I can't give you my body – because—' I swallowed before continuing with a rush of words – 'Because it isn't mine to give—'

'What the devil—'

'Look – *look* – *watch*—' I repeated desperately, 'I'm a *dancer* – to the sky and the sea and the mountains, to sadness, and joy and – and—' Words faded. I was dancing then, by the window – dancing with all the anguish, unfulfilled emotion, longing, passion, desire and the hunger for life that was in my blood. The shadows round me became dreams. The exotically scented room faded as my limbs responded to all the hidden impulses of spirit and body, and I was no longer merely Anyana, but the beauty and rhythm of flying clouds and the winged flight of birds soaring and dipping above the singing music of wind-blown trees and grass blowing. I was love, I was death. All I had, I gave to him – that stoutish affluent figure seated,as though entranced, watching, his bland broad face a mere blur in the light and flying shadows of the background.

Then, quite abruptly, the tune ceased.

I fell, breathless, on the chaise longue, waiting.

For some seconds there was no movement. All was silent and still.

Very still.

I lifted my head. He was still motionless, with no expression on his face at all.

'You see,' I said, in a low voice. 'Oh! I *hope* so. That is my gift to you, Mr Black. You are the very first.'

He spoke at last.

'Call me Theodore,' he said.

'But—'

'No buts.' He rose to his feet and regarded me critically, no longer the slightest sign of erotic desire on his face. Then he nodded.

'Very well, young lady. You are pert to the point of insolence, a tease and a natural coquette. But, above all, you are a dancer born. You are the first woman who has ever dared to trick or bribe me. But you have done it. And I'm prepared to take you on – for your talent alone.'

A great sigh of relief broke from me. I rushed towards him. 'Oh, Mr Black—'

He put up a defensive arm.

'Theodore, remember? And don't come too near, mademoiselle, or I may break my word. Now put something decent on, for heaven's sake, and we'll go down and have a word with Madam.'

And that was how I gained my first introduction to the genuine world of ballet.

## 7

It would seem strange to most people, I suppose, that Theodore Black – or to give him his real name, Sir Beverley James – who had visited me primarily at Madam's in the hope of sensual and sexual purpose, should become at that time my greatest and trusted friend, and responsible for launching me after a year's intensive training under the tuition of a friend of his – the brilliant ex-ballet master, de Revelle – as a dancer in one of Meyerbeer's Operas. I only appeared in the last act, but the role gave fire to my imagination. It was one of the spirit rather than the earth, but enabled me full emotional expression for conveying a hint of hungry dedication to the elements – the quality that later was to make the name 'Anyana' famous in the annals of ballet.

I was noticed.

Theodore, of course, was delighted. Until his death years later, I called him Theo, at his wish. The familiarity came naturally to me. Since our initial introduction he'd treated me more as a daughter than a woman he'd momentarily desired, and during my year of training, which had been strict, taking up six hours of every day, I'd lived under the protection of his unmarried sister in London's West End. Through all that period I'd given myself fanatically to mastering the technique of ballet, although de Revelle encouraged me also to obey my instincts of free moment, which held, he said, a 'pagan' quality unlike any other ballerinas of the age. I had a few male acquaintances, naturally, but no intimate friends; indeed, even had I wished for any I wouldn't have had the energy for socialising following the exhausting schedule of the work which had become my life.

I had written to Drake, giving no address, but informing

him I was well, and training for a career that might surprise him one day.

– but don't worry [I added in conclusion] I'm living as respectably as a nun, and you need have no fears for my future. I think often, when I'm not too tired, about everyone at Heatherfield, especially you and Papa Justin. I wish you could send me news, Drake, but it's safer not to give an address yet. As soon as I'm free and independent I'll get in touch with you. At the moment, though, it would be awful and quite distressing if mama should somehow find out and come rushing up to London to look for me. Those scenes we used to have were awful. No wonder Uncle Richard – I always think of him as 'uncle', never my papa – and mama hated each other so much. In a way, although he behaved so badly, I'm sorry for him.

Take care of yourself. When I think back I see you as the only completely sane and dependable character among the whole bunch of us.

With love, Rosanna.

I hadn't even mentioned Rupert. I couldn't. Any faint thought of him could still be hurtful and cast a shadow that temporarily distracted me, like a dream clouding reality.

So the months had passed.

In 1833 following my appearance in London I was launched as a prima ballerina on the stage of the Parish Opera, where my intuitive sense of dance was given full expression in *Snow Ballet*, through the brilliant choreography of the famous Perrot, combined with my partner's – Olaf Karn's – understanding and mastery of his role.

I danced as the Ice Queen surrounded in the first act by her court of dancers representing snowflakes – all quivering white against a background of pale blue.

In the final scene the Queen was overcome by the appearance of Karn's brilliant blinding Sun God and succumbed tragically following her symbolic seduction.

There were a few brief moments of resurrection as the Queen raised herself from the ground, only to sink again, and be finally lifted up triumphantly, an ethereal limp shape, white and shining, in the Sun God's arms, with a few dancers, flakes of her court, gliding downcast and sad to mourn her.

There was a pause, an awed silence, before the curtain came down, a pause shattered suddenly by such wild applause the whole Opera dome seemed to shake, reverberating with cries of '*Encore – encore – magnifique—*'

I was breathless, in a daze, trembling and only half-believing the wild enthusiasm could be for me, as Karn took my hand, and led me to the front of the stage where the oration continued until we made the last exit.

That was the point when I fully realised my true vocation was accepted – not only by the one or two individuals who had sponsored and believed in me, but by a large European public which eventually, with luck, would spread to world-wide fame.

And it did.

During the next few years following my triumphant short appearance at the Paris Opera, I danced in Vienna, Naples, Milan, London, and several other European cities. Mysticism and romance blended with a touch of sensual paganism were the craze of the day. I performed such established roles as 'La Sylphide', entirely in my own fashion which meant, naturally, comparisons were made between Taglioni's version and mine; even Théophile Gautier was guardedly complimentary, although his darling of the period, of course, was the vibrant and beautiful Fanny Elssler.

At first, naturally, I expected criticism from some quarters, and received it. But nothing could check my growing success.

At twenty-four I was established as one of the greatest prima ballerinas of the age.

Many men praised and wanted me, including dukes, a count, and even a king. I welcomed the attention, the flowers and the toasting, the lavish presents and adulation; but I gave neither my body nor my heart in return. The image of Rupert, even, was fading; my sole love was my work and talent to stir the imagination and emotions to fresh dimensions of passion, loss, and rebirth of the spirit through rhythm and awareness of beauty.

This single-mindedness of course had a price. All contact with my family during those glowing years was lost – or rather wilfully broken. Two incidents only occurred to remind me consciously of the past and the Cornwall I'd so passionately loved as a wild young girl. Once, in London, after taking my curtain, when a face registered briefly from the audience – a white, handsome, cold face under piled-up black hair glittering with jewels. The woman, wearing red, was seated beside a black-bearded, stout, affluent-looking man, equally richly attired, with a flash of diamonds glinting from his cravat. In spite of the painted lips and make-up, there was no mistaking Katrina. And for a second my heart missed a beat or two; the recognition between us was mutual, her dark eyes held mine for an instant – condemning and cold. Then I saw a white hand come up elegantly wafting a fan before her scarlet mouth.

Oh! for that dreadful brief moment it all registered – the dislike and jealousy, the blame for Justin's accident that had built up through the years. Had there, then, been no pride? Was there a chance, perhaps, that she might come to my dressing room later with a small word of congratulation? But no. I knew instinctively she would not, just as I sensed the quick glance was the last I would ever see of my mother.

And I was right.

However, that same week, following the finale of a performance of *Snow Ballet* at the Drury, I was informed in my dressing room that a gentleman wished very much to see me.

I was very tired that night, and having become sufficiently important to dismiss one gentleman from the many so eager to congratulate me without impairing my popularity, I shook my head and told my dresser, 'No, please give my apologies and say I am too exhausted.'

The message was delivered, but the doorman returned saying, 'He is rather insistent, madam. He says his name is Trengrouse, Mr Drake Trengrouse, "please tell her that I'm her—"'

I didn't allow him to finish. Despite my tiredness I jumped up and said, '*Drake* – Drake, you said? Show him in then. Of *course* I'll see him.'

And that is how I learned news of Heatherfield for the first time in years.

When we'd recovered from the pleasurable excitement of meeting again, I took my brother's hands, and standing a foot or so away, regarded him almost unbelievingly. Not that he'd altered very much; even in his dress clothes he was still the same Drake I recalled in a flash of memory – clear-eyed, fresh-faced, handsome in an out-of-door's way, but somehow strangely, wonderfully incongruous, in that small rather stuffy over-heated perfumed dressing-room packed with bouquets.

'Dear, *dear* Drake!' I exclaimed, 'And I didn't care any more. But I *do*, of *course* I do—' I waited breathlessly for him to make some reciprocative extravagant gesture; but he merely kissed me warmly and gently, gave me a brief hug, and said with a quiet smile, 'You're looking wonderful, Rosanna. That last scene – the finale—' He took a programme from his pocket, studied it briefly, and continued, 'Ah – that's it – "Death of the Ice Queen" – it was – it reminded me of that little bird I had, do you remember? The one with the broken wing when we were children? I mended it, but it died—'

'You're just the same,' I said wonderingly. 'You haven't changed a bit. Still the same kind Drake.'

'*Oh* no!' he exclaimed drawing himself to his full height and throwing out his chest. 'I'm a man now, Rosie – a real farmer with the estate to manage. I'm sure father – my *real* father would've approved.'

'But—' I indicated a chair. 'Sit down, Drake.' He did so. 'But what about papa Justin and Richard?'

'Uncle Richard's turned into a real boozer, I'm afraid, forgive the word. Doesn't care about anything but the bottle. And Justin lives alone except for an old housekeeper at Rookswood now. His only thought's about the mine. He's – odd, Rosanna. Strange. A real tyrant he'd be if the workers let him. The fact is ore's running out all the time. Caswell, the manager, knows it, so do the miners: tut-workers, all of them now! The adventurers have taken what they could, and left. It's sad. Sometimes he even moves to a hut near the engine house and stays for days on end, arguing with Caswell about new levels and sinking still another fresh shaft. He may be rich, Rosie, but no one, not even a millionaire can go on for ever losing money on what isn't there.'

I sighed. 'And Katrina? My – our – mother?' I averted my eyes before Drake spoke. I had already guessed so much.

'She left him. You couldn't blame her really. Life was pretty awful—' His voice faded unhappily.

'It must have been.'

'She's all right, though,' he said a trifle defensively, 'money wise, I mean. She has a—' he swallowed before adding, '—a protector. A rich merchant who's seen she's well provided for with a house in the country where he spends half his time. He's got rooms in London, too. She's there often.'

'Yes. I see.'

'You're not shocked?'

'I don't care, Drake,' I stated calmly. 'As a matter of fact, I saw her in the audience only a few nights ago. It was just a brief glimpse, but she recognised me. She hates me still. It was quite obvious, from her eyes and set expression – sort of condemning. Oh, what a pity. Families shouldn't be like ours, should they?'

Drake shrugged, gave a half smile and replied, 'I suppose there's no "must" or "must not" about it. Things happen, and that's it. It's only the dull ones like me who manage to survive without too many scratches and wounds.'

'You're not dull. You never were. Just sound and commonsensible.' I paused before asking, 'Do you see her still? Mama, I mean?'

'Naturally. She still likes to hear about Heatherfield, and her old man isn't a bad sort. Owns some kind of shipping line, I forget what it's called. But he's used to country life too, and gives me a few valuable hints now and then. I need them, I can tell you. It's no joke being the only one properly responsible for tenants and everyone. Of course, I've a good bailiff, Herrick. He took over for the first year after mama left, and I went around with him learning what it was all about.'

'What about University?'

'Oh, I never went. What point was there? Things being as they were?'

'And the twins?' I asked suddenly recalling I had another half-brother and sister. 'Is Dominic helping you.'

'Dominic?' Drake seemed amused by the idea. 'Dominic's at University. Like Justin, his father, in character, but with Katrina's looks. No – he's not the farming type; never will be. Studying law, but my bet is that as soon as he's got some degree or other he'll be off to foreign climes. As for Juliana—' His fact softened. 'She's lovely. Rosanna; the only one of us papa Justin shows any affection for.'

'What does she look like?'

'Well—' Drake's brows came together thoughtfully. 'I'm not very good at words, but you could say something like a—a young fawn, or sea-nymph, maybe—'

I laughed. 'Nymph? How? What do you mean?'

'She's not like any others or us. Her hair's sort of fairish-brown, and very silky, and her eyes are clear grey, like pools. She's soft-voiced and shy, and so *kind*, Rosanna. She's always riding to Rookswood to see papa Justin's all right, and that the funny old housekeeper he has is cooking the right things for him. She loves the land, too, and the sea. I suppose that's what reminds me of sea-nymph, her long pale hair and the way she sits on the rocks dabbling her toes in the water whenever there's a chance to get to the coast.' He didn't look at me and added, after a moment, hesitantly, 'Then, of course, there's Rupert.'

My spine stiffened.

'Yes?' I managed to say with apparent indifference.

'He's married well. The daughter of Lord Drewslake. They live at his place in Devon. I think they're happy in a conventional way, although—'

'Yes, yes. Enough of Rupert,' I interrupted sharply. 'Tell me more about *yourself*, Drake – why you're not yet married. Or *are* you?'

He shook his head and said drily, 'It will take a very wily girl to get me to the altar. From what I've already seen of marriage I'm not impressed.' He sounded faintly reluctant and I was momentarily sad for him.

'Oh, you just wait, Drake,' I remarked tritely. 'You're made to be a settled husband and father, and when the right woman appears you'll know it.'

'Maybe. Anyway what about tonight? I wondered if we could have dined somewhere together? That is if you're not already promised to some rich gallant or lord.'

'If I was it wouldn't matter,' I told him. 'I wouldn't go. But luckily I'm not. So where shall we dine? – Have you an idea?'

He shook his head. 'I don't know London. I've only been twice before – just for a day or so to see mama.'

'Very dutiful of you,' I said cattily.

His fair complexion coloured slightly. 'Oh well – there's no use judging people. Life's too short. And anyway, believe it or not, she missed you when you left. Behind all her tempers you meant more to her than the rest of us.'

'No. Papa Justin came first – always,' I said bitterly. 'She *did* love me once, I suppose, when your father was alive. But—' I suddenly realised the futility of going back into the past, and changed the subject abruptly. 'Drake, dear, if we're going out. I must hurry and dress properly. You'll have to wait in the wings for a bit, then we'll take the cab to a little place I know – the Green Cockatoo. Now—' I gave him a gentle affectionate push. 'My dresser's outside. Tell her she's needed, and take a turn to the right, you'll find a chair or stool or something. And if you have trouble with any hopeful male lurking about, give a call to Harry. He's the doorman and used to handling any awkward beaux.'

Looking slightly bewildered Drake left, and presently, when I'd dressed as inconspicuously as possible, with a black velvet hooded cloak covering my hair and violet gown. I was seated by him in the waiting vehicle, on its way to the restaurant.

During the meal Drake did his best to rise to the occasion and present a sophisticated front. But it was an effort for him, and being tired I felt slightly strained, hoping I'd be unrecognised and spared further adulation from any admiring public present. Luckily, I was. The plain unobtrusive manner I'd insisted on having my hair arranged, the lack of ornament or jewellery, had completely changed my appearance, and except for the waiters, no one showed any interest in the quiet restrained couple we represented.

Strangely, I could conjure up no enthusiasm in the memories of Cornwall evoked by my brother. I tried hard, but I was tired, and after all, years had passed. The wild coast and sea were very far away; away in another life.

When we said farewell later at the door of my hotel it was with no real regret. It had been lovely seeing him at first. And I was glad for his sake he seemed so content. But we no longer had much in common. My one touch of sadness was for papa Justin.

As for Katrina! – I was careful not to think of her at all.

A quick glimpse of her bold imperious face in the audience had been sufficient to rekindle a brief dislike that was as quickly dispelled into negation. She was nothing to me but a shadowed memory to be erased from my life for good.

Rupert's mother. And mine.

Strange, I thought once, such a fact could alter the whole course of two individuals' lives. And stranger still that it should be responsible for my fame.

Destiny?

Perhaps.

And I recalled at that point the ancient gypsy woman – Katrina's grandmother who had handed me the locket I still took with me wherever I went. Her words, also, as she'd forced it on me: 'Take this, dordi, 'tis thy true heritage'.

When I was next in France, I decided, I would make enquiries about the de Marchère family – Louis de Marchère in particular, whose noble face was so finely depicted opposite that of my smart grandmother – Anyana – on ivory in the ancient trinket.

Vicomte Louis de Marchère – my forebear by blood, if not by law; or had he been executed with his father before he could inherit?

That I would find out.

So it was, that a few months later when I was to appear once more as the Ice Queen in *Snow Ballet* at the Paris Opera, I attained all relevant facts concerning the de Marchères, and went one spare afternoon to visit their ancient stately mansion not far beyond the outskirts of the city, where the house itself still stood as a museum containing priceless relics of the once-proud family.

## 8

The château was grey and Gothic-looking with small towers and statuary that must have had a certain grace during the prosperous pre-Revolution days when its surrounding park-lands sloped gracefully to distant cornfields and vineyards. Now a wide road had been cut through the gardens for visitors and tourists wishing to inspect the relics of past elegance, and when I arrived, although near to closing time, one or two broughams still waited outside for their occupants to leave. The late autumn afternoon sun was sinking in a ball of fire below the horizon as I paid a somewhat hostile-looking elderly woman, whom I took to be the caretaker, for my admittance. She evidently didn't recognise me, for which I was grateful. '*C'est late*,' she said grumbling, glancing at an ornate grandfather clock standing in the great hall.

'I shan't be long,' I told her, paying my entrance fee at the same time, keeping my head inclined downwards so my features were shadowed by the fur of my collar. '*Merci, madame*.'

She gave an abrupt little nod, dangling her keys obtrusively. I passed on turning into the first door on the left. A couple passed by me as I entered, and I stood for a moment or two inside the room staring round.

At first I thought I was alone. There was no movement at all; not a ripple of wind from the tall window, facing a stretch of lawn, which was slightly open. All was permeated with a faint smell of potpourri, reminiscent somehow of long-dead things. Transient shadows flickered over the soft warm carpet which had once been richly piled, patterned in a design of roses. Above the immense marble fireplace delicate porcelain figures caught the glow of evening. On an ornately carved Louis Quinze rosewood table leaflets bearing the history and numbers of the items on show seemed to mock French heritage.

In a flash of imagination I could imagine the room as it had once been, when bewigged men and women in costly, extravagant attire, drank from the delicate goblets, and ate from the exquisite gold plate, laughed, chatted, flirted behind jewelled fans, filling the perfumed air with frivolous laughter and gossip. Glancing up at the high-domed ceiling, where baby angels, gilded, but faded now, were intricately merged with clouds and birds, I thought, 'You have stared down for so long, gazed from your blank round eyes on so much that was real; yet what are you now but effigies of power turned to dust?'

And I shivered; the atmosphere seemed suddenly chill as though the ghosts of those who'd gone to the tumbrils stirred with the brush of cold phantom hands on my face. The waft of a fan – the phantom shadow of waving plumes, coronets, a lace cuff – could be imagined briefly, resurrected to life through golden shafts of the dying light. Then all was still again, save for the light tinkle of a small gold clock, and the buzz of an intruding bee caught from outside.

Slowly I wandered round the interior, inspecting but not entirely appreciating the relics stored there – miniatures, the finest porcelain, pearl and silver duelling pistols, the most delicate crystal, and snuff boxes, all engraved with the de Marchère crest of a fleur-de-lys, entwining a coronet and griffin's head.

There were gowns, too, of exotic silks and satins richly embroidered with pearls. And I – somewhere far back had had a share in it, been born of the de Marchère blood! The genes were deep in my being, just as were those of the gypsy Petra's, the ancient crone who had thought fit to reveal the truth.

What a mixture.

As I stood quite still for a moment by the window staring out at the darkening sky, there was the low creak of a door opening, followed by the muttered undertone of a woman's voice which I recognised as that of the caretaker who'd admitted me. A grunt came from someone in reply. I stiffened, keeping myself in the shadows of the curtain, where presumably I'd not been seen. After a short conversation in muttered French, the woman departed, and when the sound of her footsteps had finally faded I took a soft, furtive step forward, with eyes focussed on a shadowed alcove at the far end of the room.

It was then that I realised with a shock, someone else had been there, probably watching me all the time: the static shape of a very old man seated in a carved high-backed chair, thin ivory-pale hands resting on the arms, head thrust forward, chin sunk below the high collar of his coat. I went forward tentatively, and when I was sufficiently near, stared into his face. It was lined and imperious. A proud enigmatic countenance with the patrician features coldly set. He could have been carved in stone or wax, had it not been for the fierce, dark, hungry eyes under the bristling white brows. I had never in my life seen him before, but knowledge intuitively stirred and woke in me. He was a de Marchère, a survivor, probably the last of his line, of whom I was his bastard kin.

I said nothing, simply stared. And then, at last, after a prolonged pause, he whispered, 'Anyana?'

I bent down, and nodded, and a deep flame lit his eyes; I touched his long cold hand, and it seemed a frail pulse beat conveying recognition between us, although I knew it was not me he saw but my ancestress of the same name.

I knew then what I must do.

'Shall I dance for you?' I asked.

The flame deepened. He tried to nod, but the effort was too much for him, and I guessed he was paralysed. So ignoring the fact, and uncaring that the harsh-voiced woman caretaker, or whatever she was, might reappear any moment, I slipped off my cloak, hood and boots, divested my hair of pins and combs and ran again to the window which was already reflecting the green glow of twilight.

And there I danced; not the 'Ice Queen', but the true flamenco with which the gypsy girl, the first Anyana must have entranced him in the past. And as I danced passion flooded my veins for all the love I'd known and still had in me to feel again. On that old soft carpet my toes and limbs skimmed and flew, pirouetted with delight, while my arms reached, wavered, and fell, like a bird's wings driven by cloud. And all the time I was singing, humming – an old, old tune I'd first heard played on the fiddle by gypsies near Rookswood when I was a child.

I wasn't aware of the woman's return. But when at last I

stopped, breathless, she was there, standing by the old man's side, open-mouthed in astonishment. I went over and ignoring her, stared into his face. He was smiling. I even fancied there was a faint inclination of his head in appreciation.

'Tch!' the woman said, speaking in a flood of French. 'How can you? He is paralysed. And you – who are you? You should be *gone*. They are all gone but you. You are an interloper – a – a—'

She broke off, and I said quietly in English, 'No. Your master knows me. Look at him. He has come alive again, the part that matters, the heart. I am – Anyana. The dancer.'

Uncomprehendingly the woman threw up her arms, shaking her head partly in disapproval, partly in grudging acceptance.

'You mean – the ballet? Is that eet? Eh? The famous one? Then why did you not say? Eh? Eh? English, too. And me all on my own. And not knowing and my husband out, the lazy one.' She paused to get her breath. 'Monsieur Louis, too. Oh, *c'est mal*; all worry. I tell you there's what you call – trouble coming. Ah! *mais oui*. Trouble – trouble.'

After a further tirade half in English, half in French, she calmed down, and presently I left.

The greenish glow of early twilight was deepening as I made my way down the wide straight drive to the main road below. I glanced back once, and saw a flickering light like that of a candle from window to window – probably the woman going through the house and locking up. I wondered about the old man's life there – confined in the deserted, lofty rooms. He must be lonely, existing with only his memories. Were there servants? And, if so, how many? Or were the old couple – the wife with the keys and the errant husband whom she'd described as 'the lazy one' the sole employees, acting as caretakers not only of the house, but of the ancient heir himself – of that once stately château?

Through the darkening night and with my mind swimming, I didn't at first notice a tall dark figure in a cape approaching the gates where my cab waited. Swaying, elongated shadows from poplars threw a constantly changing pattern across the landscape, and I had to draw up with a jerk to avoid bumping into him.

'I'm sorry,' I said, glancing up at him. 'I didn't see you – careless of me.'

'But there is no need for apologies, mademoiselle,' he replied with only a faint suggestion of French accent. His voice was rich and pleasant, reminiscent, faintly, of another voice I'd heard in the past – a voice I'd managed to erase with so many other things from my memory. What made me hesitate for a second, and take a closer look at him, I really don't know. For so long I'd been hiding from that other life. But in the brief moment of time, when he removed the tall dark hat, resolution faltered, and faded into shock. A shaft of light from a lamp somewhere lit his strongly carved, kindly but arrogant countenance, and it was as though Rupert stood facing me; an older Rupert with lines of experience and a suggestion of suffering cutting deeply from high cheekbones between aquiline nose and compressed lips above the strong jaw. The dark eyes, guarded at first, became suddenly alive, blazing at me with a questioning flame that must have found response in my own.

Dark wild emotions stirred me, whispering, 'This is he – you've always known him – always – always—'

The impact between us was so ridiculous, so overwhelming, I felt in that short moment of awareness, my whole future was threatened, and tearing myself from his gaze pulled the cloak firmly to my chin and fled; fled to the brougham which stood only yards away, with the horse already restive and the driver anxious as I was to be away.

I did not look back, and the next minute there was the grinding of carriage wheels on gravel and clip clop of horse's hooves along the lane leading to Paris.

\*

The next evening, following the performance at the Opera, he was there, waiting at the dressing-room door. And his smile told me everything. This time I would not be able to escape.

Except for a high white-frilled collar, and white silk shirt and waistcoat, he was dressed all in black – black cut-away tailed coat and tightly-fitting narrow black trousers. But this detailed impression registered only later. It was the eyes that held me – dark eyes flashing warmly into mine; eyes that said everything – everything that I too felt.

He took my hand, bending forward to touch it with his lips. 'Mademoiselle,' he said then, 'Anyana. So it has happened at last.' When I did not speak, he continued, 'We will go for supper, will we not? Some quiet place where we can talk perhaps of what is to be done?'

With my senses and head reeling I replied feebly, 'But there's someone calling for me later. I'm already engaged, monsieur—?' My voice died on the question.

'De Marchère,' he said quietly. 'As you will know, I believe. But you will call me Louis, of course. I bear the name of my great relative.'

'I—'

'As for your – appointment, shall we say? Appointments are made to be broken, I believe, except when they are for me.'

His effrontery dazed but dazzled me.

'You take a great deal for granted.'

'Yes.'

'I'm afraid I—'

'Please get your cloak, Anyana; I have a cab already waiting; to argue is so futile.'

'You take great liberties,' I retorted, with my cheeks burning.

He merely smiled. 'As you say.'

I was so bewildered, so fascinated, so taken off my guard, I could find no suitable reply, and in a daze of excitement found myself minutes later being escorted to the cab and on the way to a small, discreet but expensive restaurant in the vicinity of Montmartre. There we drank wine and dined, although I can't now recall the menu or topics of conversation discussed, only the wonderful magic of being together, the knowledge that nothing in the world, ever, could be quite the same again. Certain fragments of knowledge I gathered, naturally: that he was a great-nephew of the count – the old man who'd somehow managed to survive the Revolution, although the rest of the family had gone to the guillotine; that their lands and wealth had been confiscated by the state, until later when Louis and his uncle had been allowed to return to the family home on the proviso it was retained as a museum for the public.

'So!' he said at last, with a shrug, 'that is the not-so-pretty story. Still, fate, after all, has made a pattern of it.'

He reached across the table and took my hand. I could feel the warm blood, the pulse beating strongly beneath the firm fine skin.

'You and I, Anyana. There's no need to put it into words, is there? We belong.'

I nodded.

'And the dance? The dancing will stop, except for me?'

I didn't reply directly, but remarked, 'At the end of this week, in two days, the *Snow Ballet* closes. I have another week for resting, and then there'll be rehearsing in London for the Drury.'

'Perhaps,' he said enigmatically. 'In the meantime we will spend time together – yes? Time in which to get to know and love each other. Ah, Anyana, it is not good to look too far into the future. I have a small place in mind – not so very far from here – Le Cheval Blanc. There you can stay, my most beautiful love, and we will find together all the secret wonderful places of nature, and of our hearts.'

He paused briefly, his eyes so alight with life and desire my whole body and being trembled.

Such was the beginning of a phase that was to reshape my whole life.

## 9

The pension, although so conveniently available to Paris, was situated on the outskirts of a village in a gentle verdant valley of undulating country, against a background of farmlands and cornfields washed to golden, green and brown in the changeful autumn light. Louis, who knew the owner and manageress well, a jolly, ample-sized woman with bright black eyes, a wide smile and welcoming manner, introduced me incognito as a friend of his; Mademoiselle Lafargès. Whether she believed him or not, I do not know; it was impossible to tell. But she was discreet, asking no quesitons, and from the very first did everything possible to make my stay there enjoyable. The food was excellent – and would have pleased any epicure. My room, low-ceilinged, with white walls and light oak furnishings had two windows, which provided sunlight for most of the day. Oh, it was a pastoral, quiet, dreamlike place, and I loved it. From the kitchen below, at times, the tempting smell of savoury dishes cooking wafted up the twisting stairs. But mostly, with my windows open, there was the drifting faint scent of flowers – late honeysuckle and earthy, rich vegetation that hovered sweetly on the calm mild air.

For the first three days Louis rode over in the afternoons, and we would wander the countryside until we found some secluded spot where we could rest, talk a little, then be close in the rich lush grass, lost to everything and everyone else in the world but the wonderful, magical experience of being together. Bees droned; there was the chortle of birds from the trees, and sometimes the distant lowing of cattle from the fields. No words can adequately describe the happiness that encompassed us. I think I sensed it must end one day – or perhaps not. I don't know. We made no plans for the future; our relationship remained delicately poised between romantic mutual adoration and deepening passion – until the fourth day, which was a Thursday. It was then that I realised something different in the atmosphere, that Louis was going to put a question I had to answer. The moment for decision had arrived.

We lay in our favourite glade, romantically linked, my head on Louis' shoulder, one of his arms beneath my shoulders, the other across my body with his head raised so his lips could kiss my cheek, lips and neck, then fall away suddenly, while he sighed, glancing up at the hazy film of sky. I was aware of his quickened breathing, the passion that consumed him, and the tumultous beating of my own heart. He was not really a young man any more – fifteen years my senior, at least; but the tiny, almost indefinable lines about the corners of his eyes and nobly sculptured mouth somehow added to his attractions. He had lived and suffered, and must have known many women during his life. But I knew instinctively his desire and need of me surmounted and far exceeded any previous experience he might have had.

'Ah, Louis,' I thought, 'I'm not glass, I won't break. Speak – something – anything – but love me, Louis. Please love me.'

He glanced down again, unsmiling, staring long and deep into my eyes, then smoothed a tumbled lock of hair from my forehead.

'I can bear this no longer, Anyana,' he said. 'Either you come to me as I would have you, for my very own – every inch of you, all the subtle sweetness of your lovely body, and warm rich flame of your heart, or I get up and walk away out of your life, for good.' He paused, before adding, 'You understand? I'm no man for half-measures, or brief romantic encounters. I yearn, long, and lust for you. You are my obsession – my dream.'

'Of course—' I whispered, neither thinking nor caring of the future. 'Of course, Louis.'

He was trembling as he unbuttoned my gown and under-garments, and prepared himself for ultimate union. His flesh then was firm and smooth against mine, his thighs strong. Unconsciously my arms were about his neck, and while he entered to possess me my whole body arched to receive him. We made love, damp and glowing, with the wine of the gods, it seemed, spilling rich and warm through our veins. The rest of the world faded in a whirl of delirious, delicious ecstasy as we rose to the heights soaring, dipping, and soaring again until exhausted, he gently withdrew, and lay glistening and golden brown in the sensuous drift of feathered ferns, one arm over my naked stomach, travelling slowly upwards to cup a breast. I lay with my eyes closed, waiting for him to speak. Presently he remarked.

'This is for ever, Anyana, my dearest, my darling, my sweetest beloved.'

'Forever,' I echoed, although the words for a fragile second held a hint of sadness – an uncertainty I could neither express nor understand.

He kissed me once more, his warm lips traversing every curve and secret recess of my body, lingering eventually on the soft triangle of moist hair, precious symbol of my womanhood and gift of my most sacred self while I murmured constantly, 'Oh, Louis – Louis – I love you so—'

Later, how long I do not know, still half-bemused, we got up and dressed, and as the sun's last rays pierced the distant horizon, made our way back to the pension.

With forced practicality, Louis said, before leaving for Paris, 'I will see you tomorrow, darling, at the same time, yes? And you will remain here – at the Cheval, until we find a cottage somewhere.'

'Tomorrow, Louis, I would bid adieu to many friends,' I reminded him. 'There are others of the company like me, who have stayed on in France before going to London to prepare for the *Snow Ballet* and a new ballet at the theatre there—'

'Ah! but – have you not yet told them?'

'What, Louis?'

'That you are no longer one of them?'

'I didn't know though, did I?' I said weakly, rather helplessly. 'It's – it's a big step, Louis. It was only today we found out. I mean—'

'I would like to know what you really do mean,' Louis said solemnly – even with a hint of severity.

I shook my head mutely. How could I say? When I didn't even know myself. for so long, purposely, I had been a virgin – for my art, the dance. Now, suddenly, the shell had been shattered by this one 'exciting' wonderful man. My whole future had become uncertain – a mysterious limbo of erotic and spiritual fulfilment that was temporarily sundered from the real world of practical living.

I was his, completely. And yet – and yet—

'Yes?' I heard him saying with some urgency.

'I can't think,' I said. 'Don't let's make plans, darling – just believe in me. I love you so terribly—'

'Tomorrow then,' he insisted. 'Later, if you like – in the evening I'll come, to the pension. Then we can talk, yes?'

I had to agree, although my mind was confused, entangled in the wild impetus of my heart's longing. It was as though I'd trembled in the glow of eternal sunlight for a brief time, knowing in a deep subconscious way that the world wanted to pull me back; the ruthless practical world of my own choice.

And so it was.

That evening, in the pale flare of candlelight, I sat in my pleasant bedroom at Le Cheval Blanc and wrote a letter to Louis.

Dearest Louis, my darling. When you get this note I shall be gone. Please – please forgive me. It is not that I do not love you, inded I love you more than my own life, and if sacrificing it would help you in any way I would do it willingly. But, my love, without my dancing, I should be nothing, either to you or myself. I wouldn't be the Anyana you fell in love with – and at being mistress, either, of a cottage or ancient château like the one you were born to – I should be a failure. I'm not domesticated, Louis. A coward maybe because I can't even try – yes, I admit it.

Dancing is my life; but knowing and loving you has been the most beautiful thing that ever happened to me, and will remain so, always. I hope and pray you will understand, or at least try to. You have said you must possess me utterly, but darling – *no* man can do that for a lifetime. For those precious hours we were together, *you* did, and no one else ever will. Let that wonderful time remain as it is, bright and glowing, something perfect that can never fade.

Dearest heart, I shall remember you always.
Adieu, Anyana.

I folded the paper with hands that trembled, put it in an envelope, sealed it, and wrote just the name 'Louis' on the outside. Then I packed my clothes ready for an early departure the next day, and when morning came, after an almost sleepless night, I gave the note to Madam Lafargès, and requested her to deliver it to monsieur when he arrived later.

Dew still sprinkled the grass and hedgerows when I left early after breakfast. A great sadness filled me, holding also an empty sense of relief.

Once, perhaps, years ago, when I was a young girl who'd thought herself so wildly in love with Rupert, I would have acted very differently. But it was too late now for legal bondage. I had to be free. *Free* to continue on the course I'd chosen from the bitterness and disillusion of the past.

Free to dance.

And so it was.

Two hours later from the deck of a steamship I watched the French coastline disappear into the misty distance. It was a grey day, with a few gulls wheeling overhead. Loneliness was in my heart, and salt spray, with that of my own tears, brushed my face; but dimly, at the back of my brain, the pattern of a new ballet was already forming.

It never occurred to me that fate could have a different plan ahead.

Weeks were to pass before I knew.

And even then I fought against the truth.

\*

The new ballet, *Firefly*, in which I was partnered once again by Karn, went into rehearsal the following week. Because of what I had given up – the deliberate sacrifice of Louis' love, I worked and thought of nothing else but the disciplined concentrated attention demanded to make success of a role, so entirely different emotionally and in style from the Ice Queen. It was true I had rare moments of panic when brief doubt swept over me of the way I'd handled things – times when I wondered if I could not have kept both – our mutual passion for each other, and my own for the dance. But deep down I knew the latter would have been impossible, and ruthlessly dismissed the idea.

So preparations for the opening continued; and if at times I felt more drained and tired than was usual, I put this down to the underlying stress I'd been through, and it was only after three months that I realised, with shock, I was going to have a child.

My whole world seemed to collapse about me. I didn't know what to do. The opening night was over, and Karn and I had both received startlingly complimentary reviews. My understudy was a capable dancer, and would not let me down. But temperamentally she had not the pagan erotic qualities required for the certain role of 'Firefly' herself. Ultimately, I knew, I would have to give in gracefully, and allow her to step into my shoes, but in the meantime I continued, though I knew it was not good for me, and might end in my losing the baby. If so, then all might be salvaged, I told myself ruthlessly. Perhaps, indeed, this could be the way out. I'd tried others which hadn't worked, and at the time I'd been relieved, because beneath all the complexity, distress, and fear – the thought of ruthlessly killing that small something of Louis in me had been obnoxious – a betrayal, somehow, of my love for him.

So I danced, keeping my secret to myself, danced in torment, wildly, fiercely, while my body swelled slightly under the frills of scarlet and gold, unknown to any but myself, allowing life to shape its own course. I had no plans ahead, possessed nothing in the world any more, but a considerably comfortable fortune, for which I was thankful, knowing it must inevitably be needed later, unless a miracle happened.

Miracles, though, are few.

And what *did* occur, was a tragedy.

Following a particularly brilliant night, a royal occasion, graced even by Queen Victoria herself, I fainted after the last curtain, and was carried to my dressing room where I was attended as soon as possible, and taken to hospital, for, presumably, 'collapse following strain due to overwork'.

This was the message issued to the public.

The truth was, of course, I had lost my baby.

Not only that.

Due to the fall I'd twisted my foot badly beneath me, and later, when it was found to be badly fractured, I had to face the fact that I would never again be able to perform in ballet. Naturally as a dancer of free movement, not requiring the strict discipline of a prima ballerina – perhaps.

But for me, at the height of my career it was finished.

Anyana, the beloved of Europe and of vast audiences everywhere, was no more.

*

There was the expected whispered publicity, regret, and condolences offered concerning the unfortunate event which had robbed the public of 'the most popular dancer of that period'. At first it was suggested through the press that Anyana's disablement might only be temporary, and that after a prolonged rest she would once more appear before the footlights. But as the weeks, then months went by, interest died into reluctant acceptance of her retirement. In any case ballet was for only a limited public, and the style of dancing was gradually changing. There might never be another Anyana, but younger dancers were always coming along to fill new roles.

It was inevitable, therefore, that if not entirely forgotten, I was left to sink into the background, which I did, wilfully at first, travelling from one place to another, or living quietly with my loyal dresser at a country retreat near Hampstead. At first, following my accident I hoped and half-believed that Louis, hearing of it, might decide to locate me. But he never did. Later I learned why. He had died in a fire with his ancient relative, the Vicomte de Marchère, which had destroyed the greater part of the château, and had probably been caused by a candle falling and setting fire to ancient tapestries that had ignited the building.

The shock had been almost too cruel to bear.

'I should have been with him,' I said to my dresser one day, 'That would have been best. If I had let him find me the cottage we wanted it would never have happened. I should have been there.'

'Shsh!' she said. '*C'est stupide*. And where would the sense be in that? Eh? Waste. Just waste. You have a life to live.'

Life! I thought dismally. What life? Without love? Without the dance? Death surely would be preferable.

Of course, I didn't *really* believe it. I was still comparatively young, and though ballet was over, and my beloved Louis gone, an inner voice, borne from somewhere far away, whispered to me, 'There are other things – the soft sweet winds of the moors, winding lanes, and the grass blowing. Moonlit nights, and the waking of spring following the hard winter. No need for ballet shoes or wild applause – there is still the dance; the dance of the spirit, and being free.'

I knew then what I would do.

Sophisticated society was no longer for me, and I had no wish to be an encumbrance at Heatherfield or Rockswood. The thought of meeting again with papa Justin even, gave me no pleasure any more, only a depressing sense of futility.

So I made up my mind.

I would find the first Anyana's family, and make my life with them as my own people.

# IV
## Dominic

### 1

I was twenty-four years old in 1845, and bored with life at Heatherfield, which meant a daily dutiful ride on horseback to Rookswood where I worked on accounts and as a kind of overseer for the wretched mine, Wheal Clara, on behalf of my father. My salary was meagre for my position, but considered quite adequate by my sire, for a son who had failed to get a brilliant first in mathematics at University. During my young days I'd admired Justin immensely for his drive, energy, and the adventurous streak in him which had landed him with such an immense and enviable fortune from his perspicacity in the goldfields abroad. But bitterness concerning the break-up of his marriage to Katrina, my mother, and her outrageous behaviour in London, had turned him into a sour, single-minded fanatic, who had no thought or affection for anybody except, perhaps, my sainted sister, Juliana, who cherished and cared for him as though he was some deity descended from heaven to grace the family with his presence.

And, of course, the mine.

After Uncle Richard's death when I was at Oxford, Juliana, despite her youth, had shouldered the role of playing mother to us all managing the servants and household with a gentle dignity that however commendable, irritated me profoundly sometimes. She was clever, too, artistic and good to look at in an ethereal way. Very different from myself, her twin, who must have inherited something of my mother's wild hot streak, as had Rosanna, my older half-sister. I remembered Rosanna well – the 'Anyana' of ballet, who'd run away to be a dancer and later disappeared mysteriously, following some accident or other to her foot.

In looks, I suppose, I must have appeared rather a cuckoo in the nest, being neither fair nor handsome like dependable Drake, or sturdily reminiscent of the hard-headed pioneer my father had once been, but merely of average height, very thin and craggy-faced, with eyes so dark they gave me a look of great fierceness. In character, I suppose, I was a loner – I got a peculiar feeling sometimes of not belonging, of wanting to sail the seas in exploration of other lands and other people. Maybe that was my father in me speaking – maybe. But he never gave the possibility consideration when I expressed the ambition to start and run a shipping line.

'You've no experience of shipping,' he said abruptly. 'Foolhardy! And idiotic for one like you with a good education behind you, and a fine mine needing all the attention you've got. What do you know of the merchandise business, or the first thing of how to handle a good ship – even recognise one if you saw it?'

'I could learn,' I said stubbornly. 'Besides – what knowledge did *you* have before you went searching for gold in America and Africa?'

'I had a nose for it. I was strong and hefty, with no background, nothing behind me to lose, whereas you have everything.'

I gritted my teeth. 'I've nothing,' I said grimly, trying to stifle my rising temper, 'except something planned for me; by *you*. Your mine; your fanatical obsession that it's going to pay off, when all it does is just tick over with a minimum of copper, and not always that. It doesn't matter to you, I suppose – you're rich enough to stand the loss. But I don't happen to have a bean of my own, and I don't like mining. I'm twenty-four, and got nowhere. Don't you *understand*? I'm your *son*. If you can afford to go on year after year losing money over a white elephant, couldn't you back me for once, for God's sake – put your hand in your pocket and give me the chance I want? It wouldn't take much, comparatively speaking – two good ships and a bit of business advice—'

'You don't know what you're talking about,' my father said shortly. 'Gold, copper, tin – *ore*. That's my line, as it should be yours. You've the ability. So no more of it, Dominic. Understand?'

Yes, I understood all right. But *he* didn't; and I knew he never would or could possibly comprehend the frustration I felt – the urge either to lash out at him, or walk away that very moment, find a boat somewhere along the coast, and learn about ships the hard way. If something hadn't happened about that time to catch my attention, I should have taken off just as my half-sister, Rosanna, had done and said goodbye to Heatherfield for good. I'd already wasted too much time.

But the following week a queer trick of fate, the unexpected, occurred in the person of a woman – a girl called Elizabeth Payne. She was tall, brown-haired, well-made, with swinging well-curved thighs, a cream skin, and green eyes under rather heavy dark brows. Her lips were full and ripe, what I'd call hungry, or else inviting. I don't know. You can't analyse these things. She wasn't beautiful as Rosanna had been, or delicately feminine like Juliana. But by God! from the word go I wanted her.

She was the daughter of a famous mining expert and engineer in Bristol, and had come along with her father to Heatherfield on a visit for discussions with Justin over his eternal problems concerning Wheal Clara. My father left Rookswood to be with the rest of us at the house during the week of their visit, so I had limited opportunities of getting to know her in the evenings, and any other leisure time possible when the two men were discussing business and the pros and cons of further development for the mine. Drake was a stumbling block because I saw from the first glance he was impressed, but I wasn't bothered about his interest. He was the farming type, and always would be – devoted to running the estate, and to the land and cattle almost exclusively. At that time he was nearing thirty and still unmarried. Once or twice some young woman or other had appeared to take his fancy, and there'd been conjecture that he was about to take the plunge; but gradually the possibility had fizzled out, and Juliana had remarked to me whimsically – oh, yes, my sister had quite a sense of humour, 'I think Drake's far too fond of his pigs and cows for divided loyalties.'

So I didn't really fear Drake, and as the days passed his brief interest in Elizabeth seemed to fade. It was autumn, a busy time for harvesting and the estate, and more often than not he was occupied even in the evenings, either helping the men, concerned with the tenants, and the business of buying and selling stock. So I felt I was beginning to know Elizabeth quite well during that first week. I went riding with her when the chance came along of deserting Rookswood for a bit, and sometimes we went walking. We'd both speak of our youth; her father apparently was a self-made man who'd married above him, as she put it laughingly – the daughter of an impoverished earl.

'So I'm quite a mongrel,' she said laughingly. 'But rather more on the commonside, I think, than the noble.'

'I wouldn't say that,' I remarked, throwing her a sidelong meaningful glance. 'I think you're quite – stunning, Miss Payne.' My near hand touched her arm just above the wrist. It felt warm and strong, and glowing.

'And I think *you're* very accomplished at flattery, Mr Pencorrin,' she said again with a quick hint of that rich laughter. Her hand was drawn away firmly. I shrugged. I didn't mind the slight rebuff. An easy woman was no challenge to me. I'd no doubts at all that if I gave my mind to it, I'd eventually have Miss Elizabeth sweet and willing in my arms.

But for the time being I held my behaviour and feelings in check. There was no reason in the world to rush the fences. I'd already overheard my father discussing a further meeting with old man Payne a month or so ahead, and I had a shrewd idea Elizabeth would accompany him. If she didn't, I'd concoct some reason for taking a trip to Bristol myself, on my father's behalf, concerning Wheal Clara. The truth was that I was already considering marriage for the first time in my life, partly, I suppose, because I sensed a girl of her type would settle for no less. She was proud, and in giving her body she'd demand everything in return. And it was her body that set me alight – the giving of her thighs and pointed up-thrust tilt of rounded breasts – rich and ripe as luscious pears, when the wind blew the cloak from her shoulders, leaving her bodice strained tight against its constricting row of tiny buttons. She had called herself 'common', but of course she wasn't. She was just splendidly free and desirable, of the earth, earthy – a fruit ready and willing to be plucked by the right man at the right time, and for the right purpose.

And I meant to be that man.

Once the idea had firmly formulated in my mind I went for it 'hook, line and sinker', as they put it. By devious means, and my playing up to Justin and old man Payne, visits between Heatherfield and the Payne place in Bristol became frequent and quite sociable affairs.

Drake, a little bewildered, but gratified to find our sire less of the mad hermit we'd feared he'd become, relaxed into his usual air of equable friendliness, though he appeared perhaps a little more withdrawn than usual. Occasionally I felt his eyes on me with a faintly puzzled look in them as though he sensed something of my feelings for Elizabeth and couldn't quite accept I was sincere. Good old Drake, I thought. Little he guessed the torment of impatience that consumed me – the longing to get everything settled, with Elizabeth accepted by both families as my bride-to-be. I never doubted that she reciprocated my own feelings; there was a warmth about her when we were together that spoke more than words. Yet every time I came near to blurting out the truth, she somehow evaded the subject by joking and laughing – acting what could have been called 'coy' when applied to any other woman I'd known, except her. There was nothing of the obvious temptress about her, no posing or coquetry or deliberate effort to impress by displaying her best features with a lift of the head at a complimentary angle. She seemed totally unconcerned about whether or not I admired her. And this, though irritating in one way, added fire to the challenge.

Did I love her? Yes. In the only way I knew – physically, and with appreciation of her vitality and the practical attributes that I knew would make her a good wife and mother. Also the marriage would doubtless bring a certain financial security that would be of considerable benefit to my ambition in the shipping business. In return I would be faithful, and as attentive a husband as possible. Viewed both from the romantic and practical angles, the union appeared eminently desirable. So I continued making plans, at the same time cultivating a relationship of bonhomie with her father, who luckily seemed to like me well enough, and occasionally even gave a knowing wink when Elizabeth and I left to go riding together.

It was on a golden day in late October that I brought the matter up, abruptly, and quite on the spur of the moment. We'd ridden from Heatherfield to the high ridge of the moors and along to a point from where, in the distance, the rugged tongue of coast below Rookswood was visible. The air was tangy and exhilarating filled with the pungent smells of bracken, damp earth and brine. Ancient standing stones stood grey and primitive against the stretch of russet and green landscape, tangled with gorse and briar. Smoke from Wheal Clara far ahead lingered with a haze of thin mist along the grey horizon of sea and sky.

A wild remote land, this patch of Cornwall that was the heritage of the Pencorrins and others like us.

The power of things to come, of new life stirring beneath the passing year's decay brought a thrill to my blood and a racing of my pulses that after tethering our horses to a windblown sycamore, made me suddenly approach Elizabeth and draw her fiercely to me. The action was so forceful and unexpected her hat was accidentally knocked from her head to the ground, and as my mouth burned her lips, her hair fell from its combs loose and free over her velvet jacket. She struggled ineffectually, while I murmured, 'I want you, Elizabeth. God! how I want you. You'll marry me, won't you?'

I could feel the force of her strong limbs fighting, trying to free herself, and thought at first she was acting, just for the fun of it. The pressure of our two bodies increased. One of my hands was round her buttocks – fiercely, possessively.

'Dominic,' I heard her gasp, 'let me go – what on earth's got into you?'

I laughed. 'You – *you*. *And* you know it.' My mouth was hot again on her cheeks, temples and lips, and all the time desire hardened in me so her body was arched backwards, full-pointed breasts crushed under my chest. A second later she'd tumbled into the heather with me on top of her, and it was then, for the first time, looking down, I saw her face. Soil spattered it at one side. Her lips were curled in contempt, her eyes wild and staring, so filled with dislike – even hatred – I was suddenly shocked into sobriety. The manhood in me that a second ago had been lusting, and hard as the granite-faced menhir standing nearby, exploded and collapsed. I tried to help her up, saying feebly, 'I'm sorry. I didn't mean to – don't look like that, Elizabeth. No harm's done. I want to *marry* you. Don't you understand?'

She pushed me away violently, struggled to her feet, smoothing automatically a film of twigs, earth and small dead leaves from her gown. Then she rounded on me like a wild-cat and said contemptuously, 'You *fool*! You ridiculous clumsy fool. Don't you ever dare touch me again, you understand? You've no manners, no pride, nothing. Why!' She gave a contemptuous laugh. 'I've never even *liked* you. But as Drake's younger brother, I tried to be friendly, hoped we'd get on—'

It was then the truth – or *part* of it, hit me.

'*Drake*?' I echoed, with the hot blood creeping up my spine and coursing through my veins so my whole body was drenched in sweat. 'Did you say *Drake*?'

'I did.' She lifted an arm, smoothed her hair as best she could, picked up her hat from the ground and placed it on her head.

'*Now*, if you don't mind, untether my horse,' she said like a queen addressing a serf.

'Damned if I will,' I told her curtly, breathing heavily. 'Do it yourself before I put you over my knee and beat you. That's what women like *you* deserve.'

'And you're the type of man quite capable of doing it,' she answered curtly. 'But you won't, because you need help, don't you? Papa's help.' Her voice softened significantly when she said, 'Oh, come along, Dominic. Now don't look so insulted. I won't tell, if that's what you're afraid of.'

'*Tell*?'

'That if I hadn't been a particularly tough female you'd have raped me on the moor.' She forced a smile to her lips. 'Anyway, you didn't. So the best thing is to try to forget about it, for both our sakes. Drake and I plan to get married before Christmas. Maybe I should have said something before, but being the thoughtful kind – my husband-to-be was just waiting for the right moment to let the news out. You know Drake. He likes things on an even tempo and to be planned properly before announcing any great decision.'

Yes. I knew Drake; devious, dull, but with the fair out-of-doors kind of good looks, that could charm any girl, I guessed, if he really gave a mind to it. And he'd certainly done that pretty slyly in the case of Elizabeth. Damn him. Oh, damn him, I thought savagely. One day I'd get my own back, by God I would.

Even in that angry moment of defeat though, I recognised the senselessness of revenge, and that I didn't really want it. Somehow there had to be a different way of working the passion out of my blood.

That same evening I found it.

I didn't eat at home; humiliation and anger were still too hot in me to face Elizabeth with any show of continued respect and dignity across the dining table. I felt also a certain degree of shame, knowing my threats had been mostly bluff. I would never actually have hurt her physically. She could have made a scene, though, I knew that. A word in Drake's ear or papa's, and there'd have been hell to pay. I suppose I should have felt grateful for her conciliatory mood following our little struggle, but her kindly manner of 'big sister to little brother' affronted me far more than her temper had done. So after a show of having my horse stabled I set off again for a further mad gallop over the moors to ease the fire.

I rode westward, over an expanse of brown moorland dotted with patches of bog and dark furze, from where, at the highest point, a jagged tongue of rock near Land's End was visible, cutting into a glassy sea. A wind was rising, sending a fleet of black cloud chasing across the lifting moon. I had no care or reason for where I went. It seemed as though the bounds of hell were with me, and the Demon Horseman of legend himself not far behind. At one point, when I cut inland, my stallion stumbled, and I was thrown, cutting my head against a rock. But I wasn't harmed seriously, or even conscious of the wound, except for the warm trickle of blood coursing from one temple down a cheek.

I mounted again and went on. At intervals glimmers of remote cottage windows, of hamlets and small farms, winked from secluded valleys below, but for the most part all was a lonely dramatic scene of light and dark, of slipping shadows giving way momentarily to streaks of sinister clarity from the moon's glow. I reined my horse at an open patch where a half-circle of tall granite stones stood gaunt and tangled from creeping briar. Their bleak forms sent long fingered shapes clawing down the hill.

I took a brandy flask from my pocket, lifted it to my mouth dramatically and called mockingly, 'Here's to you, my friends, whatever you are, and may your ghosts thrive well. Good luck to you.'

All nonsense of course, and I was halfway to being drunk already. But it did seem to me for a second or two that one of them swayed and came towards me, and I remembered the tale of one such relic that tore itself from the ground at certain nights and went to the stream to drink.

I started laughing, and the sound alerted my horse, Bruno, who stamped and reared. 'All right, all right,' I cried placatingly. 'Off we go.'

And at a sudden mad pace we were galloping away again, ahead at first, then down, down, over stones and bushes, past bog and furze, missing a derelict mine shaft by inches, although by then I didn't care.

I had no knowledge of any whereabouts when I fell. The last thing that registered was of a high-pitched neigh, and of tumbling forward over my horse's head, a flash of light, and then darkness.

*

Hours must have passed before I regained consciousness, and at first all was blurred, with a warm, animal kind of smell about it that was somehow comforting. Then, as my brain registered, memory returned slowly, with a feeling of pain at one temple. I eased myself up, and looked round blinking. There was a lamp glowing nearby, I was obviously lying on hay, and I was not alone.

From the shadows a woman's form emerged – or rather that of a girl – for as she came close and looked down, I saw she was young, with a broad face, not uncomely, and in the fitful glow welcoming and kindly.

'You all right, then?' she asked. 'That cut isn't hurtin' too bad?'

She had a low pitched voice with a Cornish burr in it.

I put a hand to my head and felt the bandage there. 'I shan't die,' I said with an attempt at humour, dimly remembering the fall from my horse. 'Did you – how did I get here?'

'I pulled en,' she answered. 'See'd ee from my winder. A real bad tumble 't'was, too. So I camed out an' theer you was, all covered in blood an' muck. This ole farm was near, so all I c'ld do was to walk thee a bit, an' make thee comfortable like – an' that great horse o' yours took off. Sorry 'bout that. But you jus' lie a bit an' I'll nip back f'r a bit o' food. Don't you worry now. No one knows. 'Tis only 'bout three o'clock. So doan you get startin' movin' now, before I've seen that there cut's healin' proper.' She broke off as I stretched out and took her hand. It was firm and rough, but warm and strong.

'What's your name? And where exactly is this place?'

'Crippledon Farm's the house – a field away, and I be Farmer Cockington's niece – lived there since I was a babe when mam died an' father took off f'r Americky. This ole barn ain' used much now. So doan' you worry, 'fore marnin' come we'll think o' how to get thee back. Where d'you come from, mister?'

I told her, and she said with a kind of awed wonder in her wide grey eyes. 'Ah! I see'd you wus a genleman. An' Heatherfield be that big place miles away up over, bean't it?'

I nodded.

'Hm, well,' she went on, 'we'm must be careful like. My uncle – he doan' much care for *genlemen*. A Methody he is – all strict and proper. A good man. But,' she sighed, 'it does seem to me sometimes that goodness doan' always bring happiness.'

Her voice was sad then; in the dim shadowed light her country features took on a wistful kind of beauty that was balm in a strange, subtle way, for my hurt pride and the aching of my head and limbs. Instinctively, without thought, I drew her closer to me.

'You're a kind girl,' I said. 'Gentle. I guess you're good with animals.'

She smiled. 'Ah! the dear critters. Uncle Amos says it's soft I am 'cos I cares when they'm go to the slaughter – like Sammy the pig. He was a dear thing, Sam. I cared for him y'see but theer wasn' nuthen I c'd do.'

Perhaps it was the after-effects of the brandy working in me, I don't know. At that moment though I felt nothing but a desire to comfort her, to somehow erase the loneliness and sadness of her repressed feeling for suffering and helpless things.

'What's your name?' I asked her once more.

'Bethany. They do call me Beth.'

I swallowed hard, 'Well, Beth, I'm sorry about Sam, but these things do happen, as you said, and it's true; there's nothing we can do about it.'

'I reckon not. But it doan' help, do it?'

'*No*,' I replied, 'nothing. All of us – even gentlemen, as you call them, like me – have to take what comes along and make the best of it.'

'Like *you*, mister?'

'Yes. In a way. Life can be pretty grim sometimes.'

Hardly realising what I was doing, I drew her head to my shoulder and stroked the soft pale hair framing her warm cheeks. She didn't pull away, but rested quietly, staring up at me once, to say more practically, 'That cut'll need proper attention, mister. If it wasn't f'r Uncle Amos I'd tek you back to the farm, but marnin'll be comin' soon, and he'll be up an' 'bout afore five. There's the chickens to feed, too, an' the milkin' – I'll have to be busy.'

I made a gesture to rise, but she pushed me back. ''Tes not four yet. You'm a bit o' time to rest on. How's the head now?' She stared into my eyes searchingly, with concern. 'Hurts bad, do et?'

'Nothin' to speak of – thanks to you. You should have been a nurse, Beth.'

Even through the dim light I noticed the colour deepening in her round cheeks. 'Theer's no need for flattery, mister. Flattery edn' good for a maid. Sinful, my Uncle Amos says, an' I reckon he' mebbe right, 'cos I do get awful sinful thoughts sometimes—' Her voice faded as she looked away. I could sense the longing in her, the vulnerability of a rare inborn innocence that in spite of the knowledge of nature and animals she must have, moved me strangely. I wanted to run my hands down the golden skin of her body, and give warmth for warmth, taking her to me not with lust or passion, but richly, quietly, so mutual need was satisfied – at peace – in fulfilment of her loneliness, and as appeasement for my chaotic experience with Elizabeth.

'I can't imagine any thoughts you have being sinful,' I said almost in a whisper. 'You're a lovely girl, Beth.'

'Lovely? Me?'

'Yes, you.'

My arm drew her down, close and warm, and smelling faintly of hay and her own feminine earthy odour. The softness and throbbing strength of her released a flood of desire between us that was completely natural and uninhibited. We made love as the wild things did, without conscious thought or any man-made concept of morality; and when it was over we lay side by side until senses eased, and she got up, straightening her skirt and trying as best she could to tidy her thick straw-gold hair.

Until I left a quarter of an hour or so later, we said little. Mild regret tinged with a hint of shame touched me that my one thought then was to be away, and somehow erase the incident from my mind. I hadn't meant to seduce the girl, neither did I feel that in doing so I'd in any way cheapened her. She'd wanted it as much as I had at the time. But the moment was over. It would be better now, I told myself coldly, reassuringly, that we never met again.

So just before the first thin line of a grey dawn lit the horizon, I set off along a path leading to a lane which after five miles or so she told me, would land me in the vicinity of Heatherfield.

My head had started to throb again, and my legs felt heavy, but I plodded on resolutely, never looking back, and at a turn of the narrow road, luckily, came across a pedlar who offered me a lift in his donkey-drawn cart to a hamlet not far from my home.

The stallion was already back, fed and stabled, and, of course, there was a probing questioning from Drake who'd just returned from an early morning search after hearing I was missing. He was glowering, and anxious, and we came pretty near to an uncharacteristic row where Drake was concerned. Generally he managed to keep his temper well under control.

'You stink,' he said coldly, smelling the brandy. 'A bit inconsiderate of you under the circumstances with the Paynes here, *and* father. What happened?'

'I went out for a canter and had a fall – as you can see—' I said, indicating my head with its bloodied bandage.

'For Heaven's sake, Dominic,' he said, 'get that thing off and have a good wash. I'll be up presently and see if old Doctor Webb should have a look—'

'You needn't worry,' I told him. 'It's only superficial.'

I pushed by him and went to my room. Later there were dark glances from my offended papa, but with old man Payne around he couldn't – or *didn't* – choose to say anything. So by the time the Payne visit was over, curiosity and tempers had simmered, and with my father returning to Rookswood life became comparatively normal again. 'Comparative' is the only word to use, although with things as they were, concerning the mine and my presumed duties there, it's an understatement. The brief incident with Beth – you could hardly call it an affair – had left me more than ever conscious of the futility of my present existence. I hated it. The effort of trying to interest myself with men burrowing through the earth like moles just to satisfy one man's ineffectual greed for gold – or tin, copper, whatever you liked to call it – dulled and bored me. It wasn't even as though Wheal Clara paid, or was worth it. Justin was quite irrational, a fanatic about it, and he was *using* me, accepting any knowledge I'd gleaned through studies and work on the site, as his due, and his right for having fathered me. I'd done my best during the first year or two, but at the back of my mind always was the passion for open skies and to satisfy my repressed ambition to sail and captain my own ship when I felt like it. Something in me was bursting for freedom – free of bondage and family, and Heatherfield itself, which was presently abuzz with the news of Elizabeth's forthcoming marriage to Drake.

Although humiliation at her reception had killed any desire for her that I'd formerly had, the constant visits and sound of her name irritated and annoyed me. So for a brief time I *did* concentrate more on the mine, and ironically it was in doing so that a real confrontation with my father arose.

Caswell, Wheal Clara's captain, had taken it on himself to dismiss two tut-workers who he said weren't pulling their weight. The real reason, I guessed, was because they'd become involved with the new Union, and also because I'd taken them on in the first place.

Without involving Justin, since it was my job presumably to take overall responsibility, I re-employed them, whereupon they were refused admittance when they appeared for early shift on a Monday morning.

I accosted Caswell on the first opportunity, and he was derisively belligerent.

'You tek your complaints to the master, young man,' he said, 'and see what he says. I reckon I know what his answer'll be. I tek my orders from him an' no other; so the sooner you come to accept it the better.'

He'd stuck his cap on his head and stumped away. He was a shortish man, with tremendously broad shoulders, and somehow his whole appearance and manner affronted me beyond reason. I strode after him and faced him with set jaw and a determination to settle the matter for good.

'You'll listen to me if you don't mind,' I said, placing myself squarely in front of him, thus barring his progress along the narrow path. 'Mine captain you may be, but not manager. You've had your way all along, but not any more, Caswell. In future I'm going to see that when I say a thing, I mean it. If not, you'll take the consequences.'

He laughed outright in my face. 'Indeed? *Indeed*?' his tones were contemptuous. 'And *what*, my young buck, will *they* be? Eh? Come on, now. Out with it. From the moment the master had you here you've bin no more than an interferin' liability. You with your high phrases an' college eddication. What do *you* know about the business and workin' of a mine? Eh?' He spat.

And it was then I hit him.

Not hard, the first time, but sufficient to flare the hot temper in him. He lunged back and seconds later we were in a tough battle of fists. The result was that, quite unintentionally on my part, Caswell crashed against a boulder, fracturing a leg and an arm, and was laid up for an indefinite period.

Justin exploded when he knew.

'You fool! You ill-mannered filthy-tempered fool!' he exclaimed, and worse. 'What the devil did you think you were doing? My best man gone — maybe for good, and for no earthly reason at all except I had the ill-luck to breed an oaf for a son with no thought in his head but for the bottle and womanising—'

I tried to interrupt, but he silenced me with a threatening gesture that I realised was genuine. 'Hold your tongue and let me finish. As far as *I'm* concerned it's over, understand? You'll just pack your bag and get out as quickly as possible. I don't want you here, and I'm quite sure Drake has no use for you at Heatherfield. You wanted a ship. Right? Well – you'll have to work for it. I'll give you enough to get you to Plymouth or Bristol, London – or better still, come colony wanting men to build and populate the land there, with sufficient to tide you over and find lodgings for a week or two. But don't you ever show your face here again unless you've a million in your pocket as I had when I bought Rookswood land. And that's final.'

It was good – or bad – enough for me. As I stared into his lean hard face with the cold eyes so ruthlessly on mine, I no longer felt any bond – any love or admiration, only a bitter sense of regret, and perhaps loss; loss of something I'd never really had from either of my parents – affection and understanding.

'Very well,' I said. 'If that's how you feel, there's no more to be said.'

He went to his old secretaire, opened the deep top drawer serving as a desk, pressed a knob that flung out a secret compartment where he kept his money, and small duelling pistols, took out two small leather bags filled with coins, and flung them at me. 'More than you deserve,' he remarked, still with the set uncompromising expression on his countenance. 'Now go. I've more than enough to attend to with the additional worry on my hands of finding a replacement for Caswell.'

I was ready enough to give him my hand; but he kept his firmly behind his back and stood staring straight out of the window as I picked up the bags, and without another glance at him strode out of the room, banging the door sharply behind me.

That evening, meaning to leave Heatherfield early in the morning, I said farewell to Drake and Juliana in as practical and commonplace a manner as possible.

'There's no point in mincing matters,' I said, with a lifeless kind of grin. 'My presence is redundant. Father doesn't want me, and I'd be no good as a farmer if a place even could be found for me here. I've no feeling either for wallowing in sentimentality. A time comes when a man has to make his own choice, and—' I shrugged, '—this is it. Don't worry about me. I shall find something to my liking – somewhere.'

Drake appeared slightly concerned, but with the forth-coming marriage so close he was probably relieved to be free of the continual bickering between Justin and myself.

He gave me a very straight look, and after a pause said, 'Yes, I think you will. I believe you've the determination to fend for yourself, especially with that nice little handout from father. But don't waste it, be a bit – circumspect, and let us know how you get on.'

That was that.

With Juliana it was a little different. Being my twin and a girl, her lips trembled, and at one point I had the ghastly fear she was going to weep.

'Now look here,' I said, with forced lightness, 'don't, for goodness sake, make a tragedy out of something that was bound to happen anyway; I'll be back – someday, you bet I will, and maybe with that million in my pocket. Who knows. So—' I tilted her pert little chin up and gave her a brotherly kiss, and dabbed one moist eye with a corner of my handkerchief.

'It seems so *wrong*, though,' she said, 'for us to be parted like this – as a family, and all because of *Caswell*.'

'Oh, maybe I *was* too tough with him,' I said, 'and papa's a funny old stick – kind of doted on him. I didn't really grudge Justin his rage. Look at it this way, Julie. Except for you I've always been the odd one out. Never fitted in, and this—' holding up the money bags, '—is maybe Fate's way of putting me on the right track.'

'But what are you going to *do* with it? It'll take more than that to start your shipping idea. And if you just fritter it away—' she sighed, and continued, '—I shall worry about you, Dominic.'

'You needn't. I'll keep in touch, once anything's decided. Now, sea-nymph—'

'Don't be silly! *Sea-nymph*.'

'That's how I'll remember you – dabbling your toes in the

water with your hair flying in the wind. But when we next meet you'll probably have changed into a very competent young matron with a devoted husband and maybe a youngster in your arms.'

'And probably not,' Juliana retorted quickly. 'I don't think I'm the marrying kind, and I didn't know you were the practical sort, either. *Sea-nymph!*' she giggled, then suddenly sobered again. 'Oh, Dominic.'

Before she could fling herself into my arms, I gave her a light kiss on the forehead, picked up my bag and hurried to the drive where the landau waited to take me and the rest of my few belongings to the nearest station of Carlake.

I looked back once and gave a brief wave, then I was off – off to find a new destination and a new way of life, but not to Plymouth or Bristol as Justin had directed, but to London where I had a pal from my university days – Edgar Willis. He had graduated with a brilliant first in Law at Oxford, and now practised – fairly nonchalantly, I'd gathered – in the West End. He was handsome, cultured, of an impressive family, and extremely rich, with all the credentials for introducing me to a select social set. I had no intention of squandering my father's farewell legacy on buying one mediocre second rate ship, but had made up my mind to reap all the advantage possible by living for a limited time available as a gentleman of means – savouring the existence of a popular gallant with access to wealthy homes where eligible young ladies swooned in delight at the attention of handsome beaux.

I was not exactly handsome, no. But when elegantly dressed had the capacity, I knew, to stir feminine hearts by my certain dashing dark charm.

When – or rather *if* – I found one available and willing from such an elite circle, who could both please my senses and my ambitions, I might even contrive by subtle means to lead her to the altar. Who could tell? The rest, then, would be easy. I had no conscience about the matter. Elizabeth had scorned me. My father had cast me off; Drake hadn't wanted me. So it was all out for myself now. And should I achieve my end in the brief time finances allowed, I'd be fair and give any wife of my bosom the allegiance and connubial attention she demanded – outwardly, at any rate, which was all that could be expected from wedlock in a marriage of convenience.

\*

Edgar's – or rather the Willis – home was situated in verdant parklands in Hertfordshire. But he spent most of his time at his select club near Piccadilly, or his own lavish bachelor apartments in the West End where he entertained friends both of the nobility and artistic order, including, on occasion, young ladies whose exotic painted beauty excluded any possibility of serious commitment on Edgar's part. The latter, I discovered, were generally connected with the theatre, of which he was a popular patron. His business offices were nearby, but provided more of a respectable façade for his extravagant and somewhat eccentric social life, than as a provider of income which was a mere irreverence where the heir to the Willis fortune was concerned.

To look at he was tall, fair, mostly impeccably, if colourfully, attired, reminiscent of the late Beau Brummel though his height of six feet six made him more spectacular. He had a frank, boyish gaze and manner, with a fresh complexion and blue eyes which, innocent as they might appear at first glance, were nevertheless shrewd and worldly wise – and already slightly bagged beneath from certain self indulgences and overmuch good living.

We had not been exactly *intimates* at Oxford; our backgrounds and ambitions had been so widely different, and I was a year younger. But because Edgar had the collector's instinct for curiosities, and regarded me possibly as something of an oddity, coming from remote Cornwall where miners and smugglers abounded with a smattering of small gentry intermingled – I had been singled out for his comradely attentions and introduction to University life.

So up to a point we'd been friends. But only up to a point. There were certain devious practices and extravagances both sexual and social that I'd avoided, not merely through lack of funds but from choice.

However, the point had now arrived when I was only too willing to use any advantage he cared to offer. And one certain aspect of his character was generosity. Edgar, whatever his individual quirks of behaviour might be, had always been over-generous to the point of the ridiculous.

And it was this I meant to play upon.

So when I made my ambitions clear – not specifically mentioning the limitation of my pocket, he was all eagerness to oblige.

'First of all, dear boy, if you really want to savour London society at its most titillating, you must be decently attired,' he said, 'and of course we must find acceptable rooms for you – in the vicinity of Chelsea perhaps. Not *too* expensive. But – within reason?' His brows arched in a question over his appraising blue eyes, despite the knowing quizzical whimsical tilt of his well-sculptored mouth which was one-sided and I guessed had both charmed and bewildered many women.

'I have funds from the old man,' I said ambiguously, with a casual debonaire manner meant to match his. 'Don't worry about me.'

'My dear fellow, I wouldn't dream of it,' he retorted lightly. Then he patted my shoulder meaningfully, saying lightly, 'If you're going to be one of us you mustn't lack for the wherewithal. That would really be too atrocious. A whisper in my ear from you, a hand in my pocket, and there you are. Eh?'

I wasn't a fool. I knew Edgar's off-beat fancies, and although I'd not the slightest intention of indulging them myself, at the moment I meant to tread warily not wishing to kill too soon the goose that laid the golden egg. So I replied, staring him very straight in the eyes, 'You put things very concisely, Willis. Thanks.'

So it was arranged. Bachelor apartments were found for me with a discreet butler-cum-valet to fill my needs. I was introduced to Edgar's tailor, fitted and equipped with clothes sufficiently elegant for any wealthy man of fashion, and the relentless course to social success and the realisation of my ambition set in motion.

From the first I assessed my financial situation with a hard-headed astuteness that would have astonished my father. What I possessed moneywise, without having to approach Willis would probably, with luck, see me through a month of the lavish living required of the young buck I was supposed to be. After that I should have to take an extremely subtle line with Edgar.

*So!*

I forthwith started my search, during a series of conventional and unconventional little 'get-togethers' provided by my rich sponsor, for the lady of means who hopefully was destined to become ensnared in my matrimonial net.

I wasn't proud of myself. In Drake's eyes, I suppose, I would have been considered a cad of the most contemptible order. But at least I was honest with myself, and once my object was achieved there'd be no false sentimentality or soft spoken lines of eternal faithfulness and adoration. Any woman I married must be sophisticated, yet sufficiently enamoured to accept me with no false assumptions of high-handed virtues I didn't possess.

Somewhere in Edgar's wide circle of friends and acquaintances there must surely be such a one.

I found her in the person of Isabella Colbert, the only daughter of an American multi-millionaire, John Hartley Colbert who'd made a fortune from cotton and shipping, and was a prominent figure in Boston's business and cultural life. She was a pink-cheeked, bouncy, voluptuous-looking girl of twenty with slightly prominent blue eyes, very white teeth, and a capacity for seeing the comical side of life that put me instantly at ease with her. Both she and her sire apparently adored – her own words – anything truly British, and being a widower and except for his one daughter, childless, Hartley adored *her*.

From our first meeting at Edgar's place, we got on. There was no false modesty or pretence about her, and obviously she was in need of a husband. Preferably an English one – which was the reason, so far, she hadn't been snapped up. I admit I saw the advantages of filling the tempting role, given the chance, with a considerable amount of pleasure, not only for financial reasons, but because Isabella's gusto for life would obviously compensate for any innate lack of refinement. She was of the New World, and her outrageous sense of humour combined with the practical ability inherited most probably from her father, was proof enough to me that I'd have to suffer none of the moods and megrims that could make marriage a bondage within the uppercrust of English society.

In love with her? No, I certainly wasn't, in any high-flown romantic way. Sexually, though, I knew she could be fun and would probably breed fine sons to carry on the Pencorrin name allied to the Colbert inheritance and tradition.

Isabella Colbert-Pencorrin!

The double-barrelled name sounded good. What better?

Oh, yes! with most of what I'd aimed for looming so tantalisingly near on the horizon, I'd become, I supposed, something of a gratified cynic. All illusions I'd had in the past were discarded. In a few short weeks I'd become a businessman, more ruthless even and determined than my father.

I tried not to think of him. Whenever his image rose as a shadow to the back of my mind, I thrust it away. Except for Juliana, my family meant nothing to me any more.

Whether Colbert himself realised my deviousness in the courtship of his daughter I didn't quite know, but I guessed he must. A man of his calibre, physically and mentally, must have learned to know people pretty well in his long and successful business career. To look at he was large, genial, always the benevolent host, but with that certain assessing shrewdness in his small darting eyes that said more clearly than any words, 'Don't try and fool me, young man. I know very well what you're after. Whether you get it or not depends on how clever you are.'

So I had to be bright. And I was. While making quite clear to him my passion for the shipping business, and this certainly pleased him, I spent every minute possible in charming Isabella. First it was a restrained affectionate touch of my lips on her warm cheek – the brotherly kind which left her wanting something different. The second was more directly intimate, and the third, in the conservatory of the weekend mansion rented by Colbert for the season, was definitely of the sensual order to which she responded with more than normal warmth. At the same time I allowed a hand subtly to slip down the inviting low cut bodice of her gown where it lingered pleasurably on one white breast.

She had a very good skin.

She possessed, as well, a husky voice with the kind of she-animal tremor in it, that told me I had won.

'Oh, Dominic!' she breathed, before I released her. 'You sure are *awful*!' but her eyes were mischievous, and her pert mouth though mocking, was moist with desire.

'Will you marry me, Isabella?' I said on the spur of the moment.

She gaped in assumed astonishment.

'*Marry* you! – But – *marry* you? What an idea. I don't even—'

'Shsh¡' I became bold, and put my fingers over her lips. 'Don't dare to say, "I don't even *know* you",' I continued, reckless now the dice was cast. 'I wouldn't like to think you'd been playing with me, Isabella.'

Suddenly she laughed, richly, gaily, the kind of laugh I really did appreciate, and dug me in the ribs quite fiercely.

'You're sure a quick worker, Mr Penniless-Pencorrin, aren't you?'

That stung me.

'All right. So we'll forget it. If it's money you're after, I haven't got it. But in decent English society such things aren't generally referred to under circumstances of this kind. Allow me, Miss Colbert.' I offered my arm. 'Shall we join the others?'

For a second I think she was taken aback, her smile faded, then, with a rush, she flung her fine form against me with such force I nearly struck my back against an immense plant pot.

'Of *course* I'll marry you, silly,' she breathed into my ear. 'But—'

'Yes?'

She studied me for a pause in which I noted an unexpected series of different emotions cross her face.

'You don't love me, though, do you?'

It had come; the question I'd dreaded. I didn't want to lie to her. Despite her wealth, her background, her forthright realistic attitude to sophisticated circles, she appeared for those few seconds suddenly curiously vulnerable and young. So I answered her query in the kindest, subtlest way possible.

'I *want* you. I like your looks and wonderful body. I want to be with you and give you children. If that's love – well, you know the answer. But if you need more, if that isn't enough, say so, and we'll forget it. I think we'd get on together, though, and that should count quite a lot.'

I waited, and when she spoke, her voice was so low I hardly recognised it.

'Yes. It's enough, Dominic. I guess I'm not the romantic type. Just—'

'Damned desirable,' I interrupted and meant it when the words were spoken. 'I only hope your father agrees.'

'He will when he knows it what *I* want,' she assured me. 'I'll *make* him.'

And she did.

We were married at St Paul's Cathedral a month later, with all the important personages of the period Hartley could muster in the congregation. I hadn't wanted the show, but Isabella, gloriously happy and proud, looked quite – splendid, I think is the apt word – in white satin fitted to show off the seductive lines of her figure, with a veil yards long carried by six small child attendants. Where she got them from, heaven alone knew. But I had already discovered that however proud certain families of aristocratic lineage might be, most of them were seldom averse to having their names mentioned in any fashionable event. And Hartley was certainly lavish but only in the spending of money for this very important occasion, but in cunningly contriving to obtain the utmost publicity.

Personally I would have preferred a quiet affair; but from the very start Isabella had been bouncily determined otherwise. She had got what she wanted – an English husband with a dashing air and of good family, though the family – except for Juliana, whom I'd notified – was not present to drink a toast.

Drake, she'd told me in answer to my letter informing her of my news, was unable to accept because Elizabeth was already *enceinte* – somehow the word irritated me – and Justin, my father, seemed uninterested.

He's not himself these days [she'd explained] always grumbling and on the defensive about something or other. I do my best to brighten him up, but since Drake got married he's become more than ever a hermit at Rookswood. Anyway, I'll be in London for the great day, although I shall only stay for the one night. If you can book me in at an hotel somewhere I'd be grateful.

    With love, Juliana.

When he heard of the proposed arrangement Hartley was characteristically opposed to it, and insisted that my sister should stay at their town house.

I could hardly refuse – a decision which I knew that although not to Juliana's liking – she would gracefully accept, for the sake of family harmony.

I didn't relish the idea. It would have been good to have an intimate chat with my twin somewhere quiet and away from the charade of celebrating, wining, dining, and eternal gushing from ladies and back-slapping of the men. Still, wishing even for a second's blissful pause in the colourful cavalcade proved indeed to be a pipe-dream.

Following the reception at the Café Royal after the wedding, we were whirled off to the Colbert Mansion where a second celebration and feasting was held.

Juliana, looking fawn-like – or nymph-like – as ever, and very lovely in muted grey silk and greenish blue – hadn't changed since I'd last seen her, except perhaps to appear a little more thoughtful with a wondering half-anxious look in her large eyes.

I managed to have just a few words with her in a corner of the vast drawing room away from the buffet and rest of the crowd.

'What's the matter?' I asked. 'Don't you approve?'

She smiled.

'Oh, Dominic, if you're happy – if this is what you want, of course I approve.'

'It's what I want,' I said stubbornly, making myself believe it. 'Anyway it's only the beginning. It'll give me the chance to make something of my life, something that'll stagger the old man. I *had* to get away, Julie, you know that. He just – *despised*, thwarted me.'

She squeezed my hand. 'I know.'

'And Isabella? What do you think—?'

'She seems fun.'

'Fun? Yes, but—'

'Oh, she's charming and very pretty, Dominic. I'm sure she'll make you a good wife—'

More could have been said, and doubtless would have been, if Edgar hadn't blundered in at that exact moment and started his 'charming' process with Juliana. He really was rather entranced, but she wasn't. Behind her shy quiet smile I glimpsed a faint withdrawal and coolness, a certain strain that told me she was already longing for the weekend to be over, and to be back with her moors and menhirs and the soft sting of winds from the sea brushing he cheeks.

For a brief time I almost envied her. But hours later when I was alone at last with Isabella in the lush bedroom allotted to us for the one night before setting off on our Continental honeymoon, any lingering regrets of the past were dispelled.

Yesterday, financially, I had been a nobody – *presumably* a young gallant of means, but *practically*, except for a few remaining guineas, with no means at all.

Tonight was different; tonight, with a breathtaking dowry at my disposal and quite an exciting young wife to bed, a successful and very rosy future indeed were mine for the taking.

I'd make the most of it.

By God I would.

And to hell with Justin Pencorrin.

## 2

To say my first night with Isabella was exhilarating would be an understatement. There were moments indeed when it became almost a riot. To begin with, her sense of humour and obvious delight over her initiation into wifely duties dispelled any sense of restraint between us, and although – somewhat to my surprise – she was proved to be completely virginal – no sentimentality on my part was required, and would probably have aroused guffaws of laughter. Under other circumstances perhaps – if, for instance, my bride had happened to be Elizabeth – I might have been mildly disappointed feeling a sense of loss at the lack of romance, but with Isabella there was no time or need for displays of words or manner. Our mutual fulfilment came as the natural outcome of an enjoyable tumble under the Colbert silken sheets, which would have been equally acceptable and suitable in a hay loft.

Next morning, though, as I caught the pride of possession in her blue eyes over the breakfast tray, I realised that her single heartedness could be a nuisance if I allowed it to be. The thought was momentarily daunting, until the fact registered that business would play a large part in my future life; there would be weeks – months perhaps – when I should be away on trips, leaving my wife to pursue her own hobbies – cultural or otherwise – in her select Boston set.

A town house had already been planned for us in the Massachussetts capital on the order of Hartley himself, which would be ready for us following an extended month's holiday trip on his luxury yacht aptly named *The Isabella*.

'And when you get back my boy, there'll be a time of learning and work,' my father-in-law had stated with an affable wink and one of his characteristic slaps on my shoulder. 'My little girl deserves the best, and you and I are going to see she gets it, eh? Fame, boy. And money. Security so

the Colbert-Pencorrin line is something for the kids you'll
have to be proud of. They talk of Kingdom Brunel now; but in
not so many years ahead you'll be neck and neck with him, if
you put your heart into things, and with my backing, boy.'

Oh, yes, the old man was very sure of himself. And of me,
thanks to Isabella. But I noticed he put the Colbert name
before the Pencorrin, and although that was all right for me
temporarily, a decision was already hardening in me that it
would not always be so. I was under no illusion that Hartley
was not a fanatic where success was concerned, and would
expect a good deal of me. This didn't worry me an iota. Had
Justin given me the chance to pursue my own line I'd have
worked as hard for him. That he'd made a mistake I was going
to prove, one day.

Yes, I have to admit it. There were odd moments when old
wounds still festered.

He and his mine! God help him.

What a fool he'd been.

Once, when I was standing on deck staring over the water
during our cruise of Europe and further afield, Isabella came
up to me and asked, 'Why so solemn, honey? You look kind of
– glum.'

'No,' I told her, 'I was only thinking.'

'About what? Me?' Her arm slipped round my shoulders, I
could feel a warm fresh cheek against mine. She was a tall girl,
making us both about the same height, and there were
occasions when I'd have liked more inches to give a sense of
male superiority. This was one of them. Just for a second I was
mildly irritated by her feminine vitality and her assumption
that she had a right to share my most secret thoughts.

'No,' I answered, more shortly than I'd intended. 'I was just
looking back. On the past.'

'Oh.'

I glanced at her quickly. She wore an expression – almost a
moué – of disappointment like that of a child that had been
snubbed.

I forced a smile.

'There are other people and things in the world besides you
and me, my love,' I pointed out.

'Such as?'

'My father, my sister who you've met, Drake, my brother, even my missing mother. Then there's Cornwall itself—' Perhaps my voice held a hint of nostalgia, for she remarked pettishly:

'It seems kind of strange for you to be dwelling on *Cornwall* when you've a whole new life in America ahead, with me.'

'That's *why*, I suppose. I'm saying a long goodbye.'

'And your mother? All the time we were engaged you hardly mentioned her—'

'Such a *long* time, wasn't it, our engagement?' I said jokingly. 'A whole month.'

'Don't laugh, Dominic. I'd have *liked* to hear about her, sure I would. What she looked like, I mean? And why she ran off.' When I didn't speak, she resumed, still with her eyes unswervingly upon my face, 'Was she that bad? A disgrace in some way? A – a—' She broke off tentatively.

'She was a law unto herself,' I said abruptly. 'She was bold and fiery and sweet all at the same time – that's how I remember her. I was just a young boy when she left, and it was because of my father. They didn't get on. To look at? Well – think of heather blowing in the wind, and gulls swooping across a stormy sky – of great cliffs dashed by wild white spray, and I guess you've got the essence of Katrina. But all that must sound phoney to you, because you've never known those things or her. So let's forget it, shall we? I'm a bit of an ass to go maundering away like any milk-sop poet.'

'I don't think so, honey. And poets aren't necessarily milk-sops. What about Emerson?'

'Emerson?'

'Ralph Waldo Emerson. The great poet and philosopher. There, you see?' she broke off triumphantly. 'You've never even *heard* of him, have you? He's famous *every*where now, even in Boston.'

'Why do you say "even in Boston"?'

'Because Boston's not only well-known for its seaport and industry, but its *the* cultural centre of the States,' Isabella informed me proudly. 'It has a *marvellous* Museum of Fine Arts, and a Symphony Orchestra known by musicians everywhere throughout the world. *Really*, honey!' she grinned at me chidingly, 'you do have a whole heap of learning in front of you. A deal of knowledge is going to be expected of you – just because Bostonians have this – *feeling* – if you like – for the British way of life. And poetry's *sure* to be brought up at tea parties and receptions. So it would be just terrible if you didn't know about Emerson.'

I groaned. 'Tea parties, did you say? Oh, God! surely not. Now just get this into your pretty head, Isabella, my love – you may have captured a fairly respectable English husband, but this one happens also to be Cornish with no intention whatever of being on a lead and taught to beg and bark prettily in ladies' drawingrooms. You can have your little cultural do's and enjoy them, with my blessing, my darling, but *not* with me there. Understand?' I tried to look severe, but it was difficult. Isabella looked so pretty that day, in blue which was her colour, emphasising the shade of her eyes, fair hair, and fresh bloom of her cheeks, whipped rosy by the salt breeze.

She made a face, and my arm tightened round her waist.

'Come on,' I said. 'I can think of better things to do than conversing about your precious Emerson. To the cabin with you – wife!'

Laughingly, she made a mock attempt to dodge me, conveniently allowing me to catch her the next moment and escort her, not unwillingly, to our luscious cabin, where we made love exuberantly in an entirely physical way that drove everything else temporarily from my mind.

It was on that day that our first child, a boy, was conceived.

*

During the first six months of my life in Boston, much of my time was spent in studying and absorbing the business side of Colbert's expanding shipping company. Under Hartley's genial front was a driving ruthless will which was determined his daughter's husband should acquire a sound knowledge of every aspect concerning the empire he'd already built from small beginnings. I frequently chafed inwardly, because my natural instincts were for the more adventurous side of shipping – for travel and the sea, and experiencing presumably what seemed to me the first essential factor of sea trading – of learning to manage large vessels – the exciting possibilities of exploring new ports, and new types of cargoes from far away places as yet unconsidered by established companies. I wanted the adventure of things, not the dry-as-dust calculating and perpetual discussions with clerks and business associates behind closed doors. However, I did my best to conform and knowing I had no other course.

'Soon, boy – soon – when you're properly ready for it, you'll be given the chance to take the helm yourself – metaphorically speaking,' my father-in-law told me, taking a cheroot from his lips, and smiling affably. 'I'll have you sail with Biggins, the best captain we have. Jamaica, then Britain. Cotton. Just be patient, son, I know what I'm about.'

He certainly did. And it was not long after that brief conversation that I had my first real ocean trip away from Boston's business world and Isabella's evening social life, which despite her condition she still managed to enjoy, with me in attendance. There were brief tears of regret when she saw me off from the Bay, but I knew they would soon fade. She would miss me for a bit, but for some time the connubial bed had been hers alone, since, as she pointed out – well-bred young wives were expected to be chaste following the first months of being *enceinte*. In any case, it was obvious her interest in me, physically, had evaporated somewhat since the conception of young George – or Georgina, according to the coming child's sex.

I had been somewhat relieved, somewhat flattered, and a trifle amused by the importance already given by the family to the impending little stranger's future advent into the household.

The name, too.

'Why George?' I'd asked, thinking she might have chosen Hartley or even Dominic.

'Oh, I like the name George,' Isabella had answered firmly. 'Kind of regal, when you think of it. And easy to say. After all, honey, so many *kings* have been George, and what about Washington? If it hadn't been for Washington – why! there wouldn't have been America as it is today, would there? So George it *must* be. Say you agree. Now, *say* it.' Her mouth was pouting, though her voice was firm.

Mildly irritated, I answered, 'Call the baby what you like. It makes no difference to me. But you're being premature, my love. Suppose you have a girl?'

'Then it shall be Georgina. *Yes*. And she'll have *my* looks and your wild English spirit.'

'Or *my* looks, and your bounciness.'

'*Bounciness?*'

I'd grinned then. 'Your *charm*, love, *and* your beauty. God help any poor little chip off the Pencorrin block. Having my name will be more than sufficient.'

My wife would have continued the discussion no doubt, but at that point I managed to steer the conversation into different channels. Truth to tell, the prospect of fatherhood was already beginning to bore me.

So time passed. I set off in *The United*, the newly named Hartley-Pencorrin ship, captained by Frank Biggins, for a period blissfully free of women and entertaining, facing the first real taste of the career I'd chosen.

And when I returned, my son had been born.

## 3

In the autumn of 1848 I was shocked to receive a letter from Juliana telling me of my father's – Justin's – death. Another piece of information also left me momentarily off balance.

Please don't fret too much about papa. As you know he had been emotionally ill for some time, ever since that terrible scene with mama. When she left Heatherfield he pretended not to care, but I know deep down that he did. The final blow was an accident at Wheal Clara. One of the newest levels collapsed – an adit was blocked, and three men were drowned. Papa did his best to help, but the effort was too much for him. He had a massive stroke from which he never recovered consciousness.

Anyway, the mine is closed for good now, which means, of course, that men will be out of work. Drake is going to find employment for one or two – the ones with young families, and apparently three others are talking of either going up north to the cotton mills or emigrating to the States.

It's all very distressing, and really to no purpose. Wheal Clara had been failing for so long. And would you believe it? – more than three quarters of our father's money has been lost over that 'white elephant'?

The estate now of course is legally Drake's. When Uncle Richard died, Rupert wasn't interested in anything to do with Heatherfield, and it was legally handed over to papa. Rightly so, since papa had to cope with all the debts and renovations necessary. Papa saw that Drake inherited and I am provided for.

Rupert and his rich wife made an unexpected visit recently. He is still handsome, but portly, and at times seemed bored and uneasy. I expect he was wondering about Rosanna, although he said nothing. It's strange, isn't it, that she could disappear so completely after her fame as Anyana? And Katrina! I often wonder about mama, but she never writes. News of her sometimes filtrates to the vicinity and the gossips lap it up. Of course, the manner of her life in London is no secret. I saw a picture of her once with her friend – the first I believe of many – Sir something-or-other. She appeared handsome and much befrilled. I felt so sad, Dominic. How long can such an existence last? And once she and Justin were so much in love.

Oh dear, forgive me for sounding morbid. No more of it. I have something else to tell you which will be a surprise.

I have a *son*, Dominic. Just imagine it. Oh, no, I haven't done anything silly, and I'm not married. Nymphs don't usually marry. do they? And you always called me a sea-nymph.

What happened was that a young girl, obviously pregnant and ill-nourished, called at Rookswood one day last summer asking if there was any work she could do, such as helping in the kitchen or even in the fields? I had a quiet talk with her; apparently her uncle, a farmer and something of a religious fanatic, from Crippledon way who'd brought her up, had turned her out to fend for herself when he'd discovered her condition. She showed me her back where he'd beaten her first. The weals were terrible. Somehow she'd found food by helping occasionally on the land, or else grovelling for turnips at night, but no one, so far, had thought fit to employ her. Naturally I asked her about the father-to-be – the man responsible for her plight, but she wouldn't say. Through loyalty, I suppose. I'm sure she must have been very fond of him. Her name, by the way, was Bethany. Rather appropriate, don't you think?

Anyway, I gave her a home at Rookswood, and she helped cook very efficiently. But when the baby was born, the effort of a difficult birth was too much for her, and she died.

I told Drake I wished to keep the little boy, and he agreed, so arrangements were made for me to adopt him legally, and he is now the newest member of our family – Jason Pencorrin.

Oh, Dominic, he is so enchanting and strong – beautiful to look at, fair-haired, and bright – quite wilful in fact, and I do so love him. I only wish you could be here for a bit – pay a visit to make his acquaintance. I have moved now to Heatherfield since father's death, Drake would like to see you too.

The letter ran on, turning to more general affairs of life in the district but none of it made any impact.

Only one fact registered.

I had not only one son, but two. George born in legal wedlock, and Jason of a gentle, kindly girl who'd given me comfort and understanding when I most needed it.

When my mind had calmed I was seized with a sudden irrational desire to know and see this fruit of my loins, who in my sister's words was so beautiful and bright and enchanting to look at – then commonsense asserted itself abruptly. My course in life was set. At whatever cost I must retain the goodwill and respect of the Colbert family. No shadow of my past life must be allowed to endanger it. Therefore it was best for all concerned that I stayed safely away from Cornwall.

Which meant that most probably I would never see my sister Juliana again.

\*

Once I had forced myself to the irrevocable decision of sundering myself completely from Heatherfield I became more dedicated than ever to the Pencorrin line. Hartley was impressed, but showed faint concern on one occasion suggesting that I might perhaps be foregoing too much of my social and domestic life with Isabella.

'Don't drive yourself *too* hard, son,' he said. 'Remember you have a wife who needs cosseting now and then. I'm proud of you and your aims. But—' and again the characteristic slap on the back, '—a woman's a woman. Don't do to make 'em jealous or feel neglected.'

'I've given no cause for Isabella to be jealous of anyone,' I said shortly. 'And she knows it. So do you. She's got young George to occupy her – which he does pretty thoroughly. She dotes on him.'

'Don't we all? I wasn't talking of the boy, though. A son's a son, but a husband's a different matter. Going all right, is it? Life between you. In the bedroom, boy, the *bedroom*?'

I was surprised he should doubt it. Isabella had always been capable of having what she wanted of me, sexually, although it was true, that at times, frequently, I'd sensed a mild irritation in her manner, a certain pettiness that didn't suit her still ripening looks.

'Do you still think I'm beautiful,' she said once, before the habitual mating process. She was standing perfectly naked before the mirror, staring at the magnificent lines of her voluptuous figure, which had developed considerably since the birth of George. She was heavier, I thought, a little overweight.

'Of course you're beautiful,' I replied, mildly bored.

'Then why don't you say so sometimes? Other men do.'

'Other men? What do you mean?'

'Guests. The folk we have around here when there's anything on. There are always compliments flying.'

'Naturally. You're an extremely handsome and desirable woman, and there shouldn't be any need for me to tell you so.'

'I like to hear you say it. You know—' she turned round suddenly and considered me with uncomfortable scrutiny from her prominent blue eyes, '—you've changed, Dominic. There was a time when the sight of me with just nothing on like this would have sent you into a frenzy. Now it doesn't affect you at all, does it?'

I happened to be very tired that night. But I made a pretence of passionate need that eventually appeared to soothe her. After the love-making was over she lay staring at the ceiling for a few moments, then said à propos of nothing at all, 'Have you wanted any other woman on these recent long trips of yours, Dominic dear?'

I was glad she'd said wanted instead of 'had', because I wouldn't have wished to lie to her.

'*Wanted*? Don't be *absurd*. Now just stop asking damn-fool questions, will you; of course I haven't wanted anyone else. Not seriously.'

'And what does that mean?'

'It means that you're the tops, darling. There are other beautiful women in the world, sure—' I was becoming quite au fait with Americanisms by then, 'and I'd be nuts not to notice and admit it, but after a glance or two I'd think, "compared with my Isabella, they're just nothing".' I gave a derisive wave of my hand, 'Mere shadows, that is all. Now. Are you satisfied?'

Whether she was or not I couldn't tell. But she snuggled close to me, her scented plump body half smothering me, and said, 'I do love you, honey. On the next long trip maybe I can come with you.'

I was spared that luckily, because when the time arrived, Isabella was once more *enceinte* – it was one of her snobbish little foibles to use the French word instead of pregnant, and I was free to travel once more the world unencumbered by wifely attentions.

*

I suppose it would be considered regrettable by most that as time passed the mental gulf between Isabella and myself gradually widened. I couldn't blame her. She had always liked entertaining, and being the focal point of the select little social set milling round her, whereas I, at heart, was something of a loner. At first, when other men eyed her covetously, and she responded with her bright smile and the offer of a jewelled hand to kiss, I felt a mild stirring of jealousy, but that was all. At that time I was quite certain of her fidelity. She thrived on attention and admiration, but let things go no further. To the Colberts, being a conventional family, any shadow of a scandal on Isabella's name would have been obnoxious. Later, after the birth of our second son, Alexander, two years following George's arrival, I was not so sure. By then, though, so long as she was discreet, I did not particularly care. Her bright buoyancy had become so habitual as to be wearying, and I no longer made any pretence of enjoying her eternal round of bridge drives, parties, and high-flown Bostonian intellectual meetings, avoiding them as much as possible.

Naturally our intimate life became cooler, although during the next ten years she bore me four other children, Conrad, a son, then William, and two girls, Eleanor and Frances. All bore a marked resemblance to their mother except Frances, who was a pert, dark, impish little thing with green eyes and an elfin smile above a pointed stubborn little chin. She was undoubtedly a Pencorrin – or rather a true grandchild to my mother, Katrina and was from the very first my favourite, and the only one I could take an acute interest in, though I made a point of treating the youngsters with equal fairness. She wanted to be an actress.

So the years went by. My children grew up, graduated successfully at college and the boys launched with careers of their choice – the two elder, George and Alexander, being initiated into the Hartley Colbert empire. It was, I suppose, a successful period, if somewhat dull, marred only by one family incident.

In 1871 Frances ran away, and somehow managed to reach Britain travelling as a stowaway on one of the Pencorrin boats and escaping to a hide-out in Falmouth, from where she made her way eventually to Heatherfield.

I was dismayed and worried until Juliana cabled me that she was safe with the family, and there was nothing to be concerned about. She would be writing later.

'*Concerned!*' Isabella gasped. 'The insolence of it – when my own daughter deserts her mother and father and good home in such a manner. You were always too lenient with her, Dominic. I'm no believer in corporal punishment as a general rule, but that girl sure *does* deserve a good old-fashioned spanking, and right now I could give her one. Discipline. She should have had more of it when she was small.'

I *could* have pointed out that in their youthful days Isabella herself had taken little trouble in dealing with the youngsters – all that had been left to governesses. But I didn't. I simply reminded her that Frances was like me in one way – very single-minded and that she'd begged continuously to be allowed to train as a dancer and actress, and that it had been refused.

'Refused? I should just think so,' Isabella exploded. 'The stage is no place for a well brought up American girl – a *Colbert.*'

'A Pencorrin,' I stated. 'Something you could do well to remember on occasion. Now calm down, while we think what to do.'

'*Think?* There's no question of what. You'll set off right away for that benighted place in Cornwall and bring her back. That's what any responsible parent would do, and before any more time's wasted.'

'I see,' I answered coldly. 'But I don't take orders from anyone concerning my own flesh and blood, even *you*, Isabella. However – in this you may be right. But from now on – and I mean it – you'll pay considerably more attention to what the girl herself wishes to do, and incidentally what *I* think is right for her, and control that bullying manner of yours which is becoming all too frequent these days.'

She was staring at me flushed and hot, too angry to speak, when I continued after a short pause, 'I hope you understand.'

'Do you realise who you're talking to?' she demanded then.

'Perfectly. My wife.'

'If papa heard you, he'd—'

'Probably agree with me wholeheartedly,' I interrupted before she could finish. 'Now don't look like that, Isabella. Tempers don't suit you. You're no longer a young girl.'

'And what a perfectly nasty thing to say.'

'Why?'

The blunt question took her aback. Her mouth dropped, giving her a sulky, petulant look.

'Making out my looks had gone. All my – my allure.'

I threw up my hands in despair.

'For heaven's sake, grow up, woman, and forget your damned vanity for a bit. It was our daughter under discussion not your appearance, and I've taken your suggestion. I'm going to pack right away and make the first Transatlantic crossing available.'

I strode to the door of our room, but she rushed after me and caught my coat.

'You can't go like that,' she said fiercely, passionately, 'I won't let you.'

I stopped, turned, sighed, and said wearily, 'What is it you *do* want, Isabella?'

'You, of course, and for us to be like we once were – happy and close.'

I kissed her for the sake of peace, and said with a hint of impatience, 'Nothing goes on in the same way forever. We've a family now, and I'm about to do the best I can to see that our youngest is brought back safely to the fold. There's a vessel setting off at noon under Captain Falkes. I shall wangle a berth, and hope to reach Falmouth in the least possible time. *If* we're lucky.'

'Oh well. All right. Go then – yes, you *must*, of course. Shall I help you pack?'

I laughed outright.

'My dear Isabella, whenever have you done that? And I'll hardly need a wardrobe. Don't look so – so *desperate*, for goodness sake. It'll do you good to be rid of me for a bit again. Go on now, tart yourself up; haven't you a soirée on or something tonight?'

'A poetry reading,' Isabella replied smugly, with a touch of hauteur. 'Brinsley Arnold is going to give a talk on the psychology of Walt Whitman as opposed to that of Ralph Waldo Emerson.'

'Arnold? Is he the rather long-haired chappie with a fancy for floppy bows?'

She flushed. 'He's a very clever man. *Creative* and sincere.'

'My love, I take your word for it. Now, Isabella, if you please—' I gently but firmly pushed past her and strode down the passage to my own private sanctum. Once my door was closed I gave a sigh of relief.

The next moment, despite anxiety for my daughter, jubilation rose in me.

For a time, anyway, I would be free of my wife.

I was going to Cornwall.

## 4

Despite the worldly-wise realism – one might almost say cynicism which had developed in me during my years in the States, a rising excitement filled me as I mounted the few steps leading from the terrace to Heatherfield's front door. The old manor house which had originally been Elizabethan, had changed with the years, and in the past I'd been mildly irritated by renovations and additions which had included the removal of cosy little porches, turrets, and bays for dull square windows.

The twisted chimney pots had been surplanted by plain square stacks which had destroyed a good deal of the picturesque quality that must have characterised the building in earlier times. Only one turret, erected probably in the seventeenth century existed, designed Roman style as a small round temple with a lead covered dome supported by wooden columns. This erection must have been designed mostly for effect, although it contained a hanging bell.

The overall result was confusing in design, especially as an early Georgian wing had been added in my grandfather's day. However, it was Heatherfield, our ancestral home, and thanks to Drake and my father's money, I saw at a glance that during the years of my absence everything about the building had been repaired and brought into good order. The grounds surrounding the drive looked neat and well-cared for. I had no doubt that the estate generally had thrived since the period of Richard's long neglect.

My deductions proved correct, and my greeting with the family – Drake, his wife Elizabeth, and Juliana – was welcoming and warm, if a little restrained, except for Juliana, who flung her arms round me, hugging me as though I'd been resurrected from the dead.

'And you must meet Jason,' she exclaimed with a rush,

following the first enthusiastic interval. 'Well, you will – as soon as he gets in – he's sort of deputy bailiff now, and will take over when John Cardew leaves. Old John's getting on now – he's retiring next year. So—' She broke off as the lounge door opened revealing the figure of my errant daughter, Frances, who stood on the threshold looking like some shy cautious woodland creature, her large eyes turned upon me bravely, but holding also a haunted look – almost fear.

My heart went out to her; she looked so young and defenceless in a loose green gown with her silken hair tumbled about her slim shoulders. Like her eyes, her hair was neither dark russet brown nor black, but of an elusive smoky shade holding glints of amber, and that transient misty blue of woodsmoke against autumn sunlit skies. How Isabella had ever borne such a daughter I'd never been able to fathom, and suddenly, with a very uncharacteristic – for *me* – rush of emotion, I knew that everything had been worthwhile: the tense years of keeping up with Hartley's aims; my bored existence with my wife; the endless sessions of flattery and pandering to her whims following the fading of mutual sexual enjoyment; the whole practical hardheaded business of adjusting from being a Pencorrin to a Colbert. It had all paid off in the end, through the begetting of this one unique and lovely creature.

'Frances,' I said a little huskily. 'Come here, love – there's nothing to worry about.' I held out my arms, and she rushed into them.

'Oh, papa, I felt awful leaving you. I am so sorry – in a way. But it had to be, don't you *see*? It simply *had* to, because mama would never – she never loved me like she did the others, *never*. She would listen to what I said or even *try* to understand. So what else – what could I *do* – papa—?' She broke off, looking up with the tears of emotion bright in her eyes. I noticed Drake glance at Elizabeth and Juliana conspiratorily, then Elizabeth said quickly in the rich voice I remembered so, 'We'll leave you two together for a while. Then, when you've got everything off your chests we'll have a cup of something to celebrate the coming-together.'

My brother, who despite the greying of his crisp hair and a few lines carving his handsome face, looked little different from the Drake I'd left behind all those years before, strode to the door, opened it for the women to pass through, and a moment later Frances and I were alone.

'Now, young woman,' I said in tones meant to be firm, 'we're not going to hum and hah, and go into a lot of needless fuss over this business. I know very well why you took off in such a desperate manner. And I can guess too that maybe you've fretted a bit in causing such a rumpus at home—'

'I didn't *want* to do that,' she interrupted quickly, 'and it was *awful*, leaving you, papa. But mama!' Her small chin came out stubbornly. 'I'm not sorry about *her*. It isn't as if she cared – not really.'

'But she did, and *does*, Frances. And you *should* care. Now – no more scolding. We're going to talk this whole matter over sensibly and decide what's to be done about it. You've got this passion for the stage, for acting and dancing. I know all about that; from being a little thing of only two feet tall—' I couldn't help a reminiscent smile touching my lips, '—you had a fancy for showing off and putting on acts—'

'Oh, it wasn't showing off exactly, papa. I liked *acting* – being someone else than just myself and that's what it is, you see. On the stage you can be anyone you're interested in – a queen in Shakespeare, or Puck, or someone more modern—' She broke off briefly, to get her breath.

'*If* you're lucky,' I pointed out. 'Only a few would-be actors and actresses make the grade. There are many out of work, and countless ambitious girls like you who never even get a chance of an appearance – just an *appearance* before the footlights in a crowd.'

'How do you know all this, papa? It hasn't been your wish, has it? You haven't read like I have about it all? And it isn't that I just want to *look* nice and get applause and all that sort of thing. There's something in me, here—' she tapped her chest, 'that wants to understand everything about life, and people – from earliest times, all through history – and give what's in myself to give. Oh! it's so difficult to explain. But life in Boston is so *flat*, papa, and so *smug*. There've been times – can you imagine?—' her eyes brightened, and for a moment the spirit of mischief itself hovered on her lips, '—why I wanted to jump on the table at one of mama's ghastly tea-parties, and dance a jig or give a speech from Portia or *The Taming of the Shrew*. I was so horribly sickeningly, terribly *bored*! So there! That's why I ran away. To save anything like that really happening.'

'Yes,' I agreed drily. 'Including your mother's finest bone china teaset.'

She giggled briefly, then became solemn again.

'I think you *do* understand,' she said at length. 'In some ways we're rather alike, aren't we, papa?'

'Now what makes you think that?'

'I just feel it – *know*,' she answered, gaining confidence all the time. 'Only the difference is you have your escapes, don't you? When things get too much for you, you can always concoct a business sea trip to other parts of the world. Whereas *me*! if I stayed in Boston I'd probably end up by making a respectable marriage – *if* the husband turned up, of course – that would please mama and get me off her hands for good.'

'Most girls want marriage and children,' I pointed out rather feebly.

'Yes. But I'm not most girls. I'm me. It isn't that I'm *against* it – marrying, I mean. But it would have to be someone I *loved* – awfully. And I'd far more likely meet him in my own kind of environment – dancing or acting – than in the stuffy business world created by grandpa.'

'On the other hand, you might quite easily choose a bad hat.'

'What's that?'

'A rotter,' I answered shortly. 'One who's out for your money and fame – if you make it.'

'The man I loved wouldn't be like that,' she protested, with the naivity of youth.

'And what exactly *would* he be like?'

'Oh, gentle, but firm, and strong. Someone with – with the sunshine in him,' she answered evasively.

I shook my head. 'You speak in riddles, Frances,' I said.

'Perhaps that's why I can't properly explain,' she admitted. 'When I say sunshine I mean the real deep art of loving and caring and suffering, and *giving*, and – and someone to laugh with. Oh, I don't know—'

'Neither do I. But even if you should find this paragon of your young dreams, would you agree to give up any successful career you had, just for him?'

She nodded. 'I think so. *Probably*. Because that's what marriage should be, isn't it? In a way rather *like* an act or dance on the stage – going from one thing to another – step by step, or running sometimes – experiencing just everything that comes along, together? Don't you see, papa? I want so much. Not just to take, but *be*. *Being* is what we're born for—' Her voice trailed off, leaving me astonished and bewildered by the poetical, yet inherent, sagacity of my nymph-like daughter.

One thing registered, though, she had won. I would not take her back with me to America, I would defy Isabella, and see Frances settled in Drama School in London before returning myself to Boston.

When I told her of my decision she was at first so stunned with joy she couldn't speak. She gave a great gasp, then a smile like sunshine irradiated her face.

'Papa, papa—' Her hands were reaching to my shoulders again, and I could feel the soft sweet scent of her pressed against my coat. 'I'll work hard, I really *will*. I'll make you proud of me.'

'Hey, now!' I eased her away. 'First things first, honey. You're the only one of my kids not yet fully schooled. Besides this acting business you're so keen about, there'll have to be a few lessons to complete your education. That's only right and proper. Your mother would expect it. And you never know – after a bit you may not fancy the stage so much. You may get a yearning for home, and another thing—' I paused before adding, 'There's no telling yet whether the Drama School will accept you.'

Her face fell. 'Why *shouldn't* they? Anyway – if it wasn't acting it could be dancing. Dancers are generally small girls. And I'm good, papa – really good.'

'Maybe. But don't get conceited, young woman. Just try and quieten down a bit now, until we get everything in proportion and some sort of plans clear.'

She agreed reluctantly, and went out into the garden to sniff the air and presently wander off across the moors.

When I informed Drake and Elizabeth of the news – Juliana had disappeared upstairs – Drake as usual raised practical points.

'*Your* difficulty, as far as I can see, is explaining and making peace with your wife,' he told me doubtfully. 'As I've never met her personally, it's not for me to make any judgement, but from what I've heard of her, from you and from Juliana's brief contact at the wedding, she's a pretty strong character, and may not appreciate the line you're taking.'

'She certainly won't. But she'll have to lump it. For once, in any domestic crisis I'm having my way. Frances is completely different to the rest of the Colberts. She wants a chance to go her own way which doesn't happen to be theirs, and I'm damn well going to see she has the chance.'

'She's a lovely child,' Elizabeth remarked, and there was a wistful note in her voice that made me wonder how it was she and Drake, both fit and strong, had never succeeded in starting a family. If *I'd* married her, I thought a trifle wrily, it wouldn't have been like that, and a momentary shadow of bygone jealousy touched me. She was still a fine looking and lovely woman, and though the years had streaked her rich hair with silver and brought a few fine lines to her face, her figure and stature were still perfect, her head as proudly held, and her complexion clear. Glancing at her overtly for a second I wondered if she'd ever regretted the humiliating scene of my rejection, and decided not. Her expression, when she glanced at Drake, was warm and trusting. The marital and emotional bond between them was indisputable – something I'd never found with any woman, least of all Isabella. I was about to leave the room and stretch my legs looking for Frances, when Elizabeth glanced sharply round saying, 'I believe that's Jason come in.'

There was the slam of a door from the distance, the tread of strong footsteps down the hall, followed by the yelp of a dog, and a man's voice. 'Down, boy, down.'

'Jason,' Elizabeth called. 'Come here – there's someone to see you.'

The lounge door opened, and there he stood – tall, fair, handsome – a young man bearing the look of some young Viking god, rather than a Celtic Pencorrin – Jason, my oldest son, having not the slightest resemblance to me except a certain thrust of his chin perhaps, and the aquiline nose beneath his wide brow. Ironic that he could be taken so easily as an offspring of Drake, my half-brother, and passed over where I was concerned.

I held out my hand as Elizabeth introduced us, and almost simultaneously Juliana entered.

'This is your Uncle Dominic, Jason,' she said breathlessly before Elizabeth could finish with the formalities.

'So I understand,' I said somewhat stiffly. 'I'm very glad to meet you, Jason.'

He grinned.

'So am I.' His manner was frank, friendly, trusting – reminding me in a flash of nostalgic memory of a girl long ago, who'd given me comfort in a hayloft, for which she'd paid with her life through the begetting of this magnificent specimen of humanity – our son.

'I've heard you're more or less major-domo here,' I said somewhat tritely. 'Congratulations. You must find plenty to do.'

'Oh, I like it. You could say, I suppose, that fresh air, country folk, and getting down to practical everyday problems are my sort of thing.'

'Splendid.'

'He went to Oxford, of course,' Juliana put in, proudly, 'and took an honours degree in languages.'

Jason's fresh complexion turned a shade deeper in tone.

'Don't embarrass me.' He gave his winning smile. 'I guess I just happened to be born with a "yen" for talking – French came easily to me during my schooldays. But I wouldn't want the scholastic life. So—!' he shrugged, '—it seemed the right thing to learn how to carry on here when old Cardew turns it in. And I do a bit of studying – agriculture, drainage, crops – there's a heck of a lot to learn about the land if you're going to get the right results from it.'

'He's right,' Drake remarked, 'and when I take you round the estate later, Dominic, you'll see what improvements have been made during the time you've been away. How long are you staying by the way?'

'Not long. Just a breather – maybe a week or less even, before I take Frances to London. Now the decision's made I want to see things settled as soon as possible and then off home again to face the music.'

As things turned out, however, tragedy, by a bizarre twist of fate stepped in, and prolonged the period at Heatherfield.

\*

Two days following my arrival in Cornwall, on a quiet late afternoon when the sun was only a fading glow behind a rising mist, I had a sudden unpredictable urge to take a look at Rookswood which was by then empty, the housekeeper and staff having left following Justin's death. I went to the Heatherfield stables, got the groom to saddle me a horse, and was soon cantering with a rising sense of rejuvenation beyond the lane, over the miles of moorland which were dim purple and brown now, and holding the damp nostalgic tang of heather, fern and fallen leaves. At a high point I reined in for a few moments and stared across the landscape to where Wheal Clara had once stood, above the sea to the far right. Nothing remained of my father's obsession now, but a ruined black chimney stack standing like a crooked giant finger against the lonely hill. A monument, I thought wryly, to what? A man's senseless greed and ambition that had finally destroyed the work of years of his own life. Strangely, I felt no sadness, only relief that I'd taken the plunge and left before it also devoured me.

A moment later, I kicked my mount to a gallop, turning to the left where the trees bordering the dark shape of Rookswood were soon visible. Like witches' hats, two turrets appeared against the grey sky, and presently I had reached the short drive leading to the front door which to my surprise was ajar.

I dismounted, and tethered the gelding to a windblown sycamore, then marched ahead, straight into the flagged hall, my footsteps echoing with chill thudding emphasis through the silence.

In the ordinary way I cannot be called an imaginative or faintly psychic character. A sense of realism had always been my guide and mainstay. But during those first moments in the already musty-smelling interior I was aware that something – or some*one* other than myself was present.

'Hullo,' I called. 'Anyone there?'

There was no answer.

Then at the far end of the gloomy hall, as my eyes became accustomed to the gathering darkness, I glimpsed faint movement – the stirring of air that resolved eerily into the pale watchful face of a tall shape – a woman's figure approaching me slowly, almost soundlessly.

She stopped walking as I took a stride forward. Then we both stood motionless for a few seconds, like enemies – or was it friends? – in confrontation. Her face, that must once have been handsome, was haggard, lined and strained, with a greenish glow to it, cast from a tall Gothic window on her right. She was draped in a black shabby cloak that hung loosely about her thin shoulders, giving her a spectral air, that of some ghostly ethereal creature risen from the tomb. Yet her eyes burned bright and feverish – twin flames of cold condemnation above the aquiline nose and satirical faint smile on the thin lips.

'Dominic!' she breathed rather than spoke. 'It *is* Dominic, isn't it?' And her voice was a rasp through the air.

I knew her, of course. I think I'd known from my first glance, or sensed with an intuition stronger than reason that something of me – of my own kin – had emanated from the cloying atmosphere of the empty house. From outside I heard the restive whinnying of my horse, and had an impulse to turn and ride away; away from whatever threat the past could hold. Then I spoke, and everything came into proper focus again.

'Yes,' I answered. 'And you're my mother – Katrina. But what in the name of—'

She raised an arm like a thin bat's claw, silencing me. 'Don't say "God", Dominic,' she commanded, still in hard rasping tones. 'God has nothing to do with my presence here – or *yours* either, I imagine.' There was a swift glint of teeth as she smiled bitterly.

'Come and sit down,' I said practically. 'You look exhausted; I suppose there *are* chairs here still?'

I pushed the nearest door open, the door into a parlour, and ushered her in. The light by then was quickly fading, and nothing was clearly defined. But I found candles with matches on a shelf, and lit them one by one. She took the first available seat, and leaned back, breathing heavily.

'Now,' I said, seating myself on a bench, 'suppose we have a little talk. It's a long time since we met. We both must have a lot to say – and—'

'Have we indeed? And what do you imagine I'm going to tell *you*?'

Repelled by the contempt, the sudden flash of hatred in her eyes and voice, I looked away, steeling myself to continue quietly, 'To begin with why you've allowed yourself to get into such a state. The last I heard of you was that you were leading a rich, comfortable life in London. Now you appear looking tired to death, attired like a tramp and as though you hadn't eaten for a week. Mama, it's only right you should explain. God help me, I'm your son. And there are the others at Heatherfield, Drake, and Jason, Juliana's son – then Elizabeth, Drake's wife—'

'And what do you think they mean to *me*?' she almost screamed. 'Or *you* either? None of you matter. No one – there never *was* anyone except Justin. He was the only person I've ever really loved in all my life. Oh, I wanted you, when you were born because you were also his. But when he turned against me – and when he died – there was nothing left for me, *nothing*. And it was this place that did it, this damned house, Rookswood. If he hadn't appeared at the door that day, we wouldn't have met. There'd have been no suffering, no lies, no pretence, and I wouldn't have missed what I'd never had. Do you understand? But of course you don't. I've heard about you, riches, prowess, a rich American businessman! Ha!' She gave a derisive cough. 'Good luck to you. I grudge you nothing. But *this place*, this devil's haunt, it's cursed; it was cursed from the beginning, ever since I moved in with Trengrouse. And do you know *why*?' She paused to get her breath before continuing in lower tones, 'Because it was built on evil – on a *murder*, Dominic.'

Her voice faltered a little. 'And that's the truth. Thomas murdered his wife so he could wed me. I knew about it from the very beginning, and didn't try to stop him.' She got up and went to the window where the greenish luminosity of twilight lit the high dark line of moons beyond. 'Her bones lie somewhere up there at the bottom of a filled up mineshaft. No one has ever known but me – and these walls – these cursed walls—' She stood with a wild desolation on her thin face. 'In the end it got *him*, too. Didn't it? Justin, the man I've always loved more than my own life.' Something like a sob caught her throat.

For the first time I felt pity for the gaunt travesty of a woman who'd borne me. I reached out an arm but she pushed me away. 'Don't touch me. We've nothing between us, you and me. Look at me. Look *hard*.' She thrust her ravaged face forward. 'I'm *old*, Dominic. Old and wasted and shrivelled of life. Shrivelled of everything. Oh, I've existed in a certain way. I've had men in the past, and paid them out in my own fashion for what *one* did to me in the past. *Pencorrin*, when he cheapened and scorned me and sold me as a whore to the highest bidder.'

She laughed hysterically. 'You didn't know that, did you? Well, you do now. But don't try pitying me or offering your filial understanding. You could never understand – *never*. Because you inherit a smug conventional world where right is right and wrong is wrong. And I'm the latter kind – a worn-out old whore who no one wants any more, and who wants nothing, least of all your so-smug charity.'

I was shocked; too shocked to answer. But after a time, when I'd given her a full measure of neat whisky from a cupboard in the kitchen, she calmed down a little, and I learned that she'd spent all she had on a journey by steam-train and ferry to Bodmin, and from there been given a lift by a kindly farmer in his waggon carrying pigs to a certain village where she'd joined a pedlar. He'd taken her in his donkey cart to a spot on the high lane some five miles from Rookswood, and there left her to find her own way to the coast.

She'd walked the rest of the journey. Her manner became curiously quiet then. I gathered that her foot was cut, that she'd probably been a fool to come, that 'there must have been a reason', but she didn't remember what. After that she relapsed into complete silence while I took off her boot and examined her injury. Dried blood had stuck to the leather, where a sharp graze bit across the arch of the foot just beneath the toes. I fetched water, washed and bandaged the swollen flesh with a clean kerchief from my pocket; she neither remonstrated nor uttered any sign of pain. It was as though all normal reaction to feeling had withered following her outburst, leaving just the shell of an aged, bitter woman sitting like an automatom facing me.

'There!' I said when I'd done what I could. 'Now, mama, I'm going to get you to Heatherfield as quickly as possible. The horse out there is sturdy, and can quite well carry us both.'

Instantly she stiffened, and got to her feet, resting one hand on the table. '*No.*' The one word came out like the crack of a pistol shot. 'I'm not going to that place. I'm staying here. It's mine. I made it, it would have been a ruin but for me, and here I'll stay.'

'You'll do no such thing. A fine son I'd be to leave you – or any of my own kin – tired and hungry and needing attention alone in a house already damp and unhealthy from neglect and only rats probably – maybe a few bats – for company. Good God, you could easily be ill and die and no one would know it.'

'Would that matter? Who cares?'

'*I* care.'

'*You.*' Again the mockery of her hard contemptuous laugh. 'Don't be a fool, Dominic. You're like all the rest of the precious Pencorrins. You care only for yourself. So *leave* me.' She stared at me, and for the first time I was aware of a pleading that was almost agony – the agony of suffering, on the lined cold face that had once been so beautiful.

I sighed, hesitated, and at length said, 'I can't keep your presence secret. The family will have to know. Now, suppose I ride back for help. You could have a girl here – a servant and maybe a man to get the place cleaned and livable. Food, too, and clothes. You'll need food if you're so determined on staying. I could arrange for provisions and bedding. It wouldn't take long. An hour, maybe two. What about that?'

I knew deep down in my mind I oughtn't to leave her at all, at the same time recognising that if I attempted further argument anything might happen. She could have a stroke, a heart-attack, or completely lose what balance and reasonshe still possessed.

She eyed me warily. 'You would do that? Just a girl – and food – someone I don't know? No Pencorrins or holier-than-thou Drake?'

I shook my head. 'No one else.'

At length she agreed, and I set off, kicking the gelding to as wild a pace as was reasonable in the gathering darkness. Luckily the horse knew the way, having taken Justin for so many years in the past.

To say the household was astonished was an understatement.

'*Mama*?' Juliana gasped, 'at *Rookswood*? And alone, did you say?'

'Very alone,' I almost snapped, 'and quite exhausted. She's in poor spirits, chilled to the bone, and badly needing food which I shall push down her throat if necessary.'

Juliana got up, her manner swift and decisive. 'I'll come with you.'

'You'll do nothing of the sort,' I replied, in a voice I'd never used to her before – my father's voice. 'We made a bargain, and I'm not going to break it. She wants to be on her own for a bit – without any family haggling or explanations, and I don't blame her. Later, but not *now*, Julie. What she *did* agree to was some sort of help. A girl who's never known her, and a man. Can you spare one of the gardeners? Someone strong and youthful enough to shoulder a deal of hard work?'

Jason nodded. 'I'll speak to Joseph.'

Juliana appeared resentful at first. 'I really don't see why you should do all this ordering about, Dominic. I'm your twin, and her daughter. I've as much right as you to know what's going on, and why she should appear like this in such a state.' She paused, then added, 'You *know* something, don't you?'

'Only that she's destitute and proud. And proud people don't like to admit it. Now – what about the girl?'

'There's Ellen, I suppose,' Juliana agreed grudgingly, 'she's capable, and can turn her hand to most things. But I *would* like to know how long this – this separation – incarceration, really – is likely to on. After all, there's Elizabeth to consider too. She's really mistress *here*, you know.'

Just at the propitious moment my sister-in-law, hearing her name used, appeared on the scene.

I told her in as few words as possible what had happened.

'Right,' she said. 'Of *course* she can have Ellen, and I'll see about food being packed ready immediately.' She turned a reproachful eye upon Juliana. 'It's not like *you* to show resentment,' she said. 'Being your own mother, and after all this time—'

'That's just it,' Juliana's face saddened. 'I could help her – I know I could. Just like I did for papa all those years when he was rooted at Rookswood, sitting there staring for days on end at that old mine. You never knew him properly then. You couldn't possibly understand. But he and mama – whatever happened – they still *cared* for each other. It was just that. Apart, they couldn't cope. He never hated her, not really. If Rupert hadn't – if he hadn't been so stupid with Rosanna, and if she—'

'No use bringing up old history,' I interrupted. 'The thing is to act practically *now*.' I turned to Elizabeth. 'Thank you – for understanding. Maybe you'll go a bit further and explain to Drake when he gets in. He'll want to see her, of course, but if you can just put to him that all she wants at the moment is to be left alone it would help a damn lot.'

She gave me a very straight look, and once again I couldn't help thinking what a lovely woman she was. And so calm – like a quiet pool in a storm-tossed forest of emotion.

'I'll manage Drake,' she said.

But she didn't have to.

On the point of his arrival from a longer than usual round of the estate, the far horizon of dark evening sky and moorland hills Rookswood way showed a glow of deepening crimson. At first I thought it was merely a remaining reflection of the setting sun. But there'd been little sun that day, and what there was of it had completely faded before I left my mother. In any case the direction was wrong. Then what the hell could it be? Was there a fire somewhere?

I was still staring motionlessly when Drake came up behind me and put a hand on my shoulder. 'Elizabeth told me,' he said, 'about mama. The food's packed and—' His voice broke off sharply. Then he exclaimed, 'Well, I'll be damned – what's that? Has some fool set a rick alight? Or – God, Dominic, once a blaze gets hold on that moor there's no knowing where it'll stop. And it's getting worse. See those flames—'

Yes, I saw. Leaping tongues of lurid red like those of a

giant dragon's teeth blazing intermittently between curdling coils of ugly smoke.

'Very near Rookswood,' I said automatically.

'If it's not Rookswood itself. Come, brother – we'd better be off immediately. I'll get what help I can. Alert the man to get horses ready. Let's hope we're wrong, though. Heaven help us if we're not – and *her* – Katrina—'

What my thoughts were as we raced through the night towards the sweeping river of flame I can't recall. Probably I had none except a terrible sense of desperate urgency and apprehension of doom. A wind had risen, driving any lingering haze away, and in the sky above a pale moon rose like a wan lantern over the ever-reddening horizon. Once Drake's horse reared and floundered throwing him. Drake was not hurt, and to the sound of neighing mounted again and was quickly following my course which evaded the well remembered pitfalls of bog and treacherous shaft.

The air thickened, and grew rancid with the hot breath of smoke and burning timber. On reaching the house it was already a crumbling mass of tumbling blackened brick and wood. The whole of one wing had gone, and when we circled to the sea side, the thin form of a human figure could be seen at an upstairs window, lit macabrely like some gaunt scarecrow with waving arms against the lurid glow.

Drake looked helplessly at me, then jumped from his horse, thrusting the reins into my hand. 'Hold him. He'll be needed. The men are coming. Do what you can, Dominic.'

Before I could stop him he'd plunged into the holocaust with something – his handkerchief, or neckscarf – held to his face, while I battled with the terrified animals to get them securely tethered. From the slope opposite several men converged on the scene dragging what equipment they could muster to fight the fire.

But it was all of no use.

What remained of the gutted building suddenly collapsed; there was the roaring sound of tumbling granite and brick, and for a moment the whole earth seemed to shudder.

Frozen with shock and grief I couldn't move for what seemed an interminable time. Then, automatically, I joined the little group of workers in what I knew was a futile task.

The two bodies were found later. Drake badly burned and crushed, Katrina almost indistinguishable, but able to whisper before she died, 'I always loved him, you know. Always. *Always.*' I wished it was her son she referred to, but knew otherwise. It was true what she'd asserted earlier, my father – Justin King Pencorrin – was the only individual in the world she'd truly cared about.

The tragedy was that Drake should have paid for that caring.

*

At the inquest later a verdict of accidental death was recorded, there being no evidence, or question, of arson. No reason could be found for the fire, except that the 'poor lady' might have dropped a lighted candle or match by mistake which had first set fire possibly to curtains or some inflammable material that had ignited the interior, there being much old wood about.

I revealed nothing but the bare facts, and tried to dispel from memory the curious hatred on my mother's face when she'd muttered that the house was founded on evil, and was a cursed place that should be destroyed.

Yet how possessive she'd been of it, even in her bitterness. So possessive that she and she alone must have been the means of its destruction?

I believe that was so, that in her maddened mind she thought that ridding the moor of Rookswood might bring her and Justin together again at last.

By nature, though, as I've pointed out before, I'm not an imaginative man. Neither do I believe in wasting life through pondering on morbid possibilities. My first concern therefore was to busy myself with practical plans for Heatherfield, and of course Elizabeth.

She was very brave and did not break down in front of any of us, even when told of his death, though later, when she'd locked her door after going to bed, the low sound of sobbing could be heard.

'He was a good man,' she said the next day. 'And we had a good marriage. And after all—' she faced me calmly, 'that's what matters, what I must remember always.'

'Yes.'

'I don't want you to worry about me,' she remarked, with the suggestion of a tremor in her voice. 'Jason's here – Jason will continue with the estate, as Drake wished him to. He's a wonderful support, Dominic. Rather a rare kind of person, really.'

'Yes,' I agreed once more, ineffectually. 'I'm sure he is.'

A minute later Jason joined us.

We stared at each other with a conflict of emotions stirring both of us, I'm sure. But there was no recognition, and I knew in that moment I would never reveal the truth. He had a right to retain any illusions of his father built up in him during the years. And I had a right to retain his affection.

He put out a hand. 'Thanks, Uncle Dominic. You've been a great help. I'll see that Aunt Elizabeth's all right, I promise you.'

'I'm sure you will,' I agreed warmly. And that was as far as we got.

## 5

An undercurrent of gloom settled about Heatherfield during the next week, which for the sake of Frances I tried to minimise by taking her away from the house as much as possible, either walking, riding, or on brief trips by chaise to Truro. But the dreary procedure of impending funeral arrangements had to be tackled, and I spent considerable time after Frances had gone to bed each night discussing business matters, and plan for the future with Jason and Elizabeth. With a wry sense of Nemesis I had Jason's promise to act as guardian for the girl whilst she was in London, taking occasional trips to the city to see everything was well with her.

Elizabeth also accepted a certain responsibility. Juliana, I thought, had enough to contend with. Although only a middle-aged woman still, her health was failing. She had never been very strong, and the tragic loss of Drake seemed to have hit her more acutely than it had his wife. Possibly Elizabeth being made of sterner stuff managed better to conceal her grief. For the first time I realised fully her indomitable pride, and realised that perhaps after all, we could never have been properly adjusted as man and wife. There was an inner aloofness about her I'd never reached. Perhaps no one had – not even Drake.

Frances naturally was more subdued than usual during that unhappy period. The servants, like the rest of the household did their best to put on as ordinary a veneer as possible. But my daughter noticed, and said to me one afternoon, 'I think funerals are horribly morbid. Why have we all got to wear black and be miserable. It doesn't help her, does it? Not grandmama or Uncle Drake. And *she* must have been very strange. *I* don't want people to mourn over me when I die. I want to be sent out to sea and burnt like the Vikings were. Or perhaps collapse on a mountain top. Yes, that would be best—'

'Don't talk like that,' I said more sharply than I'd intended. 'Death's not the subject for a girl like you.'

'Perhaps not. I've never really thought about it much before. But when something happens like this you just have to, I guess.'

'Yes,' I agreed. 'But keep the thing in proportion. Trees and flowers put on a show in the spring, then wither and fade in the winter. Leaves fall, and animals go into hibernation. We're all creatures of Nature, Frances, and Nature doesn't mean us to be sad. Just get the best out of each day and know there's always a tomorrow ahead.'

'But we don't know, do we?'

'As much as one can know anything in this old world.'

Oh, I was quite surprised and rather proud of myself at being capable of turning out to be the helpful philosopher for once.

'Maybe you're right,' she said absently. There was a pause until she remarked, 'Aunt Juliana's offered to lend me a grey silk dress and a black velvet cloak for the – the funeral affair, with a bonnet to match. She said no one would expect me to look like a black crow. *You* won't mind, will you? Aunt Elizabeth was a bit huffy about it. She's rather conventional, papa. So dreary.'

'Drake was her husband,' I reminded her. 'You can't expect her not to want respect shown—'

'*Respect*? As if a grey dress could have anything to do with *that*!'

'Of course it hasn't. And you wear the grey,' I confirmed. 'It should suit you.'

Her voice brightened slightly.

'I don't want to be horrid, but English people – *some* of them – some do have sort of off-beat ideas, don't you think?'

'So do many Americans,' I pointed out. 'Remember the Boston bridge parties?'

She smiled.

'Yes. It's just a pity this terrible fire had to happen while we were here. I'd have liked to go to that fair. Did you know there was quite a large one on at Thalk?'

Thalk was a large village some ten miles away.

'No. I hadn't heard.'

'It ends tomorrow.'

'Then we'll go – just you and I,' I said, on the spur of the moment.

She gave my arm a squeeze.

'Thank you. But only if you think it's right. I mean – I don't want to make things uncomfortable for you.'

'Daughter dear, I can be quite hard-headed when I feel like it, as you should know by now. So let tongues wag and gossips natter. If it's what you want it's OK by me, and be damned to the rest.'

Our little conversation cheered her up immensely, a fact that even penetrated and gave lift to my own low spirits and regret for the loss of a good brother.

\*

Thalk was larger than most mining villages, having a population worthy of a small town, with a straggling main street, a square bordered by two inns, a church, hall, general stores and small cobbled lanes with shops leading either seawards, or to the moors at the back. Most of the industry there was mining, with three large mines working in the vicinity. Therefore the first impression given was of uniform greyness, a centre composed chiefly of grey granite cottages to house the hundreds of workers employed.

At times of any celebration or a fair, however, the scene changed. There were stalls and booths in the streets and various side shows at a nearby field on the outskirts. There was wrestling, a group of travelling players performing from waggons, and a raised platform, jugglers, soothsayers, fortune tellers, pedlars, and a notorious character, Doctor Bridie, selling pills and potions with a special concoction for promoting fertility and long life.

A dancing bear on a chain displayed his antics, and for the more lurid-minded cock-fights arranged in an enclosed ring. Much that went on there was illegal, and much was ignored by the authorities. The colourful cloaks, bonnets and painted faces of the gentry mingled with those of peasants and rogues. The atmosphere was one of highly charged excitement mingled with bargaining, and as the day wore on considerable drunkenness.

It was afternoon when I arrived with Frances. First of all I took her into the best parlour of the Persian King where we had refreshment of cheese, lardy cake, and each a glass of home-brewed mead.

'Your mother would be outraged at this,' I told my daughter severely. 'Don't you dare breathe a word or she'll have my head.'

Frances laughed outright.

'I certainly won't say. I *couldn't*, anyway, could I? Because I may not see her for years and years.'

'We don't know about that yet,' I reminded her. 'We'll have to wait and see.'

'*I* do. *I* know,' she stated firmly. 'You've made a promise, and if you break it—'

'Well?'

'It'll make no difference. I'm not going back to that stuffy existence; I'll get on somehow in London.'

'Not without the wherewithal. You realise that, don't you? It's going to take quite a tidy little fortune getting you decently started off as a budding Siddons.'

She stared at me very seriously.

'Do you grudge it to me, papa? Is it going to make things difficult for you?'

'You bet it is. With your mama. No way else.'

'Oh, well, I'm sure you'll be perfectly able to cope with her.'

'You're sure of far too much,' I told her. 'Now finish your mead and let us get going.'

She quaffed her drink down, and gave her elfin grin. 'I liked that. It was good.'

'You should have been a boy, Frances,' I remarked. 'And yet perhaps not. I must say, as a girl, you do look quite enchanting today, love.'

She flushed slightly. 'Thank you, papa.'

A moment or two later we were making our way through the crowd, stopping at stalls and booths, while Frances bought ribbons and trinkets, and a bag of gingerbread which she started to nibble in what Isabella would have termed a most unladylike way. Once or twice heads turned to look at her — her impudent little face beamed so engagingly from a cream-lined velvet bonnet wheedled from Juliana, which effectively matched a blue cape bordered by fur that we'd purchased on an outing to Truro, for the planned London visit.

She was throwing sugar lumps to a little monkey in a scarlet coat performing on a barrel organ when a face watching from outside a fortune teller's tent arrested my attention. The face was of a woman's – proud, strong-featured, weather-beaten to a shade of dark parchment, but with a kind of nobility about it. She was not young – nearing the sixties or even more – a gypsy obviously; but not, at that moment, begging, performing, or selling anything. She belonged most probably to the small group of travellers who'd pitched their vans and tents on the fringe of the fair ground.

I stared, with a riot of confused emotions slowly rising in me, and a sense of someone beckoning me from long, long years ago. It was the eyes most of all. The eyes – now slightly sunken – but still luminous with the dark shining quality of moorland pools reflecting violet shadows – that broke the spell of forgetfulness and I remembered.

Rosanna – my sister.

Anyana the beloved.

I'd found her.

I took a step forward, and the shawl fell from her head revealing luxurious dark hair, as yet still only tinged with grey. She smiled with odd sweetness for a woman of her years, and I was about to make a sudden dive through the constricting crowd, when a tug of my coat restrained me, and Frances's high, clear voice cried, 'Papa, there's a play starting over there – at the other side – near the wrestling. Oh, *do* come.'

I paused, and in that brief space, Rosanna, if indeed it was she – and I was sure I was right – retreated and was submerged by the pushing mob of sightseers.

Reluctantly I turned and followed my daughter, knowing that the time was not right in her company, for such a nostalgic reunion of the past and present.

Tomorrow, at dawn however, I would ride over before the group of Romanies moved on. And if they'd left I'd follow and find them. Somehow I had to see my sister again.

*

It was grey but fine the next day when I went to the stables before any of the household were about, and saddled the horse I'd been riding since my arrival at Heatherfield for canters with my daughter.

Elation soared in me, an odd excitement – indicative perhaps for a man of my years well on in the fifties – when I set off at a smart canter, cutting down a side drive, towards the moors from where a track led to the high lane which eventually joined the road to Thalk.

As I had thought probable, most of the fair people were packing up or had already gone when I arrived. But on the fringe of the rough field the gypsy vardoes were still there, half-hidden by a thick copse of trees. There was movement and the smell of cooking and burning wood as I approached after tethering my mount. Dark shawls, a flash of scarlet, and a stream of smoke accompanied by low toned voices and the chatter of children stirred my blood with an odd sense of mystery and familiarity, though I had never in my life had knowledge of these people – the itinerants of a remote and ancient race.

Power and wealth – a gambler's luck, had been my chosen course. And it had paid off. Rosanna's way had been different – her desires of an opposite nature, if indeed the violet-eyed, brown-skinned woman I'd glimpsed the previous night really *had* been Rosanna.

I passed a tent and small van, pushing bushes and protruding branches aside to have a clear view of the encampment. A young boy with a crop of black curls and solemn dark eyes regarded me curiously, then turned away to join a man carrying sticks in one arm, and a sack over his shoulder. He gave me a fleeting look, a curt nod, then cut to the left where a fire burned, surrounded by a number of men and women, young and old – their dark brows lit with flashes of rose gold from the flames. A pot simmered on the burning pile, tended by a fierce-looking old crone whose gaze was not entirely friendly.

All speech subsided when I entered upon the scene. I became aware only of eyes – numerous watchful eyes turned intently upon me. There was the faint jangle of a bracelet and tinkle of earrings at the first movement, followed again by the hushed whispered undertone of conversation in a foreign tongue. Then from the curious interplay of light and shade cast by shadows from flame and smoke, the form of a woman detached itself, and moved in my direction.

She was by no means young. But her back was straight, draped by a black shawl, her stance proud, almost imperious. Beneath the shawl her long skirt glinted scarlet, and there was a flash of gold beneath the plaited coils of her shining hair. As she drew nearer a sudden flare from the kindling fire struck sideways on the fine lines etching her countenance, emphasising also the grey and silver strands of the thinning locks that had once been so luxurious. In youth she had been beautiful. Now she was handsome, carrying herself with the regality of a queen.

She stood facing me, then touched my hand and drew me to a small clearing apart from the rest of the travellers. Looking hard into my eyes she said, 'It *is* you, isn't it? Dominic. My brother?'

I nodded. 'After all this time.' There was a brief pause between us. Then, suddenly, she smiled again, that old sweet radiant smile, and put her arms about me, while I held her close. But only for a moment. After that she drew apart and said, 'Last night I knew. I knew, too—' patting her thin breast, 'something told me, from deep inside my heart, that you would return, if only to say, "Hallo sister".'

'But *why*?' I queried trying to subdue the tumult of my own unexpected emotions, '*why* did you never write or make contact? Just a word, to say you were all right would have meant so much, Rosanna. To all of us.'

She shook her head.

'No. Not all. My mother resented me. Justin always was jealous, because I was Katrina's and not his – and the rest – they weren't *meant* to know, Dominic. They were Pencorrins – all except Drake. Poor – *poor* Drake.'

'So you heard? About the fire?'

'Of course. He was good. I cared for him as much as I could. But love! – ah, yes. I've known love also. And that is why—' She fumbled with her skirt and produced a small object wrapped in cloth. 'There,' she said. 'It is for *you* now; for you to take to that child, that lovely girl of our blood, yours and mine – the one you brought yesterday to the fair. My niece. Yes?' I nodded. 'Then give it to her and let her know of the first

Anyana and Vicomte Louis de Marchère, her love – of whom Katrina and the rest of us were descended. Open it, Dominic, and see for yourself.'

I did as she said, examined the finely-wrought crest, and the words inscribed, then snapped it open, staring at the lovely-painted miniatures portrayed so long ago.

I could hardly believe it at first, but the likenesses, in both cases, were unmistakable – the proud imperious features of de Marchère, and the exquisite beauty of Rosanna, my sister, as she had once been, and to a certain extent had been reborn in my own daughter, Frances.

'Her name was Anyana,' Rosanna continued after a pause, 'and so I chose it to make it mine in ballet. She, too, was a dancer, but of a wilder, different kind – the Flamenco. They fell in love – forbidden love on both sides, and Katrina was the fruit of it.'

She then went on to relate something of her own colourful history – of how she met the Vicomte as a very old man, danced for him, and after meeting his great-nephew by chance the story had been repeated, a passion which she had eventually sacrificed to her career.

'Whether it was a mistake, I do not know,' she said finally. 'Perhaps Nemesis played a part, who can say? But when the accident ended my dancing I knew there was only one way for me to take – the road of wandering Romanies who are also our kin.'

'But why? *Why*, Rosanna?' I queried. 'Why couldn't you have rejoined your *own* family at Heatherfield?'

She shook her head. 'Ah, no. You don't understand. It was over. When Louis died so tragically I knew I had to begin again – as another person belonging to another race. The famous Anyana was no more. I couldn't face being no one – just a shadow, brother dear. I suppose that was the Pencorrin in me.' A faint smile touched her lips momentarily dispelling the years with its sweetness.

I didn't know what to say, and after searching my mind ineffectually, realised there was nothing. She wished to remain forever apart from her childhood and youth, but in handing over the locket to me was offering all that was precious she still had to give.

'It is for the girl, remember,' she emphasised, glancing again at the trinket.

'I shan't forget.'

'A dancer too?'

'Or actress. That's why I'm here. If it hadn't been for that terrible fire at Rookswood I'd not have seen you at the fair, I should have been in London with her, but the tragedy delayed it.'

She bowed her head. 'Of course. Poor Drake. And mama. I'm so sorry; but I can't cry. Tears in me for anyone dried up long ago. And fire at least is a clean death. My Louis, too—' For a fleeting instant she softened, appeared vulnerable. Then she straightened up again and said, 'Go now, brother. That we have seen each other is good; so let it remain as a pleasant memory. Just your secret and mine, and if you choose, the girl's. Yes, tell her. Tell her, too, to follow the path of her choice, but if true love beckons, then let the rest go. Had I done so, then my life now would be very different.'

I reached towards her, offering a brotherly kiss, but she turned away.

'No sentiment, Dominic. The time has passed for that.'

I stood watching as she moved slowly through the shadowed trees towards the half glimpsed group of itinerants. Once she looked back, raised a hand, and said something in a tongue I'd never heard before. Then she was gone.

I never saw her again.

\*

I can't say it was not without a certain sense of relief that a month later, having seen my daughter settled in a suitable hostel for dramatic students in London, and arrangements made for her tuition, I set sail once more for America. The intense drama and tragic happenings of my Cornish stay had been more exhausting to a man of my years than I'd realised at the time; I felt drained, like a character recovering from some kind of nightmare unrelated to the factual realities of life.

Even the thought of facing Isabella didn't annoy or irritate me any more. There'd be reproaches and admonishments, no doubt, but I'd long since learned that a calculated dose of flattery could work wonders on her vain ebullient ego. By the time of my arrival in Boston she might even have become completely adjusted to the loss of one difficult daughter. Frances had always been somewhat of a problem and a thorn in her plump side. And no doubt she had already concocted some believable story to satisfy the gossiping matrons of her select circle. At times her mind could be surprisingly devious.

My calculations proved to be correct.

After the expected preliminary reproaches, she assumed an air of concern for me which I didn't doubt was mostly quite genuine.

'But, honey,' she said, surveying me critically, and tapping my stomach with a conciliatory hand, on our first connubial reunion, 'how *thin* you are. Didn't they feed you properly then, in that far-off wild place? Or was it just plain downright ignorance?'

Eyeing her speculatively, I remarked drily, 'Fretting for you possibly. Thought of that? No. And obviously *you* haven't done any pining.'

She made a face.

'Now that isn't fair, Dominic. What I feel has nothing to do with my weight. As a matter of fact—' She lifted her body to its maximum height revealing all the splendid contours of her fine body to advantage. Yes. She was a very large woman but well proportioned and in no way obese, 'As a matter of fact,' she continued, after a short pause, 'I *have* lost a pound or two, and I *have* missed you.'

She moved to the long pier glass and studied her reflection with a small thoughtful wrinkle between her eyes. She was wearing a flowing wrap that gave a touch of sensuous mystery to the full ripe breasts and plump curving thighs.

'Not bad, really, for my age, am I?' she queried. 'Maybe I *should* go all out for losing a bit, though. Would you like me better? Tell me, honest now. Straight from the shoulder, as you men say.'

The naivety of the question combined with the look of appeal in her blue eyes – one of which was faintly smeared with kohl – tickled not only my sense of humour, but roused in me an upsurge of unexpected affection that quickly turned to desire. God! I thought – what a relief. How pleasant to be freed of drama and death and the high falutin' business of mixed up ancestry and long-dead viscounts and dancers that didn't mean a thing any more.

I touched her shoulder tentatively. The skin was warm and satin-smooth. 'Come on, Bella,' I said, with the other hand releasing the cord of my dressing gown. 'Come to bed. Let's behave like a couple of kids. Let's make love.'

The result was pleasant and gratifying.

I slept better than I had for weeks.

'Gee, honey,' Isabella said when I went down to breakfast the next morning. 'You sure were something last night.'

'If not quite in your celebrated Walt Whitman's class,' I said quirkily.

She made a grimace behind the silver coffee pot.

'Don't be a softie. *He*'s a poet. *You*—' She broke off with a mischievous gleam in her eye, and I decided the smart black satin outfit suited her full figure remarkably well, however ridiculous it might have been considered in London society, or at Brown's.

'Yes? Me?' I queried, as I was meant to.

'You're a *man*,' she said. 'That's different.'

So looked at objectively, the Cornish interlude had added fresh stimulus to my life with Isabella. In time no doubt there'd be periods of boredom and a revival of some of the old irritations. But the present was good, and my aspects in the business world still thriving. Hartley was an old man now, keen-witted as ever, but physically going downhill. Occasionally he presided at board meetings, but merely as a figurehead. I, Dominic Pencorrin, was chairman of the Shipping Line concern, with sons to support me, and likewise of other major enterprises.

I had achieved what I'd aimed for – success and power.

It was strange to realise, on looking back, that Justin's act in kicking me out those years ago, was half-responsible.

Strange, and a little sad.

But to hell with sadness. The dead were dead, and life was for the living.

And that's what I had – *life*!

No man could expect or wish for more.

# V

## Susannah

### 1

My first vivid memory of childhood was being pushed on to the stage to appear as some poor little orphan child in one of the sentimental plays featuring my mother, Frances Levere, who was such a success with late Victorian audiences. I could not have been more than three at the most, and did nothing but stand in front of the footlights with my head bent down and a thumb in my mouth.

I was bare-footed, wearing only a shawl pinned at my neck over a ragged nightdress. Above the murmurs of approval from the audience, I did hear one clear voice shouting, 'What a little darling'. I certainly felt little, but no darling. I disliked the whole silly business because I was not allowed to skip and jump when I wanted to. Mama at that time was always elegant and gracious in the parts she performed like the mother in *Little Lord Fauntleroy*, *East Lynne*, and plays of an even more melodramatic nature. A little later she was persuaded by my father, who was also her manager, to appear in *Lady Windermere's Fan* by Oscar Wilde, which made the name of Frances Levere really famous.

Levere, of course, was not her real name. She had been born Frances Pencorrin, becoming Frances Alan, when she married papa. 'Alan' however was considered too plain for a stage beauty, and Levere sounded a bit French which suited her piquant looks. That's how reviewers and newspapers described her – piquant and lovely, and during the years of my growing up her popularity increased to such an extent that the Prince of Wales himself became one of her admirers, and asked to meet her. She received gifts from him also, and told me once, with a sigh, that if she'd wished he'd have provided a

wonderful cottage for her in the country. I'd heard this after
my papa had died when I was nine years old.

'I was too fond of your father, though,' she'd said half
regretfully. 'How could I so *blatantly* have hurt him? That is
what you must remember *always*, Susannah – to be *kind*. And
have *values*. It's *so* important. Resist any man who tries to
charm you unless you really *love* him. Never be cheap.'

I couldn't help wondering how many men mama had
resisted, or truly loved. For as long as I remembered she'd
always had a number of admirers waiting at her dressing
room door or lingering about outside when we left the
theatre.

Of course, my time with her was limited. During the
mornings I had lessons with a governess, Miss Wilkins, who
travelled about with us when we went on tour. In the afternoon I practised dancing and elocution, and rehearsed for
the varied occasions when I had to appear in a play considered suitable for my youth. Most of these, as I've said
before, were stupid parts that bored me. I really wasn't a very
good actress, not in mama's way at all. But I had a voice, and I
loved prancing about and kicking my heels high, singing the
jolly, perhaps rather common, songs that were beginning to
be popular in music halls.

'I can't understand you, Susannah,' mama said once when
I'd been discovered unexpectedly in our bedroom wearing a
top hat, a boy's jacket and a pair of boots over my bloomers,
singing, 'Oh, Mr Porter', and 'Champagne Charlie', with
great gusto, striding back and forth, in what was, I suppose, a
most unseemly way.

'—I really *can't*,' my poor mother repeated exasperatedly.
'You have the chance of being offered the role of Little Nell
in *The Old Curiosity Shop*, and all you seem interested in is to
waste time making yourself look quite ridiculous. And
*common*.'

'Perhaps I *am* common, a bit,' I said, stopping my cantering
and slumping on the bed breathless and hot-cheeked.

'How *can* you be? You're a Pencorrin.'

'But I'm other things, too. I mean great-grandmama and
*her* descendants – *they* weren't Pencorrins, were they? And
those far off Americans? We're all bits of this and that really,

aren't we? Sort of patchwork pieces.' The idea suddenly seemed so funny, I started to giggle.

Mama gave one of her great sighs. She did an awful lot of sighing; I suppose it was because of all the tragic heroines she used to play.

'It isn't a laughing matter,' she said, with a kind of sad resignation in her voice. 'I'm not so young any more, and I do so *very* much wish to see you make a dignified success of your talents before I die.'

'You're not going to die yet, not for years and years,' I said sturdily – though a little later I was to be proved wrong. 'And if you marry that nice Lord Crowther who's so much in love with you—'

'I'm *not* going to marry Lord Crowther,' my mother interrupted sharply. 'And we were not discussing my future. We were talking of yours.'

'Yes. Well – we don't know, do we? I'm not like you. I haven't your gift. And to look at!' I jumped off the bed to take a quick glance at myself in the mirror. 'I'm not exactly beautiful, am I?'

'No. Not dressed up as a clown. But your colouring is very striking and you have nice legs.'

'I know. But there's no point if I'm not allowed to show them. And my hair! – you call it russet, mama, but really it's just plain dark red and my eyes are so *green*. I wish they were like yours. I wish I were like you altogether.'

'Your dead father had red hair,' mama said, with that certain poignant break in her voice which had so stirred past audiences, 'and *he* was a wonderful man. If he hadn't been so unselfish and such a marvellous manager I'd certainly never have got where I am today.'

'Only because he encouraged you to do what you wanted,' I said rather tactlessly, 'in your own way, and in the parts you liked. But he's not here now, and you want me to act differently to how I feel. Even Ned says I'm a born comic – I mean comedienne.'

Ned Archer was the producer who'd taken mama's stage appearances over when Frank Arnold had retired a year or two following papa's death. He was middle-aged, with a round face and twinkling shrewd eyes that had been watching me closely for some time. Mama generally accepted his judgement because she knew it was sound. But this time she was annoyed.

'He had no business to encourage such ideas in you,' she said coldly.

'He doesn't have to. They're already there!'

'I won't have you talking to me in such a manner,' mama retorted, with a wild rose colour flooding her lovely face. 'Now take off those ridiculous things immediately. And remember, Susannah, you're still only a child, in my care, and entirely dependent on me for support. Unless you behave better, I may have to send you to a convent school where you'll learn good manners and further your education.'

'Wilkins wouldn't like that.'

'Neither would you. So far I've trusted Miss Wilkins to train you in the way I would wish, but I'm beginning to think she hasn't entirely succeeded.'

After that I did try to be more compliant and curb my high spirits. For the next year or two I appeared intermittently in roles that pleased mama, bored me, and made little impact on theatre-goers.

Then, in 1904, when I was fourteen, mama's hansom cab was in collision with a carriage one evening when she was returning from the theatre. The horses reared, and she was killed.

At first, when Wilkie told me, I didn't feel very much at all. It was such a shock. I stared round our handsome London apartment blankly trying to believe that never again would I see mama's graceful figure glide from sitting room to bedroom in her graceful proud way, lovely so lovely in her elegant chiffon and velvet gowns – that I would never more hear her soft, slightly husky, voice chiding or praising me. She was *mama*! – Frances Levere. Famous beauties like her just couldn't suddenly be knocked out of a cab and *killed*. It was too ghastly to comprehend. There'd been a mistake, there must have been, I told Wilkie, when her dreadful words properly registered.

But it was all true. I was left alone, under the joint guardianship of Miss Wilkins and Ned whom she trusted with the paternal raising of her daughter until I was eighteen, and Wilkie domestically.

There was no shortage of money, of course. Frances had

done well in the theatre, and possessed besides a comfortable, if comparatively small income from her late papa, my own grandfather, Dominic, whom I'd never met, but which continued in my name following her death.

Wilkie never entirely approved of Ned, who became a little more lenient in his choice of roles for me than she — and certainly mama — would have been. He was sufficiently astute to realise that my potential was not really as a successful tragedienne or romantic actress, but having a conscience and wishing to follow mama's wishes as much as possible, he was careful never to allow any chance for my displaying down-to-earth rollicking comedy for which I had a talent. I yearned for the music hall — even if it *was*, in Wilkie's words, merely 'a platform for vulgarity which no decent person would visit'.

Once I'd been taken to a show starring Marie Lloyd, when Wilkie was ill and thought I was bound for the Lyceum. The landlady of our apartment, my companion, had enjoyed the subterfuge as much as me, and although I never *directly* told lies to poor Wilkie when I returned, I behaved so well, and answered her questions so demurely and deviously, she never guessed the truth.

Oh, how I'd loved the laughter, the jokes, the singing and clapping and down-to-earth feeling of comradeship. I determined then, that one day, whatever Ned or Wilkie said, I'd appear in Music Hall. In the meantime, I put on a show of doing my best for Ned and acting along the lines mama had wished. But my heart wasn't in it. Ned knew it, even if Wilkie didn't. Anyway, after Wilkie died in 1906, things changed slightly. By then I was simply no draw at the box office of serious drama, and Ned, who was still my guardian until I was eighteen, relaxed in his attitude. 'We'll see — we'll see,' he said a little impatiently following the closing down of a melodramatic show in which I'd been a dismal failure. 'I've a rehearsal on my hands for next week's opening of the Wilde comedy. I want you along with me there, although there's nothing suitable in it for you. But no wasting time, my girl. You just *watch*, take everything in, and try and learn something.'

That's just what I did, and I learned a great deal, but not in the way he wanted.

One evening when Ned was fully occupied I left the Lyceum and made my way to an old-fashioned but still popular playhouse, featuring all kinds of highly colourful and stimulating characters such as jugglers, dancers, red-nosed comedians, illusionists, clowns and singers – oh! every type of entertainment you could think of.

I managed to enveigle myself by a side door into the wings, and there waited, near a stuffy dressing room where girls in pink and blue satin were putting the last dabs of paint and powder on their faces. There was a great deal of low chattering and common talk – yes, it was certainly what mama would have called 'common talk' – going on. But the sense of excitement, of being on the brink of a new experience was exhilarating.

One or two of the girls were already exercising their plump thighs in anticipation of the moment when the stage manager gave his cue from the opposite wings. Others were hastily adjusting their plumed headdresses, and making sure their little tails were properly in the place they were meant to be – at the rear of their glittering tights. The smell of sweat and perfume mingled with the faint odour of beer, smoke and orange from somewhere in the audience though odorous, was heady with atmosphere. A little man hurried among the cramped stuffy interior issuing orders which were instantly obeyed, although a tongue or two came out behind his back. I crouched in the shadows, until the orchestra struck up a tune – I think it was 'The man who broke the bank at Monte Carlo', followed by something newer, heralding the impending jazz era of the new American music. There was a hurried pushing and attempt at order; the next moment the girls were filing on to the stage in single order, kicking their silk legs waist-high as their feathers and little tails bobbed.

I had a wild, ridiculous impulse then – the kind of impulse I always followed – and without a second thought I grabbed a top hat lying conveniently nearby, crammed it on my head at a jaunty angle, hitched up my skirts and rushed – it was almost a leap – on to the stage in *front* of the chorus, and was doing what *I* wanted to do – a kind of comical semi-can-can, flinging my legs about here, there and everywhere, revealing a generous expanse of frilly white bloomers. I must have looked an outrageous sight. But I didn't care. It was marvellous, thrilling, to be doing exactly what I wanted for the first time in my life. I'd pause occasionally, to bow and smile, then take off again, after knocking the hat off, catching it, and replacing it coquettishly at a sideways angle.

Oh, it was fun! – fun for me, especially when the music changed to 'Burlington Bertie'. This was my *real* chance. I was suddenly no longer a mad-cap girl, but the caricature of a swaggering young buck, strolling down the Strand with a wink, and waving an imaginary cane. Not exactly Ella Shields quality, but sufficiently funny to cause a sudden roar of applause from the audience, and wild nods of outraged encouragement from the stage manager at the side.

'Encore! Come on then, let's have it – more, *more*—' the crowd called. And on I went, grinning, kicking, putting all the comedy I was capable of at that time, into my daring stolen act.

Then, in a burst of awareness I realised what I'd done, made a final grotesque bow and bounced off the stage allowing the chorus once more to take over.

There was trouble, of course. But also triumph.

In his hole of an office a few moments later the manager of the theatre confronted me severely saying, 'I suppose you know what a mess you've made of things, girl? Interrupting a perfectly good act by your damned bad manners. Eh?'

He had a large red face with a scowl on it, a beefy-looking nose like a comedian's, and was glaring at me through an eye-glass. Trying not to notice his expression I glanced at the white flower in the lapel of his black coat, and admitted, 'Yes. But it – it worked, didn't it!'

'*Worked*?' he roared. 'Is that all you're going to say? *Worked.* When it meant spoiling the whole performance of those smart girls I'd employed? They were a special act – a *draw*. But you – you had the impertinence, a mere upstart of a youngster, to humiliate and upstage them.'

'Did I? I didn't know. I thought I was rather a success.'

'So you thought that, did you? Well, I'll tell you what *I* think.' He paused before adding, 'You should have had your behind well tanned when you were younger so you'd have learned respect for your betters.'

My face flamed.

'How *dare* you talk to me like that – *me*! Susannah Levere.'

'I don't care what your damn name is, young lady. You've the impudence of old Nick himself, and—' He broke off suddenly, staring. '*What*? What did you say you're called?'

I repeated the name, adding, 'My mother was Frances Levere and she always wanted me to go in for tragedy and straight drama. I knew I was no good though and never would have been. But tonight I *did* prove something: that I could make people laugh, didn't I? They *liked* me, Mr – Mr—?'

'Crew,' he said. 'William Crew. And I happen to be responsible for the good name of this theatre. People pay to see turns that are advertised on the bills outside – not naughty little girls dressed up like clowns with the conceit of the devil in them.'

I fluttered my lashes at him. 'All the same, they wanted more of me,' I pointed out. 'And I'm not *that* young, Mr Crew. I know a lot about the stage too. And if you gave me a chance I could learn more. I could even – perhaps – make your theatre more popular than it is. Because those girls – well, they were good in their way, I suppose, but *their* sort of acts have been done so many times before, haven't they? There's nothing original in it. I am though; I *could* be – if only you'd give me a chance.'

He was quite flabbergasted, of course. But by then I knew he was considering the suggestion, realised also that his vulgar scolding had mostly been bluff. Angry he might be, but the response from the audience had certainly startled him and been something of a shock.

The result of the titillating, if unseemly, interview, was that William Crew got into touch with Ned the next day, and after a good deal of bargaining and assurances that my moral and professional future should be in no way impaired, the two men came to an understanding, the result of which gave me an opportunity under Ned's guidance to prepare for my debut in variety at the end of the next two months.

So it was that I first became involved in the magical world of the Music Hall.

*

After the first shock, Ned had been unexpectedly understanding of my erratic behaviour, even perhaps a little relieved, because it had taken the onus of decision from his shoulders. Even when my mother had been alive he must have realised my dramatic talents were in direct opposition to hers, had even suggested to her tentatively that I did seem to have a great sense of the comic. Frances, of course, backed up by Wilkie, had given him no chance of putting any such talent to the test. With Miss Wilkins' death, however, important decisions concerning my future had been left to him – although I'd determined to go my own way anyhow. Still, it was pleasant to have his backing.

There was one curious incident before I set off, under new management, on my first touring debut.

Before patting my shoulder and giving me a fatherly kiss on the cheek, he handed a small parcel to me, wrapped in tissue paper.

'Your mother left it with me to give you when I thought you were adult enough to appreciate it,' he said. 'It was passed on to her from her father, your grandfather, Dominic, who received it as a gift from his sister, Rosanna, your great-aunt. She was – someone very famous once upon a time. Take it now, there's a letter inside. I'll leave you to read it.'

He left me alone, and with mounting excitement I unwrapped the parcel and stared, fascinated, at the locket containing the two small miniatures. I gasped; the woman's face was so exquisitely beautiful – a little foreign-looking – the man's so proud and aristocratic. It was moments before I perused the letter.

Susannah, my dearest child [the message ran, penned in mama's slanting delicate handwriting] by the time you receive this memento and note I shall be no longer with you – physically. But spiritually I like to think something of me may be very near you. I am placing the locket with Ned, because I know I can trust him to see that you, and you alone, receive it. If anything happens to him in the meantime, he is making certain safe arrangements for the heirloom to be delivered to you. And it *is* an heirloom, Susannah. The portraits so finely depicted are of your far-off ancestors, Louis de Marchère and Anyana, a Romany dancer, who became his love. Incidentally, the

Prima Ballerina of more recent times, the *famous* Anyana, was in reality your great-aunt – the Rosanna referred to. I could have revealed the connection at the start of my career, of course. It would have been an immediate step to fame. But I respected the wishes of Rosanna for secrecy, and in any case I was sufficiently proud and independent enough to wish to make my own name.

Keep it safely, my darling. I happen to be superstitious enough to believe it holds some special quality which may influence your life, and hopefully be of some protection. I dearly hope also that you will do your best to follow the traditions of the theatre I have done my best to support. But if, in the end, your wishes take you in another direction, I ask only that you remain true to yourself, and never resort to anything cheap or second-rate in life. That is important.

My love to you.

Your mother, Frances Pencorrin Alan.'

My heart was beating quickly as I put the letter down. I could feel a lump in my throat, and the threat of tears very near my eyes. With the precious relic clasped tightly in a hot hand I clutched it to my breast making an inward vow to cherish it carefully all my life, and whenever possible wear it.

*

So a new era started for me – years of success which involved a good deal of touring about the country, especially the north and midlands, working off steam both physically and mentally – concocting and putting fresh acts before appreciative audiences who nicknamed me 'Sunshine Susie', by which title I was eventually billed. In 1908 I married Willie Vernon, a truly fantastic comedian, who partnered me in a new turn containing a good deal of comical miming and a funny song that gave me a chance to display any vocal abilities I possessed. It was a roaring success, and following a night in Birmingham, Willie proposed.

I was flattered and excited, on the brink of considerable fame myself, but not yet of his quality. He had been a marvellous friend to me for years, I liked him, and knew he'd take good care of me. He was almost twice my age, but that didn't seem to matter. The one important love affair I'd previously had with a handsome young juggler had failed and left me feeling downcast and rejected emotionally. There was no reason for this really – I knew I was pert-looking with my reddish-brown hair and green eyes and that men liked me. But Frankie Banes had touched my heart, and I'd determined never to be hurt again. I could trust Willie not to do that. What I didn't realise at the time was my own deep-rooted capacity for passion and loving – a passion that Vernon would never be able to reciprocate or fulfil. That our marriage failed wasn't his fault. He'd never pretended to be a romantic – any effort on his part would have been futile; he was, even off the stage, a whimsical-looking character with no pretensions to good looks, a small man with sandy hair, a long nose, and an endearing but funny one-sided smile.

Our marriage night, despite his efforts at flattery and attempts to establish a connubial relationship was a dismal failure. I'd chosen, with all the excitement of a young bride-to-be, to wear an ethereal-looking pale greenish-blue nightdress and negligée for my debut as a wife, thinking, stupidly, that at his first glimpse of me with my shining thick hair romantically loose about my shoulders, and subdued lighting emphasing the slender but enticing curves of my figure, he would somehow magically be transformed from quaint Willie Vernon into some typical gallant but forceful lover so frequently portrayed in fiction.

But such miracles unfortunately do not happen.

My disillusionment was complete.

He tried so hard I could have screamed.

In the end, following the undignified procedure of fumbling and athletic contortions on the hotel bed which had been lushly prepared with pink silk sheets to honour the occasion, I suddenly managed to free myself from Willie's ineffectual advances and leap to the floor, while he sat up shamefacedly buttoning up his nightshirt.

'I'm sorry,' I apologised, masking my fury and embarrassment under a veneer of comradely understanding. 'We're too tired tonight. Maybe it'll be all right next time.'

But next time it was worse.

And at the end of the week we both accepted that fond as we

were of each other as friends and stage partners, the private husband-and-wife business was just not possible.

Oh, perhaps put like that I sound hard and unfeeling. But I wasn't. I just felt too much – not for Willie – but for something that had lingered in me even since my break with the juggler, Frankie Banes – something that told me life could hold more – *far* more than a sterile marriage and just pirouetting and prancing before the footlights – something that unconsciously had been slowly deepening in me since Ned had given me my mother's locket. And it wasn't only physical; it was a knowledge that comprised a whole new word – an awareness of places and people my hitherto one-track mind had been far too busy even to contemplate. It was also the shock of having to accept the true complex emotional depths of my own personality.

I wanted love; of course I did. 'Sunshine Susie' was merely a facet – one side of the whole me. A stepping-stone of youth leading to – where?

Frequently, as the days passed, the question would rise to bewilder and frustrate me in my few leisure moments; whatever the answer proved ultimately to be, I knew it was not life with Willie. He began to bore me utterly. Even our dual act had lost its savour for me, although I still put the best I knew into our comical façade together.

At last, after a particularly tiring season in the midlands, I told him frankly I wanted a divorce. He was standing before the mirror of our bedroom in a dreary theatrical boarding establishment wiping a few faint traces of make-up from his face when I announced my decision, coolly, practically, just as though I was asking for a cup of tea.

At first he didn't appear to take in what I'd said; his pale ageing face with the slightly red-rimmed eyes was concentrated entirely on examining his lean reflection which was faintly blue-ish about the lantern jaws.

'Well?' I said impatiently. 'Did you hear what I said, Willie?'

'Sorry,' he muttered, putting the handkerchief down and turning. 'What was it then? Anything important?'

'Yes,' I emphasised, trying hard not to sound exasperated but anxious now the point had come to get the subject settled once and for all. 'I want a *divorce*. You and me. I'm *serious*.

Don't look like that. You know yourself it's no good. Ours is not a *marriage*, Willie — it's a — a—' I broke off, aware suddenly my statement was ill-timed and too blunt.

'*Yes?*'

I shrugged to think out an acceptable answer — say something that wouldn't hurt his pride.

'Well — a *stage* partnership. You're wonderful at that, but—'

'A failure in bed. A bloody cissy. Is that what you're trying to tell me?' His voice was bitter; a voice I'd never heard from him before, and I could see he was shaking.

'*No,*' I lied. 'I would never think of you that way. But — but you *are* so much older, Willie. You've been good to me, I know that, too. *Too* good. I'm not worth fretting about. Please try and understand. And don't think I'm not grateful, I am. But—'

'Grateful for making you a star when before you were just a saucy little nobody with get-rich-quick ideas. Oh, yes, I understand all right. I'm not a fool. However, if you're bent on this insane idea don't think I'll make it easy for you. I won't. If you take my advice you'll have a good think to find out exactly where you really stand. In any divorce between you and me, you'll take the blame. I'll see to that—'

'You'd have no evidence.'

'No?' His sandy eyebrows shot up. 'I'd soon find some, mark my words. There's many a man'd be proud to be sued for the publicity of being in on an adultery act with "Sunshine Susie". I've good friends, girl. You just remember that. And the public don't like money-grabbing little tarts — not your public and mine. They're *moral*, girl. Respectable middle and working-class folks mostly, who don't appreciate cuckolds or whores. You've got some way to go yet before you reach the randy high-ups, and by God I'll see you never do unless you behave properly and forget this stuff and nonsense. *Divorce.* You must want your head examining.'

Oh! I was suddenly so disgusted I flung on a coat and walked straight out of the bedroom into the grey city street so I could draw the cold air, however damp and smoky, into my lungs.

Freedom, I thought, I must have freedom and release. After that unpleasant threatening tirade from a man I'd always before looked upon with at least liking and respect, I knew I couldn't possibly continue working with Willie Vernon.

I must be on my own.

*Myself*. But how?

All that night I walked the streets in a whirl of mixed emotions and misery. The scene was depressing and dreary, and despite the slow crawl of traffic through the smog, the blurred lights of night cafés and clatter of wheels and horses hooves, loneliness engulfed me. I had never felt so lonely before – not even following mama's death. Occasionally, like the muted sound of a distant fog-horn, the toot of one of the new motor-car signals merged with the rest. As the mist turned to thin rain, street-girls huddled into their coats, waiting hopefully at corners or recognisable areas of their own individual 'patches'. Occasionally there was a giggle, a flash of plump net legs through the light of a cab as a man hailed a vehicle to stop and assisted the girl in.

A bedraggled bent hag of an old woman approached me with a leer – claw-like hand extended in a begging gesture. I pushed her away automatically and hurried on, knowing that she might in reality be some avaricious male in disguise – on the watch perhaps for prey concerning his filthy trade of white slave traffic. I'd long since heard of such things – life in a touring company meant a certain knowledge of the seamier side of existence, although I'd had no threat of such things, myself, always being certain of company, either Willie's or some other friend's on my journeys to and from the theatre.

Willie.

Poor, *poor* Willie. As my first anger abated, I realised his threats must have been mostly bluff caused by shame and acute distress that I wished to end our relationship. When he *knew* – really accepted – that I'd meant what I'd said, he'd give in as gracefully as possible and see matters were settled in a civilised fashion. I didn't *really* belong to his world – and this was a fact I'd been half-consciously facing for quite some time. Music hall had played an important part in my life – had been the first great challenge to face. But it was only a step.

The rest?

Sitting in a small, ill-lighted cafe sipping a cup of tea – tired but mentally alert as one often can be in the throes of physical weariness, I faced the blunt truth.

Something very important was missing.

I needed new experience in a different environment; some place to relax in and be at peace for a time; not just doing nothing – that would be intolerable, one might as well be dead, but discovering a purpose that could be exciting, stimulating in a way that meant fresh adventure every day, yet real and enduring.

Roots. Yes, astonishing as it may sound, I wanted roots. Roots to expand and grow into a pattern of rich life like those of some lovely spreading tree. It was odd that such thoughts should occur to me behind beaded curtains in a misty dreary café at two o'clock in the morning, although it was natural I suppose to long for fresh air and other sounds than those of intermittent chatter and passing traffic down a sombre city street, but I started wondering about my family that had once lived in far-away Cornwall. It had seemed odd, that when I was younger, mama hadn't visited or taken me there. In the past I'd suggested it more than once, but she'd always replied her stage commitments gave her no time to go on futile visits to such out-of-the-way places. 'It isn't as if anyone *wants* us,' she'd told me, when her fame was at its height. 'If your Uncle Jason hadn't been killed in the Boer War, I might have considered it. But Aunt Elizabeth is a stuffy, proud kind of woman, and very old now. I only met her once, and that was sufficient. Juliana was different. Rather shy and airy-fairy, but I liked her. She wasn't *really* Jason's mother, you know. He was adopted. Anyway she's dead too now, and there's no one left of our family.'

'Oh, I see. Still—'

'There's no point in thinking about the Pencorrins, darling,' my mama said in practical unemotional tones. 'One day, perhaps, when I've retired – if I ever do – we'll have a trip together to Heatherfield. But I'm sure you'd find it rather dull.'

Not long after that conversation I'd learned that Aunt Elizabeth, Drake's widow, had left Cornwall and gone abroad somewhere to live.

'She's a rich woman in her own right,' mama had said vaguely, 'but quite probably she'll sell the estate now.'

Mama's prediction proved to be incorrect. I'd heard, following correspondence between lawyers and Frances, that the house and lands had been bequeathed legally to certain authorities for some sort of an historical museum dealing with that certain part of Cornwall.

'So all that remains of the Pencorrin inheritance now is one piece of ground covering a few acres some ten miles or so away from Heatherfield that once belonged to your great grand-father Justin,' mama had stated abstractedly. 'There was a house there once, Rookswood, that was burned down. It had been left by Justin to Juliana, Jason's mother, and strangely enough now becomes yours.'

'*Mine?*'

Mama had smiled. 'Yes. It's a romantic thought, isn't it? But not much more. Just a rambling piece of moorland overlook-ing the coast. Probably completely unfrequented except by sheep and an occasional eccentric or artist wanting loneliness and quiet.'

'Just a rambling piece of moorland.' The words returned to my mind as I sat stirring my cup watching the shadowed shapes pass the steamy window outside in the street. I could picture it in my imagination, and because I was more exhausted than I realised probably, I had a sudden wild urge to leave the problems of my life with Willie far behind and say goodbye to stage life for good – to make my way to Paddington Station and get on the first available train bound for the remote South West where those few acres of ground waited that were my own.

The idea at that point, of course, was quite impractical. I couldn't just run away and hide, letting down not only my audiences and contracts with theatre managers, but friends as well like Ned who'd helped me along the road to success. No, I couldn't. That wasn't me. What arrangements and arguments concerning my future life there had to be, must be faced openly and if possible in a decent friendly way. Only one thing was certain – I had no intention of spending the rest of my days as Mrs Willie Vernon. I was as firm on that as Mrs Pankhurst was on obtaining votes for women – the current movement now that was causing such unrest and political turmoil in the country.

If I had to, I too would fight. For the moment though I couldn't decide the proper way to do it. It wasn't as though I still didn't enjoy the excitement and thrills of 'Sunshine Susie's' life. I *did*. I couldn't picture existence entirely without the warm feeling of being loved by an appreciative public. But beyond that was something else – something my senses and heart yearned for – to be adored and taken in passion by just one man – someone exciting somewhere in the world whom I'd recognise instantly when we met, and know with a leap of the heart that this was *he* – the one person on earth with the power and magic to overcome all other conflicting ambitions I had, and claim me for myself.

My lover.

My mate.

I'd no idea what he'd look like. Even in moments of secret and tormenting longing I couldn't visualise his face. But he'd be strong, and – and – at such a point in my imaginings I'd generally break off saying to myself, 'You are a goose, Susannah. Just a melodramatic sentimental copy-cat out of a paper novelette. Buck up now. Be your age. Write a song about it if you like. But for God's sake *laugh*.'

Oh, I'd generally managed to. I had such a lot of laughter in me; but during the days after my return to the theatre following that night of street wandering, much of the laughter seemed to be drying up. It wasn't only Willie and the fact that he still stubbornly refused to consider any civilised way of ending our mockery of a marriage, but a general sense of oppression and gradual deepening awareness that all was not well with Europe. Clouds of approaching war ahead, though sensed by many, were still ridiculed by the masses and public opinion. But a shadowed sense of uncertainty remained.

Edward VII, however, deviously, had succeeded in establishing and retaining an apparently friendly association with his neighbours. Following his death, however, and the accession of George V to the throne, things seemed to be changing. There were great festivities through the land for the coronation – parties, fireworks, and fairs in country districts where there was generally a greasy pole for youngsters to climb.

Something good had gone, but something new and stimulating despite the deepening cloud abroad, was starting. So we *thought*! – little dreaming of the actual holocaust ahead.

*War.*

On 23rd August 1914, Britain, under its commander Sir John French, fought its first battle against Germany on the Franco-Belgian border in reprisal for Germany's invasion of Belgium. I was then twenty-four years old.

'It will soon be over now,' was the general comment following Britain's victory. 'Give it a few months, perhaps weeks even, and we'll be at peace again.'

But peace didn't come easily. Bitterness and tragedy inevitably replaced the light-hearted optimism first expressed by word of mouth and in the press. The façade and false sense of chivalry festered in women's hearts when their husbands and sons left home for bloody trenches, death, or possibly to be gassed or imprisoned for life, faded in the face of reality.

> If I should die, think only this of me;
> That there's some corner of a foreign field
> That is forever England . . .

Fine words, from an idealistic poet, Rupert Brooke. But of little use to the millions of bereaved.

To counteract the bloodshed and the loss, the theatre itself sturdily tried to infuse additional patriotism and further comic relief into the minds and hearts of audiences. The press, too, had its lighter moments. There was the cartoonist, Bruce Bairnsfather who depicted a cartoon with two comical military heads bobbing out of holes on a battlefield, one saying to the other – 'Well, if you knows of a better 'ole – go to it.'

From the pulpit 'Woodbine Willie', a quaint looking, tremendously vital and magnetic padre, preached in strong downright language unheard of before by church congregations, and on the battlefield, instilling a sense of comradeship and hope to civilian and soldier alike. His was a message of 'togetherness' so strong, that all physical and spiritual barriers were swept away in a wave of courage and determination somehow to survive. Later he was to become a legend – a legend of fortitude and respect.

As the days passed, women became involved in all aspects of war work – on the land, in factories, forces, and nurses, VADS. There were blackouts at night; German planes, and Zeppelins flying like gigantic silver fish carrying their loads of destruction.

And everywhere, in the streets, tubes, on factory walls and on buses, were posters of Kitchener beckoning all fit men to do their duty.

Hospitals became crowded with the wounded. Frequently during the daytime individual members of theatrical companies visited convalescent homes to provide an hour or so of amusement to men without sight or use of limbs – gassed men – the scarred and burned; shell-shocked relics to whom life would never be the same again.

Willie and I patched up our long disagreement occasionally to appear together – he had at last agreed to the divorce and the legal business was in hand.

Mostly, though, any hospital visits were on my own.

As Sunshine Susie I believe I really *did* manage to bring a little light-heartedness to the grimness of reality. But the strain was taking its toll.

Many things at that period – springs of my being hitherto untouched – came to life painfully, and I knew that when peace came – if ever – I could never again spend my days as a mere prancing 'funny girl' before the footlights.

All that would be over.

For what? I did not know.

There was no time to think or plan for the future that might never come.

But in my tired dreams sometimes I saw an imagined piece of moorland stretching to a quiet sea. The tormented nightmare faces of young scarred men, faded gradually into sunlit acres of moorland lit by the small pale faces of flowers among thrusting fern. And I'd long then – long in my sleep to be there. But when I woke it was to the rattle of wartime Britain and the shrill voices of newsboys calling down busy streets of the latest victory or defeat.

I knew then that I must go on for the time being as I was.

Sunshine Susie – comedienne, nurse, and at hand always for any other task that came along. Yes. It was a busy life, exhausting, tireless even when one was too tired to sleep. But like all the rest I managed, knowing how much worse it was for all those millions of poor boys suffering and dying in blood-spattered trenches. The nurses out there, too. Oh, yes – compared with many I was lucky.

And in 1917 when I was twenty-seven years old, I met Philippe.

## 2

I remember that afternoon so well – a soft summer afternoon, windless, but with a heat haze lingering over the lush West Country where I'd been giving a solo turn of short light-hearted episodes and miming, meant to cheer the inmates of a sanatorium for the wounded.

I had to be back in Bristol for an evening show, and was already feeling tired. The sickness I'd seen had oppressed me, though I'd tried not to show it – the sense of hopelessness enlightened only by false smiles and brief enforced façades of optimism on the faces of the men – mostly young – lying immobile and defenceless in the long ward. Those certain quarters for convalescence had been converted from a stately country residence where once peacocks had strutted about velvet lawns, and well-tended paths had wound between pergolas, rose gardens and pools. Now weeds entangled the feet of stone statues – the box hedges were going their own ways, untended except for one gardener and help from patients well enough to give assistance. This latter was encouraged as therapy – an interest, the doctors said, to help reduce the pain and nightmare memories of minds shocked by the terrors enforced upon them.

I had grown used to seeing an occasional blue-clad figure clipping at branches, or weeding the soil as I passed on my way to the car waiting for me at the drive gates. These were the most hopeful cases – the ones expected to face life again one day, comparatively sound mentally and physically.

Often greetings were exchanged, with perhaps a following brief chat before I went on. But that afternoon I hoped for no encounter, feeling uncharacteristically depressed. The sky was beginning to lower, sending an ominous roll of thunder from the distance. There was no other sound but the faint rustle of a bird from the bushes. In a field beyond the grounds cattle were already moving slowly towards the hedges. Soon rain would fall, I thought, and then maybe the air would freshen and give energy to all so desperately needing it – the military, the nurses, patients, workers, and civilians like myself who nevertheless were all an integral part of the war machine.

I stopped for a moment to wipe the perspiration coursing in a stream from my forehead threatening to make a bizarre pattern of any make-up left on my face; and it was then, round a bend of the path that a figure wearing the usual hospital blue uniform, appeared unexpectedly, to stand perfectly still confronting me. His eyes were watchful, with a curious glazed look about them. He was not shaking, as so many of the shell-shocked inmates did, but there was something about his absolute rigidity that was unnerving.

I made the effort to smile, and after a brief pause said in my cheery Sunshine Susie voice, 'Glad to see you about. Do you like gardening?'

He didn't speak. I moved ahead, but he planted himself before me – he was very tall – with still no flicker of expression on his countenance. He was young, I suppose, and under normal circumstances would have appeared almost boyish had it not been for the blankness, the frozen set of his features under his thatch of crisply curly brown hair. I tried to think of something to say – anything to dispel the strain that held us there like two automatons under the shaded trees.

'It's a – it's been a nice day,' I remarked at last ineffectually. 'Were you – were you at the – at my show? I didn't see you. Well—' I swallowed hard, and smiled nervously. 'You didn't miss much.'

Still he didn't speak, didn't even move. I glanced sideways, wondering if by a quick gesture I could slip by and hurry to the car. But he forestalled me by lifting an arm like the jerky wooden arm of a puppet in a play, and almost simultaneously a loud threatening roll of thunder broke the silence of the waiting garden. He laughed then – terrified and terrifying laughter that had madness in it. His head was lifted, with the face a contorted grimace of chattering teeth. I made a dive to escape, but quick as the lightning zig-zagging from the angry sky, he lunged forward with his two hands at my throat. I screamed and screamed. He released me, tottered back, then approached again, back bent in an almost crouching position, the right arm extended in the murderous attitude of a sniper in attack.

I turned and ran; ran blindly through the bushes knowing in those few seconds a glimmer of the fear millions must have been feeling on the war-torn battlefield.

'Oh God—' I cried, 'dear God – help – help—' or maybe the words never registered, everything seemed closing in upon me like a vast cloud of horror – the air, the increasing thunder, the intermittent shouts of the poor crazed creature on my heels. At a corner of the path I stumbled, gasping, for want of breath. The ground seemed to be slipping away; the sky lowered, receded to darkness, then lifted again as something strong and tangible caught me back and my two feet found firm ground.

'It's all right,' I heard a voice saying. 'You're safe – wait there a moment. It's only Jimmy—'

I wanted to cry, 'Don't leave me'. But the words never left my lips. Instead, leaning against a tree, I watched the man, also wearing the hospital blue, make his way steadily on crutches towards the poor wreck of broken humanity. He was slumped down by a rose bush, with his head in his hands; foam spattered his lips and chin, and he was shaking violently between the intermittent fits of moaning and sobbing.

Ashamed of my weakness I made my way back to the scene. 'Is there anything I can do?' I enquired feebly. 'I'm sorry. I shouldn't have run. But I – I—'

The patient with the crutches shook his head. 'You weren't to blame. It was a shock for you. And there's nothing, thanks. Jimmy will be all right; it was the thunder, wasn't it, old chap?'

He had helped the other man to his feet, and had one arm round him while he steadied himself with a crutch under the other.

'The b-bloody war – that's what it was—' came the reply in slurred but good educated English. 'The timing was wrong. And it was me – had to go you see – lead 'em all – over the top – responsible. Oh! bloody hell!—'

It was as though the stricken eyes saw me for the first time. His face then appeared really young. Young and tired; oh, so tired. The muscles were still twitching but the glazed stare was gone. 'I *do* apol-apologise—' he continued. 'Great Scott! – what a bastard I am.'

He made an effort to stem the stream of tears and sweat, helped by the soothing presence of his companion.

'Come on, Jimmy, old pal, we'll get back to the house.'

My rescuer looked me straight in the face and in that instant something stirred in me that I'd never felt before. Recognition? Not exactly. How could one recognise another individual one had never contacted before? No. It was stronger than recognition, and far, far more bewildering and exciting; knowledge; a deep truth springing from roots lying dormant hitherto in my deepest being – and I sensed instinctively – in his.

I smiled. I couldn't help it, and held out my hand. With the crutch firmly under his armpit, he reached out and held it as the communication flowed between us, blossoming from the wilds of tragedy, like a scarlet flower on a rubbish dump.

A line from *The Song of Solomon* rushed willy-nilly through my brain – 'Oh, my beloved is fair—' and fair indeed he was, fair as sunlight over cornfields on a summer's morning in peacetime. Not in physical colouring – his hair was dark almost as ebony, but his eyes were blue, clear, direct eyes that despite the monstrosities he must have witnessed still searched and saw beyond – to the skies and deep, deep into my heart.

The conversation between us on that first occasion was brief; he had to take his pathetic friend back to the house. But during the short time I learned that his name was Philippe – Philippe Marne – that his father had been Breton and his mother English.

'We shall meet again,' he said, before we parted.

There was no question. It was a statement.

'Yes,' I answered. 'Oh, yes, of course.'

And that was how it began.

\*

During the fortnight I was in the vicinity we managed to meet most days, although the strain on my time and energy with evening shows at the threatre every evening, frequently matinees, air raids and blackouts at night, and any other voluntary jobs that came along, made regular sick visits almost an impossibility. Whenever there was a chance, however, I dashed out in the small Ford for a precious hour or half-hour with Philippe before setting off again for the city. Naturally I had to spend some part of that period chatting to others – including poor Jimmy who had been put under stronger sedation to steady his nerves. Along with Philippe he'd been wounded and shell-shocked in the terrible Somme battle in which there had been so many casualties. Philippe thought it unlikely that Jimmy would ever completely recover.

'He's just nineteen years old,' he told me one day. 'And though they may patch him up physically, what he's seen's enough to affect him all his life.' He paused before adding, 'Poor young devil. What price *war*!' For a moment the blue eyes clouded, staring far beyond me into things I'd been spared the sight of. Then he quoted quietly, almost as from a dream—

I am the enemy you killed, my friend.
I knew you in this dark; for so you frowned
Yesterday through me as you jabbed and killed
I parried; but my hands were loth and cold.
Let us sleep now . . .

I said nothing. And after a moment Philippe continued.
'Wilfred Owen. I knew him on the Western Front.'
His voice was so sad, I said, 'Try not to think back, Philippe. And I—'
He pulled himself back to the world again; an arm slipped round me, firm, strong, despite his weakness. We were standing in the garden hidden by a belt of trees clustered round a small pool. Goldfish darted there. The air was warm, although it was autumn. The heady scent of fallen leaves and rich earth seemed to hold a promise beyond all present anguish. I wanted Philippe desperately to feel the same. But then it was different for him. And in any case I'd always been an optimist, believing, irrationally perhaps, that hope and happiness were what we were born for. And sometimes – we had to laugh.
So I ended the distressing and over-serious conversation by

pulling a yellow leaf from a tree and tickling his cheek with it.

'Smile, Philippe Marne, please,' I begged. 'Smile please, for me.'

He looked down on me, and his lips for the first time were on my cheek, then my mouth. How long that kiss lasted I do not know. My eyes closed. All I wanted was to feel the sweet hungry contact for as long as possible, forgetting wounded and helpless things – tormented minds and bodies and the ugly things men did to men. All I wanted was to feel this one man's body close, and his heart thumping against mine as desire flowed through us.

Oh, but how soon it was over. How quickly it came – the stiffening of his being against the natural impulse of life – the cold jolt to reality as he said, 'You mustn't, Susannah. It's no use, my darling. I love you—'

'And I love *you*—'

'But it's no good. When I recover – *if* I do, and it's hardly likely with this damned leg – I shall be back out there again, in the trenches, that hell. If I don't the odds are I'll be incapable of doing a man's job.'

'But—'

'It's *this*,' he said, tapping the right side of his chest. 'My lung. Darling—'

'*Yes?*' I demanded stubbornly. 'Go on, what about it? You have a bad leg and a poor lung. So do others I expect, *thousands*. That doesn't mean to say they'll be wiped off as useless members of the community. And the war won't go on for ever—'

'Neither will this lung, unless they're clever enough somehow to get the bullet out.'

'They will do. Anyway, what's a bullet?'

He smiled then. 'You're so incorrigibly resilient, Susie. And in a way – so naive.'

'No, I'm not at all naive. But I know what I want, and I think – I'm sure *you* do. If you love me—'

'If – *if*—' He shook his head slowly, wonderingly. 'That's a stupid thing to say. When we *both* know. But my dearest girl, face it. You still have everything before you. Whereas I—'

'Yes? Tell me about yourself. You never really have yet,' I

interrupted, 'not about your family except the French and English bit – but nothing about your plans, the job you did, and what you *want* to do in the future.'

After a few devious remarks and arguments Philippe eventually gave me a rough history. How he'd been born in Brittany where his grandparents had had a large and prosperous farm. His father had continued with the estate after they'd died, but he had been killed in an accident when young Philippe was only three years' old. His mother, who came of a scholastic family in Oxford, had returned to the family home with her son, and then young Philippe had been brought up in the conventional style, going to Rugby school, followed by University at Cambridge. He'd taken a degree in languages, 'Not a very brilliant one, I'm afraid,' he said, 'but sufficient to get me a place as tutor in a decent school. But my heart was never in it. Then my mother – the last of my family, had a serious operation from which she never recovered. This was a year or two before the war. I sold the home for what was termed 'a song', wanting the money, because, strange as it seemed – she'd always lived well – all her capital had been gone on an annuity, and the property was all she *did* have.'

'Oh. I see.'

'I didn't want to continue teaching. It wasn't really my cup of tea – I suppose there was more of my father in me than I'd realised and deep down I had a hankering – a yen for the outdoor life. Well, that's the state of mind I was in when war was declared. As it happened everything was settled for me. Here I am! – a "wounded hero" as they like to call it, with millions of other "heroes", far luckier than most, though, with a bit of cash in the bank, but not a chance in hell of any normal future.'

'That's a depressing remark,' I said, 'that last bit – about the future. And not like you.'

He made a grimace. 'How do *you* know? You've really not the slightest inkling of what I really *am* like. I can be quite a moody bloke – selfish, arrogant – oh, yes, Mrs Vernon. Believe me, my faults are many, and frequently unlivable with.' There was a pause. I didn't look at him, but could feel his eyes upon me, as though probing, waiting for my reaction.

'Then I'm sorry for you,' I said tartly, 'and you should make an attempt to come to terms, shouldn't you?'

'What with?'

'Yourself, and other people. Oh – I'm sorry, I'd no right to say that. Another thing—'

'Yes?'

'I'd rather you didn't call me Mrs Vernon.'

'You *are*, though, unfortunately, aren't you? I have to – we must keep things in perspective. Anyway, perhaps it's as well—'

I turned round on him in a flash. 'How *dare* you say that – that it's as well? I thought you cared. I thought—'

'I *do*. You know damn well I do. But I've nothing to offer. Last night I was thinking about it—'

'And so was I. Not only last night, but every moment of the day when I had breathing space from being hearty, jolly, rollicking Sunshine Susie – servant of all, the comic, nurse, entertainer and soother of the sick rolled into one! – Do you know what it's like to be *me*? Of course you don't. As for Mrs *Vernon*—' my voice quickened, 'she doesn't exist any more.'

'What do you mean?'

'My divorce came through. Yesterday.'

'Oh.'

'Is that all you can say, Philippe? Just "oh"?'

He shook his head slowly. '*Words* my love. A scrap of paper – do they really make so much difference? Facts remain. The fact that I'm—'

'Tired and hurt and not yet recovered from the shock of all you've gone through,' I interrupted. 'I understand that. But—' a sense of despair of uncontrollable emotion surged through me, '—but don't you mind enough to believe it will pass, Philippe? Can't you give me hope that things can be right for us? I need love so much. *Your* love. Oh, please – *please*—' I could feel tears thicken in my throat and flood my eyes. I put up a hand to wipe the moisture from a cheek, and felt Philippe's cover it. 'Don't, darling. Please *don't*—' His voice was warm again and there, in the small hidden space of the garden we'd made our own, he took me into his arms.

'It's all right—' I heard him saying. 'Yes, yes, I believe you. In the end, somehow it will work out. My God, Susie – when

I'm strong enough, when I'm *really* a man again, I'll show you what love is – and be damned to this old leg.'

'You don't have to *prove* it,' I told him. 'Just be what you feel. Don't let pride spoil things. I'm not a child, Philippe, my darling – I'm nearer thirty than twenty. But when you've recovered – and you *will* recover – there's still time for us to have a lifetime ahead—' I broke off as he loosened his hold of me and stroked a strand of hair from my forehead. Then, with his very blue eyes on my face – more blue than summer skies, or the deep seas I'd imagined often breaking gently on faraway Cornish shores, he said with a sorrowing kind of longing in his voice – 'You're such an optimist, Susannah – unbeatable and brave, and so very young, despite your tremendous years. Nothing has hardened you, has it? Not yet. Pray God it never will. But me – I'm—'

'*You*,' I told him fiercely. 'Just *you*; that's what you are – the only man I want or ever will. So—' I glanced up at him smiling wickedly, though my eyes were moist, 'Shut up, will you, and kiss me again.'

He did; a long, hungry kiss holding such sweetness and passion I would gladly have drowned in it. It was as though all the life of my being was drawn into his, leaving time and circumstance obliterated. Had he asked everything of me at that moment I couldn't have denied him. But the contact was broken by the sound of voices borne on a rising breeze from the house.

We drew apart, with trembling hands still linked. 'You're a terrible girl, Susannah,' he said, in fake light-hearted tones. 'Has anyone ever told you before?'

'Oh, yes,' I replied. 'Lots. As I said – I'm not a child. I'm a sophisticated hard-to-get woman of the world. It just happens that I – that I've never been in love before.'

'And Vernon?'

'He was a father-figure, I suppose. I don't know. You see, my own father died when I was young, and I hadn't anyone else but mama. *She* was married to the stage really. And my grandparents, well I never knew them at all. Grandfather Dominic used to write from America, but he never got round to visiting Britain after his mother died in an awful fire—'

From that point I went on to describe some of the Pencorrin

family incidents that had been related to me by my mother, including the pendant and letter handed to me by Ned shortly before my first proper appearance in music hall. I told him also of the patch of land I owned where Rookswood had once stood before its destruction, and where my great grandfather Justin had spent his last days.

'It all sounds rather melodramatic and complicated,' I concluded. The exciting part, of course, is that Anyana, the famous dancer, should have been my great aunt. And the French bit, too. That's odd, isn't it? That we've both got a bit of French in us?'

'My father was Breton,' Philippe pointed out. 'Quite a different kettle of fish.'

I shrugged. 'Oh, well! It's all the same to me. But the land—'

'What about it?'

'Let us go there one day,' I said, 'and have a look at it. You never know – you said you had a yen or something for the out-of-door life. Well, maybe—' at that point my imagination went zig-zagging about in all directions, ending in the thought – 'why not? Why shouldn't Philippe and I claim it properly and live there one day?' I was too wise to put the suggestion into words at that moment, but decided at the first proper opportunity, when the time and the place were suitable, I would.

As the days passed hospitals and homes became more selective and specialised in the type of wounded cases sent to them for treatment. The shell-shocked and gassed were no longer so intermingled with straightforward convalescents like Philippe. It was inevitable that our meetings became less frequent, as I was on tour for much of the time. But there was never a week when letters weren't passed between us. The mistaken idealism that had fired the country and sent fervent young men to the trenches was relentlessly becoming outworn, replaced by increasing disillusionment. Paul Nash, the artist, who served with the Artists Rifles in France, wrote, 'I am no longer an artist interested and curious. I am a messenger who will bring back word from the men who are fighting, to those who want the war to go on forever . . . it will be a bitter truth, and may it burn their lousy souls.'

His picture of the Menin Road painted in 1917 depicted war

at its most savage and desolate. He too was a victim of poison gas from which he suffered for the rest of his life.

Inevitably 'Sunshine Susie's' early chirpiness became a mere front in the face of duty. I was beginning grimly to detest entertaining, though I tried not to show it. But I was no longer so very young, and apart from the changing values of wartime, fashions in the theatre were also assuming a different look. More and more I was haunted by an obsession for that lovely, far-away piece of land in Cornwall, and in a letter to Philippe reminded him of it.

'Perhaps you could make something of it,' I said. 'Perhaps we both could – together. You have said you wanted to marry me, darling. Don't let us wait too long. You're so much better, aren't you? Is it right to waste one precious day in indecision?'

He replied by return of post.

My dearest love – my wish for us to be together is every bit as strong as yours. Do you imagine I too haven't my dreams? But the war isn't over yet, and though thank heaven they've done the best with my lung, and got the bullet out, my foot is still a problem. They're still humming and hawing about whether it should come off or not, and if the latter – what the hell use would I be limping about a few acres of ground unable to work them? We must wait and see, Susannah. I'd *loathe* thinking you had a cripple for a husband.

In a frenzy of impatience I replied fiercely,

And what use do you think *I'd* be without you? Don't be such a sanctimonious morbid prig, Philippe. And don't dwell on having your foot off. If you stick out and damn well make those medical morons put their heads together and take more notice than they have, it's my belief you'll keep it. If you don't – you'll just have to get along with a wooden one or whatever they make the artificial ones of, won't you?'

Oh, darling, darling, I miss you so. Please forgive me if I sound bossy. I'm not bossy, really. I mustn't be, must I? Or you won't want to marry me at all. I remember you saying that in any flesh and blood successful marriage a man must be master if the occasion arose. And I agree – I agree absolutely. But a mere limp doesn't make any difference to the situation, does it? You could still sit down and put me over your knee if I kicked over the traces. I wouldn't divorce you, I promise, so think about it, Philippe – that piece of ground, I mean – and the things we could do with it perhaps – build a house, grow flowers maybe. Didn't you say your grandfather grew acres of them in Brittany? Well then! it would be quite something wouldn't it, to grow whole fields of flowers – our little bit in creating beauty, following the havoc of this awful war.

As an answer Philippe wrote, 'When peace comes, Susannah. That's my promise, and last word on the subject.'

I seethed, and in desperation threw a cup at the wall of the lodging house in the midlands where I was on tour.

Then I cried a bit, and then I stiffened, and in the end, even managed a bit of a smile, because I'd worked off steam, and recognised that Philippe after all was really proving himself to be the strong man I secretly wanted.

Peace *did* come, of course, eventually.

In November 1918 came the Armistice, and a week later Philippe and I met again.

I was almost twenty-nine years old, passionately in love, longing for a husband and the chance to start a family of my own.

*3*

The battle of bayonets, gas and guns was over; but ironically nature was macabrely involved in another – the great plague of influenza sweeping Europe claimed as many fatal victims as the military war itself.

Philippe, whose general health had improved rapidly, leaving only a permanent limp and attacks of pain in his foot, escaped. But I did not.

For many weeks I lay in a hospital bed so sick and weak from the complications of septic pneumonia that I was told afterwards it was thought I would die. There were periods of unconscious nothingness, but gradually, as my stubborn heart and will refused defeat, forms began to emerge, with the quiet intermittent whisper of voices. I became aware of the taste of brandy warming my throat, and liquid food – Bengers I think – through the stem of a feeding cup being forced between my lips. Vague incoherent thoughts and impressions swam haphazardly through my mind. It was rather like floating in some strange dream, nonsensical as *Alice-in-Wonderland*. Everything was done for me. It was only when some fiery hot kind of jacket was removed that any sensation of being a human being registered. The first impressions were of mild pain still, extreme sweating, weakness, and a bewildered sense of fear.

Then one day, Philippe arrived miraculously, and as I stared up from my pillows into his face, a wave of life and hope surged through me.

I tried to speak, to whisper his name, and reach out to him, but was restrained.

'Lie still,' he said, as a nurse gently pressed my shoulder. 'You'll do as you're told, and rest. Oh, Susie – Susie, my love – if anything had happened – thank God you're better. It's been just hell, my darling. Plain hell.' What more he said I don't remember. Maybe the words didn't sink in. All I knew was that he was there, and that everything was going to be all right. It *had* to be.

So from that moment I set my will firmly and stubbornly on conscious recovery.

I had to learn to walk again. And one day when Philippe came to see me, I said with a grin, 'You see – *you've* got to teach *me* to use my legs now. Not the other way round. A funny dot-and-carry-one pair we'll be walking up the aisle – or should it be dot-and-carry-two?'

'*What* did you say?'

I glanced at him innocently. 'You heard.'

'Yes.' He got on the side of the bed holding my hand, and playing with my fingers. Then looking up, with his blue eyes warm and bright on my face, he said, 'I give in. Just as soon as possible when you've left this place, I'll get us to the altar, even if I have to carry you.'

So that was that, although at that moment I didn't point out to him that owing to Willie there wouldn't actually be an altar – just a register office.

We were married in the autumn of 1919, in London, where Philippe had taken a Chelsea flat until he decided what to do in the future, when his periodical hospital visits were over.

I was then twenty-nine years old, and in a wave of optimism, determined to salvage what I could of the lost wartime days of youth, by purchasing a quite spectacular outfit for the occasion of a pale silver-grey knitted silk dress with a long eighteen inch frinch dangling to halfway up my calves. My hat was a tightly fitting silver turban reaching over my ears and down to the eyebrows. It had two tiny curled feathers in front, like antennae, and a whisper of veil behind. My shoes were spiky and very high-heeled, and beneath the atrocious headgear – yes, I admit it *was* atrocious – my hair had been closely bobbed resembling the shingle and the bingle which were so soon to follow.

'You must be prepared for a surprise when you see me,' I told Philippe a week before the ceremony, which was to be a quiet one at a small registry office nearby his rooms. 'Not white, darling. It wouldn't be suitable, would it? – Not for me, being divorced. And I *do* want something different. Anyway – orange blossom would be ridiculous – at my age.'

'*Your* age. Don't be a nut. Are you trying to put me off? Because whatever my short-comings may be, I certainly don't intend marrying a goody-goody middle-aged matron.'

I giggled.

'You *won't* be. You just wait. I can tango as well as anyone. Even Rudolph would approve and gnash his teeth to get me.'

'Rudolph?'

'Valentino, silly. He's all the rage. They say—'

Philippe very firmly put his hand over my lips.

'Stop it, or I'll—'

'Yes?'

'Do what no gentleman would do, in true Valentino style.'

I giggled again. Lovely, ridiculous, laughter of happiness, as Philippe drew me close, with hands warm and possessively about my waist and buttocks. Oh, I was happy then; so happy. Memories of the past few years were dispelled forcefully in the rising sense of delirious freedom hovering ahead. Whenever I caught a swift fleeting glance of sadness or retrospective pain on Philippe's face, I managed quickly to chivvy it out of him.

'It's time to forget all that,' I said once, referring to the war. 'There's no point in dwelling on horrible things. We're lucky, darling. The rest—'

'Yes? The rest?'

'Most of them are at peace now,' I pointed out. 'The rest will have all the help possible, I'm sure of that. Being gloomy won't help. A new life's beginning. And we're part of it. We must be grateful.'

'A new world for hero's to live in. I hope you're right.'

'Now Philippe—' I put my hand over his lips.

He relaxed. 'You're incorrigible. Absolutely indefatigable,' he said, before removing his fingers and pressing his lips on mine.

I laughed quietly and drew away. 'A bobber-up – that's what I am,' I stated, strolling to the mirror and regarding myself critically through the mirror. During my illness I'd lost almost two stone in weight. 'I'm really quite sylph-like now,' I observed unashamedly. 'And the effect's rather good don't you think, darling?'

'*No*,' Philippe answered, coming up behind me and nuzzling my shoulder. 'You look ravishing any old way. But just you remember to take that daily dose of cream the doctor ordered. I want a wife with breasts and flesh on her – not just a shadow.'

'Breasts are out of fashion,' I stated, having thumbed through various magazines predicting the future. 'They're even designing tight sort of body jackets to flatten them down. That's what they call it – the boyish look.'

'Well, I don't want a boy. I want my own bouncy Susie back. So you just hurry up and eat your head off, or I may desert you on our wedding morning.'

He didn't, of course. He was there at the registrar's, well before time, waiting for me to mount the steps followed by my good friend and 'dresser' of the past, Marion Harris.

I believe Philippe's wonderful eyes widened when he saw me complete with fringes and turban, as I appeared. Maybe he gasped a little – I don't know. I didn't care anyway. All that mattered was about to happen. In a matter of minutes – a quarter of an hour, perhaps, or less – the ring would be on my finger and I'd be wife to the man I adored.

And so it was.

After the ceremony we had a short celebration in a Soho restaurant, and two hours' later we were on the way to our honeymoon in Devon.

I'd chosen Devon for devious reasons. Firstly because Philippe liked it – secondly that it was in easy distance of Cornwall, and Rookswood. So far he had not responded with any enthusiasm to my suggestion we might like to make something of my small patch of land. He'd had an offer from a friend of his in high circles, to employ him as horticultural adviser on his country estate, provided he agreed to have a year's training first. The salary would be good, starting immediately. The offer was tempting. But I sensed Philippe's fierce independence would resent any suggestion of patronage. Surely – *surely*, I thought, under the circumstances I might be able to bring him round to *my* point of view, if the Cornish acres appeared in any way possible for development.

With such optimistic reasoning in mind I temporarily dispelled any doubts of the future and flung myself whole-heartedly into the delirious ecstatic business – although 'business' is hardly the right word to use – of being married to Philippe. We walked and talked, wined and dined, loved and laughed, and indulged every moment of passion possible during that first fortnight, with a zest that seemed to keep us forever on the crest of an out-of-this-world wave. The hotel was magnificently large and luxurious on the coast not far from Quaybridge. There was dancing at night – in which Philippe even, with an infectious grin, made an attempt at a 'dot-and-carry-one' foxtrot as he called it. Mostly, though, in the evenings, after dinner, we either went out for a quiet stroll, or to listen to orchestral music in the town's concert hall. Then, in quite unseemly haste we'd return to our hotel bedroom where we'd flop on to the great silk sheeted bed hardly able to get our clothes off before making love. We were absurdly, ridiculously, obsessively lost in each other, and most mornings I'd have to prise my eyes open, they were so starved of sleep.

'I love you – love you – love you—' Philippe would murmur as his hands slid over my breasts and thighs, lips on my naked flesh everywhere. And my body would arch to his, warm and wide to receive and give. It was as though, almost, the war had never been. Occasionally there'd be a twinge of pain from this man I so adored. Then I'd hold him until the spasm ceased, and the sweetness of love would soothe and heal.

That first blissful period had to end, of course – or at least relax into reasonable proportions. It was then I got my brain working again.

Three days before we were due to return to London, I said to him, 'I've an idea, darling. Let's go to Rookswood.'

'Rookswood? What? That bit of moor you mean? Your benighted Cornish wilderness?'

'Why not? We could hire a car – or get someone to drive us – easier than bothering about trains. Much more free and independent.'

'Oh, I don't know. Isn't it good enough here? A pity to waste—'

'It wouldn't be waste,' I interrupted quickly. 'I'd *like* to see my – heritage.' There was a smile on my face, but something about it – maybe the set of my chin, or sound of my voice – I don't know – made him frown.

'You're dead set on it, aren't you? All along you've meant to go. What a devious little schemer. I might have known.'

I nodded, and my smile widened. 'Oh, yes. I'm quite awful. But I have to be, don't I? Or you'd have your way every time. Well just this once, darling, *darling*. Do agree and be nice about it. After all, it's quite reasonable, isn't it? In a way—' I searched for a non-compelling excuse, 'in a way it's part of *me*. So you being such a *possessive*, autocratic kind of creature – well! I'd have thought you'd be hell-bent to have a look. There's the museum, too. Heatherfield. I want to see the old family home.'

After that he hadn't a chance. He just gave in, and the following day we found a reliable but rather ageing little Ford to drive, and early in the morning set off for Cornwall. Because the weather was misty and chill, and the car was open, I wore a check tartan cape, and a tam-o-shanter of the same material, held safely on my head by a scarf tied under the chin. Philippe said I looked 'cute' – cute was a word made fashionable by the new rag-time age from America. 'And you're beginning to put on weight again, thank heavens,' he said.

'*No.*'

'Oh, yes. And that's how I like you.'

I had to be content with what was supposed to be a compliment, but determined that never – *never* would I overstep the eight and a half stone maximum.

So we set off, and it was late afternoon before we reached Heatherfield.

During the latter part of the afternoon the haze had lifted, but now it was shrouding the slowly sinking sun a little, giving the effect of a thin dew-sprinkled gossamer curtain draping the landscape. However, as we ground along the lane towards the manor it was quite evident that the few neighbouring cottages and farmsteads in the district were in order, the small granite-walled fields under cultivation, and what hedges there were on that sweep of moorland trimmed in an orderly fashion. The land beyond, rising to its tummocky cromlech was still wild and free – as free as the sweet tangy air and freshening wind from the distant sea. A feeling of excitement rose in me.

'I *like* it,' I said. 'Oh, Philippe – see that bird? – is it a hawk? Take those horrible goggles off and look—'

But Philippe merely grinned. 'Probably a gull. Now calm yourself, for Pete's sake. If you're set on seeing the museum we'd better be quick about it, or we'll have no time to survey your precious inheritance. We've about an hour of proper light left, and I'm afraid we'll have to put up for the night at some decent farm or maybe find a hotel. There was a signpost back there saying "To Thalk" – or some funny name like it—'

'Ah, well, I don't care,' I told him. 'In fact I'd rather like it. Look out! – there's a boulder ahead!' Philippe jerked the steering wheel; there was a grinding sound, and a spatter of earth, then the car continued on its somewhat rough course.

'Funny having a museum in an out-of-the-way place like this,' he grumbled. 'What's the use of it? Who'll come?'

'People like us,' I told him, 'those naturally interested in the history of the locality. Anyway it's of *special* interest to me. Do you know – I'm already getting a queer feeling of atmosphere – of history. Odd, isn't it, to think that all *mama*'s family on her father's – grandpa Dominic's side – were born here.'

'I don't know,' Philippe said, casting me a sideways glance. 'You're a bit of a contradiction in your own funny way.'

'What do you mean?'

'In one way so caring, and adult – in the other like some wayward gypsy maid forever roaming.'

'Oh, I wouldn't want to roam if I lived here – at Heather-field, or—' I was about to say Rookswood, when the car took an abrupt turn up a drive leading between alder and sycamore, towards the house. There it stood, directly facing us, its imposing façade lit with a wash of dying gold striking sideways across terraces and gardens. There was a sign outside saying 'Heatherfield Museum. Open from 10.30 a.m. to 5.30 p.m.'

'We've only just made it,' Philippe said. 'And would you believe it! – there's someone else here.'

'Yes. Another car.'

'Rolls, if I'm not mistaken. Fancy risking such an elegant vehicle on rough land like this.'

As we left the humble Ford well at the side of the drive below the steps, a woman cut down from the front doors towards us. She was wearing a long fur coat that looked like mink; a gold and orange scarf peeped under the collar, and an orange velvet turban draped her sleek head. Long amber drops

swung titillatingly from her ears. Her slim ankles were
sheathed in finest networked stockings that I sensed were silk;
her shoes extremely high-heeled, echoed the bronze shade of
her outfit. Gold bracelets dangled about her wrists.

She was very elegant indeed.

And as she drew close I saw she was also quite beautiful, fine
featured, with long slanting eyes of vivid green. As green as
mine. Simultaneously, with her appearance, a chauffeur
emerged from the shadowed trees, making his way to the car.
She lifted a hand imperiously.

'A few moments,' she said, dismissing him briefly. He
stepped back.

She extended a hand towards me. 'Hullo. How nice.' Her
voice had the trace of an American accent.

I stared at her bewildered, and she continued in friendly
buoyant tones, 'Good to see someone taking an interest
anyway, in this old museum piece. I've come a long way to find
Heatherfield, and not a soul have I seen in this benighted
dump until now.' She paused, adding, 'It's not a dump really.
It's quite terrific – all old English and traditional. But maybe I
*would* feel that way, because you see – I'm one of them.'

My heart jumped. I almost gasped.

'You're *what*?'

'Of the old lot – the ones who made it – the Pencorrins. I was
Miriam Pencorrin before I married my first husband, Hal. Hal
Rogers *he* was. I'm Miriam Garson now—'

'But – do you mind repeating that? The Pencorrin bit I
mean? You said it was your name—'

She nodded.

'Sure. Grand-daughter of Dominic Pencorrin who married
Isabella Colbert and made his name in the States.' She broke
off. 'What's the matter? Have I said something wrong?'

'Oh, no,' I told her as the truth really registered. 'It's just that
– I happen to be a Pencorrin too, or *was* until I married
Philippe. Dominic's grand-daughter. So in that case we must
be cousins.'

There was a long pause, then she exclaimed, 'You *don't* say!'

The next moment my tam-o-shanter was crushed against a
soft fragrantly smelling bosom while Philippe strolled away to
have a man-to-man talk with the chauffeur.

We laughed and chattered for what must have been minutes. Miriam really *was* so exuberant. But then so was I.

'You must really come to the States one day,' she exclaimed, following a chaotic interchange of family reminiscences and history. 'It's absolutely thrilling to find a relation like you – a *first cousin* on the London stage—' I tried to point out that I was no longer an actress, and never had been really – just a music hall artist-dancer. But it was no use. She waved my attempt aside and continued, 'They'd go mad about your voice – the way you talk – in Boston. It's so *English*, you see—'

I laughed again, and managed to get a word in.

'I'm not only English. I'm Cornish and French – bits of this and bits of that. American too. I suppose the whole family is. We've quite a – a varied history, according to mama.'

'Now who'd believe it! *Cousins!*' Her blue eyes widened, and the smile temporarily left her scarlet lips. She looked older then. Of course she *would* be considerably my senior, being the daughter of Dominic's eldest son. 'Yes. I remember grandpapa talking about your mother when I was a child,' she went on, 'that would be my Aunt Frances – and how famous she was. She must have been awfully daring to run away from Boston like that.'

'Yes.'

'Then there was – wasn't there a dancer or something – grandpapa's sister?'

'Rosanna. Yes. Anyana. She disappeared.'

'I thought there was something like that. But no one seemed to know anything definite.'

'Well,' I parried, 'it was all a very long time ago.' I could have told my handsome American cousin of the other Anyana – the one whose portrait at that very moment lay under my gown in a locket on my breast, but I didn't. There was something secret – almost sacred about it to me, that didn't entirely fit in with the eager – perhaps faintly brash – personality of the tall American woman swathed in diamonds and furs confronting me.

Would she have been interested? Perhaps; although her criticism of the museum was mildly condescending.

'Nothing terribly exciting there,' she exclaimed. 'Not what you'd expect of a great English family, only lots and lots or rock and rather dingy relics. A few rusty-looking swords, and musty books written in a funny language. No jewellery, except crosses or pendants. I expected a tiara or too – you know—' she shrugged. 'Something a bit more spectacular.'

'I don't imagine the Pencorrins were all that great – as a family,' I replied. 'And after all they were Celts; not exactly English.'

'*Celts*? What do you mean?'

I made a quick attempt to explain the difference between the Anglo-Saxon races and those of Cornwall, Wales and Brittany, but Miriam wasn't particularly interested. I don't even think she entirely believed me. Eventually she said, 'Well, honey, I'll have to be off. I promised Hal I wouldn't be late because before dinner we're paying a call for drinks, at the Dennets – they're business acquaintances of my poppa's, and have a house this way. But I tell you what – when you've finished foraging about this quaint mausoleum, make your way to our hotel and join us for dinner. It's Mortingdale Manor – back the way you've come – a real old world affair – pricey. But that's on us. You'll see a turn to the left some six miles or so – you can't miss it. There's a sign. Another thing – you can't *possibly* drive back to Quaybridge tonight. You must stay with us for the night. Then tomorrow—'

I thought up an excuse quickly, because I knew how Philippe would resent and hate having to waste precious hours of our honeymoon discussing trivialities with rich Americans. Anyway, some argument would be sure to arise, because at the moment he didn't feel too charitably towards our powerful ally who he said had only stepped into the war at the last moment for their own ends.

'I'm sorry,' I said very definitely. 'It's kind of you, Miriam, but we *can't*. When we've had a quick look at the museum we've another call to make. Really, it's impossible.'

The statuesque figure shrugged, gave a little moué and remarked, 'Just as you say. It would have been kind of fun though. We go back to the States on Saturday, so guess this is the only chance we have of getting together.'

I made hypocritical gestures and expressions of regret, and a few minutes later the expensive Rolls was purring away taking a fluttering wave of a white gloved hand with it.

I heaved a sigh of relief, and at the same moment Philippe, grinning, ambled over towards me, put his arm round me, and together we entered Heatherfield. The caretaker at the door warned us we had only five minutes. 'Have to close on time,' he said. 'It gets dark early; there'll be no use anyone else coming tonight, furriners or not.'

We didn't need much time. The relics on show, as Miriam had stated, weren't particularly stimulating, although a poignant atmosphere of days long gone lingered in the lonely house, and in the gradually fading light it was easy to imagine the trespassing influence of family ghosts stirring through the shadows. The specimens of quartz were fascinating, but my thoughts were too intently involved for a glimpse of my own inherited acres to allow concern for ghosts and long dead things.

In exactly five minutes, therefore, we were on our way to the place where Rookswood had once stood. The lane threaded in unexpected twists and turns to the high ridge of moors from where it dropped down at a more gradual incline towards the coast. Below a belt of windblown trees Philippe eventually located the particular spot we were looking for by the aid of an old map on which Rookswood House was marked by a small x. We got out of the car and stood, staring round.

'This must be it,' I said. 'There's that funny little place – an inn or something, called a kiddleywink, that the lawyer told us about – belongs to the property, too. Look Philippe – just above the sea on the other side of the track.'

Philippe agreed with me. 'Then all this patch – this headland, I suppose you could call it – is your inheritance.' He was smiling whimsically. 'You're a rich woman, my love.'

'Don't laugh. It may look wild and lonely, but it's got something – something unique. Don't you feel it? A kind of atmosphere?'

Philippe shrugged.

'You could say so, I suppose. It's wild enough.'

'Wild, yes. But not too wild to build on,' I remarked bluntly.

'Build?'

I slipped a hand into his. 'Why not? Time after time when

we've been talking you've insisted you wanted an out-of-door life. Here you could have it, without having to rely on your rich friend for a salary. We could build a house here—'

'You and I together? Brick by brick?' he interrupted ironically.

'Don't be silly. You know what I mean. We're not exactly paupers – and there'd be nothing to pay for land, it's already mine. With what my mother left I could pay for the building—'

'Oh, *no*, my girl. Get that out of your pretty head for good. Wherever we settle I'm not having you squander your little fortune on our home. I'll be *my* responsibility, and that's final.'

I sighed, but with a sense of triumph filling me that he'd not turned the idea down flat.

'All right,' I agreed cheerfully. 'If you're so stupidly proud and independent and determined to do things *your* way, well—' I broke off to add more gently, in pleading tones, 'Let's consider it, darling. It's such a chance. Look—' I waved an arm towards the west where small dells and hollows dipped in verdant pockets of earth between patches of heather and furze – 'there are sheltered spots. We could grow *flowers*, Philippe, like your grandfather did in Britanny. We could do – oh, so much cultivation; make a living from it if necessary. And there's a village not far away – you remember? Where the lanes crossed?'

He nodded, but said nothing.

'It could be our own new beginning,' I said after a pause. 'A rebuilding on – old roots. *My* roots. They began here.'

Philippe stared at me thoughtfully. 'You really *mean* it, don't you?'

'Of *course*. I think it would be *wonderful*. I've got a kind of – sixth sense, here—' I tapped my breast, 'that tells me it was meant – I can imagine all the years ahead, you and I – with a – family round us, creating, expanding, making new things from this lovely – lovely patch of ground. Take a deep breath, sniff the air, Philippe, it's full of sea and freshness and promise, and heather—'

I waited expectantly, hopefully, for his answer.

At last it came.

'Have you any idea what you'd be giving up, Susannah? You *think* you know. At the moment you're in a state of reaction; we all are – escapists wanting to forget the war. It's nature's way of survival – like a conjurer's trick producing a flash of idealism to blot out reality. But behind it all, facts remain. Commonsense facts. I expect the remote simple life would suit me. I had a "yen" for it before the bloody massacre, and there's a perfectly good post waiting for me if I agree – a chance in a million. But *you*! you belong to a different, wider world. You have audiences waiting—'

'Oh, damn audiences,' I cried, 'and damn your smug pi-preaching words, Philippe Marne. I'm more than just a playgirl – I'm *me*, Susannah Marne! Your wife. I'm also a Pencorrin born, and this is my inheritance. *And* yours, my love.' I lifted my face to his. '*Please*, darling.'

He gave in, of course. Not only because of my impassioned plea, but because deep down I knew he really wanted it.

And so it was that a new triumphant, healthier Rookswood came eventually into being. A home that in the future was to ring with the chatter and tears and laughter of children.

As we walked back to the car on that far-off evening Philippe said, 'If we have no kids – and not all couples do – how will you fill your days then? It's lonely here, Susannah?'

'It won't be,' I said confidently. 'With or without children there'll be you and me, and the flowers we grow. The trade for flowers is growing, you know. I got a booklet the other day. They do well with them in the Scillies. And after all we're not *exactly* paupers, either of us. Oh, I can visualise quite a business-like future ahead. Most of all though—'

'Well?'

'Our life here will be some sort of justification – for the past. There's quite a lot of exorcism to be done of old ghosts and misdeeds. I don't know all the facts; but from hints dropped by mama, and allusions in old letters and things like that, some pretty violent things happened.'

'So long as you don't expect everything to be perfect, all the time,' Philippe said guardedly.

'Of *course* it won't be. Nothing ever is. Besides – perfection's a stupid word. Dull. We don't want that, we want *life* and loving, fighting a bit perhaps and making up. Sun and rain, the sea and salt winds, and heather on the hill. Oh, Philippe, Philippe – just imagine it.'

His tired eyes brightened suddenly with their inborn natural vitality and in the blue brilliance of their blaze I saw all that I had ever wanted in life, or ever would.

I had won. Not only me – both of us.

\*

Slowly the last glow of sunlight died, a fading flare of crimson and gold over the horizon. Rocks and undergrowth were taken into encroaching grey.

From a distant headland a coil of smoke spiralled from bushes near the skeletal fading shape of an old mine stack.

'Gypsies, probably,' Philippe remarked, following my gaze.

I said nothing. But a sense of strange and ancient knowledge stirred in me. I knew then my decision to rebuild Rookswood had been right. It was as though the mystery and past of this wild and lovely land had stirred from forgotten years to welcome me.

There could be no explanation in words. But I knew that whatever had happened once, had not been in vain – either the tragedy or the joy. Perhaps everything of colour and experience – of suffering and happines is written on the ether, for all time, like a vast storehouse of emotion with nothing completely lost.

I like to think so, and that they wait somewhere, those others of my kin – just out of sight, perhaps – but as much an integral part of earth and air as the boulders and breaking sea round this far tip of rugged land.

# RIVALS

## *Janet Dailey*

FLAME BENNETT is a woman of contrasts; as fiery as her copper-red hair, yet as cool as her clear green eyes. Ambitious, successful and sought-after, she moves in the most glittering San Francisco circles. And she is looking for love . . .

CHANCE STUART, multimillionaire real estate magnate, has come a long way from an unhappy, poverty-stricken childhood. His dark good looks, electric blue eyes and devastating charm have made him supremely sure of himself. And now he is sure of his love for Flame. The attraction between them is immediate and intense . . .

Their passion deepens and develops – and then erupts into a white-hot hatred. For Flame and Chance are the unknowing inheritors of a vicious family feud; a quarrel that spans a continent and stretches back for a century. They are the heirs of a turbulent story of intrigue and betrayal, of a history that is about to repeat itself. Locked into a deadly battle of wills, they are destined to become the bitterest of RIVALS

Also by Janet Dailey in Sphere Books:

THE GREAT ALONE
THE GLORY GAME
HEIRESS

GENERAL FICTION
0 7474 0292 2

# FALSE PRETENSES

## *Catherine Coulter*

### IT BEGAN WITH MURDER . . .

Elizabeth Carleton, beautiful and talented concert
pianist, looks certain to be convicted of her millionaire
husband's murder; until a mystery witness provides her
with an unshakable alibi . . .

Newly acquitted, she struggles to rule her husband's
financial empire, confronted on all sides by her vicious
and scheming in-laws. In the hostile world of Wall
Street, Elizabeth battles against all odds. And when she
meets Jonathan Harley, both success and happiness are
within her grasp. But her husband's murderer still
stalks . . .

GENERAL FICTION
0 7474 0459 3

All Sphere Books are available at your bookshop or newsagent, or can be ordered from the following address: Sphere Books, Cash Sales Department, P.O. Box 11, Falmouth, Cornwall TR10 9EN.

Please send cheque or postal order (no currency), and allow 60p for postage and packing for the first book plus 25p for the second book and 15p for each additional book ordered up to a maximum charge of £1.90 in U.K.

B.F.P.O. customers please allow 60p for the first book, 25p for the second book plus 15p per copy for the next 7 books, thereafter 9p per book.

Overseas customers, including Eire, please allow £1.25 for postage and packing for the first book, 75p for the second book and 28p for each subsequent title ordered.